The
Survivor

The Survivor

Sean Slater

SIMON &
SCHUSTER

London · New York · Sydney · Toronto

A CBS COMPANY

First published in Great Britain by Simon & Schuster UK Ltd, 2011
A CBS COMPANY

1 3 5 7 9 10 8 6 4 2

Simon & Schuster UK Ltd
1st Floor
222 Gray's Inn Road
London WC1X 8HB

www.simonandschuster.co.uk

Simon & Schuster Australia
Sydney

A CIP catalogue record for this book
is available from the British Library

Trade Paperback ISBN 978-0-85720-038-9
Library Hardback ISBN 978-0-85720-187-4

Typeset by M Rules
Printed in the UK by CPI Mackays, Chatham ME5 8TD

The Survivor is dedicated to:

My wife, Lani, who has given me two wonderful children and
always makes our house a happy home,

And to my mother, Jo-Ann Oakley, who puts everyone else
first and is always there with her endless love and support.

Acknowledgements

Special thanks go to:

My partner, Constable Kirk 'O.M.T.' Longstaffe, for being the perfect soundboard and first reader (and safeguard).

Constable Warren 'The code word is "hot dog"' Tutkaluke, for his expertise in ammunition types and operations.

And to Sgt Steve 'the Silver Fox' Thacker, for his expertise in department structure and investigative techniques.

Any mistakes made from their assistance are mine alone to bear.

I would also like to acknowledge the following people, who have long supported (or in some way suffered because of) my writing career:

Luke and Riley, for sitting there beside their father so many times, writing their own little stories and reading their own little books. You are always so good and you make me so proud.

Larry 'Poppa' Oakley, who has been there for everyone since day one.

Bill and Jamie.

Cindy – I'm sorry about the typewriter . . . (No, I'm not).

My father (I miss you) and Mary (I just saw you), and Adamo and Nick.

Lydia and Gail and Yen Yen.

Dean and Lori Methorst, who offered support and an Oscar-winning show of interest throughout the early years.

Harry Methorst, who suffered through every one of my first drafts.

Rita Methorst, for her support (and for putting up with Harry ;o).

Dietrich Martins, who let me drag him to every local book-store Vancouver owns.

Helga, Joe, Ian and Paula, who make up the best critique group in the world.

Jason 'a green flash of light' Gallant.

Joe and Margot Cummings, with whom Lani and I share memories of story and Stella.

Lisa and Phil 'Watch out for those Tic Tacs' Webb.

Gramps and Grandma, who helped me pay for some of those writing courses.

Dean and Kris, who took off the blinders and showed me what voice was.

Taffy Cannon for her encouraging words during a difficult time.

My college professor Chris Rideout, who in one semester showed me what passion for story truly is.

Daniel Kalla, John Fuller and Ros Guggi, for setting up the wonderful time and experience I gained during the Sunday Serial Thriller(s) in *The Province* newspaper.

Kasia Behnke, Rosanna Bellingham, Madeleine Buston and Zoe King, who make up the wonderful staff at Darley Anderson Agency.

My talented editor at Simon & Schuster UK, Libby Yevtushenko, and my copy editor, Joan Deitch, who helped turn this good story into a great book.

Suzanne Baboneau at Simon & Schuster UK for taking a chance on me.

And last – and definitely not least – my superb agent, Camilla Bolton, whose tireless work helped perfect this novel, and who was the first person to see promise in my career as a novelist.

I thank you all.

If there's anyone I have overlooked, please forgive me. It is a crazy time.

Sincerely,
Sean

The Survivor

Wednesday

One

Dying is easy; living is the hard part.

Homicide Detective Jacob Striker knew this too well. Although 'surviving' seemed a better word than 'living'. How could it not? The past two years had been cruel. His wife was dead. His daughter was an emotional void. And now, just an hour into his first shift back from a six-month stress leave, the day was turning to shit. God, it was barely midmorning, just ten minutes to nine, and already Principal Myers had called about his daughter. The last thing Striker wanted to do was pull himself and his partner, Felicia Santos, from the road, but Principal Myers had been adamant. Striker had no idea what Courtney had done this time. Or what punishments her actions would merit.

But whatever the outcome, it wasn't going to be good.

Striker steeled himself for more bad news as he marched down the mahogany-walled corridor to Caroline's office – yes, they were on a *first*-name basis now, he and Principal Myers – passing under the fighting gold gryphons of the St Patrick's High School banners.

All around him roamed ghosts and goblins and Jokers and Batmen – a sea of eerie spooks getting ready for the festivities. Most of the students were taking the opportunity to dress up for the occasion, though a few still wore their school uniforms.

The kids, ranging from thirteen to seventeen, were loud and boisterous. Their overlapping conversations mutated into one loud din in the high-ceilinged antechamber of the walkway.

Excitement was in the air. Striker could feel it.

Halloween was coming.

He stopped and looked back at his partner, who followed a few steps behind. Despite his annoyance at being summoned here again, he tried to keep things light.

'That guy over there with the hockey mask,' he said. 'Looks a lot like your last boyfriend.'

Felicia brushed back a few wayward strands of her long brown hair, and smirked. 'Technically, *you* were my last boyfriend.'

'Like I said, good-lookin' dude.'

Felicia let out a soft laugh, and Striker felt an uncomfortable moment envelop them. It had been this way since their break-up a few months back. He looked away from her stare and led her on through the mob of Grade Eight to Twelve students.

Principal Myers was waiting in her office. Her chic, cream-coloured business suit looked out of place with her Sally Jessy Raphael, Coke-bottle glasses that were barely a shade redder than her short curly hair. She held a manila file in her hands, a thick one – Courtney's student file, no doubt – and upon seeing Striker, she offered a forced smile.

He cleared his throat. 'I heard you needed tickets to the Policeman's Ball,' he joked, and when she didn't laugh, he dropped the act. 'Oh Christ, Caroline, what's she done this time?'

'What do you think she's done?' the Principal responded. 'She skipped out. Again. Fifth time this month.'

Striker felt his jaw tighten. 'Any ideas where she went? Or who she was with?'

Before the woman could respond, a series of loud bangs came from somewhere down the hall, near the school's assembly hall or cafeteria. Principal Meyers stiffened at the sound like she'd been slapped.

'Halloween is two days away,' she said, 'and I can't wait till it's over. All day long, the firecrackers. They never stop.'

As she finished speaking, another series of explosions rocked the room. This time, the sounds made Striker stop cold. The explosions were sharp – like the crack of a bullwhip.

Ka-POW—Ka-POW.

Ka-POW—Ka-POW—Ka-POW.

He spun around and found Felicia in the doorway. One look at her hard expression and he knew he'd heard it right.

Not firecrackers.

Gunfire.

Something heavy and automatic.

Two

'Jesus Christ, we got an Active Shooter.' Striker turned to Principal Myers. 'Call it in, *now*!'

But she just stood there with a look of disbelief on her face. Striker snatched up the phone, dialled 911 and thrust the receiver into her hand.

'Tell them we got a shooter in the school!'

He reached into his shoulder-holster, left side, and found the grip of his gun. Sig Sauer, forty cal. Twelve rounds in the mag, plus one in the chamber. He looked at Felicia, saw that she had already drawn her gun, and gave her the nod.

'On me,' he said.

'Just go.'

With his partner at his side, Striker aimed his gun to the low ready and left the cover of the office. He swung into the hall. Kept close to the wall. Turned right at the first corner. Stared down the long corridor.

For the briefest of moments, there was only silence. No gunfire. No explosions. No screaming. Just nothing. And everything felt oddly surreal. Previous nightmare incidents flooded him – the Active Shooter situations everyone had seen on their TV screens a million times:

Dunblane.

Virginia Tech.

Columbine.

But St Patrick's High?

Somehow it didn't ring true for this peaceful community. He wondered if he'd heard the noise wrong. After all, it was his first day back to work in six months. Maybe he was out of sync. A little rusty. Maybe—

The explosion echoed through the hall, killing Striker's doubts. The blasts were deep-based, heavy enough to feel in his bones. They resonated with power. Combat shotgun. Every cop's worst nightmare in a close-quarters gun battle.

And it sounded close.

Striker looked at Felicia. 'Shoot on sight.'

'Take left, I got right,' was all she said.

So Striker took left, and together, the two of them swept down the hallway, clearing each room as they went. They'd barely turned the first corner when they heard the screams – high-pitched, frantic wails.

Just ahead. On the left.

The cafeteria.

Striker checked his grip on the Sig and took aim on the double doors. They were wooden, painted in a cheap latex blue, and had inset wired-windows. As if on cue, the doors swung open and teenage kids came running out. Streams of them. Dressed as Iron Men and Jack Sparrows and cheerleaders and princesses. They were screaming. Crying. Hysterical. One girl, a small blonde all of fifteen, stumbled out. Her white school shirt was splattered with blood and she had peed down her legs. She wobbled towards them on clumsy feet, stopped, and found Striker's eyes.

'They're shooting. They're *killing* everyone . . .'

Her left knee buckled and she collapsed, landing face down on the beige tiles of the hallway floor. Striker looked down at her twitching body, saw the red meaty exit wounds on her back.

Hydra-Shok rounds.

'Oh Jesus Christ!' Felicia gasped.

She went for the girl, but came to an abrupt halt when the firing started again. Striker yanked her back. Bullets exploded through the steel-wired glass of the cafeteria doors, sending glass and steel fragments everywhere.

'Down, stay down!' Striker ordered.

A second later, when the shooting lulled, he gripped Felicia's shoulder, then pointed to the door on the far side. She nodded her understanding, and the two of them took sides. Once set, Striker readied his gun, eased open the nearest door and scanned inside the cafeteria for the gunman. To his horror, he didn't find one.

He found *three*.

Three

Gunsmoke owned the cafeteria. It floated through the air in thin waves. The greyness brought with it the stink of burned gunpowder. And urine, and blood, and shit.

The smell of fear.

Striker blocked it all out. With beads of sweat rolling under his collar, he scanned the rest of the cafeteria for any other immediate threats, found none, then focused on the ones he had already located.

Three gunmen. Thin builds, average height. Instinct told him they were males, but it was impossible to tell. They were all dressed alike. Black baggy cargo pants. Black hoodies. And hockey masks – one white, one black, one red.

A scene from a real-life nightmare.

The sighting damn near froze Striker. He'd expected to find one gunman, two at the most. But definitely not three. He scanned the corners of the room. Teenage kids were trapped everywhere. Balled up on the floor. Huddled beneath tables. Sprawled out behind the serving counters. Many of them were already dead.

Or dying.

One girl, dressed as a pixie, lay face down on the floor, a stone's throw from the entrance doors. Redness surrounded her, spilled all over the beige floor tiles. At first glance, Striker was shaken. The girl looked a lot like Courtney – long, straight, auburn hair; creamy skin; lean build – and he'd almost lost control, forgotten his training and run from cover to her side. But then a horrible relief spilled through him; his daughter wasn't in school today.

This girl was someone else's daughter.

Numbness overtook him. The girl was dead – she had to be, with that much blood lost. But then she shifted. Lifted her head. Looked at him through empty, milky eyes.

'*Help me*,' she got out.

She was directly in the gunmen's path.

Striker felt his stomach rise against him, fought it down. Every second wasted meant another dead child. He forced his eyes away from the girl and found the closest of the three gunmen – the one with the black hockey mask. He had another kid pinned in the corner of the room, behind the serving line entrance. He was pointing a machine gun at the boy. Yelling things Striker couldn't make out. Then suddenly, he stopped yelling, angled his head towards Striker and raised the machine gun.

'Down, down, down!' Striker yelled to Felicia. 'He's got an AK!' He ducked low and right, taking cover behind the nearest wall, and a series of explosions echoed like cannon-fire in the small room. Striker didn't hesitate. He waited for the lull in gunfire, peered around the cafeteria doors, located Black Mask—

And blasted off three shots.

The black hockey mask exploded inwards and the gunman's head snapped back. A spray of hair and bone and blood and brain painted the wall behind him. The machine gun flew from his fingertips, spun through the air and landed somewhere behind the serving counter. By the time his lifeless body hit the ground, Striker was already aiming his Sig at the second gunman. At White Mask.

But the gunfire had alerted the second shooter.

White Mask saw Striker. Raised his own pistol. Opened fire. And the gun went off with a heavy sound.

The wall behind them cracked apart, and white-painted brick exploded through the air, along with bits of dust and plaster fragments.

'Shit, he's got a forty-five!' Felicia yelled from behind the cover of the doors.

Striker raced forward. He dropped low and left, slamming into the wall and taking shelter behind the nearest row of lockers. It was poor cover, and would never stop a forty-five. White Mask kept firing. The first round buried itself in the thick wood of the cafeteria door behind Striker; the second round penetrated the thin steel of the lockers and let out a shrieking metallic clatter as it ricocheted somewhere next to him.

'Down, down, get DOWN!' he heard Felicia yell, and suddenly, she was right there beside him, covering him, firing madly.

He dropped to one knee. Took aim on White Mask for the second time.

Opened fire.

His first three shots missed their target, flew somewhere high and wide, but the last round hit centre mass. Right between the pecs, base of the throat. And White Mask let out a strange, agonised shriek. The pistol locked tight in his spasming fingers, his arms dropped to both sides, and his body rolled forwards and plopped on the ground like a puppet whose strings had been cut.

'Two down,' Striker said.

From the far end of the cafeteria, Red Mask let out an angry cry and levelled his shotgun at them. Striker grabbed hold of

Felicia and dived right, pulling her into the kitchen area. The moment they hit the ground, a deafening boom filled the air.

'You get hit?' he asked Felicia. But she was already rolling left, reloading.

Striker let her go, then mirrored her. He rolled right, peered out the kitchen doorway into the cafeteria, and caught sight of Red Mask. The gunman was marching towards them. Closing in. Just a hundred feet away.

Time enough for an emergency reload.

Striker hit the mag release, ripped out the mag, and was in the process of reloading when he registered movement. He looked up and watched the gunmen do something that took his breath away.

Reloading, Red Mask sprinted up to the body of White Mask. He stood above him, aimed the single-barrelled shotgun downward, and blasted two rounds through the shooter's face. He then racked the shotgun and pumped one more round through each of White Mask's hands.

'What the *fuck*?' Striker heard Felicia say.

Before he could respond, Red Mask raised the shotgun and blasted off another round at them. Striker swung back into the kitchen, taking cover as the fluorescent lights above him shattered. Dust and smoke filled the air. He tasted blood. Kids were screaming.

He peered out again and located Red Mask – the gunman was fleeing, escaping through the exit doors at the far end of the cafeteria.

'He's running, he's running!' Striker yelled. 'Cover me!'

He jumped up and sprinted past the two dead gunmen, in between the huddles of terrified students, across the smears of fresh blood that now painted the floor. He raced up to the rear window and scanned the area beyond.

Outside was the front of the school. In the parking lot, he saw Red Mask hop into a small green car. A mid-90's Honda Civic, one of the many that dotted the parking lot. The engine started, and the vehicle accelerated down the driveway.

'He's mobile,' Striker said.

He raced out into the parking lot with Felicia fast in tow. Already the Civic was pulling onto the main road and turning north. Striker ran into the middle of the driveway. He took aim and opened fire, and the rear window of the Civic shattered. The car swerved all over the road, almost losing control and skidding into one of the storm ditches that flanked Pine Street, then it managed to navigate the slide and regain control.

It straightened out and accelerated north.

Striker ran after it, firing until he could no longer make out the licence-plate. Firing until the vehicle grew smaller and smaller, and finally disappeared from view behind the tall sweeping hemlocks and firs of the nature reserve. Firing until his magazine had run dry and all he heard was the *click-click-click* of a goddam empty magazine clip.

And then, as quickly as the nightmare had started, it was over. Only a horrible silence filled the air.

Without thinking, Striker automatically ejected the spent mag, let it fall to the wet asphalt of the roadway, and reloaded. A sheen of sweat masked his fair skin, and steam rose from his overheated body in the misty October air.

Away, Striker thought. Jesus Christ, he got away.

The gunman wanted to live – a highly unusual trait for an Active Shooter on a killing spree. To Jacob Striker, a ten-year Homicide Detective, that one action scared him more than anything else. It confirmed his greatest fear.

This nightmare had only begun.

Four

Damp wind blustered through the bullet-smashed windows of the Honda Civic, its wails as loud as those of the murdered schoolkids. Red Mask drove on, his attention focused on the road ahead. Blood saturated the black cotton of his kangaroo jacket; it bled from the open wound in his left shoulder and ran down his arm, across the black leather glove. He angled his body, trying to leave no blood on the seat.

When he reached the south lane of Ninth Avenue, he found what he was searching for – a narrow alley crammed with cars and garbage cans. The backyards lining it were padded with green sweeping trees.

Red Mask cranked the wheel hard, his left shoulder tearing, and felt the Civic shudder when its rear-end collided with a row of garbage bins. Despite the coldness of late fall, perspiration dampened his brow. Not far away, sirens wailed.

They would be here.

Soon.

Red Mask drove on down the lane. Halfway along it, he found a wider stretch of road that sat beneath the high overhang of a willow tree. He glanced at the tree. Backed by an ice-blue sky, the bark looked black.

The tree was dying.

Red Mask killed the thought. He forced his eyes away from

the horrible tree, and backed the Honda up until the rear bumper banged into the tree trunk. His mind felt hot, over-cooked, and a low hum buzzed in his ears – the leftover echoes of the shotgun blasts. Even his heartbeat sounded too loud, pulsing through his temples like a hammer on steel. He tried to think, but a mechanical grinding noise tore him from his thoughts.

At the next yard, a garage door was rising.

With his right hand, Red Mask snatched his Glock off the passenger seat. Pistol ready, he fought open the driver's door and rolled awkwardly out of the Civic. He slipped in behind the willow tree.

Watched.

Waited.

An engine started inside the garage, then a black Lexus backed out. An expensive model. Golden chrome, shaded rear windows, glistening black paint. The driver, a small old man, seemed oblivious of Red Mask's presence. He was fidgeting with his mirrors as he reversed.

Red Mask stepped into the centre of the road, shouting, 'Do not move!'

The old man looked up. Confusion filled his eyes.

Red Mask gave him no chance to think; he moved forward and pointed the pistol. In response, the old man raised his hands, slowly, cautiously, keeping his trembling palms facing forward. The bright gold of his wristwatch shimmered against his tanned and wrinkly skin.

'Now just be easy there, son—'

'Remove yourself from vehicle!'

The old man bit his lip, then the sternness in his face crum-pled away and he did as ordered. Once outside the Lexus, in the middle of the lane, the smallness of his frame became apparent. Dressed in a dark green tailored suit, his body was thin and frail. His breath came in fast and shallow gasps.

'Now just . . . just be calm there, son, don't go—'

'Discussion is not permitted.' Red Mask ordered him into the Honda Civic, then made him park the car inside the garage. Once done, Red Mask flicked the gun. 'Turn off engine.'

The old man obeyed.

'Give me keys.'

The old man did as ordered, with shaky hands, and Red Mask grabbed the keys. He took a pack of cigarettes from his pocket – Player's Filter Lights – and leaned into the car, tucking them between the seat and console. Then he stepped back and raised his pistol.

The old man gave him a pleading look, and when he finally managed to speak, his voice sounded very soft and very far away.

'I've got money, son, I've got lots and *lots* of money . . .'

Red Mask shot him once in the face.

'Not about money,' he said.

Five

'We should have stayed at the school,' Felicia said to Striker as they raced north on Imperial Road. It was the third time she'd made the statement in the past five minutes, and her words were grinding into him.

'We have to pursue.'

'But kids are dying back there, Jacob – they *need* us.'

He gripped the steering wheel so tight his knuckles blanched.

'This prick gets away, he'll kill even more kids. Another school, another place. Who knows how many he'll hit before the cops can get him?' He gave her a hard look. 'Make no mistake about it, Feleesh, it was a fluke we were on scene when it happened, and that fluke probably saved fifty more lives.'

'We don't know if he'll kill more – but we do know there are wounded kids back there. Shot, dying. We can *save* them, Jacob.'

'Other units are already on scene.'

'But not enough of them.'

Striker's jaw tightened. She was right; he knew that. By leaving St Patrick's High and pursuing Red Mask, they had guaranteed some kids an early grave. But if Red Mask got away, there was no telling how many more children might die. He had to be stopped. At all costs.

Either decision was the wrong one. A no-win situation. And

no matter what choice he made, the consequences would be dire. His actions would be questioned by all. The sickeningly sweet odour of Felicia's perfume was making his headache worse. He powered down the window, let air bluster through the car.

'Jacob,' Felicia started again.

'We're looking for the gunman.'

'Fine. Target Three it is.'

'Call him Red Mask. We're looking for Red Mask.'

Felicia frowned at the words, but nodded her agreement.

Striker followed the same route Red Mask was most likely to have taken. It wasn't easy. Fall's frosty moisture slickened the roads, and the wheels of the undercover police cruiser skipped on the asphalt as they rounded the bend of Imperial Road.

Directly ahead, in the faraway distance, were the North Shore Mountains – blackish peaks of uneven rock, covered with white patches of snow. Above them was pale blue sky. The image suggested a calm that didn't exist.

A storm was coming.

Striker could feel it in the air like a static charge.

Slowly, methodically, he drove on. He scanned the next alley to his left, saw the wideness of the road, the lack of open garages, and the minimal number of areas of possible conceal-ment. Not the best place to dump the vehicle. So he continued north.

'Clear left,' he said at the next lane.

'Clear right,' Felicia responded.

And so they went. It had been less than ten minutes since Red Mask had escaped, and already the memory felt surreal. The adrenalin from the shootout was thinning in Striker's blood, and the shakes were hitting him hard. His palms sweated. His mouth was dry. And his chest felt hollowed out. He stared at the GPS, studying the map.

'Where are the quadrants set?'

Felicia was on the radio with Dispatch, ordering more emergency units to the school – Ambulance, Fire, Ident, the whole gamut – and broadcasting the last known direction of travel of the suspect. When done, she hung up the mike and rotated the terminal to face him.

'We got a weak box. Just six units in all. From Sixteenth to Thirty-third Ave, and from Blanca Street all the way to Dunbar.'

'That's a lot of land. Any mobiles?'

'Just two.'

'*Two*? But that makes only eight goddam cars.'

Felicia shrugged helplessly. 'All units not in containment have been ordered back to the school. The Emergency Response Team is doing a full clear.'

'How many units there?'

'Four.'

That still made for only twelve units in total. 'Where the hell is everyone?'

Felicia brought up the unit status, frowned. 'Most are coming from way down south.'

'Why so far?'

'They had a gun call in Oakridge not an hour ago. Couldn't be any further out. Real bad timing.'

Striker cursed. The timing of the gun call was too convenient, and he wondered if it was a diversion tactic. He looked down at the computer map. The box they'd set up was too large, and there were too many holes in it. To make matters worse, many of the roads serpentined through and around the forest of the nature reserve – which was another problem in itself. Even if they had the proper number of units – which they didn't – visual continuity would be a bitch.

'We need more units.'

'They're making requests from Burnaby North.'

That was RCMP territory. Mounties. Any help was welcome, but they were still too far away.

Up ahead was a blockade. Striker hit the brakes and they came to an abrupt stop. He looked both ways. Scowled. Sixteenth Avenue was a long line of gridlock in each direction. In the middle of the traffic, city engineers were tearing up the median.

Striker scanned the area and saw numerous flagmen in bright orange reflective vests amid tall stacks of blue tubing and clusters of yellow work vehicles. It was construction chaos.

'No way he got through this mess,' Felicia said.

Striker bit his lip, doubtful. He drove up to the nearest construction worker – a fat guy with tangled grey hair that hung down to the crack of his ass. The man looked back at them through mirrored sunglasses and nodded.

'Dude,' he said.

Felicia flipped open her wallet, exposing the badge. 'You see a green Civic pass through here?'

The flagman brushed some hair out of his face. 'Across this friggin' nightmare? You kiddin' me? No, I ain't seen no one.' He turned away, then started waving the westbound traffic through. A motorcycle swerved around a reversing dump truck and the flagman started screaming.

'He didn't come this way,' Felicia said to Striker.

Striker didn't respond. He just reversed out of the work area, back to Sixteenth Avenue, and studied all routes.

'To go west, he'd have to cut across the gridlock and drive against the traffic.'

'Which he likely wouldn't do,' Felicia said.

Striker agreed. 'It would bring him too much unwanted attention.'

'So that leaves only east.'

But Striker didn't like that either.

'A right turn here is the natural turn,' he said. 'Especially when driving fast.' He took a long look at the gridlock on either side of the construction zone, then grunted. 'If he broke Sixteenth, we're screwed.'

Felicia's voice was harder this time. 'He didn't break it. And we've still got tons of lanes to cover to the south. Let's do a grid search, lane by lane, right down to Dunbar.'

Striker dragged his sleeve across his brow, wiped away the perspiration. The air smelled strongly of Felicia's perfume and of molten tar from the fresh blacktop. It left his skin feeling sticky.

'The grid,' Felicia pressed.

Strike finally relented. It was the logical thing to do, even if instinct told him otherwise. He cranked the wheel and made the turn.

Twenty minutes later, the grid search of the north-east quadrant was complete, and they found themselves back at the intersection of Sixteenth Avenue and Imperial Road. Exactly where they had started. The results were SFA.

Sweet Fuck All.

'Too much time has passed,' Striker said.

Felicia didn't respond. She just got on the air and broadcast the areas they'd cleared, then slammed the mike back into its cradle. Her voice was gruff, tired. 'Okay. Let's start west.'

But Striker looked at the long procession of backed-up traffic and didn't take his foot off the brake. He sat there, immobile, for a long moment, thinking. Debating.

Felicia punched his shoulder. 'Earth to Jacob.'

He rammed the steering column in park, climbed out, and felt the cold winds bite into him. They blew his short brown hair in every direction. He bundled up the charcoal flaps of his long coat and marched towards the work crews at Sixteenth Avenue. The median and surrounding grasslands were torn up, with mounds of dirt and chunks of concrete scattered throughout the passageway, making it difficult to traverse.

Halfway across, Felicia caught up to him. 'We should finish the grid,' she said.

Striker gave her a quick but dismissive shake of his head. 'He didn't go that way. He knew the natural turn was to the right. And he knew we'd search that way for him.'

'You're giving this guy too much credit.'

'Am I?' He knelt down, raked his fingers along the ground and felt something sharp. Scattered across the brown-grey earth was a line of small dirty opaque cubes. He picked one up, rubbed it between his fingers, analysed it.

Safety glass. From a shattered rear window.

He turned to Felicia, held up the glass, and gave her a look of frustration.

'Shift containment north,' he said. 'He broke the goddam line.'

Six

Within minutes, containment had shifted north, all the way to Fourth Avenue. Three more patrol cars arrived from the Oakridge area. They stayed mobile, patrolling the lanes and side roads. Striker was happy about the increased manpower, though he feared the response was too late.

Discovery Drive was a long, snakelike road, cutting through the thick clusters of maples and oaks and firs. On either side, million-dollar homes stood tall on oversized lots. All boasted creamy stucco, dark wood and old red brick. Walkways were flanked by sea-green lawns and gardener-tended flowerbeds.

Land of the elite.

Striker steered his cruiser down the slanted hillside while dialling his daughter's cell phone. The line was in use, and the busy signal annoyed him. It should have gone directly to voice-mail, but it didn't, so someone else must have been leaving her a message, too. He took in a deep breath. Courtney was safe, he knew that. She had skipped school. But that didn't make him feel any better. He wanted to talk to her. To hear her voice. But all he got was an automated voice telling him that the person being called was not available.

He snapped the phone shut and drove on.

Now on the north side of the construction zone, he started another grid search. Four blocks into it, he spotted a middle-aged man dressed in blue jeans and a white polo-shirt standing in front of a white garage door. He was spraying off the roadside.

'Clear right,' Felicia said.

Striker didn't reciprocate.

Quiet, focused, he slowed the car to a stop and hit the power button to roll down the driver's side window. As it unrolled, the foul stench of rotting garbage blew into the car. Striker ignored it and looked at the man before him. He was of Middle Eastern descent. Tall, probably six foot three – an inch or two taller than Striker – and beefy, even in his limbs. He probably weighed in at two-forty.

The man let go of the nozzle, the spray from the hose cut off, and he turned and stared at the unmarked police car. When he found Striker's eyes, he spoke without an accent.

'Can I help you?'

Striker badged him and nodded. 'You see a Honda Civic drive by here? Dark green. Had a smashed-out rear window.'

The man shook his head. 'No. Nothing.'

'How long you been here?'

The man shrugged. 'Long enough to clean up the garbage. Maybe ten minutes.'

Striker looked past the man, down the lane. It was a dark alley, shaded almost entirely by the narrow three-storeys that dominated the north side of the road. When he saw nothing of interest, he looked back at the wide-bottomed garbage cans and knew where the stink was coming from.

'What happened to your garbage?'

'Friggin' racoons.' The man showed his first hint of emotion, his voice rising. 'Gonna get a permit, set up some traps.'

Striker nodded like he didn't care one way or the other. 'If you see that car, don't approach it, just call 911. Immediately.'

'Sure.'

Striker drove on. Heading north. Always north. After four more blocks, he felt something tugging at the rear of his subconscious. He hit the brakes. Thought for a moment. Rapped his knuckles on the steering wheel.

Felicia gave him a curious look. 'You got something?'

'Hold on.'

He u-balled and drove back up the road just in time to see the Middle Eastern man enter his backyard. Striker rolled down the window once more, got his attention with a quick wave, and the man walked back over to the cruiser, his face looking tired and irritated. Like he had better things to do.

'What now, Officer?'

Striker pointed to the wet pavement. 'Racoons dump that garbage?'

The man nodded. 'Yeah, I told you. They're a damn nuisance.'

'They ever do it before?'

'Too many times to count.'

Striker looked at the righted garbage can. It was a large canister, heavy. There were no visible dents in it.

'They normally knock it over like that, or just get inside?'

The man turned and looked at the garbage can, scowled. 'Usually they just get inside.'

'These racoons you got round here, they *ever* tip over one of those cans?'

'Well, no, actually . . .'

Striker met the man's eyes. 'You *see* them knock over that garbage can?'

'Nope.'

Striker nodded. 'Thanks. Take care.'

The man walked away without saying more. Once he was gone, Striker turned to Felicia and saw the strange look she was giving him. He gestured towards the lane.

'Those garbage cans are damn near full,' he said. 'Must weigh sixty pounds each. They don't tip easy.'

'And you think our guy did it.'

'Sure as shit wasn't Rocky the Racoon.' Striker backed the car up a few more feet to give them a better view. He pointed. 'Look at where the cans are placed,' he said. 'Right at the mouth of the lane. It's exactly where Red Mask would hit one of them if he was driving too hard, too fast. Think about it. He comes down this way, north on Discovery. At the last second, he sees a good place to dump, or maybe a flash of red and blue lights. Who knows? Either way, he cranks the wheel too hard, takes the corner too wide, and what's he gonna hit – anything that's placed on the north side of the road at the very mouth of the laneway.'

Felicia raised an eyebrow. 'You're reaching.'

'You got to reach if you wanna grab something. Get your gun ready, we're clearing this lane.'

He gripped his pistol in his right hand and steered with his left as they edged forward into the alley. For the first third, he saw nothing. No good places to dump. No movement of any kind. Certainly no green Honda Civic with the rear windshield blown out.

Then, near the halfway point where the road widened, he spotted something. A small patch of torn-up grass on the south side of the road – a muddy portion that looked disturbed.

Striker hit the brakes, pointed it out to Felicia, saying, 'Cover me.'

He got out and approached the breezeway.

It was a small patch of land, rectangular in shape, maybe thirty feet by fifteen, and it flanked a closed garage. The land here was a mixture of mud and gravel and crabgrass, running from the kerb all the way back to a giant willow tree that fronted the yard.

Striker walked over to the willow tree and looked down. In the mud, there were tire tracks, fresh ones. Their deep grooves were wider at the base of the tree, as if a car had suddenly and violently shifted. Lying across the tracks were a few willow tendrils. Striker looked at the tree and saw a horizontal gouge across the bark.

Right about bumper level.

'Something hit this tree,' he said to Felicia, 'and not long ago. These marks are fresh.' He knelt down on the cleanest patch of grass and looked at the impression in the mud.

'Is it a Civic tire?' Felicia asked.

'How should I know?'

'You'd think five years in Ident would do something for you.'

He gave her a dry look. 'Only way to know for sure is with a casting, and that's a job for Noodles.' He analysed the tread prints. The impressions were clean, the near-frozen mud of the lawn holding the shape together. The lateral edge consisted of two longitudinal striations; the medial sections were composed mainly of 60-degree chevrons.

Felicia came up beside him, bent over for a better look. 'You getting anything there, Columbo?'

'First off, I prefer Sherlock,' Striker said coolly. 'Or at the very least, Matlock. Secondly, it's impossible to tell if it was a Civic or not. But whatever it was, the tires are probably one hundred and ninety-five millimetres, which would translate into a fifteen-inch wheel diameter. Most likely.'

'And what the hell does that mean?'

'It means,' he said, 'that a smaller vehicle made these impressions. Something like a Honda Civic or a Toyota Tercel. Anything more specific than that requires lab work.'

Felicia nodded, and Striker looked back down. Something else in the mud grabbed his attention. He took a closer look, blinked. Dark brownish flecks coloured some of the blades of grass. They were indiscernible in the churned mud of the tire tracks, but against the greenish-yellow of the crabgrass, they became visible in the mid-morning light.

'We got blood.' Striker took out a pair of blue latex gloves from his suit-jacket pocket. Put them on. He reached into the darkest area of the mud, where there was a faint glint of something silver, and took hold of a small object. When he pulled his hand back, he held a key-ring. Attached to it by three separate chains were a grey fob, a small plastic happy face, and one ordinary key.

The make was Honda.

In the half-second it took for Striker to stand back up, Felicia had already gotten on her portable radio. She broadcast their location, requesting a second unit. Once she was off, Striker got her attention. He pointed to the north side of the garage, where the bay door was located, and she nodded. When she circled to the lane, he readied his pistol and approached the side door of the garage.

Both exits were covered.

The side door was white, freshly painted, and matched the stucco on the walls. Striker pulled his Maglite flashlight from his inner jacket pocket, turned it on and set the beam to cone. He gripped the cold steel of the door knob, turned it, felt it click.

The door fell open an inch.

Inside it was black. Still. Silent. And the air smelled of gas.

Striker seized the moment. He kicked the door all the way open and swung inside the garage, keeping low and moving right, getting out of the ambient light and blending into the darkness as fast as possible.

'Vancouver Police!' he announced. 'Make yourself known.'

But no one responded.

He moved the flashlight in large wide circles, hitting all four corners of the garage. The room contained nothing but a small car. One flash from the Maglite showed Striker the car was green. A second flash caught the stylistic *H* insignia of a Honda Civic.

Striker shone the light inside the vehicle. Someone was sitting in the driver's seat, their head tilted back at an unnatural angle. The body was completely still. And too short to be Red Mask.

Striker stepped closer, looked.

It was an old man. Small. With thinning white hair.

His face had been shot off.

Seven

Fifteen minutes later, Striker stood ten feet back from the Honda Civic, where the driveway met the lane. The harsh fall winds had lessened, but they were just as cold, and went right through him as if his coat were nothing but porous cheesecloth.

He dialled his daughter, put the cell to his ear and listened to a busy signal. His pulse escalated. It was the third time since the shootings that he'd tried to call Courtney, and the third time he hadn't been able to reach her. He wondered if her voicemail was full.

'For Christ's sake, pick up.'

Courtney hadn't been at the school when the shootings occurred; Striker knew that. Principal Myers had already told him she'd skipped class – yet again – and he had little doubt she would be at one of her two favourite malls, Oakridge or Metrotown Centre. Striker didn't know what he was going to do when he found her: hug her, or rant and rave. He'd already called his neighbour, Sheila, and she was now scouring the malls looking for Courtney.

But so far no word had come back.

He swore, and slid the BlackBerry into the pouch on his belt. He tried to focus, to get his head back into the game. Work was always the best diversion; it had gotten him through the worst of the last six years, and besides that, he was damn good at it.

He assessed the scene.

Inside the garage, the interior light was now turned on, revealing the true extent of the damage the Honda Civic had taken. The rear window was partially shattered. The rest was full of holes and spider-veined. The driver's side window had been blasted right out.

One of the bullets was still embedded in the frame of the windshield.

The sight brought Striker a small sense of comfort. He would have smiled, if not for the bleakness of the situation, and also because a bad feeling gnawed away at the back of his mind.

They were missing something.

He could feel it. Sense it. Something important. Right here in front of them. The car itself felt like a puzzle, but one with a missing piece. He stood there like a statue, and studied the scene before him. The seconds ticked by slowly.

Felicia walked into the garage from the yard.

'Courtney's not answering my calls,' Striker told her. 'Send her a text, will you?'

'She probably won't even read it if I send it,' Felicia said. 'Sometimes I think she's got more anger at me than at you.'

'I don't think that's possible.'

Felicia offered him a grim smile. She sent the text, then put her phone away and looked at the car.

'Good find, Jacob. Really. The alley was a good call.'

He nodded half-heartedly. Breathed in. Coughed.

The garage stunk. The death of the old man – now known as the deceased, Henry Charles Vander Haven – was fresh and not overly pungent. But the car itself reeked of gas and a combination of something else he couldn't define. The fumes were overpowering, made his head light and his lungs heavy. The fumes were the only reason Striker had opened the garage's bay door, instead of keeping everything secure from public view.

Striker understood the significance of the fuel. Red Mask had been planning on torching the vehicle; of that there was no doubt. But something must have startled him, changed his plans, made him improvise. Striker wanted to know what. Maybe the gunman was injured. Maybe one of the shots had made a critical strike.

He turned to Felicia. 'You talk to the wife?'

'The woman's a basket case,' she said, squinting against the vapours. 'Not that anyone could blame her. Got Victim Services and the paramedics with her now, but it ain't helping much.'

'She tell you anything?'

'Yeah. Hubby here's got a brand new Lexus. LS600. Flagship of the fleet, apparently. It's glossy black with lots of gold and chrome.'

'Get a plate?'

'Fox-lima-lima three forty.' Before Striker could say more, she held up a hand. 'Already broadcast it. Everyone out there's on the hunt.' She studied the car. 'What you get in here?'

Striker moved further out of the garage, away from the fumes. 'Go run the plate of the Civic.'

'Already did over the air. It's stolen. Obviously.'

'Run it again. On our computer.'

Felicia gave him a queer look, then walked over to the undercover cruiser. She hopped in the driver's seat, rotated the terminal, punched in the plate, then hit send. Ten seconds later, the computer beeped when the feed came back:

ON FILE.

Felicia turned back to face him. 'Like I said, it's stolen.'

'The car's not stolen, the *plates* are,' Striker corrected. 'Look when.'

She did. 'Stolen just this morning. Seven hundred block of Howe Street. That's the north end of District One.' She scanned the report. 'Without keys. No witnesses. No video. No nothing.'

Striker was silent. He moved back inside the garage, up to the driver's door, and stared through the front windshield. Through the cracks and lines he made out the Vehicle Identification Number – the serial number unique to every vehicle.

'Run this VIN for me,' he called out to Felicia. He read out the eighteen letters and numbers, and she typed them into the computer, then read them back for confirmation. Again she hit send.

'It comes back the same,' she said, a few seconds later. 'A ninety-four green Honda Civic, two-door. Stolen.'

'When was it stolen?'

She looked at the screen, and her brow furrowed. 'That's odd . . . says here the car was stolen over *nine* days ago.'

'That's because it was.'

'How—'

'This is a different car from the one the licence plates were stolen from, just the same year and manufacturer.'

Felicia drummed her long clear fingernails on the terminal. 'Why go to all the bother of stealing this car a whole week ago when they could just have stolen it today? Either way, the cops are gonna run the plate and find out it's stolen. Makes no sense.'

'It made sense to them. There's a reason.'

Felicia's dark eyes narrowed. 'If anything, it actually *increases* their chances of getting caught – they had a stolen car

with them for over a week.' She stopped drumming her fingernails on the computer terminal, let out a tired sound, climbed
back out of the cruiser. 'Any ideas, Sherlock?'

'Just one, but I need some time to think about it.'

Striker approached the vehicle. The Civic had already been
searched once, but only cursorily. It needed more. He put on
new gloves, then moved to the driver's side door, which was
already wide open. He looked around the immediate area,
being careful not to disturb the dead body of Mr Vander
Haven. A pack of Player's Filter Lights was wedged under the
driver's seat against the middle console.

Strange.

When the gas fumes got to be too much, Striker leaned back
out of the car and gasped for a breath of fresh air.

'Any history on the registered owner?' he asked Felicia.

She shook her head. 'RO's just some ordinary Joe from
downtown.'

'Get a hold of him. Find out if he smoked or not, and if so,
what brand.'

She gave him a long look, her dark eyes holding a spark of
resistance, then nodded reluctantly and turned back for the
cruiser.

Striker continued rummaging through the car. He did so
carefully. Vehicle searches were always a double-edged sword,
not just because of the legal ramifications, but because of the
difficulty in obtaining untainted evidence. DNA, microfibres,
cellular material – it cross-contaminated with the slightest
touch. Best case scenario would have been to leave the vehicle
untouched for Ident, but Striker knew if he didn't get in there
now and search for clues, the passing time could be detrimen-
tal to finding Red Mask.

It was another no-win situation.

Striker did his best not to touch anything, not even the broken cubes of window glass. He deftly lifted the floor mats, opened the consoles, flipped through CD cases and registration papers. With two fingers, he picked up the pack of cigarettes and opened the top flap. When all he saw inside were ordinary cigarettes, he closed it and put it back down on the passenger seat.

Last of all was the key he'd found in the bloodied mud. It was a possible source of fingerprints, though everything Striker had seen so far suggested that Red Mask would not have been foolish enough to leave any prints behind.

Certainly not on the key.

Striker removed the first pair of gloves he'd touched the cigarettes with. Once he had a new pair on, he took the key from his shirt pocket and looked it over. It was black and silver with an *H* at the base, but there were no scuff marks on the steel, meaning it was new. He then studied the grey plastic fob and the yellow plastic happy face, looking for clues.

Felicia returned from the cruiser. 'The registered owner's name is Taylor Drew,' she said. 'He doesn't smoke, and he says no one ever smokes in his vehicles.'

Striker looked up. 'Good. Don't touch the cigarettes, we'll see what Noodles can find on them.'

She gave him one of her *you-think-I'm-an-idiot?* looks, and turned her attention to the items in his hands.

'That's what you found in the mud outside?'

Striker nodded.

'Lucky,' she said.

'Strange,' he corrected. 'Even stranger is the fact he had a key at all. The car's a stolen, right? Taken without keys. And there's damage on the driver's side lock, so we know how they got in.' Striker held up the key. 'But this is a Honda – the same key that starts the ignition also opens the door. So the question is, why break the lock to get in if you got the key that opens the door in the first place?'

'Maybe the key that starts the car *isn't* the same one that opens the door.'

'Exactly,' he said, then gestured at the steering column. 'And why aren't we finding a broken ignition plate and some loose wires in there?'

Felicia shrugged. 'We're dealing with extremely careful guys here. They know if any cop sees a broken ignition, they'll think it's a stolen vehicle.'

'But the stolen plates would already tell them that.' Striker turned the key-ring over in his hand, looked at the fob. It was a small grey thing. Completely generic. He pressed the button, but none of the doors or trunk unlocked. 'The fob's for something else.'

'Garage?' Felicia asked.

'Maybe. Or an elevator. Or a building entrance.' Striker looked at the yellow key-ring charm. It was connected by a short chain. He flipped it over. On the opposite side was a happy face, though someone had painted a bullet-hole between the eyes, with a red blood trail running down the centre.

Felicia scrunched up her face. 'How quaint.'

Striker said nothing. He just kept thinking it over and rolling the happy face between his finger and thumb. He was in the same position, still thinking, when a marked patrol car pulled up. The engine was overheated, and it died with a rattle.

Constable Chris Pemberton stepped out, all six foot six and three hundred pounds of the man. Striker was six foot one and worked out hard with weights, yet Pemberton made him look ordinary. Pemberton was a five-year guy, solid for patrol, and soon to be on his way to a specialty squad.

Striker briefed him on the situation. 'No one comes in or out except us and Ident. Keep a ledger with precise times. If Deputy Chief Laroche shows up and pushes his way in, make sure he signs the ledger. That prick has a pattern of contaminating crime scenes.'

Pemberton nodded.

'When more units get here,' Striker continued, 'I want them to canvass the entire area, north and south. Witnesses, video, everything. Call my cell if you get any hits. It's always on.'

'Will do, Boss.'

Striker took one last look at the happy face key-ring. It was part of the solution, he knew. There was a reason for it being there, one he just couldn't yet understand. He also wondered how Red Mask had lost it in the mud. Had he simply dropped it? Or was he hurt? Making his first mistake?

Striker placed the key in a brown paper bag, sealed it, then left it on the passenger seat for Noodles. He stood back from the Honda and peeled off his gloves, then met Felicia's stare and didn't bother to smile.

'We've done all we can do here,' he said.

She nodded reluctantly. 'He's gotten away.'

'Not for long.'

He strode back to the cruiser, and Felicia followed. They drove out of the alley and headed south. Back to ground zero. Where the nightmare had started. Where they would have to find their next lead in the case.

St Patrick's High.

Eight

Courtney Striker stood in front of the dressing-room mirror in Warwick's Costume Rentals and frowned at her reflection. The nurse costume was sexy – and she wanted that, wanted something that would attract the eyes of every boy she met during the Parade of Lost Souls on Friday – but it was a pretty common costume, clichéd, and well, just not her.

Besides, Raine had already gotten one. And if Raine was gonna wear one to the Parade of Lost Souls, then there was no way she was going to wear one too. With the exception of Courtney's abs, Raine definitely had the better body. She was a half foot taller and had long slender legs; Courtney's were shorter and more muscular.

Raine had bigger boobs that looked ready to pop right out of the costume; Courtney's were small and perky.

Raine had skin like caramel; Courtney's was white as milk foam.

And Raine had dark chocolate fuck-me eyes, as Bobby Ryan, the captain of the hockey team, had put it yesterday. Courtney's eyes were blue. Not radiant blue. Or iceberg blue. Or even winter-sky blue. They were just an ordinary plain blue.

Hell, when it came right down to it, *none* of her features compared with Raine's.

The thought soured Courtney's mood. She reached behind

her back and began unbuttoning the dress. She'd barely gotten it halfway undone when Raine tore open the curtain and stuck her head inside the small change room.

'What you think, Court?'

Courtney shrugged, made a face. 'Something else maybe.'

'But we could go as twins. Two nurses – it would be, like, *sooo* cool. Especially later when we're at the concert.'

'No. Something else.'

Raine switched bags. 'How 'bout this then? That Disney Princess, the redheaded one – Ariel. It's perfect for you!'

'You mean the Little Mermaid?' Courtney looked at the picture on the bag and saw nothing but a low-riding tail and a green-clam bra on the supermodel displaying it. She felt her cheeks get hot. 'That shows like *waaay* too much.'

Raine grabbed another bag. 'Little Bo Peep?'

Courtney felt her cheeks get even redder. 'Why does it say *Adult Fantasy* on the corner of the bag?'

Raine looked down. 'Ooops, this one is crotchless.' She giggled, then said, 'Oh, I know! I know for real this time.' She swished the curtain closed and disappeared again.

Courtney said nothing, she just kept undoing the buttons behind her back and wondered if a push-up bra would help to even her and Raine out. Probably not. It wasn't fair. Raine was gorgeous. Voluptuous. Everything.

Christ.

Courtney stripped off the dress, hung it on the hook and slumped down on the dressing-room bench, wearing nothing but her bra and panties, and waited for the next costume Raine could dig up.

The change room was small, a cubicle Courtney could barely turn around in, and it had a cinnamon-like smell from some scented candles or perfume or something. It bothered her allergies. She sat there, feeling a little chilled from the store air-conditioning and wishing Raine would hurry up, and wondering if she was ever going to find something that looked hot on her.

'Try this!' Raine said as she burst back through the curtain.

The unexpected movement startled Courtney, and she giggled from surprise. She looked at the costume in Raine's hand and saw dark red satin and black silk.

'What is it?'

'Little Red Riding Hood. It goes perfectly with your hair.'

When Courtney held it up and saw how short the skirt was, she swallowed nervously. 'I dunno, there's not much to the skirt.'

'Exactly. And it comes with super-high-heeled boots. Trust me, it'll be *hot*.'

'You sure?'

'Of course I am. Look at how the red silk sticks to your belly. You got the flattest stomach out of all the girls – the guys'll love it. They'll wanna drink margarita shooters outta your belly button.'

The comment made Courtney smile, and she looked at the dress again, this time feeling a little more confident. She was about to try it on when her phone rang. She hoped it was Bobby Ryan – God, he was, like, Jonas Brother hot – and frowned when she read the caller ID.

DAD.

Raine saw. 'Don't answer – you'll have to go home.'

'Believe me, I'm not.'

She waited for the phone to finish ringing, then scrolled through the missed calls. She saw his number on there four times.

'Principal Myers must've called him,' she said.

'So your dad knows you're skipping.'

Courtney leaned back against the change-room wall, slumped down defeated. 'I'm dead. I am so dead. He's gonna ground me for sure. He'll ruin everything. The party, the concert . . . I wish Mom was still around.'

For a moment, both girls said nothing. Then Raine took control. She grabbed the dress and held it against Courtney's chest. Made a whistling sound, and her lips took on a mischievous grin.

'Deep dark red, baby. Brings out your hair. And red is hot, hot, *hot*!'

Courtney grinned. 'You think?'

'For sure. Bobby Ryan's gonna *love* it!'

Both girls broke out into a series of excited giggles.

'Come on,' Raine urged. 'Try it on.'

Courtney took the dress, looked at the price tag and almost choked. 'Have you seen this?'

'So?'

Her cheeks flushed. 'I don't . . . I don't have that kind of money.'

'Who says you need to?'

Courtney gave a nervous look towards the sales clerk who was standing just outside the curtain.

'I'm not stealing anything,' she whispered.

Raine let out a high-pitched laugh. 'Well, duh. I'll buy it for you.'

'It's almost two hundred bucks.'

Raine smiled. 'Being sexy don't come cheap, Court.'

'You're missing the point – it's almost *two hundred* bucks.'

'Hundred schmundred. It's nothing.'

Courtney looked at the dress, then back at Raine. 'You got that kind of money?'

Raine laughed again. 'My mom does.' Before Courtney could say more, Raine wheedled, 'Come on, Court, put it on.'

Courtney finally gave in. She stepped into the dress, felt the silk and satin slide up her body, and felt good in it. Felt sexy. She turned around so Raine could zip up the back, then pulled her long, reddish-brown hair free so that it spilled all around her shoulders.

'Friggin' perfect,' Raine said.

Courtney looked at herself in the mirror, stared where the material clung to her like a second skin, her belly showing through the thin red satin. Raine was right. She *did* have a flat stomach.

And she *did* look good.

Her phone vibrated against the hard wooden surface of the bench, and she reached down and turned it off.

No way in hell Dad was screwing this up too.

She needed the costume. They'd gotten front-row tickets for Britney Spears on Friday, and it was gonna rock hard. But before that, they were going to the Parade of Lost Souls party. They had to.

Bobby Ryan was going to be there.

Nine

As Striker drove back to St Patrick's High, he felt as if they were on a House of Horrors ride at the carnival. Small swells of anxiety crept into the back of his heart, causing it to beat a little faster with every mile. He felt hot. His skin was sweaty.

He pulled at his shirt collar to get some air, then gave Felicia a quick glance. He saw the relaxed expression on her face and the casualness of her posture, and he wondered how the hell she could be so cool all the time.

Her ability to distance herself was unnerving.

They drove on. The weather was cold and blustery, but the eleven o'clock sky remained clear and bright. Sunny, even. Unusually beautiful for such a fall day, especially one so late in October.

It seemed wrong, given all that had happened.

Imperial Road curved lazily around the woodlands as they followed it south, the road surface uneven and slippery. They passed through the swerving tunnels of maple trees until the north end of the school came into view.

A mob of people had gathered. Clusters of mothers and fathers massed near the roundabout. A handful of officers were speaking with them. Most of the parents were as white as sheets. Some of their faces were filled with fear and longing.

Others were loud and hostile, ready to riot at a moment's notice. An explosive tension filled the air.

Striker felt sick for them. From this day forward some of their homes would feel empty, filled with an unnatural silence; a grief too deep to be explained. He knew this because he had felt it after Amanda died. Even after two long years, there was still a strange emptiness inside his core. A dark and hollow place.

He looked ahead and spotted a white unmarked Crown Victoria, parked out front of the school. The White Whale, everyone called it, because there was no colour less operational than white.

The Crown Vic belonged to the road boss. Car 10. Meaning the Inspector of the day. There were many of them that ruled the road, and most of them were men Striker not only respected but admired. Guys like Jean Concorde who had been one of the best investigators the Department had ever seen, or Reggie Yorke, who was as operational as men come, spending the bulk of his time with Strike Force and the Emergency Response Team. Hell, even Davey Falk was a good man, lacking the operational and investigational skills the other two Inspectors had, but making up for it with his steadfast support of the men and women under him. All were exceptional men, and Striker hoped to see one of them behind the wheel of the White Whale.

But as he and Felicia drove nearer and the occupant came into view, Striker's hopes faltered and were replaced by a morbid feeling of something between frustration and disgust. It was the Deputy Chief himself.

'Oh Christ,' Striker said. 'It's *Laroche.*'

'Avoid him,' Felicia said.

'Just what we need now. The one guy in the Department who can make even an Active Shooter situation worse.'

'He's not *that* bad.'

'Of course you would say that.'

Felicia shot him a fiery look, as if preparing for an argument, but then let the comment go.

Striker slowed their speed as they passed the white Crown Victoria. Inside the car sat Deputy Chief Laroche. His dyed black hair, which was slicked back over his head in an oily smear, contrasted with the unblemished white of his skin. As if to counteract the glare of his face, he'd adorned himself with a pair of gold-rimmed sunglasses with overly dark lenses. He wore the standard white shirt that all Deputy Chiefs and Inspectors wore, starched so strongly it looked like white cardboard rather than a cotton-polyester blend, and had adorned himself with all the medals he'd earned during his time in the Army – a time which everyone knew he'd spent on *this* side of the ocean in field management despite his claims that he'd seen battle in the Kuwaiti wars. In one hand, Laroche held a steaming hot cup of Starbucks; in the other, a sandwich overflowing with cheese and lettuce. He took a huge bite of it as they drove by, and Striker turned his eyes back to Felicia.

'Kids are dying in there and that prick's out here eating sandwiches.'

The earlier defiance of Felicia's face crumbled away. 'Well, he's . . . he's got to eat sometime, I guess.'

'Have *we* eaten yet?' When she didn't respond, he added, 'We've been on the road since eight.'

'I'm not getting into this, Jacob.'

'No, you wouldn't, would you?'

She gave him another hot look, and for a moment, she seemed ready to say more, but changed her mind.

They left the White Whale parked a half block behind them and drove into the roundabout at the school driveway, past the front entrance. Striker parked, climbed out, and had a flashback of chasing Red Mask. He could still hear the loud bangs of the gunfire, still smell the lingering scent of burned gunpowder.

He closed his eyes, attempting to suppress the frantic blur, and flinched when a door slammed shut.

To the south-east, where the gym was located, a gaggle of paramedics exited the building. They came in twos, each pair rolling a gurney. On the gurneys were victims, some as young as thirteen.

The paramedics hurried in different directions to many waiting ambulances that were parked all over the school's front lawn. Striker watched one girl being loaded up. She was about fifteen. Dripping with a redness that managed to seep through the medics' blankets. Her eyes were out of focus, her face slack and without colour, as if there were no more blood in her body to redden her cheeks. The rear door of the ambulance closed and it accelerated away.

'That should be it,' a nearby voice said.

Striker turned and spotted a row of men snaking out of the building. It was a parade of combat boots and ballistic helmets and heavy weaponry – MP5 machine guns, sniper rifles, and close-quarter combat shotguns. The Emergency Response Team. All wore black padded uniforms, covered with dark grey, reinforced-ceramic plates. The lead, Zulu Five-One, was Tyrone Takuto, a Eurasian cop Striker knew well. Takuto had a distant look in his eyes, detectable even behind the protective goggles.

Striker met his stare. 'Any more kids in there?'

'Just bodies.' Takuto spoke with machine-like precision, without emotion. 'All the injured have been evacuated and all the uninjured are being staged in the gym. Dogmen are running the halls right now, giving it a final clear – just to be sure we got every one of them.' He glanced back at the school. 'There's a lot of bodies in there still . . . a *lot* of bodies.'

Felicia stepped forward, and for the first time, she looked shaken. 'How bad is it?'

Takuto just kept looking at the school. 'Things like this make you fear sleeping,' he murmured.

Striker understood him completely. Night terrors.

'How many?' he asked.

'Last I heard we had eleven confirmed dead, over thirty wounded.'

Striker scanned the line of ERT members. Each one of them looked exhausted, like they'd just been on a ten-day mission, not a two-hour school clearing.

'What else you find in there?' he asked.

'Just carnage. Pretty much what you'd expect.'

'Any traps, any explosives?'

'IEDs? No, none.'

'Not even a homemade rig?'

'None yet. But the dogs are still searching.'

Striker thought this over. No booby traps. Unusual. IEDs – or Improvised Explosive Devices – were the norm nowadays. And that was mainly because of an Active Shooter's intent. Terror wasn't the only goal here: inflicting the maximum number of casualties was a high priority. The more carnage, the more coverage. The better the headlines.

The media spotlight was everything.

Striker watched Takuto tell his boys to take five, then strip off his ballistic helmet and goggles. He used his forearm to mop the sweat from his brow, then sat down on a kerb and leaned back against the cream stucco of the school's outer wall. Striker was about to ask him more questions when Takuto looked across the parking lot and sneered.

'Look at that prick.'

Striker glanced back and spotted Deputy Chief Laroche in the White Whale. The man was brushing his hair back over his head and checking out his teeth in the mirror. It wasn't until the three media vans pulled up – one for BCTV, the other two Global – that Laroche finally lumbered out of the vehicle.

The mob of reporters rushed towards the school, microphones and video cameras ready. They reached the yellow crime scene tape and stopped hard, bunching together, almost crawling over one another. There was excitement in their faces, a palpable buzz in the air. Children had been slaughtered in the safety of their school.

Story of the Century.

Without thinking, Striker neared the mass. Watched the reporters fixing their make-up. Positioning themselves for the cameras. Making sure they got their best angle.

Moments later, Deputy Chief Laroche strutted in from the north. He marched stoically up to the crime scene tape, his pressed hat held gently in both hands, rim down – just the way Striker was sure he'd practised in front of the mirror a hundred times. The lineless perfection of Laroche's hair told anyone who cared to notice that he never wore the damn hat. It was just a necessary prop, a part of the intended image.

Striker listened to the beginning of the speech, the Deputy's voice dripping with cosmetic grief, his words laced with heavy pre-planned pauses, and Striker wondered if the man had taken the same long pauses while sucking back his Starbucks sandwich in the car.

'I was on scene in *minutes*,' the Deputy said.

And when one of the reporters asked him if he'd ever faced an Active Shooter before, Laroche looked him in the eye, offered a steely expression, and reminded the group of his wartime experience, being carefully vague so as to never really explain what he did during the war, and adding at the last moment: 'There were children, dammit, *children* – how couldn't we respond?'

It was too much for Striker to take, and he knew he had to do one of two things – expose the man for the fraud he was and make a scene in front of the media, or remove himself from the situation. Common sense and compassion told him that the last thing the families needed at this time was a police drama. So he gritted his teeth and turned away. With a heavy heart, he marched through the school's front doorway and stepped back into the carnage that this day's insanity had wrought.

Ten

An hour later, Striker finished helping the paramedics check the last of the unresponsive bodies. Then he made his way to the boys' changing room. It was just after twelve noon. He stood alone at one of the sinks, looked around. Everything in the room felt too small – the green lockers, the yellow benches, the white hand-dryers on the wall.

His body shivered uncontrollably. His suit jacket was gone, left behind somewhere in the chaos – he'd draped it over one of the exposed children – and his shirt was so saturated with blood it looked more red than white, sticking to his skin wherever it was stained.

The blood wasn't his, and that pained him, filled him with a strange revulsion. More bodies had been discovered, some by the dogs, some by police. Some of the wounded, in an effort to hide from the gunmen, had hidden themselves from help as well, and it had been their demise.

Striker had done his best to save them all – the wounded, the dying – and to his credit, his actions might have saved a few lives. He understood that. Deep in his heart, he understood that. But more of the wounded had died than been saved.

A lot more.

Felicia's earlier words now haunted him: 'We should go back.'

And he wondered if she had been right. After all, what had they gained by pursuing Red Mask?

The horrors of the cafeteria still filled his mind. The heat of the gun as it kicked in his hands; the hot smell of gunsmoke; the shrill cries of the teenagers.

They would be with him forever.

It made him think of Courtney. Again. Word had come in through the student grapevine. She'd been seen by friends at the mall, but it was Metrotown, not Oakridge. She was safe and unhurt, and by the sounds of things completely unaware of the school shootings.

It didn't make him feel any better.

With trembling hands, he reached down and snatched the BlackBerry from his belt. The screen was smeared with sticky redness. He wiped it on his trousers. During the past half-hour, he had called her ten times, but she had yet to return his call. And he was getting *mad*. He dialled her number yet again, and this time it rang through to voicemail:

'Hey there, you've reached the Court! Don't get *toxic* on me 'cause I can't take your call right now – I'm out getting ready for the concert. Just two more days til BRIIITNEEEY!'

The concert . . .

The Britney Spears concert.

What else could matter in the life of a fifteen-year-old girl? Were it not for the hell around him Striker could have laughed.

The greeting ended with a loud beep. Striker tried to leave a message, but couldn't. The message box was full. He hung up, called home, and got no answer there either. Just Courtney's small voice on the answering service. It made him feel sick.

'For Christ's sake!' He slammed the cell down on the sink.

'She'll call, Jacob.'

The sound alerted him. He looked up at the reflection in the mirror and watched Felicia as she entered the boys' changing room. Unlike him, her clothes were almost blood-free. She wore blue latex gloves and held a bundle of rumpled clothes and some brown paper bags. He hadn't heard her open the door, much less sneak into the room. She was like a goddam fox sometimes. But a tired one now. Despite the sharpness of her Spanish eyes, everything else about her appearance looked haggard. Her shirt was sloppily half-tucked into her trousers, and her face looked older than it had this morning.

Almost as old as he felt.

'First I can't get through at all,' he explained. 'Now her message box is full.'

Felicia closed the door, came nearer. 'Well, she wasn't here when the shooting started, twenty people have testified to that. She's out with her friends at Metrotown. Skipping school. Safe and sound. So don't freak on me.'

'I don't *freak*.'

The BlackBerry screen was sitting on the lip of the sink. The bloodied screen stuck out amidst the white porcelain. Striker willed the phone to ring. It didn't, so he stood there silently.

Felicia came right up beside him, touched his arm. 'Look, you gonna be okay?'

'I'm fine.'

'You're shaking.'

'You excite me.'

She frowned. 'You know, Jacob, if it's too soon for you after your wife's—'

'It's not.'

'I'm just saying, it wasn't all that long ago that Amanda died, and—'

'Jesus Christ, Felicia, we were just in a shootout this morning, and now we're back where it all happened. It's got nothing to do with Amanda! You sure as hell never thought it was too soon when we were dating.' He gave her a challenging look, then felt the wind go out of his sails. He closed his eyes. 'Let it go, okay? For just once, listen to what I say and let–it–go.'

'*Fine.*'

Striker turned on the hot-water tap. The trickling was loud in the boys' changing room – amplifying the fact that no boys were there, getting ready for gym class. There was no laughing. No joking. No chatter. Just a harsh, overbearing silence.

When steam rose from the basin, Striker put his hands under the hot water and watched the white enamel turn pink. For the first few teenagers, he had worn latex, but soon the gloves had become so slippery, he'd abandoned them. Now, his hands dripped with redness. It was everywhere.

He sniffed softly, winced. The coppery smell of old, dried blood was all around him now, overpowering, and no matter how viciously he scrubbed his skin, more blood seemed to wash off of his hands.

Felicia cleared her throat. She dropped the bundle of clothes on one of the change-room benches, shifted from foot to foot. 'Got these from Holmes. He's your size, more or less. Either way, it's some new clothes.'

He kept scrubbing. 'Don't need them.'

'Your shirt is *soaked*, Jacob. In blood.'

'I'll change later. At home.'

She let out a heavy breath, as if debating something, then made eye-contact with him in the mirror's reflection. 'Look, they're seizing your clothes.'

He stopped scrubbing.

'Because of the shooting,' she said. 'It's an order. From Deputy Chief Laroche.'

'Laroche.' Striker almost spat the word. 'That spindly little fuck. Spent half the morning in front of the camera while we were looking for kids.'

'Jacob—'

'Christ, he even realise we got dead kids out there, or he too busy getting his hair to look just right?'

'That's a bit harsh.'

'Is it?' Striker held out his arms, showing the blood. 'Look at me, Felicia. *Look at me.* You see that? It's blood. Children's blood. You see Laroche? He's been on scene for damn near two hours, and his shirt is still white and pristine. Not a friggin' splatter on his shirt, not a wrinkle in his slacks.'

'It's not his job—'

'His job? His *job*? He took an oath to save lives, first and foremost. End of discussion.' Striker gave her a sideways look. 'You should stop and listen to yourself once in a while. Ever since you worked under that guy, you act like he's the goddam Pope or something. I don't know if he's going to retire at year's end or ascend to the heavens.'

Felicia's lips tightened at the comment.

'I just hope he doesn't hurt himself when he falls off his pedestal. It's a long way down, baby.'

'That's enough.'

'Damn right it is.' He unbuttoned the shirt and stripped it from his body. He saw Felicia looking at him, and threw her the shirt. 'He gonna seize my underwear, too?'

Felicia said nothing, she just bagged the shirt. When she met his eyes again, he gave her a defiant look.

'What else?'

'He wants your gun.'

Striker recoiled. 'Over my dead body,' he started. Then he lost the words and zoned out.

Something bugged him. Something was wrong here. As

much as he hated to admit it, especially with Laroche being involved, seizing his clothes was normal procedure – who knew what trace elements he'd picked up from the kids he'd been trying to save? – but seizing his gun before the incident was over, now that was another matter entirely. He stopped washing the blood off his hands and arms, and turned around. Saw nervousness in Felicia's eyes.

'What the hell is going on, Feleesh?'

'There's a lot going on, Jacob, I'm not privy to every—'

'Don't mess with me. Not now.' He stepped towards her and spoke with slow deliberation. 'What – is – going – on?'

Her lips pressed together, as if she didn't want to speak. Her eyes took on a thousand-yard gaze.

'The first kid you shot . . .'

'What kid?'

'The kid, the gunman – Black Mask. He might . . . he might not have been involved, we think.'

'We?'

'Well, the Deputy Chief. Laroche.'

Something spasmed inside Striker's chest, tightened like a steel band across his heart 'The kid had a hockey mask on.'

'It's Halloween week.'

'And he was holding a gun – a fucking machine gun.'

Felicia raised her hands in a helpless gesture. 'I don't have all the answers, Jacob, I'm just relaying the message.'

He let out a shocked laugh. '"Relaying the message"? Jesus Christ.' He leaned on the sink and replayed the scene over and over again in his mind. Black Mask had held a gun, there was no doubt about it.

A friggin' machine gun.

Right?

The exact details eluded him now; the entire morning was a

blur. And after a long moment, he gave up trying to recall it. He snapped out of the memory. Made the water colder, then splashed some on his face. Dried himself off with a paper towel.

Felicia opened another paper bag for his trousers. He pulled them off, handed them to her and put on the new ones Holmes had lent him. When he attached the gun holster to his belt, Felicia gave him a hard look.

'Jacob—'

'Laroche ain't getting my gun.'

'It's an order.'

'Fuck him and fuck his orders. This isn't over, Felicia. That prick's still out there somewhere, and he's gonna strike again. I know he is, you know he is. And I'm not going to be unarmed when it happens.' He adjusted the holster, slid his Sig into the leather pouch and locked it down. 'Laroche wants my gun, he can come get it – when we got someone in custody, and not a second before.'

Felicia looked up at him, her pretty face tense and her Spanish eyes dark as black coals. 'You're playing with fire.'

'No, I'm trying to put one out.'

'Jacob—'

Before their argument could continue, one of the suits from the Tech Division poked his head into the room. The man had an extremely thin frame, a hooked nose, and an enormous Adam's apple. It was Ich – *Ichabod*, as everyone called him. As in Ichabod Crane, from *Sleepy Hollow*. Perspiration sheened on his face, and he was out of breath, like he'd just run a marathon.

'God, finally I found you guys,' he said.

Striker stopped washing his hands. 'What you got, Ich?'

'Just follow me,' he said. 'There's something both of you need to see. Something really, really . . . strange.'

Eleven

Every one of Red Mask's senses felt warped.

He marched eastward along Pender, moving deeper into Chinatown. He'd abandoned the Lexus long ago. It was no longer a concern. His entire focus was the pain in his shoulder. It pulsated, moving through his body like long jellyfish tendrils. Already it had forced him from consciousness once. Much time had been lost because of it.

He could not afford for this to happen again.

The Fortune Happy Restaurant sat in the heart of Chinatown. Its dirty gold awning was splattered with blood-red lettering. The location had been chosen by Kim Pham, not for its size or layout, but for its address.

Number 426. This was very important.

Red Mask pushed through the front doors, smearing blood across the pane. Inside, the smell of ginger crab and black bean sauce hit him. It made his stomach contents rise, and he fought them down.

Seated patrons gawked as he struggled by into the kitchen area. Behind him, the mutters of anxious customers arose. A high-pitched clatter, like frightened birds. Yet in the kitchen, no one – not the chef, not the waitresses – so much as flinched or made eye-contact.

It was as if he were a ghost.

At the rear of the kitchen was the black door. Red Mask pushed through it. Almost immediately the smell of whisky found him. Mah-jong tiles rattled loudly, sounding like marbles dropping on granite. And there was cigar smoke, too. Thick and heavy.

Red Mask scanned the room. In the far corner, Kim Pham, ever the gracious host, was offering fine whiskies to the clientele. He was thirty, and dressed as he always was – in a white suit, with a white shirt, black tie, and a pair of gold wraparound sunglasses on his head. His oily black hair had blond tips.

When Kim Pham looked up, his eyes darkened. 'Fuck, fuck, fuck!' He grabbed two of his men. 'Get him downstairs – and call the doctor. Be quick!'

Two men, dressed in suits as yellow as egg yolks, wrapped their arms around Red Mask's waist and guided him with force towards the stairwell, which quickly descended into a long, dark tunnel.

Down, down, down they went.

And Red Mask let them sweep him away. His head was empty and light – a balloon rising out of reach. He was floating now. Floating far away. To that dark and horrible place where not even the spirits could reach him.

Twelve

Striker hurried out of the boys' changing room and headed down the hall. As he went, he scanned the walls and ceiling for any closed-circuit television. Cameras didn't take long to find. They were mounted high on every corner. They were old models – big black boxy things. Striker noticed that they didn't pan down or follow him as he walked.

That was not good news.

Striker followed Ich and Felicia on their way towards the security room. Up ahead, he heard Laroche's nasally tone, so he cut away through the assembly hall. Inside, the elevated stage was empty and looming, and the room had a haunted feel.

The scene before Striker shocked him. Drying smears of blood coloured the stage's front, and a yellow Star Trek costume had been left behind. Its fabric was splattered with red and torn. The sight made Striker realise he had gotten it wrong: the shootings hadn't started in the cafeteria, but somewhere down here – in the hall or auditorium. It had all been such a panic, the exact details were hard to pull from his memory.

He looked around.

High above, Striker saw another camera. This one was silver and grey. Smaller. A newer model than the ones in the hall. He needed to know what its eye had seen.

As he cut through the opposite doorway into the next hall,

before the door had even swung closed, he felt someone bump into his chest. He didn't have to look down to see the person's face to know who it was. He noted the small stature of the man's frame, and out of the corner of his eye, saw a glimmer of that unnatural black hair, gelled heavily back and patted down with perfection.

Deputy Chief Laroche.

'Striker!' he said.

Striker stopped walking and faced the man he had moments earlier tried to avoid.

The DC was five and a half feet tall and less than one hundred and fifty pounds. Small in comparison to the normal population; puny by police standards, where the average cop was five foot ten and an even two hundred pounds.

'Sir,' Striker acknowledged.

'I've been looking for you – have you turned in your clothes?'

'Of course.'

'And your gun?'

Striker forced a grim smile. 'I'm fine, sir, thanks for asking.'

The Deputy Chief furrowed his brow. 'What?'

'Just informing you of my well-being. I'm sure that was your primary concern. I mean, one of your officers being in a shootout and all.' When the Deputy Chief didn't respond, but just stood there, hands on his hips, chest pushed out for dramatic effect, Striker added, 'I didn't want the worry weighing too heavily on your mind right now, when you've got so many press conferences to attend. God knows, *those* have to be stressful.'

The Deputy Chief's lips compressed into a straight line. He looked around, as if to see who else was present. Striker looked too. He saw a few Global TV cameras just outside the front entrance, where a smear of yellow police tape blocked access.

The Deputy Chief cleared his throat. 'Well, yes, Striker, it's good. Good you're unharmed. That was my first concern.'

'Of course it was.'

When the Deputy Chief said no more, Striker looked back at Felicia, who stood beside the assembly-hall door. Her face was more strained now than it had been during the shootout.

'Felicia is okay, too. In case you were wondering.'

The Deputy Chief stood there silently, letting the words digest.

'Your gun, Striker,' he finally said.

'What about it?'

'It's being seized.'

'That's understood, sir. And you'll have it once this incident is over.'

For a moment, the Deputy Chief said nothing. His eyes narrowed. Then: 'It's not a request, Detective Striker, it's an order.'

Striker leaned forward, so that he was towering over the man. Leaned so close he could smell the oily sweetness of Laroche's hair gel and the cigarette smoke on his breath.

'Nice speech, sir,' Striker said. 'Now it's my turn. First off, you've got my clothes, be happy with that. But you ain't getting my gun – not until this incident is entirely over. And don't bother spouting out any of that policy bullshit to me because safety supersedes policy – and what we have here is a legitimate safety concern.'

'This is hardly—'

'We don't know where the gunman is, who he is, or even his motive – and I've already been involved in one shootout with him. For all we know he might come back. So the answer is no.

No one gets my gun. Not till we got an in-custody or a dead body, preferably the latter.'

The Deputy Chief's mouth twisted as if he'd eaten something sour. 'We'll get you another gun then, Detective Striker.'

'Negative, sir. My gun is heavily modified. And I'm trained on this one.'

'Striker—'

'You'll get my gun, don't worry about that, but you'll get it when the incident is over and not a second before.' Striker paused. He looked back at Felicia, who stood looking uncomfortable next to Ich. 'And don't even think of pulling me off this case. I didn't get shot at with a shotgun and an AK-47 so that you could come down here and play God. This file is mine. I'm the primary. I've had to kill over it, literally.'

The Deputy Chief shook his head. 'You're off, Striker. I have already made the decision.'

Striker leaned closer to the man, so close that when he whispered, no one but the two of them could hear. 'I got video. Of you fixing your hair while the rest of us were hauling children out of the foyer.'

Laroche stared back at him. 'Is that some form of threat?'

'And eating sandwiches, too. What was it, anyway – Ham and Swiss? Tuna Delight?'

'You want to end your career, Striker?'

Striker held up his BlackBerry. 'Not the greatest video camera I ever had, but it sure gets the job done.'

The Deputy Chief opened his mouth, but no words came out. His neck stiffened. 'This is insubordination, Striker. The Chief will hear about it. And the Police Board, as well.'

'Good. Tell them to talk to my union rep. Directly.' Striker forced his jaw to relax and let a smile break through. 'I didn't spend five years on the board for nothing, Laroche. I know my rights better than you know your policies. When you find out where the real authority stands – and ends – come find me. We'll talk more then.'

Striker turned away and walked down the hall towards the security room. He had barely gotten ten steps when he heard the Deputy Chief barking orders at Felicia.

Striker ignored them. A sense of dark excitement flooded him as he wondered what evidence Ich had uncovered.

The security room was waiting.

Thirteen

Striker walked with Ich down to the school's security room. As they passed one of the speakers from the PA system, a jittery voice made pleas for all students and teachers to gather in the gymnasium – the one place that had achieved lockdown.

The speaker crackled, then screeched with feedback. It irritated Striker. His hearing – all his senses – felt out of whack, one moment numbed, the next amplified. People's voices were either too loud or muffled, the hall's fluorescent bulbs were too bright or too dim, and everything around him smelled of fresh death.

He was drowning in it.

Felicia finally caught up, and they walked on. This was the exact same route they had taken when trying to locate and intercept the gunmen this morning, Striker noted. He looked around. He didn't recall so many bodies. There looked to be a lot more than eleven. Already he had counted four. Each one was covered by an ordinary brown sheet.

Like little sandbags dropped here and there to stifle the flow of blood.

He wondered: had he had tunnel vision at the time of the shootings, or had these poor kids tried to escape and only made it this far? The latter seemed more realistic, but he didn't know for sure. And the more he tried to recall the exact details of how everything had unfolded, the more blank spots he found in his memory.

He passed three more kids, each one covered by a spotted brown sheet. That made seven. The sight sickened him, and he wanted to look away.

But he would not do that.

Instead, he stared intently at every single one of the children he passed, taking the time to peel back the covers and see their faces. He took in the full horror of their expressions, the rictus of twisted emotions warping their features.

He took it all in, accepted the ugly truth. Embraced it. For it steeled his determination. He would remember these children forever, each and every one of them, in image and in feeling. And he would recall these images and feelings with vigour when he caught the twisted little fuck responsible for their slaughter.

'Jacob,' a voice said.

He looked up from the body of a child he was staring at in the hall – a young, brown-haired girl with skin that was slack and pale – and saw Felicia calling him into Principal Myers's office. He took one last look at the girl, then gently brushed the hair from her eyes and covered her back up. He joined Felicia in the office.

The room smelled strongly of burning tobacco and menthol. Principal Myers was leaning on the window ledge in the corner of the room. Her unstable legs looked ready to buckle. Striker marched up to her; looked her over. Her face was like a hard-boiled egg: white, hard, ready to crack. Sweat had matted her hair to her face, and her eyes looked distant, unaware. The cigarette she was holding dangled precariously from her trembling fingertips.

'Caroline,' Striker started.

Nothing.

'Caroline,' he said, this time more sternly.

It brought her from her thoughts. 'Oh Jesus Christ, my kids, my kids, my *kids*!'

Striker touched her arm, gave it a squeeze.

'I need lists, Caroline. Start with the kids who are unhurt and sequestered in the gym. Make note of all who are accounted for. Then start a separate list of the dead. Constable Kolski's already liaising with Fire and Ambulance. Just get him the pictures and he'll make the confirmations. When we have those done, we'll know who's still missing.'

She nodded numbly. 'Yes, yes . . . a list.'

'I also need you to make note of all the deceased's known connections – who they hung out with, what clubs they joined, what sports they played, who they hated, who hated them. I need all of it and I need it now.'

When Caroline didn't immediately respond, Striker looked at Felicia. 'Can you take care of this?'

'Got it.'

He moved over to Ich, who was preoccupied with the computer terminals in the far corner of the room. 'So what you got here, Ich? What's so strange?'

Ich looked up from the keyboard, the soft blue glow of the computer screens turning his pale skin into an even sicklier colour. 'It's the school's security system – it's been disabled. Happened sometime before the shooting.'

Striker narrowed his eyes. 'You mean turned off?'

'No, I mean disabled.'

'Explain it to me.'

Ich scratched his high cheekbones with both hands, as if he had a tic or maybe because Striker was annoying him. He licked his thin lips.

'All the cameras are non-functional,' he said patiently. 'They were *deactivated*. As far as I can tell, it happened sometime early this morning.' He hit a few keys, brought up the internal history logs and scanned the electronic pages. 'Probably around eight o'clock. Seven minutes after, if the local log is correct.'

Computer lingo was foreign to Striker, but he got the gist of it. He turned back to Principal Myers, who hadn't left the spot where she was standing, the embers of her menthol cigarette now reaching the filter.

'Who has access to this?'

Her eyes blinked, she came back to life. 'Well, just . . . just me. And Vice Principal Smith.'

'Smith. Where is he?'

'Uh, Cancun.'

'How long?'

'He's been there a week. And will be a week more.'

Striker didn't like the timing. He cursed. 'No one else has access to the system? No one at all?'

The ash fell off the end of the Principal's cigarette and landed on the toe of her shoe. She didn't react. 'Well, we do have some student helpers. There's two of them, but they—'

'Their names, Caroline.' Striker took out his pen and note-book.

'Nava Sanghera and Sherman Chan. But they're good kids. Nava's in the hospital right now, getting her appendix out. And there's no way that Sherman would ever—'

Striker pointed his pen at Felicia. 'Send someone to check on Nava, but see if you can find this Sherman kid yourself. Talk to him. See what he says. If you can't locate him, at least get me his picture.'

Felicia stepped back as if he'd put her on the defensive. 'I should stay here. On the investigation with you.'

'You need to find Sherman. The fewer people involved here, the better. I need you to do it. And be quick.'

Her face reddened and she gave Striker a look, as if she was pissed at being directed. For a moment, he thought he was in for an argument, but then she turned back to Principal Myers.

'Which hospital is Nava in, Caroline?'

'Saint Paul's, I think.'

Felicia wrote down the information in her notebook, then snapped it shut and jammed it into the inner pocket of her suit jacket. She left the room without saying another word, slamming the office door behind her.

Ich whistled softly. 'Wow, your first day back, and just like old times.'

Striker didn't respond. He watched Felicia through the office window as she stormed down the hall, turned the corner and then disappeared from view. What the hell was wrong now? Of all the places for them to argue, this was the worst. A goddam school shooting. He felt like going after her, but didn't.

He struggled to let the thought go and turned his attention back to the series of flat-screen monitors that were arranged in three rows on the far wall. Each one of them showed nothing but an empty, sky-blue screen, except for the three monitors on the bottom-most row, which were turned off and completely black.

Striker looked down at Ich, who was still seated at the keyboard.

'This a good system, Ich?'

Ich looked up from the computer logs and swallowed so hard his Adam's apple bobbed up and down like a yo-yo. 'It's an excellent system, even if it is analog. It's the VISION 5, made by SecuCorp, the programme the Department was lauding a few years back – though I wouldn't go spreading that around now, if I were you.'

'Secret's safe.' Striker turned his attention back to Principal Myers.

'I'll get those lists you need,' she said, and left the room.

Striker was glad when she was gone. He approached the computer screens and propped his chin between his fingers and thumb. 'I wonder, Ich, could someone circumvent the system? You know, hack it. Do whatever it is you techies do.'

Ich shook his head. 'Unlikely. Not unless you had a real whizz here. And I mean a real whizz. Like "Hi, I'm Bill Fucking Gates". This thing is high end, man. Two-five-six-bit encryption. Even for a pro with a high-end rig it would take months. Weeks at the very least. Whoever turned this baby off had a password.'

Striker studied the different flat-screen monitors, then said slowly, 'I'm no techie, but there's something here that doesn't make sense.'

Ich looked up. 'What?'

'Come with me and I'll show you.'

Ich stood up from his desk, his joints cracking loud enough for Striker to hear, and Striker led him out of the small security room and into the hallway. Immediately, the nasally tone of Deputy Chief Laroche's voice grew louder. Striker ignored it. He pointed up to the camera that was positioned in an upper corner, where the two walls met, just outside the office door. It was a big boxy black thing with a large lens, set on a mounted tripod.

'Is that camera a part of the closed-circuit television?'

Ich nodded. 'Yes.'

'And you say it's analog?'

'Without a doubt.'

Striker led him around the corner and down the hall in the direction of the cafeteria. Before they reached it, he stopped them just outside the auditorium. The entrance door was already open, the rubber stopper keeping it that way. Striker stepped aside and jerked his head towards the auditorium.

'Go ahead, take a look.'

Ich went inside, looked around the room. Saw nothing.

'Look up,' Striker said. 'Above the stage.'

Ich did, and for a moment his eyes remained lost. Then . . .

Positioned between the stage and the door, mounted on a circular swivel-bracket, was another camera. This one was very small, a silver-and-grey rectangular unit. It was almost unnoticeable, except for the blinking red light.

Striker looked at Ich. 'Is that what I think it is?'

The techie nodded, and a wide smile stretched his lips. 'You're damn right it is. They got two systems.'

Fourteen

Pinkerton Morningstar was an inside cop, carpet cop, call it what you want. He never set foot on the road, choosing to spend all his time in Investigations. It was sad and brilliant all at once. Sad because at six foot seven and three hundred sixty pounds, there was no one bigger in the Department. Out on the streets, there would have been no greater threat in patrol. Brilliant because the only thing that dwarfed his build was his mind. He had been in several levels of investigations – Robbery, Missing Persons and Homicide – for the better part of twenty years.

That was why Striker had chosen him to sort through the detained witnesses. Most of them had been sequestered in the gym; however, the priority witnesses had been relocated to the Drama Room.

Striker marched through the lifeless corridors under the soft hum of fluorescent lights, around wayward strips of yellow police tape until he reached the Drama Room. Along the way, he passed two of the remaining teachers, who looked lost and bewildered. He sent them on to the gym.

Two rookie cops guarded the doors to the Drama Room. Striker was just about to enter when Pinkerton Morningstar walked out. Next to the two rookie cops, Morningstar stood out like a giant oak among seedlings. Even his head looked large, decorated by a pair of John Lennon-style prescription sunglasses. The tint was pink.

Striker assessed the man. Morningstar looked tired. Sweat trickled down the sides of his bald brown skin, some drops sliding under the frames of his pink shades, some disappearing into the greying thickness of the beard and moustache that made his head look even larger.

'Pinky,' Striker said.

The giant Detective wiped his brow with the sleeve of his shirt and cursed. 'Hotter than Hell in there, man. Goddam air conditioner's broken and there's no windows. And Laroche won't let us take the witnesses anywhere else. Says it's a safety concern. The fuck.'

Striker fought the urge to go on another Laroche tirade. 'I'll get you some water.'

'Right about now, I'd drink your urine, if it was cold enough.'

'The water's less salty.' Striker nodded at the room. 'How's it going in there?'

'It's not.' Morningstar let out a frustrated sound. 'But follow me.' He gave Striker no time to ask questions.

'Most of the witnesses are useless,' Morningstar said as they went. 'They heard shots. They freaked out. Ran and hid. Did pretty much what you would expect someone to do with a gunman rampaging through the halls. They can't tell us anything we don't already know. And believe me, I've been over it a dozen times with each one of them.'

'What about their parents? We gotten a hold of any of them yet?'

Morningstar stopped walking, offered up a hard look.

'I got a hundred people calling for info,' he said, 'and we've had over sixty moms and dads show up, freaking out, wanting to know where their kids are.' The muscles behind the pink shades twitched. 'We got over three hundred kids in this school, which translates into damn near six hundred parents. Laroche keeps directing them to me, and I got nothing to tell them. We haven't even completed the list of the dead. Got kids sent to every damn hospital from here to New Westminster, and I don't even know which kids are where.'

'I'll help you with it.'

Morningstar shook his head. 'Got Patrol for that. You just catch this whack job and bring him in, preferably dead.'

Striker said nothing.

They stopped outside the entrance to the teacher's lounge, where another patrol officer stood guard. Striker stepped closer to the cop, a tall white guy with scruffy facial skin – he clearly hadn't had time to shave and shower before getting the mandatory Call Out – and peered through the small window in the door.

Standing at the far end of the room, her head down, her posture so still she looked like a part of the furniture, was a young Asian girl. Thin build, small face. Too much make-up smeared around her eyes, a lot of which had drizzled down her face from the tears. She was maybe fourteen.

Striker turned back to Morningstar. 'Who is she?'

'Name's Megan Ling. And she's a survivor. She tried to help the others. She's seen a lot – and she's pretty fucked up.'

'Where's her parents?'

'Mother's already on the way down.'

Striker nodded. 'Felicia will be back soon enough,' he said. 'Hook her and the mother up, will you?'

'Done.'

Striker looked back through the window. Megan Ling hadn't budged. He gave the patrolman a nod to move out of his way.

When Striker started through the door, Morningstar put his hand flat against Striker's chest.

Striker turned, gave him a questioning look. 'What?'

'Brace yourself for this one.'

'Why?'

'You're not gonna like what she has to say.'

Fifteen

Courtney and Raine walked southward through the mall. Earlier in the day, both had dumped their St Patrick's school uniform in their locker before getting into their usual attire – white Capris and a red half-top for Raine; standard blue jeans and a white v-neck for Courtney.

They stopped near an aisle kiosk. Raine pulled out her phone, tried to call someone, got no answer, then hung up.

Courtney's face lit up when she saw the cell. 'You got an *iPhone*?'

Raine raised an eyebrow. 'Like, so totally not. My mom got pissed my minutes were over, so she put me on a shitty prepaid plan. Now my minutes run out, like, the first week of every month. So I got to use this one for the rest.'

'But how'd you get that?'

'It's not mine, it's a friend's. Here, I'll put the number in your phone.'

Courtney felt suspicion rise in her chest. 'What friend?'

'Oh my Gaaawd, look at those things.' Raine gave Courtney back her phone then ran up to the aisle kiosk, grabbed a pair of earrings and held them up. 'These will go perfect with my nurse costume!'

Courtney just nodded. Across the way from them, a group of twenty or more people huddled and murmured near the television sets at the Sony store. The news was on. The group made a collective shocked sound.

'Something must be happening,' Courtney said.

Raine shrugged and tried on the earrings. 'Something's always happening around here. It's Vancouver, Court. How do these earrings look? Hot?'

Courtney looked. 'Super-hot. Like everything looks on you.'

Raine smiled. She pulled out a wad of twenties and bought the earrings.

The jewellery kiosk sat across from a small Cinnabun shop, and the whole area smelled of sticky-hot, gooey cinnamon and melting cream cheese icing. It made Courtney's stomach rumble, and she realised how long it had been since they'd eaten. She checked her watch. It was two.

She looked at Raine, who was holding a pair of black hoop earrings up to her ear and trying to see herself in the small mirror the kiosk offered.

'Those cinnamon buns smell so good, we should get something to eat.'

'We will be soon, we're meeting someone.'

'Who?'

Raine got frustrated with the mirror, turned to buy the earrings.

While waiting, and trying to divert her mind from the hell she was going to get from Dad when she got home, Courtney opened up the black Warwick's bag and stared at the Little Red Riding Hood costume Raine had bought for her. A twinge of guilt fluttered through her stomach when she thought of the cost. Two hundred bucks was a lot of money; she shouldn't have let Raine pay for it. It was too much.

Raine counted her leftover cash. Stuffed it in her purse.

'You're gonna look delicious in that costume, Court. Bobby's gonna be drooling all over you.'

'If I can keep him away from *you*.'

Raine laughed. 'Bobby's nice, but he's yours. I'm into older boys myself. *Men*.' She spoke the words softly, giving Courtney a quick sidelong glance.

And then Courtney caught on. The phone, the money, the avoidance. 'Who are we meeting?' she asked, almost cautiously.

Raine flashed a mischievous smirk. 'What can I say? I'm weak.'

'Oh Gaaawd no, not him.'

'Uh huh.'

'Quenton Wong?'

'Uh huh.'

'You're with Que again?'

Raine let out a nervous laugh. 'For real this time.' She leaned closer to Courtney, then, and as if everyone else in the mall was eavesdropping, she whispered, 'We did things last night. I did things for him.'

Courtney knew what things Raine was talking about, but she still had to ask. 'Things?'

'With our mouths. You know.'

'You mean . . .'

Raine smiled. 'We're going all the way tonight.'

Courtney said nothing at first. Aside from her heart skipping a beat, she felt divided. Part of her was excited, turned on. She knew Raine was still a virgin – hell, she was a virgin herself, hadn't done *anything* so far. And how depressing was that? She wanted to know more, to hear all about it, the things they did, how it felt, what he said to her, how he touched her. She wanted it all, too. Just thinking about it made her body hot and tingly, and her thoughts turned to her supreme fantasy.

Bobby Ryan.

But another part of her was scared about this whole thing. The first time was exciting and all, but this was Que Wong they were talking about. He was a dropout, and three years older than them. And you knew for sure it wasn't *his* first time. Que had already broken up with Raine two times over the last three months, and Courtney had little doubt that the moment he got into Raine's pants, he'd be gone for good, leaving her broken-hearted again.

'You sure you want him to be your first?'

'Come on, Court, don't get all nerdy on me,' Raine said impatiently. 'You're starting to sound like a man-hater. Like my mom.'

Courtney bristled. 'Your *mom*?'

'Yeah. She hates any guy I like. Hates my dad, too. She's always trying to get me to go against him. That's why she gives me so much cash lately. As if she could buy me. *Right.*' Raine thought it over. 'Man, I don't even wanna go home now because of it. I'll just sit there and listen to her bitch.'

Courtney said nothing for a moment, the image of Que intruding into her thoughts. Every time she saw the guy he was either showing off his new tattoos, or flashing the wads of cash he always had spilling out of his wallet, despite the fact he had no job. And he was always touching her, especially when Raine wasn't around. Brushing his arm against her side. Touching her cheek with his hand. Just little things. Subtle things. But enough to creep her out.

Courtney opened her mouth to say more, but before she could speak Raine let out a squeal and waved. Coming up the walkway towards them was Que. He was a short guy, just a few inches taller than Raine, maybe five foot seven at most, but he was broad and muscular, built like a gymnast. On his lower body, he wore a pair of baggy black jeans with a Chinese dragon snaking down each side from the hip to the knee. Above, he wore a designer hoodie – white, with pistols and skulls stencilled in gold across the front and back.

Totally cheese.

Raine hurried down the walkway towards him, her quick skips seeming light and giddy in contrast to the determined strides Que was taking. He was always like that. Each thing he did seemed to have purpose, every movement calculated.

Courtney moved slowly up the walkway, keeping behind Raine and studying Que as he approached. His round face was divided only by the tuft of hair under his lower lip. A soul patch. His dark eyes were covered with bright green contacts. Last time he had worn blue. The contacts made his eyes stick out like little lights as he turned his head left and right, studying the mall like he was searching for something or someone other than them.

Raine finally reached him. She flung her arms around his neck and gave him a long hug, followed by a deep probing kiss. He gave her one back, his eyes never finding hers but instead roaming the mall.

When Courtney caught up to them, he said, 'Hey, Creamy.'

She hated it when he called her that.

'Quenton,' she replied, because she knew he hated that, too.

'We're starving, babe,' Raine said. She rubbed her fingers down the side of his face, then pointed at a small bamboo restaurant called Yoki's. 'Sushi?'

Que took less than a second to scan the place and shake his head.

'I got a place,' was all he said.

He steered them towards the east wing of the mall, his head constantly turning left and right, his green contacts searching for something that just wasn't there. Courtney watched him closely, felt like bad news was on the way. Like something was wrong. Had it not been for Raine, she would already have left the situation.

But Raine was her best friend.

What was she supposed to do?

Sixteen

When Striker entered the teachers' lounge, the air inside was chilly, and the smell of old, burned coffee was strong. At the far end of the room, the window had been left wide open, and Striker's first thought was that a student might have escaped through it.

This thought, and the cold, made his skin mottle with goose bumps. He reached behind him for the door knob, but the wind picked up and slammed the door shut. The noise was sharp and unexpected, and it startled him.

But Megan Ling didn't so much as flinch. She wavered where she stood, in front of the open window, staring outside with the freezing wind ruffling her burgundy school dress. The only thing remotely Halloween-like on her attire was the earring that hung from her left lobe – a jack-o-lantern with an angry smile. The one from her right ear was missing, lost somewhere in the chaos.

Striker stepped closer, noticed small splatters of red on her white shirt.

'Hello there, Megan,' he said softly.

But he got nothing in return.

The girl was zoned out. Completely. So Striker moved forward, slowly, because the last thing Megan Ling needed after all she'd been through was someone sneaking up on her. He got to within ten feet of her, stopped, and stared out the window to where she was looking.

Out front, parked all over the main road and on the school lawn, were litters of emergency vehicles – ambulance, fire, police. Red and blue lights flashed in the midday mist, tinting everything red and blue. Lines of crime tape ran everywhere, draping from post to post, tree to tree, car to car. Like yellow Kerrisdale Day banners.

Striker moved forward, reached out and closed the curtains. It turned the window into a plain white tapestry.

'Megan?' he said again.

When she didn't respond, he gently touched her arm. She flinched.

'Megan?'

She finally blinked, nodded slowly. Like she was there, but not there. In and out. When she spoke at last, her voice was quiet, raspy. 'My father died last year . . . in a car accident. On Knight Street. There was a lot of blood. In the car. A lot of blood.'

'I'm sorry for that.'

She didn't reply; she just turned her head and looked back at the window, as if she could see through the white drapes. Striker gently ushered her away from the windowsill, to a chair at one of the lounge tables. She dropped into it, folded her hands in her lap, and looked down as if she were some demure Japanese exchange student, and not a kid born right here in Vancouver, Canada. Her pretty face showed not a glint of emotion. It was as if an off-button had been pushed.

Striker sat down opposite her. He chose his words carefully. 'You've been through a lot today, Megan. It's been a very bad day, the worst day of your life. But you survived. And things are going to get better from here on in. All that matters now is that you're all right. Your mother has been contacted and she's already on the way down. My partner is meeting up with her as we speak.' He gave her time to let this information digest. 'But all that will have to wait, Megan. Right now, I have to talk to you about the bad stuff. The stuff you probably don't want to remember . . . I have to ask you about what happened here today.'

The girl twitched, as if she had just come out of a bad dream.

Striker waited for her to say something – anything – but she remained silent. He got up, crossed the room, plopped the last of his change into the drinks machine and hit the Coke button. The machine let out a loud mechanical *cha-chunk* and the bottle dropped. He brought it back with him and placed it on the table in front of her.

Megan made no move to touch it, and suddenly spoke. 'They were shooting . . .'

'Everyone, I know.'

'No. Not everyone.' She shook her head but continued looking down. 'They were asking . . . asking for people. Specific people.' Without raising her head, she reached across and grabbed the bottle of Coke. She didn't open it, but held it tightly between her hands.

Striker leaned closer across the table. 'Who exactly were they asking for?'

'Conrad MacMillan.'

'Conrad MacMillan?'

'And Tina.'

'Tina?'

'Tina Chow.'

The names rolled over Striker like a cold wave of water. He knew them.

Conrad used to live down the road, before his family moved

to the Dunbar area just over a year ago, and Tina had been on Courtney's dance team when the two were children. He hadn't seen them for years now, but that didn't soften the blow. Images of the two kids flooded him as the ice he'd formed around his heart melted. He wondered: had they made it out alive?

'That's all I know,' Megan whispered.

'That's okay.'

'I want my mother.'

'She's on her way. Be here real soon.' Striker reached out and placed a hand on her hand, but she flinched away from him. 'You did good today, Megan. You did real good. No one could've done any better.'

He'd barely finished speaking the words when the lounge door opened and Ich poked his head into the room. He caught sight of Striker and swallowed hard, his enormous Adam's apple rising and falling in his throat.

Striker looked up at him. 'We're doing an interview here, Ich.'

'Sorry, but I just had to let you know. You were right about the different cameras. It's a whole new system.'

'Meaning?'

Ich smiled. 'We got video.'

Seventeen

It was exactly two fifteen when Ich pointed to the bottom row of monitors. They all showed frozen-framed, black-and-white scenes of the school cafeteria. No date marked the tape, no legitimate marker of any kind. Just a generic time string starting at zero and ending at 451. Striker wrote down the numbers in his notebook, then looked over at Ich.

'So what we got, Ich?'

'The video security system was definitely deactivated by the gunmen. Of that there's no doubt. But that would be the old system, the VISION 5 by SecuCorp – the analogue one.' Ich let out a soft laugh, one that held no joy. 'Turns out you were bang on right about the two types of cameras. The school was in the process of upgrading to digital. Keeping up with the times, right? I mean, shit, this is Saint Patrick's High. A private school. How could they not? And they couldn't have picked a better time to do it.' He tapped the closest monitor of the bottom row. 'That's why these three screens were all blank when we first got here. They weren't turned off or disconnected – the loop was in the process of cycling.'

Striker scratched his head. 'You're talking nerd again, Ich. What does it all mean?'

'What it means is we've got evidence. Those new cameras you found in the auditorium weren't the only ones, there were some in the cafeteria, too. It's a good thing you pointed those cameras out when you did, or else everything would've been erased and recorded over before we figured it out.' He pointed to a small black box that sat up high on one of the office shelves. 'Hard drive's in there. Friggin' terabyte times two. An image raid.'

'Sure, a raid, whatever. Is it backed up?'

'Of course. And I've already disconnected the drives from the rest of the system, so they can't be erased or tampered with.'

Striker put his hands on the desk and leaned closer to the wall, where the series of monitors hung. He stared at the still image on the screen: there were two figures wearing hockey masks, one holding a long gun, the other a handgun. Exact models were difficult to tell.

Striker took a closer look. From this detached viewpoint, the physiques of the shooters looked solid. Lean, wiry, but in no way dangly or awkward. There was muscle beneath those clothes. If he had to guess, the shooters looked full-grown and strong.

Not boys, but men.

It made no sense. Why would some adults break into St Patrick's High and start shooting everyone? A disgruntled kid on drugs made some sense. So did a mentally ill outcast. But not this. It fell completely outside of what was expected. And Striker felt his fingers ball into fists.

He studied the still-shot of the cafeteria, then the auditorium, and searched for a third suspect. He couldn't find one. Sweat slicked his palms and he quickly became aware that this thrown-together security room was too hot, too small, and it still held the menthol stink of Caroline's second-hand cigarette smoke.

'Just make sure everything is backed up, Ich. We can't afford any mistakes on this one.'

'Like I said, it's already done.'

'Then do it in triplicate. We need this feed.'

Ich held up a Blu-ray disc, smiled. 'You can run the feed anytime you want, Detective. Just hit play.'

Just hit play. The words sounded so simple.

Striker looked at the keyboard for a moment, took in a deep breath, reached his finger out to tap the Enter button, and hesitated. Once he hit that button, the gunfight was on again. Bullets would be flying, and kids would be screaming. Bleeding. Dying. Once he hit that goddam button.

Ich shuffled in his seat, and gave him an odd look. Striker caught it. He forced his hand forward, hit the Enter button –

– and the images on the screen came to life.

There was no sound. Just a silent horror show. Two men in hockey masks, shooting everyone everywhere they went. With the film being black and white, it was difficult for Striker to make out which one was which some of the time. Not that it mattered overly. The feed went on for what felt like an eternity, and Striker watched it without moving or saying a word.

Near the end, a boy, aged about sixteen and dressed as the Joker, made a break for it. He raced across the cafeteria for the exit, didn't make it, and dove underneath the nearest row of tables. The two gunmen approached him from opposite angles. They yanked him out, pointed their guns in his face, and shook him. It looked like they were demanding something. The boy mouthed some words, then they pushed him back down. Took aim. Shot him in the side of his head.

The tape continued.

The two gunmen marched across the cafeteria towards a girl who was huddled in the corner. She wore no Halloween costume, just the standard school uniform – a pleated skirt, drab in the black-and-white footage, and a white shirt, school emblem embossed. The gunmen shoved their weapons into her face, and again it looked like they were demanding something. She opened her mouth to say something, cried out, raised her hands in futility. One of them pulled a different handgun from his waistband and shot her twice in the chest, then once in the head. She fell face down onto the cafeteria floor. No twitching, no spasms, no movement at all.

Just stillness.

Striker felt off balance as he watched. Everything looked fake on the small screen. Like kids playing. Children falling over and lying still. Sprays of black liquid colouring their clothes and the tables and the floor, looking more like motor oil than blood. And the longer the video played, the deeper and darker the fascination became. He just couldn't look away.

The gunmen stood above the fallen girl, facing each other as if the dead girl did not exist. As if she were nothing more than a lump of clothes or a discarded gym bag. They seemed to be talking under their masks. Communicating. After a long moment, they turned as one and marched on through the cafeteria, shooting students, seemingly indiscriminately. Striker counted five kids go down as he waited and watched, desperate for the image of him and Felicia to appear on the screen.

But it never did.

And then, abruptly, the feed ended.

He looked up, startled. 'Ich, what happened?'

The previously smug look on Ich's face was replaced by a sick expression. 'What? Nothing happened. That's all we got.'

'All we got?'

Ich shrugged. 'The system is brand new, Detective, and in the process of being configured. The cameras were set up only as a trial run. A test. They were never intended to be used as anything else. Hell, it was a fluke they were even recording when the shooting started.'

Striker gripped the back of the chair and cursed. 'The sound. What about the sound?'

'All we got right now is a garbled mess. Totally useless. I've forwarded a copy to my assistant in Forensic Video to see if we can clean it up. I'll check on it when I'm done here, but it's gonna take a while. This is Com-Tech material. They use their own digital codecs—'

'You're speaking geek again, Ich.'

Ich sighed. 'Simply put, it's not just a matter of the feed needing to be uncompressed *and* transcoded – it's totally garbled.'

Striker looked at his watch. 'How long is "a while"?'

Ich shrugged helplessly. 'Days.'

'We don't got that kinda time. Shit, I thought you were the Bill Gates of this stuff?'

'More like Steve Jobs,' Ich corrected, and failed at forcing a grim smile. 'Look, I'm sorry, but that's what it takes. It's all math, compressed data, and number crunching. You can't make miracles out of numbers. They are what they are.'

Striker leaned back on the desk and studied the screen. The programme used a graphical slide-bar for time control. He reached down and grabbed the mouse. Used it to scroll back through the timeline until he got to the moment where the two gunmen yanked the boy dressed as the Joker out from under the table.

The tape time read 362.

Striker replayed the scene until the two gunmen shot the girl.

The finish time was 451.

He wrote down both times in his notebook, then copied them onto a piece of paper and handed it to Ich.

'Make a second copy of the feed, using only these time

intervals. Get me audio here, during this time period, that's what's most important. The rest can follow later.'

Ich said nothing. He just nodded and wiped the beads of perspiration off his long hooked nose and swallowed hard, like his throat was as dry as Striker's. He grabbed another Blu-ray disc from the top shelf, stuck it in the disc drive, then initiated the burning programme.

Striker headed for the door, then stopped. He turned and waited for Ich to meet his stare, and didn't speak till he had the man's full attention.

'Let me know the minute – the second – this thing is done, Ich. Got it? That tape is crucial, my best lead. I need to find out who these guys are. Whether they're even students or not. And I need to know what they're saying to each other, even if all we get back is a word or two.'

'It'll be done, Boss.'

'And I need to know who that kid is.'

Ich looked at the screen, confused. 'You mean, the boy they talked to? The kid dressed like the Joker?'

'No, the girl,' Striker corrected. 'There's no doubt about it. She was *targeted*.'

Eighteen

Striker cut through the school foyer, the heels of his boots sounding loud in the empty antechamber. He was headed for the cafeteria, to check out the gunmen he'd shot – a task which was causing his stomach to rise and his heart to clench. He'd liked to have done it hours ago, but nothing this day had gone well.

He'd barely made it halfway across the foyer when the school's front doors swung open and Felicia walked inside. A soft wind followed her. The air was clean and cold and crisp; it smelled of fall leaves.

Striker breathed it in – to counteract the smell of old, dried blood. The metallic stench was all around him. On the walls, the floors, in the air. Even on his body, making him feel sticky, grimy.

He wiped the thought from his mind, waved Felicia over. 'How'd it go?' he asked.

She had a pissed-off look on her face, and a stack of yellow papers in her hands. She walked over, not bothering with the pleasantries, and said, 'Here you go. You can rule out Nava Sanghera. She's in Saint Paul's Hospital getting her appendix out as we speak.'

'And the other kid, that student helper, what was his name – Sherman Chan?'

Felicia shook her head. 'Can't locate him. He hasn't reported in with any of the teachers and he isn't on the list.'

'What list?'

'This one.' She held up the yellow bundle of papers and beamed. 'List of the dead.'

'Jesus, Felicia, you don't have to say it with such enthusiasm,' Striker said. 'These are dead kids we're talking about.'

For a moment the words just hung there. Then Striker reached for the list. 'Let me see that.' He took the pages, and Felicia gave them up, almost unwillingly. Lists of injured and lists of the dead. The bundle felt thick in his hands.

The list of the dead was sorted by surnames, with the additional info of where the body had been found. Striker ran his finger down each page, stopping on page six where he found the heading: *Cafeteria*. Just the sight of the word made his stomach queasy. When he read on, he saw that only three girls were listed in this section, and before he could figure out which was the one from the video, Felicia spoke up.

'Chantelle O'Riley.'

Striker looked up from the list. 'What?'

'The girl from the cafeteria. The one they shot in the corner. Her name is Chantelle O'Riley.'

'But how did—'

'I talked to Ich.' She pointed at the stack of papers. 'All the names are right there, updated as little as five minutes ago. I got it directly from Principal Myers.'

Striker ruffled through the pages, stopped, let out a heavy breath. 'How is Caroline holding up?'

'She'll make it.'

Striker nodded absently. 'She'll have to.' He scanned through the names. There were now twenty. But only three names stuck out to him:

Conrad MacMillan.

Tina Chow.

Chantelle O'Riley.

The first two kids were ones he knew; the last one was a stranger. These three had been targeted. After talking to the witness, Megan Ling, he was sure of that. But why? What was the connection? He stared at the pages, desperately hoping for something to jump out at him. A familiar ethnicity, a social link, a similar age or class.

But nothing did.

He had no idea what Chantelle O'Riley was about as a student or a person, but he did know Conrad MacMillan and Tina Chow. At least, he had four years ago. And they couldn't have been more different. Conrad was in Grade Twelve now, and by all accounts, popular; Tina was a Grade Ten kid and relatively unknown.

Polar opposites.

So why these two?

There was something there. An unknown connection lurking somewhere beneath the violent surface. There always was. The body of the iceberg, so to speak. Striker took out his pen and circled their names.

'We're missing something with these three.'

Felicia crossed her arms. 'There's over twenty dead kids on that list, Jacob, not to mention the dozens injured. There could be a hundred different connections.'

'But these three were singled out.'

'We're assuming.'

He didn't respond right away. He just looked over the pages with a despondent feeling. This was no longer just about the case, it was about these kids' lives, and the lives of their families. Striker wondered how many of their parents had even been notified yet? Being a father himself, he could understand the devastation the news would bring, and the thought of informing these parents was unbearable. It hurt even to imagine it.

'Follow me,' he finally said to Felicia.

'Where we going?'

'To the cafeteria. I need to see the bodies.'

Striker moved quickly down the halls, and Felicia followed silently. The mention of the cafeteria had done something to her; Striker could see it, as easily as the deepening lines under her eyes.

And he understood it completely. He felt it, too.

Now, filled with cops and paramedics, the entranceway seemed ordinary and safe, if not a little cluttered and disorganised. It certainly felt nothing like the war zone it had been earlier this morning. Striker stopped. He turned and looked into Felicia's face.

'You okay?'

She nodded. 'Yeah. I'm fine.'

'Good, good. *We* okay then?'

She gave him a sideways glance. 'Why wouldn't we be?'

'You acted kinda funny back there, in Caroline's office. When I sent you to check up on that Nava Sanghera kid.'

Felicia sighed, like he just didn't get it, then said, 'You gave me an order, Jacob. A fucking *order*. And in front of everyone.' When he didn't apologise, and instead looked back at her in confusion, her face darkened. 'I'm not being mentored here, Jacob, I work here. And I have for the past six months. I've been the primary on more files than anyone else in the office and I've got the highest solvability rate – you'd know that if you'd been around for ten seconds.'

She finished venting, and Striker let the air clear for a moment.

He smiled. 'Wow, you really go for the jugular, don't you?'

'Hey, I'm part-vampire, right? What do you expect?' She crossed her arms, went on: 'And don't talk to me about being fair. You're never fair. Not once, in as long as I can remember, have you ever been fair.'

'We talking about work again, or our relationship?'

'There you go again, always with the jokes.'

'I was just trying to lighten—'

'You can't lighten *this*. I'm not the rookie any more. Not in Homicide, and certainly not on the job. And I don't like being treated that way. Hell, you're the one who just came back. If anyone should be giving orders around here, it's me.'

He let out a bemused chuckle. 'I'm a ten-year Homicide vet, Feleesh, what do you expect? Shit, I got more time on lunch than you got on the job. Which makes me senior. I'm the primary on this case and I always will be.'

'Self-appointed.'

'Maybe so, but by right.'

Felicia opened her mouth like she was going to say more, then gave up. Her posture sagged, as if all the fight had drained out of her system. She looked down the hall, in the direction of the cafeteria, and when she spoke again, the fire in her eyes had gone out, and her voice was quiet.

'Let's just get this over with.'

Striker agreed. He reached out, touched her arm. 'Look, Felicia, I'm sorry. Really. I didn't mean a thing by it. I didn't even know I was doing it.'

She just nodded.

'I talked to some kids,' she said. 'They knew where Courtney was. Said she'd taken off to Metrotown Mall. Gone looking for costumes for the Parade of Lost Souls party on Friday. She's been seen there since the shooting started. So she's fine, Jacob. She's safe. She's just ignoring you like always.'

He exhaled slowly. 'Thanks.'

'I thought you should know.' When he didn't respond, Felicia gave him a puzzled look. 'You know, it's okay to be relieved. You're human, after all. Far as I can tell.'

He tried to smile at her comment, but couldn't. Learning that Courtney was safe was paramount, even if he had believed it from the beginning. But it didn't relieve the stress he felt, the burden that weighed heavily on every decision he made. He looked back at Felicia and said, 'I tagged him.'

'What?'

'The gunman, the one who escaped – Red Mask. I tagged him once, when I shot out the rear window of the car. I know it, I can feel it. I got him. And he's hurt.'

'I know,' Felicia said. 'That's great.'

'It's *not* great, it's a disaster.' When Felicia gave him a confused stare, he continued: 'There's nothing more desperate than a wounded animal. If he was planning on killing more kids, I've just done the worst thing possible – I've sped up his plans.' As Striker finished speaking the words, a cold, dark feeling filled his core. And he knew instinctively that something bad was going to happen. Something for which he would be responsible. Something he would regret.

There was no doubt about it. More death was coming.

Nineteen

Red Mask lay on a table. He opened his eyes. Looked around.

The room he was in was small, lit by bulbs bright as the winter sun. In the far corner by a greyish wall stood a small, old man. He was bald. With wrinkles carved so deep his face looked wooden.

It was the doctor. Jun Kieu.

Red Mask ignored him. He lay, staring up at the glaring whiteness above. Suddenly, Kim Pham blipped into view, snapped his fingers at the two men who stood guard by the door and said, 'Get the fuck out.'

The room cleared, and then there was only Red Mask and Kim Pham and the doctor.

'Release me,' Red Mask said.

The doctor came forward and placed a hand on his shoulder. 'Be still.'

Red Mask could not. He had gone back in time.

In his mind, Kim Pham's white suit fell away and was replaced by a green cap and a grey buttoned-down jacket. There were screams coming from outside the window, from where the women were kept. And a machinelike voice spoke.

'You are a special agent of the Central Intelligence Agency.'

'Sister,' Red Mask replied, and in his mind he was eight years old again. 'Where is my sister?'

'You are an emissary of the United Socialistic Soviet Republic.'

'No. No. My family—'

'You have shit in the food supplies to make the others sick.'

'What?'

'You have falsified medical documents to undermine the reputation of this hospital because it is an icon of its kind and a great testament to the glory.'

'Mother! I want my mother!'

And then, like an evaporating mist, the vision dissipated. And Kim Pham stood there. The muscles of his face were tight behind his padded cheeks.

'Fuck, this is bad. Bad, bad, BAD. Nothing is finished! The bosses won't be happy.' He paced back and forth, balled his fists against the sides of his head, then stopped. He leaned back over Red Mask and spoke in English, as he always did, for their dialects were too far apart. 'Can you hear me? For fuck's sake, can you hear *anything*?'

The words were too loud and too soft. But Red Mask responded. 'I am here, I am awake.'

Kim Pham's voice deepened. 'What the hell happened over there? Did you get the job done?'

Red Mask felt the images overtake him, wave after nauseating wave. 'A man appeared. Like a ghost. He came from nothing.'

'A man? What man? What are you talking about? Was he a cop?'

'A soldier, yes.'

Kim Pham became silent. He looked up at the flat-screen monitor that hung on the far wall. The news was on. The entire focus was St Patrick's High. The images were blunt: yellow police tape; dead kids; frantic parents; lots of cops. Pham watched for a long moment, then nodded in acknowledgement of what was happening. He turned around slowly and gave Red Mask an odd look.

'Where is Tran?'

The words hollowed out Red Mask's heart. 'Tran is no more.'

'Stop talking in fucking riddles!' Kim Pham yelled. He paused. 'And what about Sherman Chan?'

'Dealt with. As planned. But not . . . not Que Wong.'

'Not Que.' The words sounded flat as Kim Pham spoke them. 'You let him get away?'

'He did not show. That is why Tran had to come.'

'Fuck! Another fucking failure. There's gonna be a lot of heat over this, a lot of *heat*. They will not tolerate this.' Kim Pham got on his cell, dialled and had a quick conversation in a dialect Red Mask could not understand. When he closed the flip-phone, he asked, 'Where is Tran's body?'

'Where it fell.'

'Stop talking in chicken fucking English – *where did it fall*?'

'Saint Patrick's.'

Kim Pham's eyes took on a faraway stare. Eventually, he nodded. Gave Red Mask's uninjured shoulder a gentle squeeze. 'Rest, my friend. You need to heal.' As Kim Pham turned to go, he gave the doctor a sideways glance. The old man nodded back. The movement was minimal, but Red Mask noticed the exchange.

And he acted.

When the doctor came towards him with the syringe, Red Mask grabbed the old man's wrist. 'What is name of medicine?'

The doctor tried to pull away. 'It's . . . it's an antibiotic.'

'What is name?'

'. . . Naxopren . . .'

'Liar!' In one quick motion, Red Mask bent the old man's wrist back until a loud *crack* filled the room. The doctor screamed, fell back, and Red Mask sat up. Kim Pham turned from the door, his hand going for his gun.

Red Mask was quicker. With his good arm, he pulled the Glock from behind his waistband and fired three times from the hip.

Pham's white suit exploded with redness and he let out a strangled sound; he fell forward, landing hard on the dirty green vinyl. Almost immediately, the stairwell door burst open and the two men who'd brought Red Mask downstairs raced into the room.

Red Mask shot them both. By the time they hit the ground he was rushing across the small room. He locked the stairwell door. Spun and found the doctor. The old man was crouched in the corner, the needle still clutched in his broken right hand.

'I have done nothing! *Nothing*!' he whispered.

Red Mask neared the old man. 'Untrue. You have done much, Doctor Kieu. In Vu Nuar, and Anlong Veng. Yes, you have done much horrible things. What is name of medicine?'

'Naxopren! *Naxopren*!'

'Inject yourself.'

The doctor's eyes became rounder. 'I . . . am not sick.'

'Inject yourself!'

When the doctor did not move, Red Mask snatched up the syringe and drove the needle into his shoulder.

The old man screamed. 'Please, please, *Mok Gar Tieun*!'

But Red Mask did not listen. He depressed the plunger.

The old man gasped. Trembled. Started to cry.

Red Mask's face hardened. 'Tears from *you*, Doctor? An irony – and an insult to your victims.'

The old man opened his mouth to speak, but only spittle came out. He clutched at his chest, then fell forward and slumped in the corner like a child's doll. His breaths came deep and heavy; soon he began to shake more violently. Foam bubbled all around his lips. And then he became still.

The threat was over.

Red Mask struggled to get up and let out a cry when he put pressure on his injured shoulder. He focused on the TV screen. The news was on, showing a photograph of the cop who had ruined everything. The one who had manifested from nothing. Beneath his face was a name: Detective Jacob Striker.

Red Mask stared at him with dead eyes, this man who had killed Tran.

Let him come, he thought. It will change nothing. I will find the girl. And I will finish the job.

He headed for the exit with this one thought on his mind. The girl was still out there somewhere – the only one who had escaped him. Now that Tran was gone, her death was all that mattered. He would find her. And then he would kill her.

Twenty

Striker approached the cafeteria with Felicia beside him. The doors were open. Standing out front of them was a young cop – male, East Indian, easily six feet tall and square-jawed. A solid guy, no doubt, but still a rookie. Had to be. Only rookies got stuck with the shittiest of all posts – guard duty. When Striker got close enough to see the badge number on his shirt, he nodded with understanding. The kid barely had six months under his belt.

Six months, and already this would be his worst day on the job.

Striker badged him, then grabbed a pair of protective booties and slipped them over his shoes. Felicia did the same. They gloved up and stepped under the police tape.

The first thing Striker noticed was the smell – not of blood or of urine or of anything bad. It was a sweet smell – almost caramel-like. He looked ahead to the kitchen and saw the blown-apart racks of Coke bottles. Black liquid was stuck to the floor. Memories of dropping to the ground with shotgun blasts impacting over his head hit Striker, as explosive in his mind now as they had been in reality six hours ago.

He jerked in response to the memory and slowed his steps. Then he felt Felicia's heavy stare upon him. No doubt analysing him. If he stalled at all, the questions would begin:

Is it too soon, Jacob?

Do you need some time, Jacob?

Are you coping, Jacob?

Without meeting her eyes, he said, 'It's sticky here,' and made a point of walking around the tacky goo. He marched into the eating area where the gunfight had erupted, and immediately spotted four covered bodies. Students.

He turned away and saw another body. From where it lay, he knew it was one of the gunmen.

'White Mask.'

Dark fascination overtook Striker, and he moved forward.

The body of the gunman lay face up between the first and second row of cafeteria tables. The bloodied-red vinyl around the body had been blocked off by red cones and bright strands of yellow tape.

Another crime scene within the crime scene.

Emotions hit Striker. So many of them. They mixed into some strange concoction he could not define. Suppressing them, he walked right up to the police tape, crouched low, and looked at the body.

The gunman's head was completely gone, as were both his hands – obliterated in response to the shotgun blasts Red Mask had pumped through them. Even now as Striker stared at the carnage, he could hear the violent explosions reverberating through the room: *ka-boom, ka-boom, ka-BOOM.* Up this close to the body, he could now clearly detect the unique stink of death – the urine and blood and shit. And the faint trace of burned gunpowder, which lingered as a dark reminder.

'There's not much of the prick left,' Striker said.

Felicia came up behind him. 'Yeah, he kinda lost his head over the whole ordeal.'

Striker leaned back under the tape and stood up. He analysed where White Mask had fallen, then considered where Red Mask had been standing. He pointed to the area beyond the body. 'Look for teeth over there. We gotta find something, some way of identifying this bastard.'

'Ident's already done that.'

'They find any?'

'No, but they combed this place down.'

'Doesn't matter. Keep looking.'

Felicia started to say more, stopped. She just shook her head, turned around, and walked between the second and third row of tables. After a few steps, she leaned down and, with a gloved hand, picked up one of the rounds that had been expelled during the firefight. She inspected it. A brass casing with an inset head on the bullet. Frangible. She held it up for him to see.

'Hydra-Shok,' she said.

Striker recalled the meaty exit wounds he had seen in some of the students.

'Bag and tag,' he said, and Felicia continued her search.

With her out of the way, Striker could better focus. He examined the top of White Mask's neck. It was an uneven fleshy ridge. The edges glistened, and here and there spots of whitish bone and yellow cartilage could be seen – some of them blown deeper within the body.

The musculature around the neck struck him as odd. There was too much muscle bulk for a teenager. Striker grabbed hold of each clavicle and tried to move them. The joints shifted, but very stiffly, and he wondered if it was ossified near the sternum. That would mean the John Doe was older than they thought. Maybe even over thirty. He wasn't sure, but it was something to bring up with the Medical Examiner.

Fanning down the left side of White Mask's neck was a

strange, golden design. It added colour to the copper skin. Striker leaned close and studied it. Calligraphic lettering, he thought, or perhaps an artistic design. Something tribal.

It was hard to tell because most of the design was blown away. The part which remained was clear around the edges, and the colours were vibrant. It had been done by a professional, no doubt. Unfortunately, eighty percent of it was gone, along with the rest of the gunman's neck and head. Striker took out his notebook, noted the location and design, and drew a copy of what he could make out. Then he called Felicia over. She looked unimpressed.

'That look gold or yellow to you?' he asked.

'Amber sunshine.'

The small stab at humour felt good, and Striker managed a weak grin. 'I'm serious, Feleesh.'

'Gold. Definitely gold.' She knelt down and leaned under the police tape for a better look. 'But there's red in there too, at the uppermost edges.'

'Red?'

Striker took a better look and realised she was right. He'd thought it was dried blood, but the colour was too bright compared to the rest of the crusted goo. It was ink.

'Good call.'

After writing this information in his notebook, his eyes fell upon the area where the neck met the chest. Just below the collar bone, left side near the heart, was a crudely tattooed number 13. Striker noted this too. Wrote it down.

He scanned the rest of the chest.

Located perfectly in between the collar bones, at the top of the chest bone, there was one small dark hole, barely noticeable in contrast to the sundered flesh of the neck. This was the first point of impact – where his bullet had gone through, dead centre, then carried out via the rear of the throat, tearing through the gunman's spinal cord.

Striker stared at that spot, and the recollection hit him all over again. The moment had happened so fast, more reaction and muscle memory than intention. And he couldn't help but wonder what the outcome might have been, had this first shot not landed with such pinpoint accuracy.

The thought left him sick inside.

Felicia stood beside him. She dropped her hand to her holster and rested her palm on the butt of her pistol. 'That's the shot that dropped him. Probably saved our lives. And God knows how many others.' She spoke the words calmly, logically, without a trace of emotion. As if she were talking about a shot he'd made at the range, or even in a video game.

It drove Striker nuts. Here he was, struggling not to have a meltdown, while Felicia remained cool and composed.

'Yeah, I got him centre mass,' he finally said.

'Great shot.'

'Well, one of us had to hit him.'

Felicia flinched at the words. Striker caught her reaction, and immediately regretted saying them. You're an ass, he told himself. Why push things? As Felicia spun away from him and headed in the other direction, he said 'Look, Felicia, I'm sorry, I didn't mean—'

'Yes, Jacob, you did.'

'Felicia . . .'

'I'm looking for teeth. That is what you wanted – right, *Boss*?'

Striker stood fixed to the spot, half of him still angry, half wondering if he should go after her. He watched her search the room, clearly doing a grid, her head angled down, her long brown hair draping across the caramel skin of her cheek. She was beautiful – something he noticed far too often, but never mentioned. And for a moment, he recalled the brief time they'd shared together. It had been a wonderful two months, a temporary reprieve from the grief of losing Amanda. And though it had been exactly what he needed, he now regretted it. Nothing had been the same since. Not with their partnership, and not with their friendship.

And he wondered if it would ever be that good again.

Just then, the blue cafeteria doors swung open, stealing Striker's attention. He looked over and saw a short cop walk through. He had a full head of jagged white hair, big white bushy eyebrows, and a stomach that hung way down over his belt. Looked like a mad professor.

Striker counted him as a good friend. It was Jim Banner. Noodles, as everyone called him – ever since he'd almost choked to death while eating a creamy linguine at the Noodle Shack in Burnaby. Noodles worked in Ident. Hell, he *was* Ident. Worked seven days a week and damn near twelve hours a day. He carried the usual blue-light device and associated tool box, and upon seeing Striker he waddled faster and hollered across the room: 'Hey, Shipwreck, stay the fuck out of my crime scene!'

Shipwreck. Few people were allowed to call Striker that, but Noodles was one of them. Which was only fair, considering that the eighty-thousand-dollar speedboat Striker had sunk on the team getaway ten years back had belonged to the man.

Striker smiled at him. 'This is *my* crime scene, Noodles.'

'Not yet it ain't.' Noodles reached the body of White Mask. 'Last thing I need is more of your goddam DNA screwing up my results.'

'I'll try not to jerk off in the scene.' Striker looked at his watch. ''Bout time you got your ass down here. It's only been six hours since the shootings. What the hell took you so long? Someone open an all-day buffet down the road?'

'Yeah, your mother did. Wanna know what I was eating? I'll give you a hint – I'm not a vegetarian.'

Striker laughed, and let the banter go.

Noodles put down his tools. 'Already been and gone twice, numb-nuts. Here to get some more blood samples.' He looked down at the blown-apart body. 'Shouldn't be a problem.'

Striker followed his gaze to the corpse. All the humour he had felt moments ago dropped away. 'What have you got for me so far?'

Noodles shrugged. 'The kid had a wallet in his back pocket. Nothing's confirmed, but the name on the ID is Quenton Wong. He's nineteen. Born December twenty-fifth.'

'Oh joy, a Christmas Baby.' Striker looked the body over. 'Nineteen? Sounds a bit young for what I'm seeing.'

Noodles nodded in agreement.

'What kind of ID?' Striker asked.

'Just the standard stuff. Driver's licence, BCID, some bank cards, and of course, an old Saint Patrick's Student ID Card. His primary residence is listed as Kerrisdale – Balsam Street. I've already sent the ID upstairs for prints and trace evidence.'

Striker thought of the gunmen. It looked like they were connected to the school in some way. Ex-students maybe. 'You run him, Noodles?'

'Yeah. And he's got nothing. No history, criminal or otherwise.'

Striker frowned. 'Completely negative? Tattoos and all?'

'Fucking everything.'

Striker looked at White Mask's ribs. On the left side was a series of thick white serrated scars, each about three inches in length.

'What about those marks?' he asked. 'He's got some on his inner arm too. Really odd scar formation.'

'They look odd because he got them when he was still growing.' Noodles looked back at the corpse, gave a shrug. 'I dunno, Shipwreck. The guy's a complete non-entity in the system. And by that I mean every damn database: CPIC, LEIP, PIRS and PRIME. Haven't checked across the border yet, but I've done enough of your job. You can do that later.'

Striker turned silent for a moment. The fact that this kid had no police history, criminal or otherwise, was disturbing, if not unbelievable.

Noodles strapped on a pair of latex gloves. He nodded towards Felicia, who stood across the room with a pissed look still marring her pretty features, and said with a smirk, 'What's with my Spanish fantasy? Seems kind of sour. Or is she just picking up the better parts of your personality?'

'The world should be so lucky.'

Noodles laughed. 'You two at it again?'

'Like the Inquisition.'

'Jesus, isn't this your first day back?'

Striker sighed. 'Call me when you get some results.' He wrote this latest information into his notebook. By the time he'd closed the book and stuffed it back into his pocket, Felicia had joined them.

'Hey, Noodles,' she said.

'My Persian Princess.'

'I'm Spanish, not Middle Eastern.'

Noodles shrugged as if to say, *What?* After that he went to work on the body. Felicia addressed Striker. There was no warmth in her voice.

'Grid search done, Boss. No teeth found, Boss. Anything else, Boss?'

'No, that's all,' he said. 'Due diligence done.'

He turned away from Felicia and Noodles and marched steadily back across the room to the north-east corner – the one area he'd been avoiding since he'd entered this damn cafeteria. That was where the other gunman was still lying.

The shooter Laroche had deemed 'possibly innocent'.

Black Mask.

Twenty-One

As Striker approached the body of Black Mask, he searched the floor for the machine gun. It had been an AK-47. A Kalashnikov. He was certain of that – or at least he had been – but as he scanned the area, it was nowhere to be seen. He recalled seeing it fly over the serving counter behind the hot food racks, right after he'd plugged the shooter.

But nothing was there. Just blown-apart pop cans, jars of Jell-O, and Saran-Wrapped sandwiches.

Doubt lingered in Striker's mind, like the beginning of a migraine. He shrugged it away, pretended it didn't exist, then spotted another round on the floor near the serving counter. It was longer than the one Felicia had found, and pointier, tapered near the front. The cartridge was grey steel, the bullet jacketed with dull copper plate.

An AK-47 round.

The find killed Striker's doubts. The gun must have been secured by the first attending officers, he rationalised. Had to be. Sure as hell couldn't leave a machine gun sitting around unattended. Not in a school of all places. It was a detail he would have to investigate later.

Even if a part of him didn't want to know the answer.

The lighting above Black Mask was dim, because the overhead fluorescent lights had been shattered by the ricochet of gunshot blasts. It was fitting, if not poetic. Black Mask, out of the light, dead in the shadows.

The body was lying in the exact same position as the last gunman – on his back, hands out to the sides, face up towards the ceiling. Yellow crime scene tape formed a box around the tertiary crime scene, looking like an evil Christmas ribbon. Striker gloved up with fresh latex.

'I'm not finished over there!' Noodles called out.

'You never are.'

'Don't fuck with it, Shipwreck!'

Striker was too deep in thought to respond. Red Mask had taken the time to de-face and de-hand the other shooter, White Mask – the one with the Quenton Wong ID in his pocket – but not this gunman. So why? It didn't add up. Striker leaned over the body and studied it. This gunman's physique was less muscled than the other. Thin. Not fully developed. It was not implausible that he was a teenager. A student.

Striker studied the mask of the fallen gunman. It was pitch black in colour, moulded to fit the face, with two horizontal slots for eyes.

Two bullets had struck Black Mask, one just left of the centre of his head – a perfect lethal shot – and one in the chest bone. Striker inspected the path of the first round. The fatal bullet had entered through the gunman's left cheek, the shock of the impact shattering one third of the black hockey mask.

Striker recalled what Laroche had told Felicia: 'The boy might have been innocent.'

Impossible, Striker thought. And yet, the words haunted him.

With gloved fingers, he reached out and gently peeled the mask up and over the gunman's head. Dried blood had stuck the plastic to the young man's face like a second skin, and it came off with a soft *pop* sound.

He was exposed.

Striker studied the face. The shooter was definitely a teenager. One he had never seen. Asian, young – maybe sixteen. Something tugged at the back of Striker's mind.

'Felicia,' he called. She was standing by Noodles; the two were going over something. She stopped talking and looked over.

'Yeah?'

'Get Caroline.'

Felicia didn't respond verbally. Maybe it was the tone in his voice. She nodded and left the cafeteria. When she returned with Principal Myers five minutes later, Striker saw that Caroline's eyes were clearer now, but her face remained ghostly white. She walked across the cafeteria on wobbly legs.

'Over here,' Striker called.

Felicia marched along, unruffled and unconcerned; Principal Myers followed slowly, as if every step was painful. Her eyes scanned the cafeteria, stopping on every covered body that filled the room. The grief on her face was damn near palpable. Striker could tell what she was thinking:

Which ones of my kids are under those sheets?

Hardened cop or naive civilian, it was too much for anyone to assimilate.

Principal Myers came to within a foot of the crime-scene tape, where Striker was crouched, and she shivered as if cold.

'Caroline—'

'You want me to look?'

'I've got a hunch who this kid is, and I think you know too.' He looked up at the Principal. 'Be warned, he's been shot in the face. Most of the damage is out the back of the head, where the bullet exited, but still . . . it won't be pretty.'

'Okay,' she managed.

Slowly, Striker stood up, to reveal the body behind him.

'You recognise this kid?'

Principal Myers said nothing for a moment. She just wavered on the spot, and Felicia had to grab her arm for fear the woman would careen over. After a few seconds, tears slid down her face as she whispered, 'It's Sherman. My student helper.'

Striker nodded. 'Now we know who turned off the video.' He ducked out from under the crime scene tape. Spoke softly. 'Who was this kid, Caroline? I mean, really. Who did he hang out with?'

'He . . . he was a good kid. Really, he was. A good kid.'

'Good kids don't murder other kids.' Together with Felicia, Striker guided the Principal away from the fallen gunman, to the other end of the cafeteria where there were no bodies or blood to distract her. Once there, he sat her down and said straight to her face: 'Whatever image you had about this kid is gone, Caroline. Forget it. He's not what you thought. I need you to be sharp here. Think hard. Who was Sherman Chan, and who did he hang out with?'

The woman reached into her suit jacket and pulled out a package of Kool Lights. Menthol.

'Not in here,' Striker said. 'It's a crime scene.'

She put them away. 'He . . . he didn't have a lot of friends. Sherman was a computer kid, a bit of a loner, really. Though he did hang out with two other boys. One was from the computer lab, and the other was his friend's friend. An older boy by a few years. Previous drop-out.'

'Their names?'

'Raymond Leung was one of them,' she said. 'He was Sherman's friend in the computer lab. A foreign kid. Exchange student from Hong Kong. Doesn't speak a whole lot of English. I can get you his details.'

'Good, we'll need them.' Striker wrote down the name in his notebook, then looked at Caroline. 'And the other kid? The older one – the drop-out.'

'Que Wong.'

'Que Wong?' Striker's eyes shifted back to the crime scene behind them, where Noodles was taking swab samples from the headless gunman. He gave Felicia a quick glance, making sure she said nothing, then focused back on Principal Myers. 'I need to speak to these kids, Caroline.'

She nodded. 'I think they live together,' she said. 'I'll get you their contact information. And photographs.'

Striker stopped her. 'They haven't been located yet?'

'Raymond never showed up for school today, and as for Que – well, he's been gone from this school for a long time now. Never really was in attendance, even when he was here.'

An electric sensation pulsed through Striker, but he said nothing more. As he ushered Principal Myers out of the cafeteria, he told her he needed their yearbook photos, or whatever else she had that was more recent. On the way down the hall towards her office to get him the printouts he required, she stopped, leaned against the wall, and wept.

Striker looked away and sighed. She was damaged goods now. Nothing would ever be the same for her again. Certainly not in this school.

And maybe not in life.

Felicia came up next to him. 'Good instincts about Black Mask. You were bang on right about the kid.'

He turned to face her. 'I know that. I *always* knew that. You should have known it too, instead of listening to Laroche.'

She let out a tight breath. 'Look, Jacob, I never said I didn't believe you.'

'And you never said you did, either.'

'You're picking at straws.'

'Am I? Look at the dead kid over there and tell me that.' Striker tried to suppress his anger, but couldn't. '*We're* the only reason more kids aren't dead, Felicia. Us, not Laroche. And here Mr White-shirt wants to take my gun away. Un-fucking-real.'

'Jacob—'

He turned away and grabbed his cell. He looked at the screen, saw that there were no calls, and grimaced. He dialled Courtney's number again, got the latest Britney message, something about someone being a womaniser. That was good, it meant she was fine, though more concerned about changing her voice messages than contacting her father. Again, he tried to leave a message but couldn't. He shut off the phone. Cursed. Caught Felicia's stare.

'She's still screening her calls,' he said.

'She probably doesn't know what happened yet – you know how teenagers are with the news – and she sure as hell doesn't want you to know she's skipping school. She probably has no clue about any of this. Otherwise she would call, Jacob. You know that.'

He looked at her like she was crazy. 'How couldn't she know? It's been *hours* since the shootings.'

'I don't know. Maybe her cell died, maybe she left it at home, maybe she's turned it off to avoid you because she knows she's in shit. Who cares? We know she's all right, people have already told us that. One of those girls – Marnie Jenkins – spotted her on a bus near the mall not an hour ago. She's out there having fun.'

Striker moved to the cafeteria window, stared outside. The sky was losing light, everything looking colder and darker. It felt like it had two years ago when the problems with his wife, Amanda, were at their worst. Just prior to her death.

'What time is it?' he asked.

'Almost four o'clock.'

Christ, he thought. Over seven hours since the shootings. It felt like days. Another life.

And now, maybe it was.

He drew his Sig and slid out the mag. He replaced it with another full one, out of habit, then put the pistol back into the holster. When he looked at Felicia, she was eyeing him warily.

'What are you thinking?' she asked.

'I'm thinking the world has gone crazy.' Striker scanned the cafeteria, took one last look at the hell he would never forget. At the blood that was everywhere, turning the floor into a giant red-and-white checkerboard. At Noodles, who was still taking fluid samples from one of the gunmen. At Sherman Chan – Black Mask – the student helper Striker had shot dead.

At everything.

It was too much. All too much.

'I've had enough of this,' Striker said. 'I'm drowning in the shit. I need to leave this goddam school for bit. Clear my head. Everything here is too close.'

Through the double-doors, Striker spotted Caroline at the end of the hall. She had returned with the yearbook pictures, and Striker went out to meet her. He took them, thanked her, and left her standing and staring at the crime scene in front of her.

When Felicia caught up to him, Striker spoke aloud: 'Sherman Chan was Black Mask. That fact is undeniable. And as far as we know – at least from the ID in the gunman's pockets – Que Wong was White Mask.'

'Which leaves only Red Mask,' Felicia said.

'Right. According to Caroline, Raymond Leung lived with Quenton Wong. He was also known to hang out with Sherman Chan. So it can't be a coincidence that Raymond was absent from school today.'

'You think he's Red Mask.'

'There's only one way to find out.'

They headed for Kerrisdale.

Twenty-Two

Courtney sat opposite Raine and Que in a small secluded booth. It faced the front door, which led directly into the north lane of Kingsway. An unusual entrance anywhere else, but it seemed to make sense with this restaurant, the Golden Lotus. Everything about the place felt secluded and secretive. No sign lit up the parking lot, telling the world the restaurant even existed; the iron-barred windows were blocked from view by dark green hanging drapes, and there were no printed menus. Que had ordered everything for them in Cantonese.

When the food came, Courtney had to admit he'd done well.

Raine pushed a plate of pan-fried prawns towards Courtney. They smelled of garlic and green onions. 'You got to try one of these, Court, serious. They're to die for.'

She took one and broke off the tail. Put the meat in her mouth. It tasted strongly of chilli pepper and something sweet.

'Isn't that just so damn good?' Raine said again. 'I could eat, like, the whole plate myself. Serious. The whole plate.' She plucked up another one and stuffed it into Que's mouth. He let her, not really looking at either of the girls but keeping his eyes on the doorway.

It had been like that the entire meal, and it was making Courtney nervous.

No one would ever have accused Que Wong of being a social

butterfly, but he had barely said two words since they'd gotten there. Hell, he'd said more to the waiter when ordering their food. And as for the food, he'd hardly touched a thing, instead choosing to sip from the bottle of Wiser's Deluxe he had ordered with the meal. He just sat there, sipping whisky, waiting and looking out the front window. He chewed the prawn mechanically, then caught Courtney's stare.

'Want more?' he asked.

She shook her head.

'Then what is it?'

'You're sweating.'

He tilted his eyes up, as if he could somehow see the beads of perspiration dampening his brow, and grabbed a napkin. After wiping his forehead, he muttered something about the restaurant being hot.

But the restaurant wasn't hot. If anything, it was cold. So cold that Courtney had put on her jacket. She looked to Raine for a response.

But Raine was smelling the glass of whisky Que had poured for her and wincing. She caught Courtney's stare and giggled. When Courtney didn't respond, she gave her a look that said, *What now?*

Courtney said nothing. She looked outside to where Que had been staring all meal long, and saw the growing darkness of the sky. A quick glance at her watch told Courtney it was now half past four, and she let out a surprised sound. In an hour, Dad would be finishing up his shift in Homicide. An hour after that, he'd be home. And given the fact he knew she'd been skipping, he was gonna be in one hell of a mood. The thought soured her, and she wished her mom was still around. Missed her terribly.

'Hey, you okay?' Raine said.

Courtney looked up. 'I have to go.' She pulled out her wallet.

'Don't bother,' Que said. He reached into the left pocket of his designer hoodie and pulled out his wallet. It was a fancy one, black shiny leather, maybe eel or snakeskin, and covered by a red and gold design she couldn't make out. More noticeably it was bulging with green, easily a couple of inches thick.

Que got up from the table, pulled out a pack of Player's Filter Lights cigarettes and lit one up. Took a long drag. He walked to the register, where a slender Asian girl was adding up receipts behind a Cash Only sign. She touched his arm several times and smiled a lot. Que didn't seem to notice. He paid for the meal, all the while keeping his head craned to the alley outside.

Courtney leaned across the table. 'You see how much money he's got in his wallet?'

Raine shrugged. 'Always does.'

'How's he get it?'

'His dad's a businessman overseas. In Hong Kong. Makes theme parks or hotels or something like that. Something fancy. Anyway, he's loaded. Don't worry so much, Court. God, you always worry!'

When Que returned to the table, Raine got up, excused herself, and went to the washroom. With her gone, a silence filled the air. Uncomfortable. Courtney listened to the clatter coming from the kitchen, looked up and found Que's fake green eyes staring heavy on her. He took another deep drag on his cigarette, blew out a long trail of smoke, and grinned.

'I should take you out for dinner sometime, too, you know.'

'What?'

'Take you out for dinner, just you and me.' He leaned forward and rested on his forearms. 'One night when you're really, *really* hungry, Beautiful.'

'I don't think I'll ever be *that* hungry.'

'You might be,' he said, and smiled.

Courtney leaned back in her chair, away from the table, away from Que until Raine got back from the rest room.

'What you guys talk about?' Raine asked.

'Food,' Courtney said. She let out a long breath. Her throat was dry, her water glass empty. She refilled it from the pitcher, drank a third of a glass, and looked back at the register, just in time to see Que get up and pay for another bottle of whisky. As he did so, he leaned forward across the counter and his white hoodie rode up at his waist.

Courtney blinked. There was something underneath the back of Que's hoodie, something about the size of a man's hand. And it brought back all the bad feelings she'd been experiencing ever since they'd met him two hours ago in the mall.

It was a gun.

Courtney knew it. For sure. She'd seen her father's Sig too many times to count when he worked plainclothes or undercover.

'Raine,' she started, then cut herself short when Que returned to the table.

He didn't sit down. Instead he took his wallet back out, grabbed a pair of fifties, and handed them to Raine. 'Take a cab home,' he said.

Her smile weakened. 'But I thought . . . Well, I thought that tonight . . .'

'I have to go. Meet me at the usual place tomorrow night.'

The smile slipped a little more from Raine's face and she gave Courtney a confused look. Que grabbed her, pulled her close. He gave her a long kiss, one so deep Courtney's cheeks grew hot and she turned momentarily away from them. When the kiss ended, Raine let out a gasp, laughed softly, and touched his face.

'Are you sure—'

'I have to go,' he said again. His voice was distant, faraway. 'Wait here for ten minutes before you leave.'

'Wait?'

'Just do it,' he said. 'I'll be gone a while.'

'But I thought tonight was going to be—'

'*Enough*!' he snapped. He rubbed a hand over his face and muttered something in a language Courtney didn't understand. 'I should never have gotten this close to you.'

Raine gave him a lost look. 'I don't understand.'

Que looked back at her, said nothing for a long moment, then he touched her face softly.

'It's nothing,' he said. 'It's me. Go home.'

Raine nodded. 'You'll call?'

'Meet me tomorrow, like we'd planned. We'll talk more then.'

He kissed her again, hard, then turned away and grabbed the bottle of whisky. He spoke to the young Asian girl at the cash register, and she led him through the kitchen out the rear entrance. The door slammed closed, so loudly the girls heard it in the eating area, and then they were alone again, just the two of them in a strange back alley restaurant that had no menus or sign or name. A place where people left by the back door.

Twenty-Three

Striker drove.

They took the soft decline of Dunbar Street, heading south towards Kerrisdale. Traffic was heavy, the narrow roadway clotted from the rush-hour flow. Everyone was fighting to make their way home under the dark shroud of cloudbanks. Road conditions were poor. Striker felt the car slip on an oily patch of rain, and he eased off the gas.

No point in dying just yet.

'We should be calling the Emergency Response Team.' Felicia spoke the words with authority, and it was the fourth time she had said this to Striker.

'And like I've told you, there's no time for that. We call in ERT and this will turn into a six- or seven-hour standoff. You know how it is with those guys. Next thing you know we'll have dogmen on scene, and Laroche will show up and call for a negotiator – and then we'll have a real wait on our hands.'

Felicia rested her head against the window. 'Fine. Your call, Jacob. But Laroche is gonna freak, and you know it.'

'All the more reason to do it.' When Felicia didn't respond, Striker explained his reasoning. 'Look, all we got on this Raymond Leung kid is circumstantial at best. Friendship and absenteeism. Nothing. We don't have one bit of hard proof that Raymond Leung is involved in anything worse than skipping class.'

Felicia bit her lip. 'Still, Laroche should know.'

'Forget Laroche.'

'I'm just saying—'

'You're always "just saying". Haven't you ever noticed how the guy never makes a decision? Not on anything? He just shows up for the news conference and reiterates decisions other people have made. Gets his fat face on TV and takes absolutely no responsibility for anything. Not ever.'

'Can I finish a sentence?'

'Who's stopping you?'

'You are, and you'd know that if you listened to yourself as much as you want other people to.' She took in a deep breath, then continued, 'All I'm saying is, yes, the man has flaws. We all do. But for some reason, you've got it in for him. You provoke him. Like you did back at the school.'

'Back at the school?'

'Yes.'

'I provoked *him*?'

'You were a bit harsh.'

'He wanted my gun.'

'He has a right to it, Jacob. A legal right. Hell, an obligation. And you challenged him on it, right in front of everyone. You gave him nowhere to go, no way out. Like you always do with anyone who so much as blocks your way.'

'You saying I'm a bull in a China shop?'

'More like a rampaging rhino.' She let loose a soft laugh, then stopped talking for a moment, as if replaying the scene in her mind.

Striker held his tongue on this one. Because he had to. It was typical of Felicia to never leave anything be. She would just pick and pick and pick until there was nothing left. Sometimes, with her, it was better to let things go.

The light changed to green, and Striker drove south on Dunbar. When they crossed Forty-First Avenue, he reached down and made sure his gun was snug in its shoulder-holster. Just feeling the grip brought him a sense of calm. He gave Felicia a glance.

'We're getting close. Call for another unit – preferably plain-clothes. We'll need them stationed out back in case this prick runs.'

Felicia got on her cell, called Dispatch, got a unit started up.

A few turns later, on Balsam Street, Striker killed the head-lights and pulled over. The twilight was deepening, the dark sky purpling under the growing reaches of night and angry cloud. Striker stared through the darkness, thankful for the few street-lights that splattered the road.

Far down Balsam Street, at the end of the roundabout, stood a large, square, two-storey house. It was a modern special – made up of big dark windows and grey concrete walls – and front-lit only by the weak light of the streetlamps.

Striker pointed ahead to it. 'That's Quenton Wong's resi-dence, or at least where he's listed as staying.'

'What about Raymond Leung?'

'Leung is an exchange student. Apparently, he lived with Quenton in his parents' house.' Striker shrugged. 'That's all I could get from Caroline.'

He pulled out his cell and called Information. After obtain-ing the telephone number for the residence, he called it, let the phone ring a dozen times, got no answer and hung up.

'No one's home,' he said. 'Or no one's answering. No machine either.'

Felicia never took her eyes off the house. 'No lights are on.'

'Means nothing. God knows, if I was on the run, every light in the house would be off and I'd be as heavily armed as possible.' He located the magazine release on his pistol, he pushed the button and slid out the mag, made sure it was topped up, then reloaded. He glanced down at Felicia's chest, looking for a trauma plate bump.

'You wearing?'

She rapped her knuckles over the centre of her chest, and it made a hard *thunk*! 'Momma didn't raise no fools.'

'Good.' Striker reached into the back seat and grabbed the shotgun. He racked it once, chambering a round, and gave Felicia a grave look.

'Time for some people to face the Reaper.'

When backup was in place – all of them plainclothes units – Striker gave Felicia a nod and she drew her pistol. His palm felt wet, almost slippery now, and he tried to convince himself it was just the rain wetting his skin. But he knew better. And all at once, it felt like he was heading back into the cafeteria again to battle the three gunmen.

Tactically, the situation was a nightmare. Two cops with forty cals and one shotgun. They had no distraction or dark-light devices, just a couple of Maglites and the flashlights attached to their guns. On that note Felicia had been right. The Emergency Response Team could handle this takedown better, especially if machine guns and shotguns became the weapons of choice.

But ERT needed time, and that was the one luxury they couldn't afford. As far as Striker was concerned, time didn't even exist any more. Not in a normal state. Everything was just one big rush before the next shooting.

He snuck down the sidewalk, shotgun in hand. It was loaded

with ten gauge – enough power to stop a black bear – and he rejoiced at the feel of the stock against his inner arm. It wasn't just any old shotgun, it was a combat shotgun. Benelli. A tiny piece of lightning in his hands.

Without looking back, he asked Felicia, 'You got me covered?'

She came up behind him and gave his shoulder a squeeze, indicating she was not only there, but on full alert. Striker readied the shotgun and moved forward.

Approaching the house from the front was bad tactics, even under the best of circumstances. To the west, the neighbour's exterior lights were turned off, and Striker saw no motion detectors. He opted to use the yard as cover. As he led Felicia through it, straddling the fence and searching for dogs, the thought of booby traps filtered through his mind. IEDs – Improvised Explosive Devices – were common with these nutjobs, starting back with the Columbine kids who had planned on blowing up the entire library.

Because of this, he stopped when they crested Que Wong's backyard, he turned to face Felicia and whispered, 'Eyes up for IEDs. Wires. Bottles. Containers – whatever. High and low. Watch every step.'

She nodded. Her face was blank, and her dark eyes were steady, determined. As much as a part of him begrudged her this ability to turn her emotions to ice, he also loved it. She was a rock in the field, always standing next to him when the worst of the shit hit.

That couldn't be said about all the other cops he'd worked with.

A long hedge of manicured bush, five feet high, separated the two yards. In the rain and darkness, it looked like a solid row of blackness. As Striker flanked the hedge, searching for a break in the bush, a sliver of light found his eyes. It was coming from Que Wong's backyard.

From the *ground*.

'What the hell?' Striker heard Felicia say.

He reached back and tapped Felicia, then pointed to the lit-up area of grass. Her long hair was wet, sticking to the edges of her face, and she shivered as she nodded. Striker felt the cold, too. The fall wind picked up, whistling through the greenery and blowing the rain into his face.

With Felicia covering his back, he crept along the bush-line until he found a small break in the greenery. It was narrow, but passable. He pressed between the two bushes and took in the full view of the yard.

It was ordinary, small. In the middle, near the house, was a small patio area, complete with a propane barbecue and an outdoor patio table with chairs. At the far end of that, an upright cement birdbath stood, nestled between two rows of barren shrubs. Striker let his eyes roam beyond the shrubs to a pile of old broken cinderblocks by the far fence.

The light was coming from the pile.

Striker made sure Felicia saw it. When she nodded, he moved forward and cleared the rest of the yard, finishing up with the patio. From this new vantage, he could see that the cinder blocks weren't in a pile, but were arranged in a small square design. And in the very centre of them was a hatch, coming right out of the earth. A square of dirty light spilled out around the edges.

'Well water?' Felicia guessed.

He shook his head. 'Bunker.'

'Bunker?'

'An old bomb shelter, I think. Step back. Cover me.' He dropped down to one knee and studied the door in the earth.

It was small, barely two feet by two feet. Only one person could get through that space at a time, and that was if there was a ladder going down, not steps. He took out his flashlight, turned it on, and ran the beam all around the edges of the hatch.

'What are you doing?' she asked.

'Looking for wires. Igniters. Switches.'

'You see any?'

'No. But be ready.'

He put his flashlight away and with the shotgun in one hand, he grabbed hold of the latch, the steel feeling cold and wet against his skin, and heaved as fast and hard as he could.

The door was hinged at the top, and the joints screeched gratingly as the door opened, then slammed hard against the back row of cinderblocks.

Striker stared down into the hole and saw no movement inside. A dim light from an unseen source revealed a rickety-looking ladder descending into the earth. At the bottom, a murky passageway trailed north.

'It goes towards the house,' he told her. 'Watch our backs.'

As he stepped down onto the first rung of the ladder, Felicia grabbed his shoulder.

'You're not going down there,' she said.

He never took his eyes off the cavern below. 'You got a better idea?'

'Yeah. Get a dog.'

'Forget that. No mangy mutt's going down here to tear through all my evidence.'

'Jacob—'

'Just cover me,' he said.

'It could be a trap.'

'Exactly, so don't follow. Stay here and make sure no one

locks me down there.' And before she could protest more, he descended into the earth.

The ladder went down ten feet, then ended abruptly. Once on the ground level, he could see the source of the light: an exposed fluorescent tube that ran down the centre of the far room. From its light, he could see that the long corridor he was standing in ran straight towards the house, then ended in a large open room. From where he stood, there appeared to be no other doors in or out.

Just one big underground square of concrete.

Keeping the shotgun ready, he stepped forward. The room was cluttered with things. Stacks of small water tanks lined the far wall. Wooden shelves held canned goods, survival kits, batteries and toiletries. Sheets of white plastic covered the walls.

Striker stood still. Breathed as quietly as he could. Waited and watched for movement. There were no obvious signs of threat, but that meant nothing. Situations like this were explosive and often unpredictable.

He inched forwards into the open room. Almost immediately, he detected something in the air. Something beside dampness and old rotting wood. It was a distinct smell, a familiar smell.

Urine.

He took another step forward and scanned everything.

Old planks put together to form benches and a table took up the bulk of the room, sitting out of place and centre stage. It bothered him. They were mostly covered by an orange tarp. Striker looked around. Though the bunker was old, it was still unfinished. Fraying chunks of pink insulation poked out through the white plastic sheets that stretched from two-by-four to two-by-four. Here and there, homemade wooden shelves had been nailed up haphazardly. In the far corner of the room sat a new workbench, covered in metal parts.

Everything seemed normal.

Seemed.

And then Striker took a closer look at the details. On the shelves, unlocked and out in the open, sat several copper pads, wire brushes, and dirty rags – cleaning tools for weaponry. On the far wall, overtop the fraying insulation hung a small piece of cardboard, containing handwritten directions on how to construct homemade grenades. And on the workbench, all the pieces of metal Striker had taken for scrap were actually filed-down splinters of metal filler for explosive devices. *Shrapnel.*

He had walked into a weapons lair.

'Got gun stuff down here,' Striker called up to Felicia. 'Be ready.'

He raised his shotgun, swung into the centre of the room, and stopped abruptly. Down to his right, directly beside the workbench, a leg stuck out near the front of the benches. The leg was covered by black pants and a black runner. The remainder of the body was obscured by the hanging orange tarp.

'Got a body!' he called.

He took a wide arc around the couch for a better view.

Lying there, face up on the dirty concrete, was a young Asian male. A teenager. His mouth was agape, his empty eyes wide open. The top of his head was blown away, as if he'd shot a bullet through the roof of his mouth. Clutched in his right hand was a 40-calibre pistol. A Glock. And lying beside him on the ground was a blood-red hockey mask.

Striker eased his finger off on the trigger, but kept the gun at the low ready. 'You can come down,' he called.

He'd barely yelled the words and Felicia was beside him.

She saw the damage to the gunman's head and the wetness of his crotch. She wrinkled her nose.

'Jesus Christ, another one,' she said.

'Good things come in threes.'

Striker studied the ceiling and saw a dirty spray of redness against the old brown wood. In the centre of the stain was a small hole, where the bullet had penetrated. Surrounding the hole were splinters of bone and splatters of skin and hair, and a mess of other dark things he could not define.

'Keep us covered,' he said.

When Felicia nodded, he handed her the shotgun and gloved up. He snapped the latex and leaned down over the dead kid. He took out the photocopied picture of Raymond Leung, the one Principal Myers had given him from last year's yearbook. Comparing the picture with the dead boy on the cement floor left little doubt.

This was Raymond Leung.

Striker folded up the paper, stuffed it back into his jacket pocket. He reached down, grasped the gunman's pistol with his thumb and index finger, and hit the mag release. He slid out the clip and took close inspection of the bullets, examining the casings.

'Hydra-Shok rounds.'

Felicia let out a relieved sound. 'Just like the ones in White Mask's pistol.'

'The ones he used on the targeted kids,' Striker clarified. He pocketed the clip, expelled the last round in the pistol and gently laid it back down on the floor. He then searched through Raymond Leung's pockets and found a crumpled-up piece of computer paper. He smoothed it out and looked over the page.

Felicia peered over his shoulder. 'Is that what I think it is?'

Striker nodded. 'Suicide note. "Fuck you and fuck the world".'

'Not much of a linguist.'

'Yeah. He wouldn't have made it past Deputy Chief in our Department.'

Felicia let out a strange laugh, one that resonated with relief more than humour. She took out her cell, flipped it open. 'I'll call it in.'

Striker nodded. He returned the note to the same pocket. When Felicia agreed to guard the body, Striker called for the plainclothes units to assist him in clearing the house. As he waited for them, he went over the case in his head. Everything had fallen into place: they had Raymond Leung's body. Here, in his own residence. With his red mask beside him. And his gun. Which was filled with Hydra-Shok rounds.

All the pieces of the puzzle fitted perfectly. This should have filled Striker with elation. Or at the very least, an overpowering sense of relief. But it did nothing of the sort. Instead, it left him with a gnawing sense of worry. This was a homicide investigation. Nothing *ever* fitted together that easily.

Something was wrong.

Twenty-Four

It took over an hour, but when the clock struck seven, the Wong house was cleared. No one was home. The parents, Anson and May Wong, were apparently away on vacation, visiting family in China. They would have to be contacted as soon as possible. In the meantime, the entire house and yard needed to be guarded as a crime scene, and Felicia had already started taping off the area.

Striker thanked the plainclothes units for their assistance, then walked back towards the bunker where Red Mask – now known as seventeen-year-old Raymond Leung – lay dead. He had barely set foot in the backyard when he spotted the unmarked white cruiser parked in the lane.

Deputy Chief Laroche.

Striker scanned the yard and quickly located Inspector Beasley – the biggest brownnoser in the Department. He stood near the patio. The Deputy Chief was standing beside him, just in front of the hatchway leading into the ground. He was holding a white handkerchief to his thin lips, and when he caught sight of Striker, his face tightened and he took the handkerchief away.

'I want a word with you, Detective.' He marched over to Striker, and in a flash, Inspector Beasley was at his side.

Striker glanced at Beasley. 'Brought the cheerleader, huh?'

The Deputy Chief wasn't distracted. 'Why wasn't I notified of this address before you came here? And why wasn't the Emergency Response Team called in? Jesus Christ, Striker, you didn't even go over the air with it.'

Striker nodded. 'That's what you wanted to say to me?'

'What the hell else would it be?'

'How about "Good job – you found the killer".'

'How can I commend you when your results are based on luck?'

Striker raised an eyebrow. 'Luck?'

'You didn't follow even one proper procedure on this one – not one.'

'I located the goddam gunman.'

'And jeopardised your life in the process. And the life of your partner, too. And those of however many other cops might have had to come after you if things had gone poorly. Your recklessness will be documented.'

Striker laughed darkly. It was a typical response of Laroche; why had he expected otherwise? And really, what the fuck did the Deputy Chief know anyway? The man was a carpet cop; he had put in the minimum amount of time required for Patrol, then spent the rest of his twenty-four-year career in non-operational sections – and not even Investigative units. Places like Recruiting, and Training, and Human Resources. Hell, he'd even had a stint in the Graffiti Squad. All of his placements had been positions with the least stress. Away from the danger. Away from the violence.

It was a wonder he could even fire his gun any more.

'You can turn in your gun now,' Laroche said. 'The immediacy of this incident is over.'

'Over?'

'I'm officially downgrading it.'

Striker looked beyond the Deputy Chief to where Noodles was taking pictures of the hatch. Standing next to him was Felicia. Her dark brown eyes focused on him with an almost pleading look. There was tenderness in her stare, and concern.

Striker looked away. Focused back on Laroche.

'I wouldn't be downgrading anything, if I were you, sir. Not just yet.'

Laroche gave a deep-bellied laugh. He looked back at Inspector Beasley. 'And why is that, Striker? Why shouldn't I downgrade it? Come on – enlighten us all with your wisdom.'

'Well, for one, we only *think* we have all three shooters,' Striker said. 'Nothing has been confirmed. We don't know for sure that Raymond Leung was actually the same guy we had a shootout with at the school.'

Laroche beamed. When he spoke again, there was condescension in his tone.

'We know Sherman Chan was involved. And Quenton Wong, too. We got the bodies. Now we have their best friend and roommate, found dead in the red mask. What else would you have us believe?' The Deputy Chief stepped closer and put a hand on Striker's shoulder. 'Maybe you came back too soon. Maybe you should go back on stress leave. Just for a while.'

Striker shrugged Laroche's hand off his shoulder. 'I'm back for good.'

Laroche smiled. 'Fine then. But I'll give you a little bit of advice, Striker. One that'll get you through a lot in this profession. When you're in a field full of horses, don't go looking for zebras. All you'll find is more horses.'

'I don't know about that. I already found a jackass.'

The Deputy Chief's smile never faltered. 'Always quick with the wit, aren't you? Right down to the bitter end – and this is bitter, I am sure.' He stepped forward, to within a foot of

Striker, so close he had to look up to see Jacob's face. 'The immediacy of this file *is* over, and the case *will* be downgraded. Immediately. You can turn your pistol over to your partner. Consider it seized.'

Striker's automatic reaction was to argue, but the more he thought it over, the more he had to admit that, this time, the Deputy Chief was right. If the immediate danger was over, he didn't have a leg to stand on. His firearm was evidence now – had been since the first shooting – and for him to refuse to surrender it now that all three shooters had apparently been caught would put him in breach of the Police Act.

He relented.

'You can have the goddam gun. I'll hand it in first thing in the morning – when *I* know with certainty that this thing is over.'

An uncomfortable look flitted across the Deputy Chief's face. It was as if he was wondering how much further he could goad Striker until it blew up in his face. The battle was already won; there was no need to push it further. And in the end, he opted to leave it be.

'I will allow you that,' he said, stressing the word *allow*. 'But have it done by nine. And not a minute later. Otherwise it will be seen as a breach.' He looked over his shoulder at Felicia and smiled wide. 'You hear that, Detective Santos?'

She moved closer. 'Yes, sir. Nine a.m.'

'On the button.'

Striker walked over to the primary scene, where Noodles was working. Something tugged at the back of his mind.

'You got a time of death, Noodles?'

Noodles stood up from his squatted position and said, 'He's stiff enough. Been a few hours, that's for sure. Sometime this morning, I'd say.'

'After nine-thirty – or before?'

'If he's Red Mask, it'd have to be after.'

'That's not what I asked.'

Noodles shrugged. 'We'll know more when the autopsy's done.'

'You check the lividity?'

Noodles gave him an irritated look. 'Stop bustin' my balls, Shipwreck. Check with the Medical Examiner when she's done.'

Striker frowned. 'Is Kirstin Dunsmuir doing it?'

'Yeah. The Death Bitch herself.'

Striker told Noodles to expedite what he could and keep him informed, then walked towards the back of the yard. He needed to get away from everyone. Far, far away. As he walked, his phone vibrated and he snatched it up.

Call Missed, the screen read.

Judging by the time that had passed, it must have come when he was clearing the house. He called his message box and, seconds later, heard the most wonderful sound he'd heard in as long as he could remember:

'Hey, Pops, it's me. Just got in and was wondering when you'd be home from work. I pulled out some fish for dinner – God knows you've probably chowed down on enough fast food your first day back. Anyhow, call me if you're not gonna make it, okay? The Court is *out*.'

The call ended.

Striker hung up the phone, smiled, and before he knew it, he was chuckling. Christ, Courtney had no clue – no friggin' clue – about all that had happened today. Insane, but true. And he wondered: did fifteen-year-old girls ever listen to the news? Even on the radio?

It didn't matter.

He slid the BlackBerry back into its pouch and turned around. Canned laughter from Inspector Beasley boomed again, and Striker ignored it. For the first time in as long as he could remember, he truly didn't care. Not about Laroche or the crime scene or his position in Homicide. He didn't care about any of it. His daughter had called. She was safe and waiting for him.

He was going home.

Twenty-Five

Striker left their undercover cruiser with Felicia and got Patrol to drive him home. It was well after seven p.m. and the day had been a long one. Every muscle in his back and legs groaned with stiffness as he plodded up the front sidewalk on aching feet. Since he'd left the crime scene at Que Wong's residence, the inky blackness of the night had deepened, stealing away the moon and stars. Leaving him with only icy rain and wicked winds.

He walked through the downpour, smiling. His home had never looked more peaceful, more welcoming than it did right now. And in that one moment, it was as if he had forgotten the stress of not only the shootings and the upcoming investigations, but the time off as well. Who knew, maybe one day he'd even come to terms with Amanda's death.

Maybe Courtney would, too.

The porch light was on, the front door locked. He unlocked it and went inside. The draught sucked at his coat when the door closed. The wool of his long coat was wet, so he hung it up on the rack, and stood there in his borrowed suit, which was worn and wrinkled from the long day.

He looked around. The front room was mostly dark, with just a flickering light from the television set. Courtney was seated on the couch in her blue Old Navy sweats, her eyes fixed on the TV screen. She was as stiff as a board; her eyes were swollen from crying. When Striker moved closer, she blinked, as if coming out of a bad dream. She snapped her head to face him, let out a gasp, and before Striker knew it, she was off the couch and in his arms, trembling, her breaths coming in deep and heavy sobs.

'I'm sorry,' he said. 'I'm just so, *so* sorry.'

There was nothing else he could think of to say or do, so he just stood there, holding her and telling her it was over now. It was all over. And they were here. In their home. They were together. They were safe.

And he wondered if it was doing any good.

When the worst of it was over, when Courtney finally got herself together and pulled back from him, mascara had run down her cheeks. Striker wiped a thumb through one of the trails, and found himself studying her face – her soft blue eyes, her light brown freckles, her thick and curly auburn hair that fell all around her shoulders in heavy, fluid waves. All at once the sight pained him, for she was every bit her mother. Just as beautiful. More so even.

And Striker prayed that was all Courtney got of Amanda.

'You okay?' he asked.

She nodded absently. 'Yeah. Sure. I guess. I didn't know. Not until now, like ten minutes ago.' She looked up at him with anxious eyes. No doubt she had a lot of questions, ones he didn't particularly want to answer right now – or ever, for that matter – and he just stared back at her with a father's tenderness. She seemed to grasp this, and the fact that he was exhausted from the hellish day, and her blue eyes fell away from his.

'I just . . . need some rest,' she said.

'I know you do.'

'Some sleep.'

'Is there anything I can do for you, Pumpkin?'

For a moment she was silent. She just stared at the fireplace, her mind somewhere else. Then she spoke. 'I'm sorry, Dad.'

'Sorry?'

'I know . . . I know we've had some issues and all. It's just been harder. Everything's been a lot harder . . . since then.'

A dozen responses flashed through Striker's head, all of them sounding hollow and forced. And how could they not? Bringing up Amanda was the last thing he needed right now – the last thing either of them needed, whether Courtney understood that or not.

He looked at the lines that underscored her eyes, and grimaced.

'You look exhausted, Pumpkin. Maybe you should have a hot bath and relax. Want a glass of wine or something?'

'Wine?' She laughed in a sad way.

'Guess not, huh?'

'You ever think about her, Dad? I mean, really think about her?'

'I loved your mother.'

'But do you ever think about her? I mean, any more.'

'Every day.'

'You don't show it.'

Striker detected the resentment in her tone. 'Soon it'll be two years, Courtney. I've learned to cope. You will, too. In time.'

'I don't want to *cope*.' Her words struck out at him, fast and hard, and for a moment, the anger was back in her eyes – that explosive fiery temper of Amanda's that burned everything in its path and took days to die out.

'That's not what I—'

'It's never what you meant. But that never stops you from saying things, does it?' Courtney fixed him a sharp look. 'You know what I can never get over? How you just let go of her so easy. Just, snap, like that. Like she was nothing.'

'Nothing was nothing, Courtney. Believe me.'

'Would you get over me that easy, too?'

'Don't be ridiculous.'

'What about today?' She moved closer to him, her angry face growing even tighter. 'You never even came after me, to see where I was. To see if I was okay. For all you know I could've been one of those kids—'

'That's *enough*.' He moved forward, so quickly he backed Courtney up towards the wall. 'Don't you ever give me that crap – not now, not ever. I knew where you'd gone. Other kids had seen you on the bus. And I had confirmation you were okay. And *still* I kept trying to reach you all goddam day. Patrol went by the house three times, I sent Sheila to Metrotown, and I called your cell over twenty goddam times.'

She looked away, wouldn't meet his eyes.

'You were screening your calls again, weren't you, Courtney? Don't think I don't know that. You were screening your calls because you didn't want to get shit on for skipping school again. I couldn't even leave a message!'

Courtney sucked on her upper lip, said nothing. The fire in her eyes went out as quickly as a blown match. She looked down at the ground, her long hair falling around her face. When she spoke again, her voice was resigned.

'I wasn't screening my calls, Dad. The phone died.'

'I don't believe you.'

'Don't believe me?'

'You still managed to change your voice message. Three times.'

'It's set on random.'

'Random?'

'I've got a few different voice messages – all Britney stuff. They cycle automatically.'

Striker said nothing at first. He just let out a long breath, rubbed a hand over his face, felt like collapsing.

'Christ,' was all he managed to say.

'I'm sorry, Dad,' Courtney said. 'I had no idea. Really. I had no . . . no . . .'

She covered her face and stifled a sob, and all at once, the frustration and anger Striker felt vanished and was replaced by the usual grief and guilt. His heart plummeted in his chest. He wrapped his arms around Courtney for the second time and kissed her on the top of her head, and wished to God things could go back to the way they had been years ago.

Before Amanda died.

Finally, it was Striker who spoke.

'Sometimes I think I got over your mother quicker than you did because you're so much like her. I still feel like she's around whenever I'm with you.' He looked intently into her hurting, wide-eyed face. Made sure she saw the seriousness he felt. 'You know that I would never abandon you, Courtney. Not for a millisecond.'

'I know that, Dad.'

'I only kept looking for the gunmen because I knew you were all right.'

'I know.'

'And because I believed that if they weren't found – and soon – more kids would die.'

'Dad, I *know*. I'm just . . . so tired. Stressed. God, I think I will go to bed. For the night. I'm just so exhausted.'

She gave him another hug and a soft kiss on the cheek, and

when she went to let go of him, he held on for a while longer. Finally, when he did let go, she turned and headed for the bedroom. After ten steps, she stopped and looked back at him.

'You eaten yet?'

'I can make myself dinner, Pumpkin.'

She laughed. 'Right. Pork and Beans or Chef Boyardee?'

'Better than that – Nutella.'

She grinned. 'I don't mind cooking you that fish.'

'Get some sleep, Pumpkin.'

She delayed. 'Promise me you'll eat something *healthy*.'

He held up a hand, as if pledging allegiance. 'Everything I hate and more.'

'Love you, Dad,' she said, then slowly walked down the hall.

Striker watched her go, feeling as useless and ineffective as he had after Amanda had died. In five minutes he'd gone from feelings of love to rage to betrayal – and now he was back at love again. Intertwined with a lot of guilt. Sometimes he felt like his emotions were an endless ocean, and he was a wayward buoy floating up and down on the rough waters, being dragged wherever the currents took him.

And usually those currents were unpredictable and dangerous.

'I love you, Courtney,' he said.

But the room was empty.

Twenty-Six

When Felicia unexpectedly arrived, the night was darker than a day-old bruise. The icy rain had stopped, but the wind continued – a vocal force battering every window of the house. Striker heard the soft roar of a patrol car out front – those Crown Vics had a distinctive rumble – and saw the quick flash of halogen headlights as they beamed across the bay window.

He struggled to get up from the couch and looked out the window just in time to see Felicia trudge up the walkway, her pretty Spanish face caught in the soft glow of the exterior lights.

She looked tired, depleted. Hell, she was threadbare.

And yet she was always beautiful. Striker saw that every time he looked at her. At times like this, he berated himself for ending their relationship and letting her go six months ago.

It had been a complicated time, he told himself.

A necessary decision. It was for the best.

There were a hundred more clichés he could dredge up, but none of them were true. And none made him feel any better.

Felicia reached the front door, and instead of rapping softly on the wood, she leaned around the railing and peeked inside the bay window. Dark hair framed her dark eyes. She saw Striker and a warm smile spread her wide lips.

'Amway calling!'

He moved to the foyer and opened the door. A large gust of wind snuck inside the house. It swept right through him, and he shivered. Felicia stepped inside the foyer, hugging herself to keep warm, and kicked the door closed with the heel of her boot.

Striker smiled at her. 'What's a nice girl like you doing in a place like this?'

Felicia looked over her shoulder. 'I don't see any nice girls in here.' She grinned. 'You like my Amway joke?'

'Would've preferred *Watchtower*.'

She raised an eyebrow, and the two of them just stood there looking at one another. It was a fleeting moment, and it struck Striker as funny, how they could be so different outside of work, where they were often at each other's throats.

'So we gonna stand here trading one-liners all night, or you gonna invite me in?' she finally asked.

'You don't need an invitation here.' He swung his arm outwards to guide her into the den. Spotted the clock above the fireplace. Saw it was well past twelve. 'Jesus, you're still working?' he asked.

'Just the small stuff.'

'You mean Laroche?'

She grimaced. 'Hardy-har-har. Anyhow, I'm done for the night.' She took off her jacket, threw it to Striker, who hung it on the coat-rack. 'I was down at Ident with Noodles for the past hour. Poor guy looks like he's gonna keel over any minute. He better lose some weight or he's gonna have a heart-attack. I swear, he needs to think of his health once in a while.'

'Speaking of which, you should be in bed.'

'Is that an invitation?'

'Don't tempt me.'

She ran her fingers through her long hair, loosening it, then moved into his personal space. The humour left her eyes, and was replaced by the vulnerable look of honesty. 'I was worried about you, Jacob.'

'So you're not here for my gun.'

She sighed. 'Boy, you really know how to kill a moment.'

He raised his hands, palms forward, to signal he had no intention of arguing, then offered a quick apology. He led her into the living room, where he crashed down on the couch and beckoned her to join him. Felicia sat down at the end closest to the fireplace, where she basked in the heat.

'Freezing out there.'

'I'll get you something.' From the closet, Jacob grabbed a heavy wool blanket and wrapped it around her shoulders. He then went to make them a couple glasses of rye with hot water and lemon.

In the kitchen, Striker put on the kettle, then took the bottle of Wiser's from the cupboard and put it on the counter. When he went to open the fridge door to look for lemons, something distracted him. Stuck on the outside of the fridge door was a small yellow happy face. It was just one of the many junky trinkets Courtney had stuck up there – a magnetic picture clip holding a photo of Amanda from their last Christmas together; a scattering of magnetic letters, from which Courtney had spelled out BRITNEY; and this small round happy face.

Similar to the one they'd found in the stolen Honda Civic.

The magnet was weak, and it came away with little resistance. Striker rolled the happy face between his fingers, and knew he would have to see the stolen Honda Civic again. He put the magnet in his pocket, and the kettle began to whistle.

He finished making their drinks. When he returned to the living room, Felicia looked warmer and relaxed. He offered her one of the mugs and asked, 'What were you helping Noodles with?'

She took the mug, cradling it between her fingers, relishing the heat. 'Evidence log. And tagging. They found Black Mask's machine gun, by the way.'

'The AK-47? Where?'

'Serving counter, I think. In the cafeteria. The Emergency Response Team had already seized it during their clear.'

'Ballistics—'

Felicia held up a hand. 'Already being done as we speak. Prints, swabs, ballistics – you name it. The amount of work is insane.' She sipped her drink, licked her lips, and her eyes took on a faraway stare. 'Funny, all my life I've wanted one of these calls, dreamed about being even a small part of an actual Active Shooter situation, and then – *bang!* – here I am, dead smack in the centre of it, and I just can't wait for it to end.'

'It burns you out.'

'Like gasoline.'

Striker sipped his rye and lemon, gave her a hesitant stare, then looked down at his drink.

'What?' she asked.

He didn't want to say it but had to. 'I wouldn't be so sure it's over.'

'Not this again.'

'Yeah, I know, don't go looking for zebras. I always knew Laroche was a clown, but funny, too? Wow, how lucky am I!'

'Jacob—'

'Hey, you asked, and all I'm doing is pointing out the facts. Some of them – a lot of them – don't add up with these gunmen.' He put his drink down on the table, then started counting off the problems on his fingers. 'One, why disable the security system if they're gonna be foolish enough to carry ID

in their pockets? And for that matter, why would Red Mask –
Raymond Leung – blow off Que Wong's head and hands?'

'To conceal his identity.'

'Of course. But why do that if Wong is carrying ID? It does-
n't make any sense. And why do it if he was just going to run
home and kill himself. If he's on the run, why kill himself at
all?'

Felicia shrugged. 'Panic? Fear? Family embarrassment? A
twisted sense of honour? Who knows. We're not dealing with
rational people here.'

'But that's point number two. You see, I think we are.'

Felicia grinned darkly over her drink. 'You think an Active
Shooter is rational?'

'The purpose might be irrational, but the plan itself was put
together on good logic. Don't kid yourself, Felicia, it was solid.
Think about the facts: what kind of car did they steal for their
getaway? A 1994 Honda Civic. Dark green. Not only is it the
most common stolen car on the road, but they picked the most
common year and colour.'

'Actually the Dodge Caravan is number one on the stolen
list.'

'Fine,' he conceded. 'I'll give you that, the Civic is number
two. But tell me this, which vehicle would you choose, knowing there was a chance of a police pursuit? A clunky old van
that rolls a corner at fifty miles an hour, or a small sports car
that can blend in anywhere?' When Felicia didn't respond,
Striker asked her: 'You think that's a coincidence?'

'Maybe.'

'Okay, fine, I'll give you that too. But what about point
number three: the time of the shooting. Nine a.m., on the dot –
the exact time when Alpha shift is on break. Only cars we had
on the road out there were Bravo Shift, and because it was still

early enough, no Charlie units had cleared. There couldn't have been a better time for a weak police response.'

Felicia hedged. 'The timing could boil down to pure luck.'

'All right – but then what about point number four – and this is a big one: these pricks had gun-fighting skills. Pure and simple. They were *good*. And I still have a real problem believing the gunmen we were duelling with back there in the cafeteria were nothing but a group of disgruntled computer science kids. Kids with no criminal history. No police files. Christ, not even a firearms licence.'

'I know it looks off, Jacob, almost ridiculous, but Columbine was the exact same.'

Striker let out a frustrated sound. 'Then what about the calls made before the shooting started?'

'What calls?'

'Twenty minutes before the shooting started, there were two 911 calls placed from Oakridge Mall. Fake gun calls. Robberies. We sent five of our Bravo units up there to deal with it, so they were way out of the picture when the real shootings started. What do you call that? Just another coincidence?'

Felicia thought it over, then said, 'It sounds well-planned, true. But that kind of thing happens all the time – even in the Skids. Look at all the drugged-out zombies that hang out on those streets. If they can do it, anyone can. God knows it doesn't take a criminal mastermind to divert police resources.'

'I know that, Felicia, but I'm not talking about these things on an individual basis; I'm talking about them *collectively*. When added up, the shootings appear to be more than luck and decent planning – they look like a hired hit.'

'A hired hit? You mean pros?'

'Yes, professionals. Or at the very least someone with some type of army experience. Like a disgruntled soldier come back from Afghanistan. Or a hired mercenary. Someone with real know-how.'

Felicia looked doubtful. 'Why would a hired soldier be involved with Saint Patrick's High School students?'

Striker put down his mug. 'That's a whole different issue. Despite what Laroche is telling people, we still don't know the true reason behind all this. Everything we have is speculation. Think about it. What the hell did these kids do to warrant such extreme violence?'

'Or what did they see?' Felicia said.

'Either way, something tells me this is more than high-school politics, Felicia. A lot more.'

Felicia downed the rest of her drink, looked outside at the dark night, and sighed.

'What?' Striker asked.

'I dunno,' she said. 'Some of the moments today, when you took charge, I resented you for it – but I also admired you for it. I wish I had your confidence, Jacob, your self-assurance.'

'You do.' Striker leaned forward, made sure he had her full attention. 'There's two kinds of people in this world, Feleesh. Them and Us. Too many of Them give in and break.'

'That's how I feel sometimes.'

'Bullshit. We're the other kind.'

'Other kind?'

'The survivors. And you showed that every minute of the day today, whether you were shooting it out with those gunmen or investigating Red Mask's disappearance. You did good, Feleesh. You came through. Hell, we both did.'

Felicia exhaled and a grin found her lips. 'It's good to hear you say that.' She leaned across the couch, nearer to him. 'I guess there comes a time when you just have to let go.'

Let go.

The words hit home, and Striker nodded slowly. He looked at her for a long moment, with so many emotions colliding in his heart, ones he couldn't find the right place for. Everything was a mixed-up jumble.

'You never really know what someone's made of till your life's on the line,' he said. 'Well, today you really came through for me. Gave me cover when I was down and out. And I'll never forget that.'

She reached up and placed her palm against his cheek. Her skin was warm. Soft. Tender.

'What happened, Jacob? What happened *to us*?'

He let out a heavy breath. 'You were so bitchy in the mornings.'

'Be serious.'

He leaned back and her hand fell away. 'It was just . . . just too soon. After Amanda's death.'

'Too soon for you? Or for Courtney?'

Striker looked away. 'Does it matter?'

'Everything matters. You know, Jacob, life would be a lot easier if Courtney knew the truth.' When he didn't respond, Felicia said, 'She still doesn't know, does she?'

Striker stared at the fire. 'No.'

'Amanda was her mother. Harsh or not, she deserves to know the whole story.'

'I'm going to tell her.'

'When?'

'When she's sixty.'

'This isn't a joke. It's been – what, twenty months since the woman died, and—'

'Leave it alone, Felicia. Please. For once just leave it alone.'

'I want to, Jacob, I always want to. But where does that leave us?'

The words hit him strangely, made him feel empty and alone and desperately in need of companionship. He stared back at Felicia. Saw tenderness in her eyes. And the soft wetness of her open mouth. He wanted her now more than ever. He reached out and pulled her close.

And she came easily.

She was breathing hard, her ribs rising and falling against his hands. She felt good. So real, so alive. He kissed her lips, tasted the hot booze in her mouth, the slipperiness of her tongue. Heard her say, 'I want you, Jacob.'

She straddled him, and her long dark hair spilled across his neck and shoulders, sent tingles through his body. It made him hard, so hard he could feel the blood pulsing through his body. He pulled her into him, until her firm breasts pushed against his chest, and her thighs ground into his hips. Her inner thighs squeezed him tight, and he could feel her warmth there.

'I want you,' she said, over and over again.

He unbuttoned her shirt and pulled it back off her body, revealing a lacy purple bra, which fitted snugly against her caramel breasts. In one quick movement, he reached up and tore the straps off her shoulders. He slid the bra down, away from her breasts, exposing the curve of her nipples. They were large, hard, erect, and he kissed them. Licked them softly.

'I want you inside me,' she said.

He reached down, broke open the front of her pants, and loosened them from her waist; she helped him. When they were partway down her hips, Striker reached around her waist to the small of her back, felt the silky thin strap of her panties and ran his fingers down, reaching lower and lower until he felt warmth and wetness and—

'I can't believe it!' Courtney screamed.

In a flash, Felicia rolled off of him and spun away towards the fireplace. She tried to cover herself up, adjust her clothes.

Striker sat there, frozen, and looked down the hall to where Courtney was standing in her sleepwear. Her hands were at her sides, balled into fists. Her eyes were afire.

'Courtney,' he started.

'Mom's dead not even two years.'

'Listen to me.'

'And you're with that woman?'

'Listen to me.'

'I can't believe you – you've already fucked her, haven't you? Haven't you? You *fucked* her!' She threw her cell phone across the room, the device slamming against the old white plaster of the east wall.

'That's *enough*, goddammit!'

Courtney flinched at the roar of Striker's words. Then she regained her composure; her defiance. She shook her head slowly, as if disgusted, and after a moment, she spun about and fled back to her bedroom. The door slammed shut behind her, she screamed out 'I HATE you!' and Striker could hear things being thrown around the room.

Striker stood up from the couch. He looked at the bedroom door and hesitated, wondering what to do. Finally, he turned to Felicia, who was still tidying herself up.

'Should I go after her, or not?'

Felicia did up the last button of her shirt, let out a frustrated sound. 'Just leave her be, Jacob. Give her some space and time. She needs it.'

He rubbed his hands on his face, felt the frustration spreading through him like a hot fever. This wasn't fair. Goddammit, none of this was fair. He'd done everything right as a husband. Done his best as a father. And no matter how hard he tried with relationships, no matter what he did, he failed. Always. Utterly and completely.

And Courtney was suffering because of it.

His resilience crumbled away. He moved over by the fire and came up to Felicia. He reached for her hands. Hesitated. Then he let his own hands fall to his sides.

'Look. I'm sorry. Really. I should never have started—'

'I should go.'

'Go? But it's past midnight and you live way out off Commercial. Just stay here for the night.'

Felicia glanced down the hall. 'That is not a good idea.'

'It's the only idea.' He grabbed her gently, turned her around. 'You can use the spare bedroom, the one in the basement. There's a shower down there, too. Hell, I think you still have some clothes here.'

Felicia looked out the window, at the heavy darkness of the night.

'Just stay,' Striker pleaded. 'I'm asking you to. Please.'

She said nothing for a moment, just stood there, as if mulling the idea over. After a long moment, she tucked the tails of her shirt back into her pants, adjusted her belt, and muttered, 'Fine.'

'Good. I want you here.'

She ran her fingers through her hair. She reached up, touched his cheek and smiled. Then she sauntered out of the room. At the beginning of the hall, she stopped, looked back, and offered him a slight smile.

'Pleasant dreams, Jacob.'

'I'm sure.'

She laughed softly, a frustrated sound, then walked on.

Striker stood there with a deep sense of longing as he watched her sneak down the hall, turn the corner, and make her way down the stairs. Once he heard the last soft thumps of her feet on the staircase, he moved back to the couch. Tried to sleep. Couldn't.

Aside from being horny, his mind wouldn't rest. There were too many things he still needed to deal with. Courtney. And of course there was still Laroche: tomorrow, the Deputy Chief would close the Active Shooter file and take his gun. And maybe even place him on Mandatory Stress Leave. Again. File a report with Internal.

The list of problems was never-ending.

Sleep didn't come easy, but the exhaustion helped. Eventually a deep, magnetic slumber overtook him, bringing on the nightmares. There were long red hallways and masked men. And of course there were the school kids, too. Screaming in the darkness. Calling out for him.

'Detective Striker!'

'Detective Striker!'

'Detective Striker!'

But there was nothing he could do to save them.

Thursday

Twenty-Seven

Six thousand, three hundred and ninety-six miles away, in the entertainment district of Macau, Hong Kong, the Man with the Bamboo Spine sat in a stiff-backed chair made of black walnut wood and dyed-black leather. Cigarette smoke floated all around him.

It was ten p.m., local time, and the night was only beginning on the sixth floor of the Hotel Lisbon. This was the Lotus Flower Room. The deep red walls and ornate golden decor gave away the location to anyone who understood the significance.

The Man with the Bamboo Spine was not alone. Six men sat at the table with him. Four were Chinese, and two were white. The white guys had already laid down their hands.

The game was Texas Holdem. Once non-existent in Macau, it had caught on like wildfire. And the Man with the Bamboo Spine was pleased with the game, not only because he enjoyed it, but because he was very, very good at it. He was already up forty K. And this hand was going well.

His face helped him win. It was poker perfect. The disease had made sure of that, pulling back his skin so tight that expressions did not display across his harsh angular features. With eyes as black as oil sludge, he waited his opponent out.

'Drink, sir?'

He turned his head and spotted the waitress, a diminutive girl with a pretty face and large fake breasts.

'Hot water.'

The waitress hurried off across the room, her black high-heels clicking loudly on the marbled floor.

Across the table, the younger man finally bet. He was then checked by the big blind, and the Man with the Bamboo Spine raised them both. By the end of the round, the pot was past two hundred K and rising, and the last card could not have been a better one. King of hearts, completing the royal flush. He had the best hand of his life.

Then his cell rang.

Only one person ever called this phone. It existed for one purpose. So when it went off, a loud but ordinary ring, the Man with the Bamboo Spine put his cards down flat on the table and picked up. He listened for less than ten seconds, said, 'Yes,' and hung up.

With a royal flush for his hand and over four hundred thousand dollars in the pot, the Man with the Bamboo Spine stood up from the table and said, 'Fold.' Without another word, he took the elevator down to the ground floor where his driver was waiting.

It would take him twelve and a half hours to reach Vancouver, Canada, and the length of time was disconcerting.

Every minute was precious.

Twenty-Eight

When the phone rang, waking Striker at four-thirty in the morning, he was grateful for the interruption. He sat up with a jolt and snatched up the cell. 'Detective Striker.'

The deep baritone response was as rough and smooth as sandpaper dipped in maple syrup. 'Wake up, Sleeping Beauty.'

'Rothschild?'

'Get your ass out of bed.'

Striker blinked, surprised at hearing his old Sergeant's voice. He looked across the room. Found the wall clock. Saw the time.

'Jesus Christ, Mike, it's not even five yet – what the hell's going on?'

'Just get your ass down here. And be quick about it. I'm on the Fraser. Right on the docks, south of Marine, behind the Superstore. At the C and D Plant.'

Striker scrabbled for a pen and paper, wrote down the address. Said, 'Give me twenty minutes.'

'Make it ten, the white-shirts are coming.'

Striker cursed. 'Tell me it's not Laroche.'

'Just hurry the hell up, Shipwreck. And trust me on this one – you're gonna wanna see this.'

Fifteen minutes later, Striker crossed into South Vancouver – District 3 – and neared the Fraser River. He sped the unmarked police cruiser down the slippery stretch of Marine Drive, then turned south on the old gravel road that twisted and turned, outlining the Fraser River. The road was half-frozen, and the car skidded at every turn.

If the road conditions were bad, the lighting was worse. The heavy blackness of night showed no hint of fading, and the relentless winds whipped the river into six-foot-high swells. Just ten feet away, the retaining wall gave way to the strong currents of the Fraser River. The water looked alive, angry. Striker eased his foot off the gas pedal.

No point in killing himself.

Just yet.

All along the shoreline, massive concrete smokestacks rose up like giant cannons, blasting steam into the night. Where the charcoal cloud ended and the billowing smoke began was impossible to tell. It was all one entity now, roaming slowly across the river. This was the industrial area, built up of pulp mills and gravel lots and concrete plants and import/export transfer stations.

No one but plant workers came down here.

At the next curve, Striker caught his first glimpse of the blue and red gleam. Three patrol cars were parked in the fog, in between a concrete plant and the shoreline.

Striker spotted Rothschild straight away. The Sergeant was loitering nearby, smoking a cigarillo and drinking what must be stale, cold coffee. Knowing Rothschild, the coffee would be his fifth of the night. Minimum.

Striker jumped out of the car and marched across the gravel roadway. The cold winds blew in from the water, numbing his face and stinging his ears. He zipped up the heavy wool of his long jacket, but it did little good.

'Mike,' he called. 'Hey, Mike! Rothschild!'

Sergeant Mike Rothschild turned around, the heavy winds sending what little hair he had left into a frenzy of thin waves. He stood squarely, like a wall on legs, his shoulders turned inwards, his hands balled into fists.

'Holy shit, man, 'bout fuckin' time you got here. My balls are freezing, and I mean goddam freezing! Like little sperm-sickles.'

Striker grinned. 'Tell me how you really feel, Mike, don't hold back.'

Rothschild flashed his trademark smile – wry, almost dark, with his handlebar moustache rising higher on the left side. He slurped back his coffee, grimaced, then took off the lid and poured it out on the road.

'Already friggin' cold,' he said. 'Gas-station shit anyway. But hey, the cost is right.' He laughed.

'Why am I here?' Striker asked.

'Why you think? You're Homicide, right?'

'Take a look at my badge number. I'm not exactly first on the call-out list.'

Rothschild gave him a creepy smile. 'Don't need to be for this one.'

The way he said it made Striker nervous. 'What exactly you got here?'

The smile left Rothschild's lips and he pointed his cigarillo towards the river.

'Came in as a floater. It wasn't. The body was dumped here, but didn't land properly in the water. Got hung up below the docks, half in, half out. Feet got a little eaten, but hey, what the fuck. I got here first and found a bullet wound to the back of the guy's head.' He jabbed a thumb over his shoulder at the white unmarked patrol car tucked away from the crime scene, in the darkness next to the concrete plant. 'Car Ten beat you here. He's sitting there all toasty in his White Whale. Probably reading *What's-Up-My-Ass Weekly.*'

Striker looked at the car, saw nothing but a dark windshield. 'Which Inspector?'

'Oakley.'

'That's good. He's okay.'

'*He* is. But he's already called the Deputy Chief.'

'Laroche?'

'None other. And he's on the way down.'

Striker found the notion disturbing. Homicides happened all the time in Vancouver, especially with the growing bouts of gang violence, and the Deputy Chief was never called – not unless the deceased was a person of some significance: an ambassador, or a dignitary. Maybe a celebrity. Or, God forbid, a cop.

He looked down towards the river, past the yellow strips of all-too-familiar police tape. Out there, waves crashed hard against the wooden rails of the docks, sounding angry and powerful. With the emergency lights flashing against the black waters and river mist, the scene looked like a goddam horror show.

'Who we find in the drink?'

Rothschild grinned. 'Don't fall down the rabbit hole, Alice.' He lit up another cigarillo and the leafy aroma of good tobacco floated through the air. 'You can thank me later, Shipwreck. Captain Morgan's the preference. Dark as it comes.'

Striker gave Rothschild a confused nod, then turned away and cut down towards the river.

The gravel-and-sand mixture was nearly frozen; it crunched beneath his boots. He ducked under the police tape and moved onto the walkway. The dock was old and wooden. Rickety. Made up of three separate sections, each one connected by a series of spiralling stairways leading down to the next platform. At the beginning of each section, a yellow lamp hung off a support beam, offering poor illumination to the platform below.

Being careful of his step, Striker hiked down to the lowest platform. Swells of river water slammed hard against the floating dock, rocking the structure back and forth and covering him with cold spray. The wind down here was even stronger, piercing his clothes and biting into his skin. Regardless, he marched on until he came flush with a young constable who stood at the forefront of the platform, shaking.

Striker sized him up. He wore the standard-issue uniform pants, which were about as effective in these wet winds as a pair of ass-less chaps in a snowstorm. His hands were tucked as deep into his pockets as he could get them, and blasts of warm breath steamed from his open mouth when he spoke.

'Detective Striker,' he said.

'Tough break, kid.' Striker pointed at his pants. 'Use your e-points to get a pair of Gore-Tex.' He nodded to the end of the dock where a dirty blue tarp lay spread out across the boards. There was a long lump underneath it. 'Who found him?'

The Constable shrugged. 'Some guy, a worker loading up for the cement plant. Dunno, really. Ask Rothschild, he was first on scene.'

'We got a name for our John Doe?'

The kid shrugged again. 'I just got stuck with guard duty.'

Striker left the young Constable standing there, fighting off hypothermia, and approached the rustling plastic tarp. Four large cinderblocks held it down – one at each corner, preventing it from blowing away. Striker picked up the nearest cinderblock, moved it to the side, then peeled back the tarp.

The first thing Striker noted was that the runner from the left foot was missing. In the darkness of the dock, the golden dragon design snaking down the sides of the man's jeans was almost invisible. Striker took note of it. The white designer hoodie the man wore was stuck to his thin but muscular build like a second skin. Soil and slime smeared the stencilled designs.

The body hadn't been in there for very long, but already the tissue was starting to bloat from water saturation, and tiny pockets of flesh had been pecked away from the face by sea creatures. Even so, with the tissue damage and in the poor illumination of the lower docks, the identity of the boy was irrefutable. Striker had seen this boy's picture on his own ID cards.

It was Que Wong. The one they had thought to be White Mask.

The discovery made him sick, and yet it invigorated him. They now had an unidentified body back at the morgue. A faceless, handless corpse.

Striker stared at Que Wong with a hundred questions racing through his mind. Things that had made sense a few hours ago made no sense now, but he was so tired he could barely remember what they were. He reached out and gently took hold of the boy's left hand. All the skin remained intact, connected properly to the muscles and fascia beneath. The hand hadn't de-gloved, as is so often the case with floaters. And that was good. It meant Que Wong hadn't been in the drink for overly long.

Striker took out his Maglite and shone a beam on Que's hand. He looked for ridge detail on the fingers, but it was difficult to tell outside of the lab in the middle of the night.

'Hey, Shipwreck!' a voice called out. 'Don't fuck with my body!'

Striker didn't have to turn around to recognise the heavy,

out-of-breath yell. It was Jim Banner from Ident. Noodles. Striker spun about, half-irritated.

'Christ, Noodles, even the undead sleep.'

'Like you should talk.' Noodles said this with a laugh, but his pudgy cheeks sagged and his eyes were heavily underscored. 'And you should see my pay stubs. I get to pay more tax than any other cop in the city.'

'Congratulations.' Striker was about to say more when a movement caught his eye. He looked into the murky illumination of the dock entrance and spotted Mike Rothschild leading another man down the first set of stairs. One look at the thick, helmet-like hair, the five-foot-five stature, and Striker knew undoubtedly who it was.

Deputy Chief Laroche.

'Here comes the circus,' Noodles said.

'They normally start with the clown?' Striker had barely finished speaking when his cell rang. He snagged it, turned away from Noodles, and covered his other ear with his hand to drown out the sounds of the river. 'Jacob Striker.'

'Where the hell are you?' The voice was tired and agitated.

'Felicia?'

'No, it's Fergie, the Princess of Pop – who do you think it is? Where are you, Jacob?'

'Down at the docks. On Marine. Look, they just found the body of Que Wong.'

'Wong? But we already—'

'Our headless corpse ain't him, Feleesh. And if Que Wong was a set-up, then it's pretty damn likely Raymond Leung is, too.'

'Red Mask? Are you sure?'

'Don't kid yourself, he's still out there somewhere. I know it. And we've got to find him.'

Felicia made an exasperated sound. 'What are you talking about? Jesus, why didn't you wake me?'

He shrugged as if she could see him. 'You needed the sleep. And I didn't know it was connected. Not till now. Look, I'll explain when I get back. Just get up and get dressed. I won't be long.' He hung up his cell phone, turned around and stared at Noodles. 'Keep me up to date,' he said.

'Not with your sense of style.'

'I'm serious, Noodles. This changes everything.'

'I'll call. God, just get out of here, will you?'

Striker nodded. He started to leave, then spotted Laroche sauntering down the last set of stairs. He looked back at Noodles, saw the big black Ident marker sticking out of his jacket pocket, and smiled. He snatched it up, ignoring Noodles' protest, and marched down the dock till he came face to face with the Deputy Chief.

'What are *you* doing here?' Laroche said, his voice resonating with unease.

Striker said nothing, he just handed him the black felt marker.

'What's this for?'

Striker jabbed his thumb over his shoulder, back towards the dock. 'You might want to paint some stripes on that body back there – looks like I just found you your zebra.'

Twenty-Nine

Twenty minutes later, Striker picked up Felicia and headed to the police garage. He needed to check the forensics on the stolen Honda Civic. Something was bothering him about it, and he always followed his instincts. While en route, he pulled out his cell and dialled Noodles. On the fourth ring a gruff voice answered.

'Christ almighty, Shipwreck, I got three hours' sleep and work to do.'

'I need your help.'

'Why? What now?'

'Raymond Leung's DNA – I need it compared to the blood in the Honda Civic.'

'You called me for *that*? I've already got the samples done. They just need to be submitted to the lab.'

'I need it now.'

Noodles cursed. 'You're like a high-maintenance girlfriend.'

'Noodles—'

'The lab doesn't even open for another two hours. And even if I get the samples in first thing, and even if I get a priority one rush put on it, it's still gonna take three to four days to get any results – and that's without a full report. It's DNA. You know how it is.'

'The DNA can come later,' Striker explained. 'All I need at

this point is blood type. Find out if Raymond Leung's blood type matches the blood in the stolen Civic. You can get those results for me fast if you stop dragging your ass.'

'So I should just get up and leave our floater here.'

'Noodles, I need this.'

'I thought Red Mask was found.'

'He's *not* Raymond Leung. I know it, Noodles. I just need your help proving it.'

Noodles let out a frustrated sound, but finally relented. 'I'll get to it as soon as I got the bases covered here, then I'll come back and finish the Wong body later. But you owe me huge for this, Shipwreck. Two bottles of Crown Royal. Ten-year.'

'You got it. Just call me the second you know.'

The police garage is located in the worst part of town, the Skids. Also known as the Downtown East Side – that unpredictable area occupied by only criminals, addicts and the mentally ill.

In short, it was ten square blocks of bedlam.

Striker looked around. To the west was a series of community buildings offering housing for the down-and-outs. To the east were four straight blocks of slum apartments, housing dealers, enforcers, mules, and every other type of drug-related offender who haunted the area. Homeless people – the ones who had either refused help from the nearby community programmes or had been banned from them – roamed the block, setting up makeshift camps all along the sidewalk and rear alleyways. Their numbers had grown over the past few years, causing overpopulation of the street and sidewalks. And as a result, the City had set up sprinkler systems, timed for midnight activation, in order to keep the police bays clear.

It was a sad statement of the times.

Striker checked his watch. It was almost six a.m. He parked the Crown Vic out front and told Felicia to wait. She didn't seem to mind; she looked half-dead in the passenger seat, and she made a soft *uh-huh* sound as he got out.

It was cold. The sky was still dark, and the fall winds bit into him, sent his short brown hair blowing back over his head. He looked east and west at the cardboard tents set up all along the drive and frowned. The street was one giant paper city. A few blocks down, a marked patrol car turned east, away from him, and continued driving along Alexander Street until it disappeared in the heavy murk.

Alpha shift. Had to be. God knows, no one else was out yet.

The rain had stopped, but it had failed to clean the streets of all the used rigs and dirty condoms. Striker looked away from the filth. He used his police key to enter the barred-off entrance to the garage, then let himself in and turned off the beeping alarm. Far above, the industrial fan rattled loudly. The Department had fixed the thing ten times over the past year, and here it was on the fritz again.

He stood inside the doorway of the police garage and took in a deep breath. The place smelled of dust and dampness, oil and kitty litter. A flick of the light switch bathed the huge space in a bleak fluorescent illumination, revealing a fully-stacked bay: rows and rows of vehicles awaiting processing. Fingerprints, DNA, Hidden Compartment Searches, Paint Comparisons – all needed something.

Two Escalades with shaded windows and big chrome mags – gangbanger rides – occupied stalls one and two. A bright cherry-red sports car occupied stall three. It was heavily customised, decorated with an oversized chrome muffler, spinning gold mags, and a tail fin larger than any humpback could hope for. Gang style. Probably belonged to the White Lotus –

Canada's version of the Lotus gang, made up solely of Canadian Chinese.

Striker's eyes moved on until they found the vehicle he was looking for. The stolen Civic.

Red Mask's ride.

Striker moved to the bay door and took hold of the handle. The rollers were rigid and in desperate need of oiling. The metal made a sharp, grating noise as Striker reefed down hard on the chain and rolled the steel door open. It was barely three-quarters up when Felicia drove the cruiser inside the bay. She climbed out, shivered from the cold, zipped up her suede jacket.

'Coffee after this,' she said. 'Immediately.'

Striker agreed. He closed the garage door and turned towards the Civic. The yellow copy of the Ident Form was trapped beneath the driver's side windshield-wiper. Before he could read it, Felicia snatched it up. She held it in her long, thin fingers, her clear nails digging into the paper. She finished reading, made a face, deflated.

'Not a single goddam print in the car.'

'You didn't really expect any, did you?' Striker looked inside the vehicle. One clear bag sat on the front passenger seat, tagged after processing for fingerprints and DNA analysis. It held the key-ring and keys, complete with fob and happy face. Someone had written *No Prints* in thick black felt on the bag. The member's badge number and the incident number were included.

Striker looked at the badge number, saw it wasn't Noodles, and it pissed him off. He liked Noodles. Noodles was the best. Then he looked over the paperwork and saw that the cigarettes had also been processed:

Prints positive. Subject: Quenton Wong.

Striker stared at this for a long time, then showed it to Felicia.

'It puts him in the car,' she said.

'No. It *connects* him to the car, the shooter, or anyone connected to either one. But how, we don't know.'

Striker removed his long coat and draped it over the work bench. He put on a fresh pair of latex gloves, then moved over to the metallic whiteboard on the west wall, where numerous yellow forms were hanging by clip-magnets. He shifted them all to the left side, exposing a large patch of white steel, then returned to the Civic.

Felicia joined him. 'So Que's prints are on the cigarettes, and now he's dead. Great. So aside from knowing he's somehow connected, all we got is another dead end on our hands.'

Striker corrected her. 'This has been anything but a dead end.'

She furrowed her brow.

'It's not just about the prints,' he explained. 'It's about why they stole the car a whole week before the shootings.'

'And you got an answer for that?'

'I think so.' He pulled Courtney's happy face magnet from his pocket and handed it to Felicia. 'What do you see?'

She flipped it over. 'A happy face. Where did you get this?'

'Courtney had it on the fridge, next to her Britney magnets,' Stiker said. 'Put it on something metal. Like the whiteboard over there.'

She did, and the happy face stuck. She pulled it off the board and looked back at Striker. 'It's magnetic. So?'

Striker returned to the Civic. According to the notes on the Ident bag, there were no prints on the key-ring and the items had already been swabbed for DNA. So there was no fear of cross-contamination. However, taking no chances, he gloved up with fresh latex. He took the key-ring complete with key, fob, and happy face out of the bag and held it up for Felicia to see.

'This happy face is magnetic, too.' He gave the key-ring an underhand toss across the room. When it hit the metallic white-board, the key-ring and fob fell down towards the ground, but the happy face stuck hard, holding everything up.

He looked at Felicia and smiled. 'That tells us everything.'

Felicia played with Courtney's happy face and shook her head. 'It tells *me* nothing.'

Striker tried to explain it from a different angle. 'How many keys do you see on that key-ring?'

'One.'

'Wrong,' he said. 'There's two. The Honda key, and the happy face – which is a key in its own right. Magnetically-speaking.'

'Meaning?'

'Meaning that's why they stole the car a whole week before the shootings: they were modifying it somehow.' He lowered his voice. 'There's something hidden in that car.'

Thirty

Felicia stood in the dim lighting of the police garage and stared blankly at the small yellow happy face that was stuck to the metallic whiteboard.

'You lost me,' she said to Striker. She walked up to the whiteboard. Stopped. Studied the happy face.

It was a circular piece of plastic. Dark yellow with the standard smile painted onto it. The only difference was the bullet-hole that had been painted in the centre of the forehead. The happy face was attached to the key-ring by a ten-centimetre chain, just like the fob and Honda key.

'So it's a magnet,' Felicia said again.

Striker took Courtney's happy face magnet from Felicia and put it on the board next to the one from Red Mask's key-ring.

'Take them off the board,' he said.

When Felicia tried, Courtney's came off easily. But she almost broke a nail on Red Mask's version. She swore. 'Okay, it's a really, really strong magnet.'

'And it separates from the key-ring.'

Felicia made a face, as if she was tired of playing Twenty Questions, but Striker didn't notice. To prove his point, he pried the magnet from the board, then found the snap attachment in the chain. He rolled it between his fingers, gave it a firm squeeze, and the chain broke in half, separating the happy face from the rest of the key-ring. He handed it to Felicia.

She took it. 'Early birthday present?'

'Something like that.'

Her voice took on a curious tone. 'So how's it gonna open something in the car that, so far, no one else has found?'

'The clue is the magnet. It completes a circuit, probably somewhere near the steering column or radio. If you hit the right spot, it's like plugging in a power cord. Once we got power, the fob will open the hidden compartment.' He gave her a nod. 'Go to the passenger side.'

She did. 'How do you know this?'

Striker reached the driver's side. 'I've seen it before with the gangs. And I took some courses down in Virginia with the DEA. Once I knew this key was magnetic, I suspected there might be a hidden compartment. Let's hope I'm right.'

They gloved up with fresh latex, then Striker leaned inside the car and scanned the dashboard. He took the Honda key from the Ident bag and placed it in the ignition. 'Usually, the car has to be turned on to complete the circuit.'

'What do you want me to do?' Felicia asked.

'Look on top of the dashboard, see if you can find any marks or scratches.'

Felicia started to lean inside the car, then stopped. She took a moment to tie her hair back – the last thing she needed was to leave her own DNA there for investigators. Once done, she scanned the top of the dashboard. It was dark green and made of smooth vinyl. Appeared very ordinary.

'Nothing here. No marks of any kind.'

Striker cursed. 'Put the magnet on top of the dashboard. Your end.'

She did. 'Okay.'

'The magnet should complete the circuit, the fob should activate it.' He put the key into the auxiliary position, and all the dash lights came on. 'Now slowly slide the magnet across the dash towards me, just a half-inch at a time.'

Felicia moved the happy face as requested, inch by inch, and each time Striker pressed the button on the fob. Nothing happened. They did this across the entire dashboard.

Nothing.

A frustrated sound escaped Striker's lips. He wiped his forehead on his sleeve. His skin felt itchy. The police garage was a cold, draughty place, but inside the Civic, it felt hot and claustrophobic. Small dots of sweat dampened his brow. The sweet smell of Felicia's perfume was getting to him.

He stood back from the vehicle and took a short walk to the other side of the garage. It gave him some space – room to think. He stood in the corner for a long moment, going over everything in his head.

I must be missing something.

He turned, looked back at the car and saw Felicia standing there, her coffee-depleted patience thinning. Her long dark hair had been sprayed down and combed out, but it was obvious she'd slept on it wrong all night. A thought occurred to him.

'Is the radio turned on?'

'Radio?'

'Inside the Civic. Is it on?'

Felicia looked inside, shook her head. 'No.'

'Christ. The radio is part of the circuit.'

He marched back to the car and leaned inside the driver's seat. The radio was brand new, one of those disc, radio and mp3 players, all built into one. There was no brand name anywhere on the device. Just a plain black faceplate with all the LEDs turned off. Striker pressed the power button, and the faceplate lit up in bright neon blue. The screen said DISC, but nothing was playing. He grabbed the happy face magnet, handed it back to Felicia, and grinned.

'One more time.'

Like before, Felicia placed the magnet down on the far end of the dashboard. Striker grabbed the remote, and they started the entire process all over again. When they reached the midway point of the dashboard – with the happy face magnet positioned directly above the D in DISC – Striker hit the fob and an unseen electronic lock disengaged somewhere. The click was sharp, audible, and it was followed by a soft whirring sound.

Felicia flinched. 'What the hell is that?'

Before Striker could respond, the entire front section of the dashboard came apart. The front half moved forward, away from the baseboard. It lowered towards them on a pair of automated, gliding hinges, revealing a hidden compartment that went deep under the dashboard, back towards the engine area.

Striker smiled.

'That's the jackpot.'

Thirty-One

Ten minutes later, Striker and Felicia draped brown paper over a work table, then laid out everything they'd found inside the hidden compartment. The list was brief but significant:

One Benelli shotgun, single-barrel, pump-action.
　Two 40-calibre Glock handguns. Pistols. Modified to be fully automatic.
　Ammunition, boxed and open. Slugs and 40-calibre. Hollow-tip variety and steel-cased Full Metal Jacket.
　And one ordinary brown legal-size envelope with over ten grand in cash inside.

Striker held it up, grinned. 'Coffee money.'

Felicia finally gave him the smile he'd been drilling for all morning. 'Make mine a latte.'

He gathered up all the free ammunition, stuck one of the rounds inside his pocket, then placed the rest in a brown paper bag for Ident. He left it in the centre of the table with a large sign that read: *Ammo from Hidden Compartment in Civic. Check for Prints.*

Then he called Noodles and told him about the find.

'This is fucking insane,' Noodles said. 'I was just gonna call you. I heard about the ammo issues, so I did some analysis here. Looks to me like these kids were shot with different types. Some 762s and some frangible forty-cals.'

Striker glanced left at Felicia as she stared into the car at the hidden compartment. 'I've got matching ammo here, Noodles. These guys were pros. I need you to get down here and look at this stuff.'

'No can do. I'm still covering bases here on the docks with the Wong body. Plus you got me chasing down samples on Leung's body. I'm gonna be hours still – you're making too many crime scenes for me, you prick.'

Striker cursed. 'I need you, Noodles.'

'I'm sending John Winter down.'

'Winter? He's a friggin' rookie.'

'Maybe so, but he came in second overall in the competition back East. I taught the kid everything I know, Shipwreck. He's good.'

Striker accepted it, albeit grudgingly. 'Keep me posted on everything, and get Winter to call me when he's done.'

Noodles agreed, then hung up. Striker walked back to the table, picked up one of the Glocks and scanned it for a serial number. Felicia was staring at him with a lost look on her face.

'How did you know?' she said. 'About the compartment?'

'I already told you. I'd seen it before and had taken courses.'

'But what exactly? Walk me through it.'

Striker put down the Glock. 'Well, there were a few things, really. The ignition was brand new and had clearly been replaced. That was the biggest clue. But there were other things, too. Couple of scuff marks where the dash meets the steering column. And then there was the fob.'

'But that fob could've been for anything – a garage, an apartment, another car.'

'Could've been. But it wasn't.'

She said nothing, she just stared at him. Her dark eyes were beautiful but hard to read.

Striker shrugged. 'Like I said, it was one of many factors.'

'And the happy face?'

'More specifically, the magnet inside. It was *very* strong. Kept sticking to everything. And you needed that to complete the circuit. It's one of those extra little securities these maggots use nowadays, so that patrol cops can't use the fob to unlock the compartment during street checks. That's why the radio also had to be turned on, to complete the circuit. It's one more safety precaution for dial-a-dopers.'

She nodded. 'What else?'

Striker took the other pistol from the table, scanned it for a serial. Found none. 'For two, no trinket should've been there at all. Think about it. No assassin's going to start accessorising his key chain for a stolen car he intends to dump. It was there for a reason. I just had to figure out what that reason was – though I'm still a little bit lost as to why he left the keys at the scene in the first place. Must've dropped them, been his first mistake.' He gave Felicia a thoughtful look. 'Maybe he's hurt worse than we thought.'

Felicia was quiet for a moment, then leaned against the car and crossed her arms. 'Well bravo, Jacob. Nice to see you had so many ideas in your head all this time. And thanks so much for keeping me in the loop.'

He looked up from the gun barrel he was assessing. 'You're not actually pissed, are you?'

'We're partners, and you didn't even tell me.'

'I wasn't sure.'

'You had an idea.'

Striker picked up the shotgun. The serial number had been removed from the barrel here too. It was to be expected. He scanned the steel for any grind marks, saw none, and nodded. Half to himself, half to Felicia.

'No serial.'

This seemed to distract her. 'Gone? Completely?'

'Looks like it. We'll do the DNA thing first. Check it against the databank. But that will take a few weeks at best, even with a priority rush. Then we'll see if the Feds can get some serial numbers from the barrels.'

'You said the serial was gone.'

'It is. But they didn't file it off, they used acid.' Striker held up the barrel for her to see and rubbed his finger along the black shiny barrel. The metal was smooth. 'The factory stamping leaves an impression right through the steel. Lasers can pick it up. Problem is we got none here, but the Feds do. And if they can get a serial, we'll do a trace, see if it's registered. But I wouldn't hold your breath.'

Felicia looked at all the guns laid out on the table. 'So we got no serials.'

Striker put the shotgun back down alongside them. 'Not worried about the serials. What I want to know is whether these guns were used on any of the victims. Ballistics will have to tell us that. Through the pathologist.'

'But the serials—'

'There's a billion handguns in North America, Feleesh. Registered, unregistered, it makes no difference. There's just too damn many for us to track. They fly across the borders like leaves. A gun won't lead us anywhere. What will, is the hidden compartment – there's only a handful of people in this country who can make that.'

This notion seemed to perk her up.

'And even fewer who could do it so quickly,' she said.

Striker smiled. 'Exactly. Whoever did this would need to

have the materials on hand, the tools required, and the know-how. Given the timeframe and the fact that these guys weren't going to chance it by driving around the province, that person will be somewhere here in the Lower Mainland. Has to be. And once we find out who that is, we can trace things back to the school. Find out who our shooters were. Find out who was really behind this attack.'

Felicia gave him a pointed look. 'Any other ideas you're holding back?'

'No. I don't got a clue. But I know someone who will.'

'Who?'

'Just your favourite person in the whole entire world.'

A look of disgust crept across her face. 'Please God, tell me you're not talking about Hans Jager.'

Striker laughed out loud.

'You got it, darlin. The one and only. Time to go see Meathead.'

Thirty-Two

Half an hour later, just after eight o'clock as the sun was finally coming up, Striker and Felicia pulled into the south lane of Tenth Avenue, then turned down the steep driveway that led into the underground police parkade. Striker swiped his card, keyed in his ID number and drove into the protected area of the building. The steel-reinforced gates automatically closed behind them.

Felicia grimaced at the low ceiling, which was covered with grey stalactites of fire-retardant foam. 'Feels like a tomb down here.'

Striker agreed. 'Welcome to the Bunker.' It was the first time he'd been back here at Specialty Unit Headquarters since his stress leave, and it felt good.

He scanned the area. The lower levels of the complex contained electronically-secured lockers that housed the high-tech military weaponry required for the Emergency Response Team. This place was a favourite hangout for Meathead, who planned on making the move from the International Gang Task Force to the Emergency Response Team the moment his application was approved by the Inspector. So when he had suggested they all meet here to discuss matters, Striker hadn't been surprised.

Striker drove down the ramp, around the corner, and saw Meathead at the next series of storage rooms. At six foot four and two hundred and seventy pounds, Meathead was an easy man to spot. A modern-day Viking. He had a giant head, which was covered with thick, wild curls of red hair, and a moustache and goatee to match. His arms were the size of most men's calves and they were covered with so many tattoos they looked like sleeves – a Departmental rule-breaker, no doubt, but one that the white-shirts had wisely overlooked.

How could they not? Meathead was an asset. A force to be reckoned with. He was afraid of no man, and his military background and fighting arts gave him the skills to lead any operation the Department required. He was a specialist.

Striker pointed ahead. 'There he is.'

Felicia made an *ugh* sound.

Striker parked the cruiser in the nearest stall, and they both climbed out.

'Morning, Meathead,' Striker called.

Meathead looked up and spotted them both. 'Shipwreck. Fellatio.'

Felicia's posture tightened. 'In your dreams, pal.'

'Oh, all the time, Beautiful.' Meathead barked out a laugh. 'Hell, give me a few minutes and I'll whip something up for you right now.' He closed his eyes, dropped his hand into his black sweatpants and started making perverted, grunting noises.

Felicia gave Striker one of her *Can-we-leave?* looks, and he ignored it. He stepped closer to Meathead, gave the man a swat on the shoulder.

'Knock it off.'

'Gimme a second, I'm almost there.'

'*Meathead.*'

'Oh fine, ruin my fun.' Meathead opened his eyes, offered a dirty smirk, then returned his attention to the black case he was securing. It was for the carbine, the latest long-range rifle the

Department was investing in. Meathead snatched it up like it weighed five pounds, not fifty, and threw it in his locker. Once everything was secure, he walked away and motioned for Striker and Felicia to follow him.

They did, Striker with fast steps, Felicia purposely lagging behind.

They cut across the oil-stained pavement to a small doorway located behind a large concrete support pillar. Meathead opened the door to reveal a small briefing room, complete with large rectangular table and an overhead projector, which was turned off. In the far corner of the room was a row of filing cabinets. Cheap metal ones. Opposite them, a series of computers lined the wall. They were linked together, Striker noted, but almost certainly without connection to the outside world.

Meathead took note of Felicia's expression and winked. 'You look tired, Beautiful. You need to spend some time off your feet.'

'I do. Every time I smell your breath.'

'So it's getting better then.' When she didn't respond, Meathead added, 'I've been brushing more since our last meeting. Bought a Sonicare.'

Striker grinned and moved closer to Meathead. He smelled burned gunpowder. The air was strong with it. And gun oil, too. Obviously Meathead had been up at the range today, probably his third visit of the week.

Gun oil and gunpowder suited the man.

Before Striker could say anything, Meathead removed the T-shirt he was wearing and took another one from the corner of the room. The shirt looked a size too small against his massive arms. Striker took notice of the shirt. It was a grey-green colour and it had a red maple leaf on the top left, covered over by the numbers 499.

'Four nine-nine?'

Meathead gave him a pissed look. 'Larry Young, man – how could you forget?'

The moment Striker heard the name he was embarrassed. 499 was the badge number of Larry Young, the Emergency Response Team member killed during a drug raid. His name was gospel around the Department. And rightly so.

'The shirts came out a few months back,' Meathead said, 'when you were on leave. Probably why you had the mental blip.'

'Yeah, sure. Get me one, will you?'

'Will do.'

Striker cleared his throat, then pulled the bullet he had found in the hidden compartment out from his jacket pocket. He thrust it at Meathead. 'Here. Take a look at this.'

Meathead took the round, stared it over and whistled. The bullet was made of hard-tipped, shiny brass. 'Is this the ammo they were using?'

Striker nodded. 'One type. Tell me what it is.'

Meathead raised an eyebrow. 'You don't know?'

'I want confirmation.'

'Official warfare ammo, buddy. Full metal jacket.'

Striker thought it over. 'That's what they were shooting indiscriminately.' He handed Meathead another bullet. 'They also used this, but only on some of the kids – the ones I think were targeted.'

Meathead took the next bullet and examined that one, too. 'Hollow tip, man. Hydra-Shok. Ultimate stopping power. They were taking no chances with these ones.'

Striker shook his head. 'I don't get it.'

Felicia came over, took the bullet from Meathead's hand and gave it the onceover. 'What don't you get?' she asked Jacob.

'Why use full metal jacket? I mean, these guys were there to kill, so why not go for a round that's frangible – like a Hydra-Shok. Or, even better yet, some Federal HST? That shit leaves a two-inch spiral through a man. I know they didn't need anything too fancy; these were just a bunch of high-school students, after all. No one was wearing body armour. But if you're going for maximum fatalities, why not pick the proper ammunition?'

'Maybe they weren't going for maximum kills, maybe they were going for numbers,' Felicia suggested. 'Maximum casualties. Fear.'

Striker decided she was right about that. Full metal jacket would over-penetrate, ricochet, strike more targets. Cause more casualties. But the gunmen had been careful to use the Hydra-Shok ammo on Tina Chow and Conrad Macmillan and Chantelle O'Riley. Which was part of the reason why these kids seemed targeted. So why Hydra-Shok?

A signature?

Meathead interjected, 'Semantics, man. Doesn't really matter. You got a person at your mercy and shoot enough rounds of any kind through them, they're Swiss cheese. Plus I hear these guys had shotguns and an AK-47. They want to go for fatalities, that's more than enough firepower to take down a bear.'

As Meathead finished speaking, Felicia's cell went off. She answered it, but had difficulty getting a strong signal in the underground. She lost the call. After cussing, she turned to Striker and handed him the bullet.

'It's Caroline,' she said. 'I'm gonna walk up a level and call her back.'

Striker was glad to see her leave. She'd been acting strange all morning. Distant, almost hostile at times. And Meathead's banter wasn't helping the mood. With her out of the way, there was less pressure.

Meathead watched her go and grunted. 'Man, I'd like to tap that.'

'*Tap* that?'

'Like a keg, baby.'

'You ever hear of harassment?'

'Yeah, and I been trying to get me some, Boss. But so far no luck.'

Meathead barked out another hyena laugh, and Striker sighed. He said nothing to encourage the man, because Meathead was like that; he fed off of other people's attention, and the more praise he got, the wilder and more crude he became. Striker focused their attention back on the investigation.

'I found all this ammo in the stolen Civic.'

'For real?'

'Hidden compartment.'

'No shit. Floorboards?'

'Dashboard. Which is why I'm here.' Striker moved over to the table and sat down. 'I've been out of the loop on this stuff for a few years now. You're the one in Gangs, you deal with these rejects all the time. So tell me, where do they get this work done?'

Meathead walked across the room to the fridge and opened the door. He pulled out a couple of Gatorades and threw the orange one to Striker. He kept the Berry Blue for himself. Held it up. Grinned.

'Blue – to match my balls.'

'If you're matching, it should be smaller. The shot-glass version. Now back to the hidden compartment.'

'Fine, fine.' Meathead uncapped the Gatorade, drank some,

cleared his throat. 'How long did they have to make these modifications?'

'Car was stolen nine days before the attack.'

Meathead made an interested sound. 'Well, that rules out the Blaine Brothers.'

'Why?'

'They work out east. Ontario. But they're the best. Both guys are in their fifties now, former soldiers – real ones, saw Desert Storm. Then they came home and turned private.' He chugged back some sports drink, wiped his mouth with his forearm. 'They got a whole modification business going on down there, making cars bullet-proof and adding hidden compartments. But they usually work on Escalades or Hummers, maybe even the odd Beamer. Not Civics though. And it takes time to do this stuff. A full month for anything good.'

Striker commented, 'It would take them half the nine days just to drive the car out east and back.'

'Exactly, so it would have to be local. What kind of monkey work they do to the dashboard?'

'Solid stuff,' Striker said. 'Professional. No one would know anything was there unless they removed the dash. Fresh-install, too. New ignition, new radio, and a magnetic circuit to boot. Barely a mark on the dashboard, or anywhere for that matter.'

Meathead dragged his finger through the air as if writing or counting. 'Five names come to mind,' he finally said. He told them to Striker, who wrote them down in his notebook.

'All local?' Striker asked.

'Yep. Two are in the Valley, one on the North Shore, far as I can remember. Don't know where the other two are, but they were always rounders, so probably East Side – at least, that's where they were a few years back.'

Striker read the names silently. They weren't familiar. He looked back up and met Meathead's stare. 'Anything else?'

'Yeah. Some of these guys are bad dudes, man. Pop a cop no problem. So be careful.'

Striker nodded. At that moment, Felicia swung open the door and came marching back into the room. Her pretty face looked preoccupied.

'Everything okay?' Striker asked.

'No. That was Caroline. She's gone Chernobyl on us – total meltdown.'

'Can you blame her?'

'She says the parents of some of the dead have called. They won't leave her alone. They want answers to a lot of things she doesn't know answers to.'

The notion bothered Striker. He felt for these people. And he couldn't imagine their grief. Losing a loved one was hard enough, but losing a child – well, that was life-destroying. Soon, he and Felicia would have to talk to the parents of the deceased, not only for the good of the investigation, but out of simple decency and respect. First on that list were the Chows, the MacMillans, and the O'Rileys.

But before he could do that, he needed to do their background checks.

He gave Meathead a final glance, saying, 'Keep your cell on, I might need you.'

'Will do, Boss.'

Then Striker and Felicia went back to the car, drove out of the underground parkade. They headed for Main and Hastings. To their home base.

Major Crimes.

Thirty-Three

The morning sun broke through the dirty yellow drapes and formed a thin gold line across Red Mask's eyes. He lay flat on a small wooden mat. The pain told him he was still alive. It moved through his shoulder like a worm eating his tissue.

From somewhere down below, he could hear the angry words of a couple arguing. Someone had stolen something from someone, and someone was gonna pay. Through violence or sex or maybe both. The argument was nothing unusual for this place. After all, this was the Aster, one of the worst slums in Strathcona. Anyone living here was a junkie, a whore, or one of the endless crazies littering the Skids.

And anyone that mattered never set foot in this place.

Red Mask was unconcerned. The police would never locate him. His only known living quarters was his mailing address, and that was 533 Raymur Street. In the projects underneath the overpass. Down by the train tracks.

Where Father lives.

The thought came from nowhere. Left him empty.

He could not see Father again. Not after all that had happened. How could he ever tell him about Tran? He couldn't. It was but one of the many sacrifices required to reach the Perfect Harmony.

A sad smile broke his lips. Harmony. It now seemed such an empty word.

He rolled off the mat and felt the jagged shrapnel of the bullet tear through his shoulder. He vomited, bringing up nothing but transparent fluid. When the spasms stopped, he forced himself to stand in the tilting, shifting room. With his good arm, he reached behind his back and felt the rubberised grip of the Glock.

He was armed. He was prepared.

Pain or no pain, infection or no infection, living or dying, he had to go. It was time to complete his orders. It was time to finish the mission.

Thirty-Four

Striker felt hazy as they drove for coffee. He blamed it on the lack of sleep, but knew there were deeper issues. He aimed the unmarked cruiser north and glanced east. Daylight was breaking across the sky, fighting through the thin wisps of cloud. The growing light made everything feel less harsh, almost pretty. Even in the Skids. It reminded him it was actually morning, and he called home to see if Courtney was up. She wasn't. He wondered if she would've picked up anyway after reading the call display and seeing it was just dear ol' Dad.

Probably not.

She was pissed at him. Again. Like she always was for anything he did. Whether it was because he wouldn't let her go to a late-night party, or because he had two legs and breathed oxygen – it didn't seem to matter. There was no logical explanation half the time, and no chance of avoiding her emotional outbursts. The fiasco with Felicia last night had only made everything worse. With Courtney at home. And with Felicia at work.

The memory fluttered through his brain, made his blood pressure rise. He pushed it away, drove the cruiser down to the Powell Street diversion and cut through the Starbucks drive-thru. He ordered an Americano for himself, black, and a lemon poppy-seed muffin. When he asked Felicia what she wanted, her response made him laugh.

'Grande caramel latte, cream cheese muffin and a chocolate croissant.'

'That's all?'

'It's a start.'

He blinked. 'You're serious? You want *that* for breakfast?'

'I need fat and sugar and carbs, Jacob, and I need them now.'

He made the order, got them through the drive-thru, and turned back down Powell Street towards the police station. He parked the cruiser in a Patrol Only parking spot on the south side of Cordova – where non-patrol cars were always parked, despite the nonstop email warnings – and headed for the 312 Annexe with Felicia at his side.

Once out of the elevator, they walked into Major Crimes. It was one large carpeted rectangle, divided by four rows of cubicles. Flanking the room were three soundproofed interview rooms, each one connected to a viewing room with cameras and recording equipment. Above the first door, a tiny white light was flashing.

Someone was in a session.

Striker cut down the aisle towards his desk. The work space he and Felicia shared was in the rear of the room, the northeast corner, which suited him just fine. It was away from the hustle and bustle of the front desk, and on the odd occasion when one of the white-shirts came down, he was far enough away to avoid them.

Their cubicles were on opposite sides of the walkway, his facing north and hers south, which made it easy for rehashing; all they had to do was turn around and talk.

Striker sat down, grabbed his muffin from the bag and took a bite. He handed Felicia the rest of the goods, and she immediately took out her chocolate croissant. He watched her devour it as if she had been fasting for days – and this was after she'd already crammed down the cream cheese muffin in the car. She took a long sip of her latte and let out a satisfied breath.

'Good orgasm?' he asked.

'Sweet, sweet glucose.'

Striker picked up the phone and dialled the extension for the Forensic Video Unit. It was picked up on the second ring, and he immediately recognised the nasally whine of Ich.

'You sound tired, tech-boy,' Jacob said.

There was a pause. 'Detective Striker?'

'Got my audio?'

Ich made an uncomfortable sound. 'Well, actually . . . no.'

'*No?*'

'It got pushed to the back of the line. When Deputy Laroche closed the file.'

Striker cursed so loud that other Detectives in the room looked over. He ignored them as Ich continued: 'Laroche said Project Herald was top priority now, that I was to put all my resources on the wiretap.'

Striker closed his eyes, rubbed the bridge of his nose. Project Herald was one of the Deputy Chief's babies, his own little addition to the war on proceeds of crimes involving organised gangs. The premise was simple – take away their toys and anything else that makes being a gangster fun. That way, the younglings would find the criminal life less appealing. Of course to take things away meant lots of wiretaps and surveillance, and that took resources. The project was a good thing. On a normal day, Striker would have had no problem with it.

But today was anything but normal.

Laroche had obviously changed the priority on the video tape yesterday, after believing the case was closed – but he had never reversed it. Now that they had found the dead body of

Que Wong in the Fraser River, it left them with an unknown headless shooter back at the school. All bets were off. And Laroche should've reprioritised the Active Shooter call.

Striker tried not to get angry. 'The file isn't closed, Ich. It's as hot today as it was yesterday. I need that audio, and I need it now.'

'But Laroche—'

'Fuck Laroche. Just get it going – I'll take any heat for it.'

'Your call, Detective.'

'You're damn right it is, and I say get it going. And Ich – I need it *today*.'

He hung up the phone and spotted Felicia out of the corner of his eye as she swivelled her chair to avoid his stare. For a moment he felt like getting into it with her, telling her about Laroche's – her goddam mentor's – latest actions, but he let it go. It was for the best.

He already had one angry female at home. He didn't need another one at work.

'I'll work on the kids some more,' she said over her shoulder.

'Good idea,' he said.

He called Noodles back to see if he'd had time to compare the blood samples of the stolen Civic and Raymond Leung yet, but the call went unanswered. Striker left a message for Noodles to call him back, then logged onto PRIME, the online Police Records Information Management Environment data-sharing system that every cop used to record and access information.

Meathead had given Striker the names of five individuals capable of crafting professional hidden compartments in the given time frame – Sheldon Clayfield, George Davis, Jason DeHorst, Sanjit Heer and Chris Simmons.

Striker ran them all through the system. Within a minute, all five came up as perfect scores, each one having been in and out of the system so many times they needed their own express lane.

The first two names, DeHorst and Davis, were eliminated quickly. The former was already incarcerated in Kent on robbery charges, and the latter was dead, stabbed to death in Pigeon Park nine months ago. The suspect of that homicide was still unknown, and Striker didn't give a rat's ass about it. It was just one less maggot infecting the meat of society. And two names off his list.

He read through the entries on the rest of the names, and it took some time. Heer was associated with the United Nations Gang, and his specialty was making Escalades and Beamers bullet-proof. He did the work legally, under the company name of Weldwood Enterprises, which Intel files disclosed as nothing more than a four-car garage operation, situated just off Maclure Road in Abbotsford. But Heer had no history with hidden compartments, and so Striker temporarily scratched his name off the list.

That left only two names: Chris Simmons and Sheldon Clayfield.

Both were good matches. Both had long criminal histories, both had been linked to different gangs – Simmons to the Angels, Clayfield to the Scorpions – and both had their own Autobody and Repair shops right here in the Lower Mainland. Simmons was further out, a two-hour drive to Mission. Because of this, Striker got a contact, Janet Jacobson, who worked for the Abbotsford Police, to check Simmons out. As for Clayfield, he was right here in the downtown core. Franklin Street; the 1500 block.

The location alone made Sheldon Clayfield Target One.

Striker signed onto CABS – the Criminal Automated

Booking System – and punched in the name, bringing up Clayfield's mug-shot. Staring back at him was a thin, pallid man, pushing well into his fifties. He had deep lines under his eyes and around his mouth that looked well earned by hard times. His dyed black hair was swept up on both sides like a pair of falcon wings – a ridiculous attempt to cover his bald spot.

'Who's that?'

Striker craned his neck and saw that Felicia had come up behind him.

'Hopefully, he's the man who rigged our stolen car.' Striker rubbed his hands over his face, felt his blood pressure rising.

'You okay?' she asked.

'There's just . . . a lot.'

'You need to relax.'

He laughed. 'How can I? We got too many things going in too many directions. It's like a bag of marbles someone dropped, each one rolling where it's gonna roll.'

'And we'll work through them.'

Her calmness bugged him, and he wondered if maybe she didn't see it all. He started counting off the problems on his fingers. 'One, we got a headless gunman and we don't even know his identity. Two, we got tattoos on White Mask we can't define. Three, we got three kids we know were targeted more than the others, and we don't know why. Four, we got someone out there who made a hidden compartment for these pricks, and we haven't found him yet. And five, we still haven't even heard the audio from the school feed yet because of goddam Laroche's interfering. And all that doesn't even include Red Mask. We have no idea where he is or when he'll strike next.'

'At this point, we still don't know that Red Mask wasn't Leung.'

'Raymond Leung is *not* Red Mask, Feleesh. I know it.'

Felicia's face relaxed for the first time that morning. She smiled and gently brushed her fingers through his hair.

'It's your second day back, Jacob.'

'I know that.'

'Relax. Or you'll end up back on stress leave.'

He looked around the room and felt tired. Hard to believe this was only the beginning. 'We're falling deeper and deeper into a hole here, Felicia.'

'It's an investigation, remember? One thing at a time. And right now it's ten o' clock.'

'So?'

'So let's get going,' she said. She grabbed his arm and hauled him to his feet. 'We got some parents to meet.'

The words hit Striker like a hammer.

Meeting with the parents – it was the last thing in the world he wanted to do. Talking to them was going to be as hard as the shootout with Red Mask.

Thirty-Five

They had to drive by the school, which was a bad idea as far as Striker was concerned. Too many memories were still raw, and there were too many questions to answer. As if to shove this fact in his face, a horde of camera crews sat outside the front of the school, like spiders lurking in their webs. They were filming the mass of flowers and cards and baskets spread out all over the front lawn, where a makeshift memorial had been set up to honour the dead. Streams of people were out front, most of them still looking around in numb disbelief.

Striker eyed them all with a dark foreboding. 'You recognise any?' he asked.

Felicia shook her head. 'Nope.'

'Good.' He drove on by the crowds towards the Chow house. 'How many of the parents we meeting?'

'Two.'

'Just *two*? Where are the rest?'

Felicia pulled out her notebook to get the names right. 'Conrad MacMillan, the Grade Eight kid that was killed, his parents are Archibald and Margaret. Archie's on his way back from Scotland as we speak. He was over there dealing with an ailing father when all this happened.'

'Christ.'

'Yeah, welcome home. So just Margaret's coming down.'

She read on. 'William and Stefana are Chantelle O'Riley's parents. They were all prepared to meet with us till Stefana had a meltdown. William was already on his way over, but he turned around to deal with her. Called back and said it was too soon, said they needed some time. A day or two, at least.'

'And what about Tina Chow's parents?' Striker said the words with unease. Courtney had known Tina and Conrad.

And so had he.

Felicia cleared her throat. 'Parents are Stanley and Doris Chow. Stanley's taken their youngest child away from all this, so we're just meeting with Doris.'

'Three dead kids, two parents. Christ.'

'There were other kids shot too, Jacob. Twenty-two dead, and the injured count is still unreported. We can talk to their parents too, if need be.'

He shook his head. 'Not at this point. The others were random. We'll see what we can find here first.'

They drove quickly past the school, turned right at the next corner and cruised along Hemlock Glen. They soon spotted a white two-storey with a white picket fence to match. Out front were two black Mercedes. It was the Chow house. Two women stood beside the backyard gate. One was Asian, the other white. Both were standing there as still as lawn furniture. Not talking. Not really doing anything. Just staring off into space.

The Asian lady blinked out of her stupor and held up a hand.

'That's them,' Felicia said.

Striker pulled over. The half-frozen gravel crunched beneath the car's tires. He stopped, turned off the ignition, then looked at Felicia.

'You go with Margaret MacMillan, I'll take Doris Chow. We'll compare notes later.'

She nodded her agreement. 'Focus on the Debate Club.'

'Debate Club?'

'I know it sounds odd, but after talking to Caroline and some of the teachers, it's the only link I can come up with. Chantelle O'Riley and Tina Chow were in Grade Ten, but by all accounts they never spoke to one another outside of class, and they hung out in completely different social circles. As for Conrad MacMillan, he was in Grade Eight and didn't talk to any of them – except for in the Debate Club. Conrad and Chantelle and Tina all belonged to it: so far, it's the only connection we have between the three.'

Striker thought this over as he undid his seatbelt. 'You ready?' he asked.

'No, but when has that ever mattered?' She opened up the door and got out.

Striker followed, feeling sick to his stomach. He had no idea what to say to the women.

While Felicia and Margaret MacMillan walked down the bark mulch path to the east side of the house, Striker steered Doris Chow southward into the garden. He had never met Tina's mother before but could immediately see the resemblance.

Doris was small, five foot at best. Thin, too. But not a lightweight. She looked strong and wiry, in good shape for a forty-ish woman. Her hair was naturally black, though it had a burgundy tint. It was swept back into a ponytail, held in place by a lime green scrunchie that stuck out against her hair and purple jogging suit. She wore no make-up, so the lines under her eyes and around her mouth gave away her true age, but she got away with it because she was naturally good-looking.

They walked on, talked.

Striker took his time with her. They discussed the little things first. The unimportant matters: how long she had been married, when she'd immigrated to Canada, how big her family was, and so on. Through it all, Striker kept reflecting on what losing Courtney would have done to him, had she been one of the fallen.

It was a thought that left him feeling sick.

They reached the end of the garden where a row of bare thornbushes surrounded a lone cherry blossom tree. The tree was large, easily thirty feet tall. Oddly, it was still in bloom, with many of the blossoms having fallen to the ground, mottling the half-frozen grass and bark mulch in pink tones.

Doris stooped to pick one up. She rubbed the petals between her fingers and murmured, 'This was her favourite, the cherry blossom.'

'I can see why.'

As she stood there, looking at the beautiful pink flower in her hand, all of a sudden Striker saw the other side of her. There was frailness there. Like a piece of rubber band that was stretched too far and trembling from the pressure. It pained him to push her any further. But it was necessary.

He turned to face her. 'Mrs Chow, have you thought about why? Why Tina?'

She looked up. 'There is no reason. Just evil kids with guns. They were shooting everyone.'

Striker met her stare, shook his head. 'There's more to it, I'm afraid. I think Tina was targeted.'

Doris's face paled. 'Targeted?'

'Yes. Would you have any idea why?'

'But there were so many kids . . .'

'A lot of kids were shot, Mrs Chow, yes, I know. But from the evidence I've seen, three of those kids were targeted specifically. Tina was one of them. So was Conrad MacMillan. And Chantelle O'Riley.'

Doris's face twitched, but she managed to answer and maintain her composure.

'But my daughter didn't socialise with those kids. I'd never even met Margaret before this morning.'

'I know that, and that's why this investigation is so hard. There's a common connection here somewhere, and we have to find it.'

Doris looked away towards the mountains. The soft fall wind blew her hair back, but the scrunchie kept all but a few hairs tucked in place. She stood there for a long moment, and Striker allowed her the silence. When she spoke again, she seemed flustered.

'I'm sorry, my mind is racing. I can't seem to take it all in.'

Striker helped her out. 'I've heard Tina was part of a Debate Club?'

This seemed to give Doris a jolt. 'The Debate Club. Oh, yes. She loved it so much! She excelled at using her mind, and she made friends through it. Had some wonderful experiences. They took a trip, you know, last September. All the kids went. Twelve of them, I think.'

'Where did they go?'

'Hong Kong. Tina was so excited, she talked about it for weeks.' The memory brought a weak grin to the woman's lips, and she laughed sadly. 'If there was one thing my daughter was good at, it was talking.'

'What did they debate, here and in Hong Kong?'

She shrugged. 'Normally, they would debate anything that was pertinent. And hot – they liked hot topics. Abortion. The death penalty. Assisted suicide. When they went to Hong Kong, the topic was freedom and world religions. National sovereignty. The debate was on China's rule over Tibet. It caused quite a stir – they had to cut the tournament short.'

'Why?'

'They didn't say.'

Striker thought this over. 'Did Tina speak on the subject?'

'They all did, as far as I know.'

'But you weren't there?'

She shook her head. 'No, only Principal Myers went.'

Striker wrote this down in his notebook.

'Do you have any children, Detective Striker?' Tina Chow suddenly asked.

Striker thought of how Courtney had known Tina, a small fact Doris was obviously unaware of. 'A daughter, yes. She goes to Saint Patrick's.'

This seemed to shock the woman. 'She is . . . okay?'

'She was skipping class yesterday.'

Doris smiled, as if this was funny. She let out a soft laugh, then suppressed another cry. The pink petal fell from her hand and blew away in the gentle breeze. Blew away as easily as Tina Chow's life had blown away just twenty-four hours ago.

Striker saw her face quiver, saw how she was slowly losing the battle with her composure.

'I'm sorry,' he offered quietly.

Doris nodded and the tears finally came, running freely down her thin, pale cheeks. When she spoke, her voice was barely audible.

'Enjoy every day with her, Detective,' she said. 'Every minute, every second. And appreciate her. Appreciate all the small things . . . you never know when they'll be taken away.'

Thirty-Six

For the third time in ten minutes, the phone rang, and Courtney finally dragged herself out of bed to look at the call display. The bedroom drapes had blocked out the sun and kept everything dark, and the laminate floors were cold against the soft flesh of her feet as she lumbered down the hall into the living room.

She hoped the call was from Raine. Unlike everyone else, Raine understood her. How couldn't she? They had a connection, a unique bond. Courtney had lost her mother just two years ago, and Raine had lost her dad last year when her parents broke up and he moved away to Hong Kong. It made their friendship like a kinship. Kind of.

Like sisters.

The living room was no warmer than the bedroom, though brighter with the sun pouring in. It smelled of woodsmoke and whisky and lemons. Courtney passed the coffee table where Dad and Felicia's mugs still stood and picked up the phone. She stared at the small screen.

Missed call.

She hit the missed calls button and saw *Dad Cell* spread across the screen. God, he was stubborn. She scrolled down and found the same listing three more times. Totally stubborn. Stubborn as hell.

She put the phone back on its cradle, then spotted her cell

phone lying in the middle of the room, just in front of the fireplace. The phone was flipped open, the grey casing cracked
down the side from where it had slammed into the wall. It
made her angry all over again because she hadn't even finished
paying off the damn thing, and she would never have reacted
like that, were it not for Felicia.

She picked up the cell, powered it on, and was happy to see
it still worked. There were nine missed calls. All but two were
from friends she had at school. No doubt they wanted to talk
about the shootings.

Courtney erased every one of them from the phone's
memory. She had no interest in talking about the shootings.
Not now, not ever.

All it did was remind her of Mom.

The last two calls were the only ones she cared about. Both
were from Raine. The first had come in late last night, at two-
fourteen a.m. The last one had come in about a half hour ago.

Courtney called back, got the answering machine: 'Leave a
message, but don't *Raine* on my parade.'

That always made Courtney smile. 'It's the Court,' she said.
'I'm up. Gimme a call.'

She hung up, hoped her message sounded cool, hoped her
tag name wasn't getting lame, and she linked her cell to the
charger. As she tried to think up a new nickname – something
cooler than The Court – thoughts of breakfast ran through her
mind. She decided to skip it. Her stomach wasn't ready.

She turned on the TV, and saw the shootings on every channel. Police, paramedics, teachers – all running and screaming,
some crying. There were quick flashes of blood with every
scene. *Carnage.* The sight made her heart race, made her feel
sick.

Looking away, she hit Input 2, so there was no chance of

catching any more news channels. As far as she was concerned, it was time for avoidance and denial. She knelt down and opened the hutch, grabbing the disc she had left in the far back of the cabinet. It was the video from Christmas three years ago. The last one Mom was here for. And even though it hurt like hell to watch it, Courtney always did. Too many times to count. She was like a drug addict, always needing more.

The disc tray was already open. Courtney put in the disc, closed it, hit play, and the TV screen came to life, showing the Christmas tree all lit up with red and blue lights, and Mom sitting in the La-Z-Boy between the window and the crackling fire. Toby, their calico kitty, was in the picture too, jumping up on the chair and nestling in Mom's lap. He had disappeared a week after Mom had died, as if he'd known his favourite person was never coming back. Courtney often wondered where he'd gone.

The thought saddened her, but she watched on, like she always did. She felt she had to. Like it was her duty as a daughter. To let go of the pain was to let go of Mom.

In the video, the camera bobbled slightly as Dad moved around the room, panning down on the presents, then finding her with the camera and zooming in.

'Merry Christmas, Pumpkin,' he said.

'Merry Christmas, Dad.'

'Go stand with your mother so I can get a shot.'

Mom waved her hand at Dad, almost spilling her glass of rum and eggnog. 'Oh Jacob, put that thing away for once.'

There was a pause.

'Come on, Amanda, just one shot.'

In the feed, Mom sighed and Dad chuckled, and then Courtney crossed the room and sat beside Mom, giving her a kiss on the cheek. She gestured to the rum and eggnog, gave a pleading look, and asked, 'Can I have one of those?'

Her mother just gave her *the look*, and Courtney laughed. Then her mother frowned at the camera.

'You got your shot, Jacob, now put it away. You're always such a nuisance.'

'Fine. Merry Killjoy,' Dad said.

And the camera shut off.

Courtney grabbed the remote, hit stop, and closed her eyes. She could still feel the moment like it was yesterday. The fire's warmth soothing her skin. The spicy smell of the rum in Mom's drink. The eggnog of her own drink. And the pine-scented smoke that seeped out of the fireplace and hazed the room just a little bit.

It was all so wonderful. It made her cry.

And she hated Dad for that.

She hit play and watched the feed again. The shot was a bit dark, and there was a low humming noise in the audio. The video was anything but high-def, but it was the best movie she'd ever seen in her life.

Oh, Mom.

It wasn't fair.

She missed her so much her stomach hurt and she wanted to keep crying forever. And the more she missed her, the more it bugged her how Dad just plain didn't. Oh, he *said* he did. He said all the right things, especially when he caught her watching the videos which he never watched.

'She loved you so much,' he would say.

'You made her life wonderful,' he would say.

'I miss her too, Pumpkin,' he would say.

But that didn't stop him from fucking that Spanish whore.

Courtney thought of Felicia, and Dad, and how Mom was

no longer around, and it made her feel small. Alone. No one cared. No one knew how she felt. No one understood her.

Except Raine.

Raine knew because Raine had also gone through some horrible things. Like all the fights and the divorce and her dad leaving town.

With that in mind, Courtney picked up the phone and called Raine, but again, all she got was the message service. She thought about leaving another message – still wasn't sure about using The Court for her tag – then just hung up. She watched the video two more times, and soon her grief mutated into anger.

Mom should never have died that night, she thought. Dad should have done something. Something, for Christ's sake! He was the goddam cop, he should have acted. He should have damn well *cared*.

But he didn't, did he?

And even though he said he missed Mom, and even though he'd said he was sorry a million times, it didn't mean shit. Because Mom was gone. Forever. All because of what he didn't do. Of what he chose *not* to do. In the end, there was only one way to view things.

It was Dad's fault Mom had died.

Thirty-Seven

They were in the car, driving east, when Noodles finally called Striker back at quarter to twelve. His words were quick and direct, and they made Striker's nerves fire. 'The blood types of Raymond Leung and the blood in the car don't match.'

Striker closed his eyes for a second. 'I fuckin' knew it.'

'Raymond Leung is A-positive. The blood in the Civic is type O-negative.'

The information should have made Striker feel better, since it had proven him right, but it didn't. It only brought him fear and dark premonitions.

Red Mask was still out there somewhere.

'You tell Laroche?' he asked Noodles.

'He's arguing it. Says we can't prove that the blood in the car was actually Red Mask's blood.'

'I shot him myself.'

'Hey, you're preachin' to the choir, Shipwreck. Either way, it's what we're dealing with.'

They talked a bit more before Noodles promised to relay anything else he heard, then Striker hung up and told Felicia the news.

'Well, you were right,' she finally conceded. 'Congratulations, Jacob. Great news. The maniac's still out there somewhere.'

He blinked. 'I'm not gloating. All I'm saying is, we got to

keep our feet to the fire. This thing isn't done. Not by a long shot.'

He waited for a response from Felicia, but got none. So they drove in silence. Destination: East Vancouver. Franklin Street.

The industrial section of the city.

Almost fifteen minutes later, when the silence became burdensome, Striker turned the talk back to the investigation.

The meeting with the two mothers, Doris Chow and Margaret MacMillan, had turned up some interesting information. The Debate Club, the trip to Hong Kong, Free Tibet speeches, and a cancelled tournament – the timing seemed more than coincidental, but Striker could see no involvement. It was just one more piece for a jigsaw puzzle that already had too many.

His stomach rumbled, part from lunchtime hunger, part from emotional distress. It was going on twelve noon, and Courtney had yet to return his calls. No doubt she was up, and simply choosing to ignore him. In some ways she was just like her mother.

He drove east on Forty-First Avenue, past Arbutus, and cut into the McDonald's drive-thru. There was nothing he could do about Courtney's attitude, but his hunger was another matter. The breakfast menu had ended, so he ordered a Big Mac and a Filet-O-Fish, and two more coffees – his black, Felicia's loaded with cream and sugar. The smell seemed to wake Felicia up a bit. She popped off the lid of her coffee, then looked towards the bag.

'If I eat that, I'll balloon.'

'Oh come on, you eat two pastries and two fancy lattes every day, what could this hurt?'

She made a face, but reached for the bag.

As they continued down Broadway, Striker pulled out his cell and noticed he had a missed call from Janet Jacobson, the former Vancouver Vice cop who had now moved on to greener pastures. He called her back but the line was busy and he didn't leave a message. They drove towards the industrial section where Triple A Autobody was located.

Sheldon Clayfield's business.

Felicia pulled out the Filet-O-Fish. 'So fill me in again, who is this Clayfield guy?'

Striker swallowed a mouthful, then wiped a smear of Big Mac sauce from his lips. 'Clayfield is one of the five guys Meathead told us about. I've narrowed it down to two who work in the Lower Mainland that are even capable of making a hidden compartment like that. Clayfield's got a history of it, and a long list of other shit for drug running. He made a real good compartment for a drug trafficker last year, and was caught by Drugs. They dropped the charge for information. And I got word of another one he made six months before that. It gives us leverage.'

'Great. What about the other guy?'

'His name is Chris Simmons. Works out in the Valley, on the border of Mission. Remember Janet Jacobson – used to work in Vice? – she transferred out to Abbotsford a few months back. I contacted her back at the office, when you were setting things up with the parents. She's checking Simmons out for us, but Clayfield is ours. Run him on the computer and bring up his associates.'

Felicia nodded and typed in his name as Striker drove north on Knight Street. After a few blocks, she made a frustrated sound.

'This guy's got over a hundred associates in here,' she said.

'See which ones are listed under Triple A Autobody. It's

Clayton's shop. They will be our connection to Clayfield and the Honda.'

She did. 'Okay. Got eight now. Place must be a chop shop.'

'That, and a whole lot more.'

They got stuck at a red. Striker cursed softly under his breath, grabbed his own coffee which sat unchecked in the drink holder. It was still hot.

'Check out the Intels of every associate,' he said. 'See if any of these guys have been linked to other modified vehicles.'

Felicia scanned through the reports, read for a while in silence. By the time the light turned green, she found what she was looking for. 'Okay. We got two guys here with a whole lot of history. Tony Rifanzi, and a guy named Ricky Lomar.'

Striker had never heard of either of them.

'What work have they done?' he asked.

She read on. 'Lomar's done a lot of compartments, some in the dashboard, some under the seats, and some in the floor-board and wheel-wells. Always drugs though.'

'And Rifanzi?'

'Same. Just a lot less.'

'He's done a lot less, or he's been caught a lot less?'

'Good point.' Felicia clucked her tongue on the roof of her mouth. 'Looks like Rifanzi's work is a higher level. He's been suspected of using hydraulics and electronics in the past; Lomar's stuff has always been lever activated, somewhere in the car.'

Striker said nothing, he just let this information digest.

His cell phone rang and he snatched it off his belt, hoping it was Courtney. The display told him otherwise. It was Janet Jacobson. He answered, listened for less than a minute, then thanked her and hung up.

'Well?' Felicia asked.

'Turns out Simmons has been under surveillance for the better part of three weeks on unrelated matters. He's out. That leaves only Clayfield.'

They had reached East Hastings Street, only three blocks from their destination, when Felicia made an *oh-shit* sound as she finished reading through the reports. 'We've hit a snag here,' she said. 'Rifanzi's actually on the jail slate. Been in there since late last night.'

Striker thought it over. 'For what?'

'Fight at a strip club – the Number Five Orange. Assault Causing Bodily Harm.' She skimmed the electronic pages. 'Report says he was pretty coked up. Christ, another friggin' investigative dead end.'

Striker stopped the car on the north side of Franklin Street, the 1500 block. Triple A Autobody was only a half block away.

'Dead end nothing,' he said. 'He's just given us a pass into the fast lane.'

'What are you talking about?'

Striker grinned. 'Watch and learn, my young apprentice. Watch and learn.'

Thirty-Eight

There was nothing special about Triple A Autobody. It was just a two-bay garage with two hoists per lane. Three guys were working inside, one black, two East Indian. All of them were tattooed and beefy. Hardliners. Each one of them gave Striker and Felicia a sideways look as they walked in through the back bay door and poked their heads around.

'Place smells like motor oil and freshly-smoked pot,' Striker said loudly. 'A Workers Compensation Board no-no.'

Without a word, the black guy put down the tire he was holding, turned and walked into the back office.

Striker gave Felicia a wink. 'He must be getting us the welcome mat.'

A small smile broke her tight lips, and it made him feel good.

'Or the red carpet,' she added.

Striker grinned.

A tall guy with thinning white hair came out of the office. His build was skinny, but his gut was huge – a big distended belly, like he had cancer or a tapeworm or something. He was stomping more than walking, and his hands were balled into fists. He wasn't even halfway across the garage before he said, 'This is private property. What the hell do you want?'

Striker didn't respond. He just stood there and waited for the man to get close enough so that he wouldn't have to raise his voice. When the man was a few feet away, Striker recognised him from the mug-shots. It was Sheldon Clayfield all right, but he had aged badly since the photo was taken. His thinning hair was now pure white – and not a healthy white either, but an *I-shat-my-pants-one-too-many-times* white – and the lines in his face were deeper than some canyons.

'Sheldon Clayfield?' Felicia asked.

'You know it is.'

'Somewhere we can talk?'

The man placed his hands on his hips, making his large gut look more pronounced. 'Here's as good a place as any.'

Before Striker could reply, a customer walked through the front door. Striker grinned. 'You sure about that, Clayfield? Involves stolen cars, dead children, and a few rather *sensitive* names.'

The words knocked the tough look off Clayfield's face and he blinked. Just a second really, but that was all it took.

Striker knew they had something here.

'Office,' Clayfield finally grunted. 'No point in disrupting my workers.'

He turned around and walked away with far less attitude than he'd come out with. Felicia and Striker followed. Clayfield ushered them inside, said he had to deal with the customer first, then left.

Striker listened to their conversation as they waited. He also looked around the office.

It was small, had no windows, and stank of stale cigarettes and old coffee. One desk and three chairs filled the room, all of them rickety and wooden. A black rotary telephone sat on the desk, splattered white with paint drops. The rest of the office was no better. The walls had once been cream, but time and a few thousand cigarettes had greyed them to the same sickly colour old people got when they had stage three cancer. Decorating the walls were pictures of naked women, most of them on motorcycles, with tattoos and piercings. Some of them were in bondage, strapped to the handlebars.

'How modern,' Felicia said.

Striker pointed to one of the posters that had a naked blonde bent over the back of a Harley Davidson. The tattoo across her lower back read *God Rides a Harley!*

Striker gestured to the tattoo. 'Don't you have one of those?'

'Yeah, but I had the *God* changed to *Clod*. Reminded me of you.'

'You always were sentimental.'

They shared a grin as the customer out front left the shop and Clayfield returned. He looked unhappy and didn't try to cover it. He closed the door and focused on them with dark narrowed eyes.

Striker looked at Clayfield's hands and made sure they were empty.

'Now what's this shit you're talking about?' Clayfield asked.

Striker met his stare. 'I'm talking about the stolen Honda Civic you modified.'

Clayfield walked around the office until he was on the other side of the desk, facing them, as if he liked having the barrier between them.

'Honda Civic? Shit. Never heard of it.'

'Oh, I think you remember. The one with the new ignition and stereo, and the magnetic happy face – that was a nice little addition, by the way.'

'Like I said, I don't know what you're talking bout.'

Striker looked back at the closed office door, pushed on it to make sure it was secure. Then he turned around and leaned forward across the desk.

'Here's the deal, Clayfield. Twenty-two children died yesterday at Saint Patrick's and the madman is still out there. I don't think for a second you were involved in the shootings, but I do know you were approached by someone to have the car modified. And I know you did it.'

Striker paused for a moment to let the silence weigh down on Clayfield. Then he continued speaking.

'So here's the deal: what I need from you is a name. Just a name. No one will know where we got it. And then we leave you and your shop alone.'

'And if I don't got no name?'

'Then we get a warrant and tear this place apart.'

Clayfield looked at them for a short moment, then sneered, 'If you had enough for a warrant, you'd already a got one.'

Striker looked at Felicia, forced a chuckle.

'That was true yesterday,' he said. 'When we only had *you* under watch. But now that Rifanzi's spilled his guts and is willing to cut a deal, I can get one easily. But it'll take time, and time is the one thing I don't want to waste.'

Silence filled the small office, then Clayfield spoke: 'You're a fuckin' liar.'

'I'm sure you wish that was the case. But no, I'm quite serious.'

Felicia caught on, added her own take: 'Screw him, Striker. Let's just write the damn warrant and charge this prick.'

Striker's eyes never left the man.

'Up to you, Clayfield. I can set patrol up on your shop, lock it down, then write the warrant. But I'll tell you this, I find even the smallest trace of what I'm looking for, and I'll charge you with every goddam offence I can think of – and I got Crown Counsel on board with this one. These are dead kids we're talking about. *Children.*'

Even in the poor fluorescent lighting of the office, the small beads of perspiration that were forming on Clayfield's forehead glistened. He put a hand over his lower stomach and belched. A bad whiff of beer and stomach acids filled the room.

'Ain't no law against making an extra compartment in no car anyway,' he said. 'Especially if I never knowed it was stolen.'

Felicia cut in again: 'That would be true if the compartment wasn't form-fitted for an AK-47 and a Benelli shotgun. But that means *knowledge*, and knowledge makes you an accessory to the crime of murder. Multiple counts. Children.'

'Good work, by the way,' Striker added. 'Looked damn near factory made. Almost as good as the one you did for that drug trafficker last year – what was his name, Whitebear? – or the one you made six months before that, for Jeremy Koln.'

Clayfield swallowed hard, looked helplessly around the room.

Striker pretended not to notice. He gave Felicia a look. 'What time is it?'

'Too damn late,' she said. 'Let's just lock this place down and charge this prick – it's a good stat for us anyway.'

'Ah fuck it,' Striker agreed. 'You're right.' He pulled out his cell phone and pretended to get a hold of Dispatch. Told them who he was. 'We're gonna need a pair of two-man cars down here after all. And the wagon. I got to transport someone to jail.'

'Okay, okay, *okay*,' Clayfield said. His face had gone white, highlighting the red splotches of his skin. His breath was coming in wheezy puffs. He slammed his fist against the locker near the wall and yelled, 'That fuckin' Rifanzi!'

Striker paused, said into the phone, 'Hold up on that wagon for a moment. I'll call you back.' He put the phone away and met Clayfield's stare. 'You're not the fish I want, Clayfield. I want the man who booked this job. He's the real connection to the gunmen.'

Clayfield's expression crumbled; his eyes took on a pleading look.

'It was just done as a favour,' he said. 'Honest. He gets me supplies, this guy – from Japan. I was just paying him back for what I owed.'

'I'm losing patience.'

'I never even knowed it was stolen, for chrissake!'

'Just give me a goddam *name*.'

Clayfield's eyes turned down and away, and suddenly he looked a whole lot smaller than his six foot frame. When he spoke, his voice broke.

'Edward Rundell,' he croaked.

Thirty-Nine

The moment Striker and Felicia returned to the car, they ran Edward Rundell over the computer. The man came back completely negative. No criminal history. No reports written in the PRIME database. No nothing. And for a moment, Striker felt that maybe Sheldon Clayfield was smarter than they'd given him credit for.

Striker got on the phone. He called Jimmy Hensley in Fraud, told him Edward Rundell was some kind of liaison between the car modifier and the gunmen, and asked if he'd ever heard of him.

The answer was no.

Striker then called Chogi Saurn in Drugs, Jillian Wiles in the General Investigation Unit, and Stephan Fanglesworth, known as 'Fang', who worked in Financial Crime. He asked them all if they'd ever heard of an Edward Rundell. The resounding answer was *no*.

Edward Rundell just didn't exist.

'Try Info,' Felicia suggested.

Striker did. He got on the Info channel and ran Rundell over the air. Again, no criminal history came back on the man. He did get a British Columbia Driver's Licence, but even that was a problem. There was no phone number on file, and the address listed as the primary residence was in the 1600 block of

Turner Street in Vancouver – an address Striker knew didn't exist. The thought made his head hurt, and he put a hand over his left temple. Something felt wrong in there, like he had too much blood in his brain.

Felicia nudged him. 'Want some Tylenol?'

He said sure, and she handed him some. Then she pulled out her cell phone, scrolled through her long list of contacts, and dialled. 'Rundell's got to have a number,' she said. 'It's just unlisted. I'll try a few contacts I have.'

'How many phone company sources you got?'

'About ten or so.'

''Bout *ten*? I got one.'

She smiled. 'We're women. We talk.'

Striker just nodded and let the pill dissolve in his mouth. He wished he had some water to go with it, but there was only cold coffee. While he waited, he hit the unit status button to see what else was going on in the city. He did this often. It was a habit of his, ever since his days in Patrol. He liked knowing what was happening elsewhere, especially the parts he was passing through. There was nothing worse than getting that call over the air requesting you to stay out of someone's stakeout scene right after you'd driven through it in your police car.

Nothing on the unit status grabbed his attention. He pulled out his BlackBerry and tried home again. Surprise filled him when it was picked up.

'Hello?' Courtney said. Her voice was light.

'Courtney, it's me.'

She made a sound like she was surprised, like she was expecting someone else. 'I thought you were a friend.'

'Raven?'

Courtney let out a frustrated exclamation. '*Raine*, Dad! She's only, like, the most important person in my life. God, she's my best friend and you don't even know her name – how uncool is that?'

'You've never even introduced us.'

'Because you're never around.'

'I was around for *six months*. On leave – for you. You never even brought her around once.'

'Only because you'd embarrass me.'

'What? How would I—'

'Look, I can't talk right now, Dad.'

'Can't, or don't want to?'

'Fine, have it your way. Don't want to.'

Striker felt the faint traces of anger sparking up. 'You know, at some point you're going to have to deal with things, Courtney, and not just get angry and run away all the time.'

'Run away? *I'm* the one running away? Call the bank, Dad, you need a reality check.'

'Courtney—'

The phone died, and Striker bit his lip. Wanted to yell right there in the car. But Felicia was on the phone with one of her contacts at Telus, one of Canada's largest phone providers. So he sat there, stifling his anger with the cell stuck to his ear, wondering if he'd get a friendlier reception from Clayfield and the boys back at Triple A Autobody. When he pouched the phone on his belt, Felicia hung hers up in tandem.

'Anything?' he asked.

She made a face. 'Rundell has no hard line whatsoever. He might operate primarily from a cell.'

'Lovely.'

'Well, it's not a total dead end. Janie's going to run him through all the systems, see what she can come up with. Promised to call us back sometime today.'

Striker thought it over. There were other databases they

could use to find this man, but some of them took warrants. All of them took time. It was not how he wanted to investigate matters, but regardless of his personal choice, it was a route they might yet have to take. He looked at Felicia. 'How long is "sometime today"?'

'Knowing Janie, I'd say less than two hours.'

'We'll give her the time then.' He looked around the area they were parked in. It was nothing but square stucco building after square stucco building. They were all warehouse-type businesses with the odd repair shop or processing plant stuck in between.

Striker started the cruiser and powered down the window a crack. The moment he did, he was hit by the strong smell of diesel fumes and garbage. He put the car in drive and headed for 312 Main Street. Headquarters.

At his side, Felicia took the tube of Alco-rub from the glove box and spread some of the transparent gel on her palms, rubbing it vigorously between her fingers as it slowly evaporated.

'That office was disgusting,' she said. 'I got sticky stuff all over my hands.'

Striker gave her a grin.

'Don't even go there,' she warned him.

He didn't.

When she was finished with the Alco-rub, he asked her to check the unit status again. Felicia tapped the touch-screen a few times, then waited for the computer to beep and bring up the information. When it did, she read through the District Two unit status.

'This is interesting,' she said. 'Got a Charlie unit here. They went on a traffic stop that quickly turned into a Suspicious Vehicle file. They called for radio priority.'

Striker glanced at the screen. 'They get into a pursuit?'

Felicia paged through the call. '*Foot* pursuit.' She read on, shook her head as if she couldn't make any sense of it, then muttered, 'This is strange.'

Striker shrugged. 'Foot pursuits happen all the time down here, Feleesh, this is District Two. I worked it for years.'

She gave him an irritated look. 'I know, Jacob, I worked it myself – for a year longer than you did.' When he didn't reply, she added, 'I'm not talking about the foot pursuit, I'm talking about the call itself – mainly the added remarks.'

'What's so odd about it?'

She turned to face him. 'Your name is on the call.'

Forty

The call in question was at Gore and Pender, just one block south of East Hastings Street. It was positioned perfectly between the police headquarters building at 312 Main, the heart of Chinatown, and the Carnegie Support Centre, which was ground zero for Skid Row. Striker and Felicia were only eleven blocks out and arrived on scene within minutes.

Striker was surprised at what he found. The entire intersection was blocked off with yellow crime scene tape. It looked like streamers at a Skid Row birthday party. All they needed were some condom balloons and a crack cake with heroin icing.

He shook his head absently. 'What is this – the tenth crime scene in two days?'

Felicia nodded. 'I'm going to start matching my accessories.'

Striker barely heard her. He got out. Assessed.

Dumped in the middle of the intersection was an ordinary white GMC van. Both the driver and the passenger doors were wide open, but the rear double doors were closed. Standing guard was another uniformed cop, a young Chinese guy with thick, almost spiky hair.

Striker was about to duck under the yellow tape and approach him when he spotted a familiar figure rounding the front of the van. Grizzled, experienced, and almost as tired as he'd seen him down by the docks earlier this morning. It was Sergeant Mike Rothschild.

'Hey, wrinkle-face,' Striker called.

Rothschild spotted them, walked over to the inside edge of the yellow crime scene tape. 'First off, call me that again and I'll have you stationed at the jail for the rest of your career. Second off, I was just about to contact you guys.'

Striker nodded. 'I bet. Why is my name on the call?'

Rothschild raised an eyebrow. 'Well, look who we got here – Nostra-fucking-Damus. Who told you?'

'Felicia did; she read it on the unit status.'

Rothschild smiled. 'Should've known. One of you has to be on the ball.' He shared a chuckle with Felicia and ducked under the yellow tape, stepping out of the crime scene. He pulled a package of cigarillos from his pocket – Old Port, wine-tipped – and lit one up.

'Long damn day,' he said.

Felicia looked at the van, noticed it had no front plate. 'Stolen?'

Rothschild splayed his hands. 'Who fuckin' knows. Registered Owner is some restaurant down the block. Called there, but no one seems to know who's got the van or why it isn't parked in the underground parkade.'

'Is it insured?' Striker asked.

'Temporary Operators Permit. Again, registered to the restaurant. Primary driver is listed as some Kim Pham fuckwad. He's the manager, but according to staff, he's conveniently on holiday right now somewhere back East. No contact number. No known address.'

'Why is my name on the call?' Striker asked again.

'I put it on.'

'For a stolen?'

Rothschild took a long drag on the cigarillo then exhaled, and the air around them smelled strongly of wine-scented smoke. He took another puff, sucking in as much nicotine as he could get – like his life depended on it – then dropped the cigarillo on the ground, crushed it with his patrol boot, and jerked his head towards the van.

'Come on, Alice,' he said. 'Time to go through the Looking Glass.'

He ducked back under the yellow tape, into the crime scene, and Striker and Felicia followed. Rothschild continued talking.

'So Hank and Blondie – my plainclothes car – spot this thing, see it's got no rear plate. They can see the Temporary Operator's Permit, but it's behind the rear window and they can't read it, so they decide to follow it and see what happens. They first pick it up on Georgia, going westbound, and then the driver seems to take notice. He stops at the red on Main, looks indecisive, then does a hard turn when the light changes green. Hank can't make the turn because of traffic. When the traffic clears, they gun it, catch up to the van, see it turn east again, though now on Pender, and it's fuckin' flying. So they decide to light it up. Moment they do, these pricks bail and the chase is on.'

'They in custody?' Striker asked.

Rothschild shook his head. 'Got away. And the dog track was no good.'

Striker cursed.

'They get a good look at the driver?' Felicia asked.

'Nope. Happened too fast. Two guys in dark hoodies and sweatpants.' He pointed at the projects to the south-east. 'Hopped the fence and cut through there, right towards the Lucky Rooms on Prior. But who the hell knows? Dog couldn't follow the track. And with the time delay, they're long gone now.'

Striker looked at the van. 'Which restaurant does it register to?'

Rothschild leafed through his notebook. 'Fortune Happy or something. I dunno, it's just down the block. On Pender. Big yellow awning.'

'Must be stolen. Why else would they run?'

Rothschild's face darkened. 'I can think of three reasons. You will too, if you go take a look.'

Taking his time, Striker approached the van. He reefed open the back doors and looked inside the rear cab. There, lying on a piece of stained-red plywood, were three bodies. One was partly wrapped in a rug.

The closest, curled into the fetal position, was an old man. Thin. Asian. Maybe in his sixties. The two men behind him were larger, younger, and heavily muscled. In their late twenties or early thirties. Both wore fancy suits, good quality silk, yellow with faint white pinstripes.

Rothschild grinned. 'You remember Sha Na Na.'

Felicia laughed, but Striker was so focused he barely heard the comment.

'These guys are from the restaurant?' he asked.

'Don't know.'

'Anyone been in the van?'

'Just me,' Rothschild said. 'I'm still trying to identify them.'

'Any ID on them?'

'Zilch.'

Felicia looked at the bodies. 'Coroner been here yet? Ambulance?'

'Naw, no point. They were stone cold when we found them. I put your name on the call so you could check them out first.

Thought it might have some relevance to the shootings yesterday.'

'Why?' Striker asked.

Rothschild splayed his hands. 'How often we find a van full of dead Asian guys? Proximity. Time. Nothing more than that.'

Striker nodded. 'It's appreciated.'

He looked at the bodies. The old man was already stiff, mostly in the neck and shoulders, and especially in the face, where he looked to be grimacing in death. Deep wrinkles marked his face, and where there were no wrinkles, the skin was smooth and hairless.

Felicia pointed to the purplish line of bruised flesh that snaked around the left half of his thin and wiry body. 'Lividity.'

Striker had already noticed it. Blood had pooled in the torso, legs and arms – all on the left side. Yet the deceased lay on his right side.

'He didn't die here,' Striker said. 'He's been moved.'

Felicia took a closer look. 'Any idea how long?'

'Judging by the amount of rigor, it's been a while. Probably more than twenty-four hours. Pathologist'll have to figure it out for any real time.'

Striker gloved up with latex. He climbed up on the back end of the van and tried to move the old man's limbs. They were stiff, refused to budge, and Striker feared he'd tear the tissue if he forced it. He peered around the limbs, looking for a possible stab or gunshot wound.

He found none.

'How'd he die?' Felicia asked.

'Not a clue,' Striker said.

He looked past the old man, saw the blood-stained yellow suits of the two goons near the front. One of them had his jacket open. The white material of the shirt beneath was caked in dried blood. Nothing unusual for a dead body, but the bullet wound stuck out to Striker. He moved farther into the van to investigate.

What he saw made his stomach tighten.

He checked over the first victim, finding three well-placed shots, two in the chest and one in the head. He rolled the body over to see the exit wounds, then did the same with the second victim, who had also been shot three times. Two in the chest, one in the head. And by the looks of things, they were from a forty cal. Exact same placement and the exact same kind of ammo Red Mask had used on the targeted kids at St Patrick's High.

And by Hydra-Shok rounds.

It told Striker what he had already known in the darkest corner of his heart.

Red Mask was still alive.

Forty-One

High above the Pacific Ocean, at approx thirty-seven thousand feet, the Man with the Bamboo Spine walked down the centre aisle of the 747 in an effort to stretch his joints. At just over six foot, he was tall for an Asian male, and lanky. His legs and arms were disproportionately long in comparison to the rest of his body.

On returning to his seat, he pulled out the laptop given to him back in Macau. He powered it on, punched in his password, SWORDS, then waited for the operating system to finish loading. The ticket he had purchased was for a window seat. He had also purchased the seat next to him.

When the flight attendant came by and asked him if he was thirsty, he said, 'Yes.' When she asked him if wanted tea or coffee, he said, 'Tea, black.' And when she asked him if he wanted anything else, he said, 'No.' These were the first words he had spoken since entering this plane the previous day on the other side of the world.

He waited in silence, looking at nothing until the flight attendant returned with his drink. He folded down the tray of the next seat, accepted the tea, and placed the cup down in the circular inset. He waited for the flight attendant to leave.

When she was gone, he got to work.

The laptop was an Apple, and it had a rotatable screen. He

turned the screen forty degrees to the left, so that it faced the window, where only he could see it. He brought up the file folder that was password protected and encrypted by FolderSecure. He used his second password, THUNDERBOLTS, to gain access, then opened the unlocked folder.

Images popped up.

Spread across the screen were five jpegs. Four of them were the faces of children, smiling, happy. Three of them were now dead. One was presumably alive, the whereabouts unknown. The fifth jpeg was an image of a man he had not seen in decades. Not since those bad, bad times that he never thought about any more.

The sight stirred strange feelings inside of him.

The Man with the Bamboo Spine looked at the images for a long time as the plane crossed the Pacific Ocean and entered Canadian air space. He did not shut the computer down until the flight attendant announced that they would soon be making their descent.

He sat straight and said nothing more. Stared at the back of the seat in front of him as the plane prepared to land.

Vancouver, Canada.

He had arrived.

Forty-Two

Striker and Felicia left the crime scene in Rothschild's capable hands and cruised the Skids. It was fast approaching two o'clock. Above them, any clarity of blue sky was being slowly hazed over with a depressive greyness.

It matched the areas they were searching – the Raymur underpass with its tranny hookers; Pigeon Park with its open drug trafficking; Oppenheimer with its endless fighting drunks; and now, Blood Alley with its drug-sick hypes and crazies.

At times, this city felt like a demented fun house.

Striker and Felicia were searching for someone who could ID the three dead men in the van. Their best bet was forty-five-year-old Carol Kalwateen, who went by the street name Trixie. She was a regular around the Skids, and Chinatown, and the Strathcona Projects. She had been a rounder for as long as Striker could remember.

Trixie had started out as a high-end call girl, one who was popular among the Asian gangs. So popular she'd ended up helping them in their business deals – holding six, providing a safe house, and often being paid as a go-between.

In her day, Trixie had done very well.

Then she'd become a girlfriend to a mid-level drug trafficker for the Red Eagles. A guy by the name of Ngoc. That had been a long time ago. So long it was measured in decades, not years.

After that, Trixie had jumped loyalties from gang to gang, becoming connected internationally, and getting even richer in the process. Things had gone extremely well.

Then she'd started using her own product.

Within two years Trixie had become an addict – heroine and crack cocaine predominantly, but there was other stuff, too. A little meth. A little prescription. Over the years, her habit had grown, pushing past the point of her drug-sale profits. So she'd returned to stealing and whoring, doing up to twenty Johns a day.

And it showed.

Every time Striker saw her, she looked thinner, a bit more haggard. Back when he'd first known her, she hadn't been that bad. He'd even liked her, found her more pleasant than the other crooks he had to deal with down here. But now she was just like the rest – a desperate addict. One step away from some violent form of death.

Such was the life of the Skids.

'This is another one of her hangs,' Striker told Felicia. 'Keep your eyes open.'

They drove down the old, uneven cobblestones of Blood Alley, on the north side of the Stanley Hotel, which was the last chance for any drugged-out crazy before they were sleeping on the streets. Striker looked around the laneway. Cobblestone road, old iron lamps turned green from rain and time, and a small brick patio courtyard, hidden behind the roundabout of maple trees and flower-filled planters. The scene should have seemed quaint, tranquil. But this was Blood Alley.

It held nothing but pain, bad memories, and death.

'Eyes left,' Felicia said.

Striker looked past the roundabout and spotted the woman they'd been searching for. Trixie was leaning up against the far wall in one of the narrow alcoves beneath the rusted stairwell, the shadows almost hiding her completely.

Her twitching was what attracted their attention.

'She's got the sickies,' Felicia said.

Striker agreed.

Trixie was swaying back and forth. Twisting like an old wooden building during an earthquake. Her muscles twitched. Her limbs jerked. She made nervous groans that were audible, even inside the car.

'Man, she's got it bad,' Striker said. He brought the cruiser to a slow stop, then placed it in park. He climbed out, felt the cold rush of damp air on his face. Stepped around the rusting metal staircase and marched straight into the darkness.

Felicia caught up to him. There was a guy standing next to Trixie – a clean looking white guy, no doubt here for some cheap suck and fuck. She gave him a cold stare.

'Get walking, asshole,' she said.

He didn't say a word – the guilty ones rarely did – but just spun away from them and hurried westward down the breeze-way, thankful he wasn't going to be charged. Thankful that his wife and kids wouldn't find out. When he was out of ear's reach, Striker took a long hard look at Trixie and shook his head.

'You'll get killed down here, you know.'

Trixie looked back like she recognised him, but couldn't find the name – despite the fact he'd arrested her thirty times and had dealt with her a couple hundred more. She took a weak step forward, into the better light of the old iron streetlamps, and focused on him.

'Detective Striker?'

'So you remember me.'

He looked her over, felt a tug at his heart. In the better light, the truth was harsh. She looked terrible. Her clothes were rags. Her emaciated body had no muscle left; she was just translucent skin over knobby bone. Drug eruption sores covered her flesh. Her right eye was swollen shut. The rest of her face was bruised like an overripe banana. She'd been shit-kicked, probably over a crack debt.

And down here, that meant as little as five bucks' worth.

Striker killed any emotion he felt. He had to. 'You breaching your No-Go, Trixie.'

A frantic look took over her face. 'No, no, I—'

'Four block radius from Abbott Street.'

'Please, Detective Striker, please, please, please.' Her voice was weak and desperate, but quickly turning angry and sinister. 'I'm sick, I'm really sick. I need some. Really, really *need* some.'

Striker saw her pain, but had no time for pity or compassion. He gave Felicia the nod, and they each moved forward and handcuffed Trixie. He got the police wagon to attend and transport her back to the corner of Gore and Pender.

It was time for some answers.

Forty-Three

Courtney wasn't sure what time it was, but when she looked away from the computer screen, out her bedroom window, she could see darkness at the horizon. The light was fading, the day almost gone. And the clouds had come back. It was so typical of Vancouver weather. So depressing.

No wonder Mom had wanted to move away.

A sad feeling enveloped her, and she took a sip from the herbal tea she'd made. Liquorice Spice. It was hot, and it burned her tongue a little, making her suck in a mouthful of air to help cool it down. She set the mug on the blotter, the smell of liquorice filling the room, and pulled a dark green kangaroo jacket over her shoulders, zipping it up against the cold.

Once again, Dad was screwing with her life by keeping the heat turned down. There was always something.

She looked back at the computer screen. The bluish light tinted the walls of the room around her. She was on Facebook. Lookin', searchin', bloggin' – seein' what was up. Everywhere she looked, people were blogging about the massacre at the school. At first she had to work hard to find something else because just the thought of the shootings made her feel like she was going to puke. So she logged off.

But the carnage was as darkly fascinating as it was terrible, and before Courtney knew it, she was back online. She went back to Facebook, logged in and read through what her friends were saying: that three gunmen had opened fire in the school for no apparent reason. And rumour had it that Sherman Chan was one of them.

'Sherman?' The word escaped her lips.

Courtney struggled to make some sense of it. She knew Sherman. Kind of. Well, she knew who he was. Some computer nerd. Always kept to his own little group. Always smiled at her and seemed really . . . *nice.*

It was hard to believe.

She paged through the forum, and read the list of the dead. The first three killed were people she didn't know – one she'd never even heard of, which was rare for such a small school – but the fourth hit home. It was Tamara Marsden.

The name zapped Courtney like an electric shock. And she leaned back from the computer, as if this could somehow protect her. With nervous fingers, she scrolled down the page, reading the rest of the names. When she finished reading the list, she sat there very still. Then she shuddered. Cupped her hands over her mouth. Sobbed.

And she sat that way for a very long time.

Forty-Four

Striker and Felicia arrived back at the intersection of Gore and Pender Street, where the white van that held the three dead men in it was still cordoned off.

Trixie was secured in the side compartment of the police wagon, yelling and pounding her head against the steel door. It was nothing unusual, and Striker kept her there until he was ready.

When he had finished discussing his plan with Felicia, he made his way back to the wagon. The metal door was heavy. The latch felt cold against his hand and stubborn to move. He reefed it upward, hard, and the latch finally popped. The steel hinges groaned as the door swung outward. A musty smell of body odour and piss floated out of the cab.

'Out,' Striker ordered.

Trixie was crumpled against the grey steel wall of the compartment, still banging her head softly but continuously. Striker ordered her out again. When she didn't respond, he reached in and grabbed her arm. The movement woke Trixie from her stupor, and she stumbled as she exited the wagon, almost landing face first on the pavement.

Striker caught her, held her up. He studied her as she looked around.

Her face took on a twisted look when she saw she was at

Gore and Pender – one of her familiar hangouts – and not her usual abode of the Vancouver Jail. For the first time since Striker and Felicia had found her, her dark eyes looked focused and wary. She stared at the van, then at the restaurant down the road behind it.

'Why are we here?' she asked.

'Information,' Striker said.

Trixie's face darkened. She was still cuffed, hands behind her back, and moving her arms around, trying to adjust the sharper edges of steel. Striker took her left arm and Felicia her right, and they escorted her across the road. Right up to the van.

The doors were closed.

Striker took the handle of the left door, Felicia the right. Then Striker turned to watch Trixie's expression. He gave Felicia the word and they both reefed open the doors, revealing the carnage inside. When Trixie saw the three bodies, her face remained impassive. But when Striker reached in and turned the old man's head so that she could see his face, her mouth tightened and her body twitched.

She knew him.

Just like Striker had known she would. He saw that Felicia had seen the change in expression, too.

'I don't know him,' Trixie said.

Striker squeezed her arm. 'Bullshit. Who is he?'

Trixie gave him a sideways sneer. 'How the hell should I know? Lotsa old men down here.'

'You twitch every time you see one?' Felicia asked.

'What you talking 'bout, girl?' Trixie swore under her breath, then looked at Striker. 'These cuffs are diggin' into my goddam wrist.'

He made no move to loosen them. 'Want a smoke?'

Her eyes lit up. 'I'd fuckin' love ya for one.'

'Then turn around.'

Trixie did, and Striker removed the handcuffs. He walked over to the cruiser and returned with a pack of smokes. Camels. He always kept some in the glove box for occasions just like this. He handed her one. When she stuck it between her lips, he lit it and met her stare, saying, 'Don't mess around, right?'

She nodded, held up the smoke. 'My word on it, man.'

Striker let her take a few puffs and calm down, then continued, 'I've spent ten years down here, Trixie, and I've never seen this guy before. But you've spent your entire life down here; you know everyone and everyone knows you. So tell me, who is he?'

Trixie looked back at the old man in the van. Her mouth dropped open, and she spoke between ragged breaths. 'Honest, I ain't never seen him before. I swear to God, swear to God, swear to *God*.'

Striker turned to Felicia. 'I guess you're right, we should just lodge her. You wanna go back to the wagon and start the paperwork?'

Felicia looked at Trixie, said pleasantly, 'Love to.'

When she was gone, Striker turned back to Trixie. Without emotion he said, 'Listen up. I've dealt with you hundreds of times, so you know my word is good. Tell me who this guy is and no one will ever know. *Don't* tell me, and I'll throw you in the tank on this chicken-shit breach.'

Trixie's hand trembled as she took a long drag. She blew it out with a fluttery breath, and Striker kept talking. 'I'll keep you in the tank on the Obstruct charge too, got it? For as long as I possibly can. Up to a week, for sure. Maybe more.'

She glanced at him, and a nervous tension filled her eyes.

Striker smiled. 'You're feeling it already, aren't you? I can tell. How long's it been since your last fix? Six, seven hours? Already getting your insides all twisted?'

'Please—'

'Feeling that hunger just eating you alive? Well, just fucking wait. Wait till every cell in your body is screaming out for more crack and you start getting the dry heaves and the shakes, and then you'll realise you're only one day into your stay—'

'I don't know the fucker!' she screamed. 'I don't know him, I don't know him, I don't fucking *know him*!'

Striker stopped talking. He just stood there calmly, giving Trixie an eternity to think. She was sweating, trembling, her eyes looking everywhere but at him. And he no longer cared.

This was about the kids in jeopardy, not her goddam addiction.

'Either way, I'll find out who he is,' Striker said. 'The fingerprinting will just take time, and it's time I don't have to waste.' He took a half step closer, got right into her face and whispered, 'I got kids dying out there, Trixie. And this old man might be the link I need to save them. So make your choice – tell me who he is and you walk, and no one knows any the better. Don't tell me, and you spend the next two weeks being drug-sick in a jail cell. And I promise you this: when I find out who this old prick is – and I *will* find out – I'll spread it round the streets that you were the rat who told me. So when you're finished being drug-sick in your cell for ten goddam days, you can be welcomed back to the Skids the proper way.'

The look of anxiety in her eyes turned to outright fear, and she trembled even worse. 'If they knew I told you, they'd *kill* me.'

'No one will know, Trixie – unless you don't tell me.'

Her eyes widened when she looked back at the old man. She was still terrified of him, even in death. And that spoke lots to

Striker. Finally, Trixie gave in. 'I don't know the other two,' she said. 'But the old one . . . he was a bad man, Detective. A very bad man.'

'His name.'

'They call him "The Doctor".'

'His *name*, Trixie.'

She closed her eyes, took in a deep breath, trembled.

'Kieu,' she said, and she started to cry. 'His name is Jun Kieu.'

Forty-Five

Striker did not release Trixie as promised. Instead, he sent her away – not in the back of the police wagon to jail, but in an ambulance for Vancouver General Hospital – just as he'd planned all along. She was sick, so very sick – the infection of her left arm was already so bad the limb might require amputation – and he feared that without the proper medical treatment, Trixie would soon be the next sudden death in the Skids.

When she was gone, Striker approached the cruiser, where Felicia was waiting inside. She smiled at him knowingly. 'I always knew you were a sweetie.'

He just gave her a straight look, then handed her the notebook with the doctor's name. 'Jun Kieu. Confirm it.'

She took the notebook, punched in the name, then looked back at him. 'Date of birth?'

'Put him at seventy.'

'Looks younger than that.'

'Most Asians do.'

Felicia grinned. 'You just look old.' When the computer beeped and the information came back, she reached out and angled the screen towards Striker. 'We got a hit back, if he was born in 1937.'

'CPIC?'

'No. Criminal Name Index. And unfortunately, that's all the hits we got. No CPIC. No PRIME. No LEIP. No nothing.'

Striker thought about it. CPIC was the Canadian Police Information Centre, and they had information on just about everyone right across the country, so long as that person had ever crossed the criminal line. PRIME held information on everyone the police so much as came into contact with, be they criminals or good folk. LEIP and PIRS were secondary databases, but good assets in their own right. All this, and still they had nothing on Jun Kieu. Just one hit on the Criminal Name Index.

It was disconcerting.

'What's the birthplace?' he finally asked.

'Viet Nam.'

'Does he match the descriptors?'

Felicia read through the file. 'He got a horizontal scar beneath his chin?'

Striker walked back over to the van, leaned inside and tilted the old man's head to see under his chin. The scar was there. He nodded confirmation as he headed back. 'Yeah, it's him.'

'He's got a *Do Not Release* in the field remarks,' Felicia said. 'Immigration warrant.'

'I'll make sure he doesn't run off.'

Felicia smiled, then said, 'Hang on, Jacob. There's an attachment on his file.' She pulled it up, read it through. 'Wow, never seen one of these before. Crimes Against Humanity.'

Striker stopped beside the car. '*War* crimes?'

'It would appear so.'

He thought it over. 'Viet Nam War, I guess. North or South?'

'Doesn't say.'

Striker was about to ask more when Felicia's cell rang. She answered, held up a finger to demand silence, then began talking.

Striker left her alone and returned to the van. He gloved up with fresh latex, then leaned inside and undid the shirt buttons on all the bodies, exposing the neck and shoulder regions. Their skin was cold, even through the gloves. Striker examined their flesh, hoping to find the same golden artwork he'd seen on the neck of his headless shooter.

There was none. Not on any of the bodies.

The sight deflated him a bit, made him wonder what they really had here, as far as investigative leads went. An old man wanted for war crimes, dead in the back of a stolen van, with two yet-to-be identified goons.

Little, really.

But there was some light. The two men had been murdered with the same MO as the targeted kids in the school shootings.

And with what looked like Hydra-Shok rounds.

Striker thought the scene over. There was little hope of identifying the escaped driver, so the only connection that existed was the registered owner of the vehicle, and that came back not to a person, but to a business. The Fortune Happy restaurant.

Yet another lead they would have to check out.

A frustrated sound escaped his lips. There were too many possibles in this case. It was as if each lead was another long, tangled branch. He looked at the young constable guarding the van, remembered those simple days when he was a rookie, and a part of him missed it.

He put away his notebook, returned to the cruiser and crashed down in the driver's seat, closing his eyes. They felt heavier than his mood. Felicia was still on the phone, talking beside him in the passenger seat. He listened to her, breathed in slowly and smelled vanilla perfume. He was just drifting off when Felicia snapped her cellphone shut, killing any hope of tranquillity he might have had.

He opened his eyes. 'Well?'

'That was my contact at the phone company,' she said.

'Which provider?'

'Telus, of course,' Felicia said. 'Biggest is best. She scoured high and low for us.'

Striker felt a nervous tension fill his belly. Felicia's contact was the one person who might have access to the phone records of Edward Rundell – the missing link between the modified Honda Civic and the gunmen.

Striker met her stare. 'She find us Edward Rundell's number?'

'One better,' Felicia replied. 'She found us his business address.'

'Where is it?'

'Right here in Vancouver. Trans-Global Enterprises.'

Forty-Six

Trans-Global Enterprises was on the south side of Water Street, in the 100 block, on the third floor of a redbrick three-storey. Because it sat just north of the Skids, it was one of the cleaner buildings, meaning there was no array of dirty needles and used condoms out front. In fact, it had an old-fashioned feel.

Striker and Felicia parked on Main Street, not far from the law courts. It was past four o'clock and the sun was fading, falling in behind the dark cloudbanks that hurdled the North Shore Mountains. The strongest rays hit the windows of the building, turning them completely black from street level.

'Up there,' Felicia said. 'Third floor.'

Striker looked up, nodded. Heard the loud bass thump of rock music. 'Sounds like a party.'

'Rock rock till ya drop, old man.'

Striker grinned, ignored the comment.

The building faced directly onto Water Street. Front and centre were the double doors, made mainly of tinted glass. They were locked. Striker hit every single buzzer on the panel until the owner of Rag-Dog Recording Studios answered, said his name was Treble, then buzzed open the door to allow them entry.

Inside the foyer, the loud din of rock music blasted down from above, hard and heavy, yet somewhat muffled by the old walls and floor. On the west wall was a directory – a plain blackboard with white plastic lettering. Striker scanned it, located *Trans-Global Enterprises*. It was listed as 301 – the only business on the third floor.

'All alone,' he said. 'Convenient.'

There was no elevator, so they started up the stairs. The staircase was dim and had no windows, and the wooden steps that were painted brown squeaked beneath their weight. It stank, too. When Striker breathed in, he detected an old musty smell, which was quickly replaced by the skunky scent of freshly smoked BC Bud. It got stronger as they hiked past the second floor, where Rag-Dog Studios was located.

They continued up.

At the top of the staircase was an ordinary wooden door, painted the same drab brown as the stairs and boasting a dirty-paned, wired window. *Trans-Global Enterprises* was stencilled across the face in thick black script.

They stood on either side of the door, listening for several seconds. When it remained quiet, Striker knocked. No one came. He tried the door knob, found it locked, and cursed. There was no manager on site – they'd already played that card when trying to gain access to the building – so there would be no getting a master key.

Strike stood back, assessed the strength of the door. It was decent quality, made of good wood.

Felicia read his thoughts, intervened. 'We gonna need a warrant on this one?'

He took out his police knife and held it up. 'Already got one.'

'Jacob.'

He ignored her, flicked open the blade. It was good stainless steel – sharp, strong, and eight inches long. Worked good on locks, especially ones where the wood of the frame was old. In the past, he'd used it too many times to count.

Felicia made an unhappy sound. 'If we go in like this, anything we find won't hold up in court.'

'We don't have time for a warrant, Feleesh.'

'What if it's alarmed?'

'All the better. We were just en route to Headquarters when the alarm rang out. We came to investigate.'

'Sure, after we broke in. What if there's a camera?'

'There's not.'

Striker stuck the tip of the blade in between the lock and frame, and then put pressure medially. The wood was stronger than he'd anticipated, and it resisted, making him put his body weight into it. Eventually, the frame bulged and groaned, and the lock scraped against the wood, then made a sharp clashing sound as it popped out of the slot and the door creaked open.

No alarm went off, and Felicia's face relaxed a little.

'Vancouver Police!' Striker yelled, loud enough to be heard over the rock music below.

No reply.

Inside, all the lights were on, but the place looked vacant. Striker leaned through the doorway and scanned his surroundings.

The first room was a waiting area, holding a front desk with a phone, fax, and ledger. In the centre of the waiting room was a wooden table holding an assortment of magazines, which were fanned out to show their covers. Flanking the table were two rows of ordinary waiting-room chairs. And to the north was a white oak office door with a black-and-gold faceplate on it. *Manager.*

Next to the door was a large square window. All the blinds were closed, blocking off the view.

Striker looked at Felicia and nodded. When she nodded back, they stepped inside the office. To the left, running down from the secretary's desk, was a short hallway with four more doors. All of them plain brown wood. All of them closed. None marked.

'Police!' Striker announced one more time.

Again, nothing.

Felicia signalled that she would clear the hall. He covered her as she went. One by one, she opened each door and cleared each room. She walked slowly back, her pistol hanging at her side.

'They're empty.'

'Storage?'

'No, just empty. Not even a box.'

Striker frowned. He moved forward to the manager's office, tried the door knob and found it unlocked. He swung open the door. Inside was an office containing one expensive-looking desk made of black wood that took up most of the space. The desk sat against the far wall, giving whoever sat in it a full view of the office and a perfect view of the north shore mountains. Next to it, a file folder cabinet stood in the corner.

Striker walked over, opened all the drawers.

Empty.

He went back to the desk, opened all the drawers there too. He found pencils and erasers, and staples and yellow Post-it notes. All office supplies. Nothing of investigative value.

'Maybe they closed down,' Felicia said.

Striker shook his head. 'Cigar smoke in the air – I can still smell it. Even more than the pot from downstairs. Someone was in here. Today.'

Just then, Striker heard the soft whirring of a fan. He looked over and saw a computer terminal sitting on the floor at the far end of the desk. The soft blue activity light was blinking. He moved around the desk, looked at the monitor, saw it was black. He moved the mouse and the screen blinked as the screensaver turned off.

Written across the screen was one message.

KillDisk complete. Drive Override 100%.

Striker balled his hands into fists. He had no idea what had been on those disk drives, but no doubt it had been crucial. Implicating, if not damning evidence.

It was another lost link in their case.

Felicia let out a weary sound. 'We're too late.'

'Maybe Ich can still find something.'

Felicia got on her cell and called in support – Patrol, Ident and the techies. While she was talking to Dispatch, Striker's cell went off. He picked it up and looked at the screen, hoping to see Courtney's name. Instead he saw Ichabod's number – the main line from Forensic Audio. He shoved the cell against his ear.

'Tell me it's good news, Ich.'

'Depends how you look at it,' Ich replied. 'Either way, I got your audio from the school.'

Forty-Seven

A half hour later, Striker and Felicia parked out front of the Tech Facility on Tenth Avenue. The grimy old building looked about ready to crumble. It was a completely unearthquake-proof structure in a city full of treacherous faultlines. Striker climbed out of the cruiser and looked up at one of the security cameras that panned down on him.

He wondered if anyone was monitoring it.

Felicia slammed her door. She bundled up her jacket, then turned her pretty, tired eyes towards Striker. 'Any guesses what Ich found?'

'Something's weird. I could hear it in his voice.'

He climbed the front stairs, used his swipe card to gain access, then entered the foyer and flashed his badge to the security guard inside the safety booth. The door leading inside the main building clicked open. Striker walked through it with Felicia in tow.

The Tech Facility was, in essence, the Department's catchall. It housed everything from Forensic Audio and Video to the headquarters of Vice, Drugs, and the Emergency Response Teams. Each of these divisions had long been pleading for better resources and a home of their own, which included a modern facility, but in a time of high taxes and budget cutbacks and a declining economy, they were forced to make do with what they had.

And it wasn't much.

Striker walked down the faded brown carpet that still smelled of cigarette smoke, even though the smoking bylaw had been in effect for more than ten years. The walls were no better. The off-white was now beige. Most of the doors used old-fashioned keys, not coded pass cards. And everything else had a broken-down feel to it. Yet oddly enough, it worked.

Old school at its finest.

They turned the corner and came flush with the door to Forensic Audio, also known as The Matrix to all those who worked inside, which was essentially Ichabod and his lackey clone – a guy named Bernard whom no one had ever seen. Striker didn't bother to knock. He swung open the door and stepped inside.

The room was tiny, barely twelve feet long by ten feet wide. It was further cramped by the tall support beam that occupied the centre of the room. Taped on the pillar was a picture of a soldier drinking from a green metal mug, and a quotation reading: *Have a Nice Cup of Shut the Fuck Up and Wait Over There, Asshole!*

Flanking the pillar on both sides was an array of ramshackle shelves. Each one was cluttered with micro-machines that constantly beeped and blinked. One made loud whirring sounds like it was going to explode at any second.

'That's a Personal Video Recorder,' Striker said.

Felicia grinned. 'Like you would know.'

'What? No faith in my computer skills?'

'You wouldn't know a hot spot from a g-spot.'

'I found yours a few times.'

'That's still a matter of opinion.'

'Ouch.'

Felicia smirked, and Striker knew she'd bested him. He

offered her a weak grin. He closed the door behind them, more in an effort to make some extra room than for privacy. Then heard shuffling.

As if on cue, Ich stuck his head out from behind the pillar. His gaunt face was tight around the eyes, yet slack everywhere else. His posture seemed to perpetually sag. He eyed them both with expectation, and the fatigue in his eyes was replaced by excitement.

'Finally, Christ, you're here.'

'We came right away,' Felicia said.

Striker stepped around a pile of Blu-ray discs sitting on the ground and looked at Ich's desk. It was cluttered with computer parts – flash drives, discs, wires and a collection of other things Striker had never seen before. Next to them were six cans of Monster energy drinks, all of them opened.

'Jesus Christ, Ich, you drink all that?'

'Had to. Been up all night.'

Striker nodded. 'We know and we appreciate it. Now what you get us?'

Ich waved them over to his work station. He reached up to the top shelf where a generic black box sat and hit the power button. After the green activity light flashed, Ich turned up the speaker volume, then swivelled the nearest monitor to face Striker and Felicia.

'Anything good on the tape?' Striker asked.

Ich shrugged. 'It just finished transcoding when I called. I haven't even had a chance to look at the whole segment myself yet, just the first ten seconds or so – but that was enough.'

'Enough for what?'

Ich said nothing. He just hit Play.

Immediately the blue screen flashed and was replaced with

the grainy, black-and-white pixelated footage Striker had seen back at the school. But now there was sound. Static-filled clatter. Gunshots. The shrill cries of panicking kids. More than before, it took Striker back to the moment, and his heart pounded heavily in his chest; the muscles of his hands twitched like they wanted to reach for his gun.

He glanced over at Felicia, and saw the machine-like calmness of her features. Her lack of an emotional response irritated him. He looked back at the screen just in time to see the boy dressed as the Joker dive underneath the cafeteria table. The two gunmen – White Mask and Red Mask – looked at one another, and for the first time, Striker heard them speak. It was static-filled, intermittent, and garbled.

He touched Ich on the shoulder. 'Scroll it back.'

Ich did as instructed, and Striker listened again.

'It's still garbled – can you clean it up a bit?'

Felicia stepped forward, seized the volume knob and turned it up. 'Not garbled, Jacob – another language.'

Ich grabbed Felicia's hand. Removed it from his controls. Then raised a finger in an admonishing gesture. 'No touching. This is all very sensitive equipment. Hold on a second and I'll try to diminish the background noise.'

Felicia gave him an annoyed look, but held her tongue.

Striker was thankful for it. He watched Ich bring up some software audio controls, something that looked like a row of amplifier settings. He began fine-tuning the sounds. After thirty seconds, Ich hit Play again, and the gunmen's voices became clearer. Each one of them distinct.

Felicia listened intently. 'Chinese?'

Striker shook his head. 'Technically, there is no Chinese – it would be either Cantonese or Mandarin. But the answer to that is still a resounding no.'

'A *resounding* no?' Felicia said, the irritation in her voice plain.

Striker never looked away from the screen. 'Listen to the sounds; the inflections. It's not tonal. So it's something else – something different.'

Felicia tapped Ich on the back. 'Who around here can speak Asian languages?'

He looked back through fatigued eyes. 'We got Truong in Vice. And Iwata in Drugs. They're probably your best bets. Second floor.'

'I'll see if I can find one of them.'

She left, and Striker moved closer to the screen as the feed progressed. He watched more analytically this time as the gunmen dragged the boy dressed as the Joker out from under the table, then yanked him to his feet.

'*Bah ma loh?*' they asked, several times. '*Bah ma loh! . . . Bah ma loh, Chantelle O'Riley?*'

The boy finally pointed to the far corner of the room, where the girl in the pleated school skirt lay huddled. And even though Striker knew it was coming, the moment made him feel ill. He studied the scene as the gunmen marched across the room, an air of arrogance in their stances that was overpowered only by Chantelle O'Riley's terror.

Striker knew the next part as well. Red Mask would pull the Glock from his waistband, then shoot her twice in the chest and once in the face. Her death was coming, yet again, and he wanted to look away. To close his eyes. To shut his ears.

But he would not.

Instead he prepared himself to watch and hear her death. And he promised himself he would recall this moment with total clarity, should he feel even a trace of pity or compassion when he caught the monster responsible.

But he was completely unprepared for what he heard next.

The gunman – Red Mask – pointed his firearm into Chantelle O'Riley's face, and just before pulling the trigger, he asked her three times: '*Bah ma loh? Bah ma loh? Bah ma loh!*'

The girl opened her mouth, stuttered, 'I d-don't know what you're t-talking about.'

Red Mask moved closer, and this time he spoke in heavily-accented English. 'Where is she?' he said very slowly. 'Where is *Riku Aiyana Kwan*?'

Forty-Eight

Red Mask felt sweat trickle down between his shoulder blades as he lurked amidst the maple trees of 2301 Trafalgar Street – the Kwan house. It was not a part of the original plan, but here he was nonetheless, trying to manifest order out of chaos. Again.

A light was on inside the living room. He had been watching it for ten minutes. Waiting for something. Waiting for anything. But so far nothing came.

He started for the backyard, then stopped hard when a flicker of movement caught his eye. Inside, a tall woman turned on a television set. She looked part-Asian. Late thirties. Slender in face and toned in body.

Red Mask recognised her. It was Patricia Kwan. Mother of Riku Aiyana.

With his shoulder aching like a bad tooth, he drew his pistol from his waistband and rounded the house. Out back, he cut between a pair of plum trees that flanked the deck, then hiked up the stairs. The porch was old. It screamed of his coming. When he made it to the back door, it was locked. Through the pane he could see that the news was on. Using the noise as cover, he broke the window with the butt of his Glock, then reached through the opening and unlocked the deadbolt.

The door swung open and Red Mask stepped into the

kitchen area. He closed the door. Heard the click. Locked the deadbolt.

There would be no escape for those inside.

The kitchen light was off. From the darkness, he spotted Patricia Kwan in the living room. She was watching the TV and stretching. The black spandex she wore clung hungrily to her body; she was more muscular than he had thought.

As Red Mask moved nearer, the broken glass crunched beneath his runners. For a moment, the woman remained oblivious. Then her eyes caught his reflection and she gasped. Spun about. Screamed and raised her arms—

And Red Mask slammed the butt of his pistol across her face.

Patricia Kwan dropped awkwardly to the ground, colliding with the bureau. She turned over, her eyes unfocused with shock, her face smeared with blood. On the hardwood were three of her teeth. She fought to speak.

'What – please – what do you want from me?'

'Where is daughter?'

'What?'

'Where is Riku Aiyana Kwan?'

Patricia Kwan's eyes widened, her face paled, and she scrambled backwards.

Red Mask walked after her, controlling her with his presence. Then the room suddenly tilted. A hotness flooded him, and his head was floating, lifting right off his neck.

'Stop,' he ordered. 'You must stop. Escape is forbidden.'

Patricia Kwan dove for the table, and Red Mask finally understood her intentions. She was not trying to escape, she was going for the phone. He reached out to grab her, but was too late; she smacked the emergency dial.

The call went through.

He let out a scream and ripped the phone from the wall.

'It dialled,' she said. 'I got it through.'

He moved closer. 'Where is Riku Aiyana Kwan?'

The woman reared, and Red Mask reached for her. His feet bumped into something and he toppled forward. When the gun went off – the thunderous blast of a 40 cal filling the room – he was barely aware that he had shot her.

The room echoed with the explosion.

And there was screaming. *She* was screaming.

He climbed to his feet. He stepped forward, grabbed Patricia Kwan's long black ponytail and dragged her into a seated position.

'Please . . .'

'Where is Riku Aiyana Kwan? Tell me where daughter is and she will not suffer; refuse this information and she will have much pain.'

Patricia Kwan started to cry. 'Please, oh God, please, I'll do *anything*—'

'Discussion is not permitted.'

He used his arm to wipe the sweat from his eyes, felt the room moving on him again. The infection was bad. Time was running out. He grabbed Patricia's right hand, slammed it hard on the living room table and splayed her fingers. Then he placed the barrel of the gun in the centre of her palm, grinding the steel muzzle into her flesh. He met her eyes.

'I ask you one time now, Patricia Kwan.'

'No – please!'

'Where – is – Riku – Kwan?'

Forty-Nine

Striker felt an icy coldness hit his heart. It had been over twenty-four hours since Red Mask had escaped, and all that time this Kwan girl had been one of his intended targets. Experience told Striker he was already too late, but he had never been a man to give up on hope.

'The Kwan house,' Striker said to Ich. 'Call it in now – tell them to send everything they got.'

Striker then ran for the exit, reached the cruiser, started it over. A quick computer search told him that the Kwan house was in Kitsilano, and that wasn't overly far away from the Tech Building.

He floored it.

Traffic was bad, and Striker got caught dead smack in the middle of rush hour. Everywhere he looked there were red tail-lights. He turned on the lights and siren, and made good use of the air horn at every intersection.

As Kitsilano drew closer, the traffic thinned and Striker turned off the emergency equipment for fear of alerting the gunman. He parked the cruiser in the nearest bus lane on Trafalgar. People at the stop gaped as he jumped out and raced north.

Three blocks later, he saw something that made him pause.

Parked on the roadside, three houses down from the Kwan

residence, was a blue Toyota Camry. The manufacturer and model of the car did not warrant his attention so much as did the condition of the driver's side door. The lock had been punched, and when Striker drew closer, he saw wires hanging from the ignition. There were dark stains on the beige interior.

Blood.

Striker stood back from the vehicle and analysed his surroundings. The Kwan house was just three lots down. He studied it – a one-storey Kitsilano special, plastered in dark green that matched the heavy wall of bushes flanking the yard. Everything was still and quiet, and it gave Striker a bad feeling. He drew his pistol and headed for the lot. As he was nearing, a voice startled him.

'You here about the noise?' a woman asked.

He looked over and saw an old lady, dressed in nothing but an orange cotton robe and oversized fluffy slippers. In her hands was a steaming cup, and at her feet was an old Basset Hound.

'What noise?'

She jerked her head towards the Kwan house. 'I dunno, a loud one, that's for sure. Sounded like something damn well exploded in there. Took you guys long enough, I called it in over five minutes ago.'

'Get inside,' was all Striker said.

He crouched low, sprinted down the sidewalk that flanked the frontyard bushes, and raced up the front porch steps. At the door, he stopped. He leaned around the porch railing and tried to peer through the bay window, but the curtain was drawn. The flickering glimmer of a television set caught his eye, and seconds later, a harsh sound startled him – feminine, desperate, pained. It was followed by a man's voice, neutral in tone, but direct and authoritative.

In control.

'Where is she?' the man asked. 'Where is Riku Aiyana Kwan?'

Striker stepped back from the front door, assessed the structure. It was made of oak, solid as hell, and locked by a steel deadbolt. If he attempted to kick it in, he'd have to do it with one strike; otherwise, the element of surprise would be lost and he'd be an easy target when he broke through.

No time. There was no time.

No other option.

He readied his gun and leaped forward, kicking out his right leg and driving the heel of his boot onto the inner portion of the deadbolt. The steel was strong; the lock remained secure. But the frame busted inwards with a loud wooden *snap*!

'Vancouver Police!' Striker yelled.

He used his momentum to push forward through the opening, getting out of the fatal funnel as quickly as possible. He collided heavily with the wall, balanced himself, and got his first true look at the shooter.

Red Mask was standing to Striker's right. In the living room.

Without the mask on.

The sight was almost startling. He was an Asian male, with narrow hard eyes and a face much older than Striker had expected. Definitely not a student from St Patrick's High. Instantly Striker knew he had been right.

He was dealing with a trained killer.

The expression Red Mask wore was not one of surprise or fear or even anger, but one of acceptance. His body was in a semi-crouched position, ready to bound. In his hand, he held a glistening black pistol. It blended in with the darkness of his kangaroo jacket.

'Red Mask,' Striker said, the words falling unexpectedly

from his lips. He raised his Sig to open fire, but before he could get a shot off, the gunman spun away from the slumped woman and leaped into the adjoining dining room.

He was quick, Striker thought. So goddam quick.

Before Striker could reposition, shots rang out. Loud, rapid-fire: *bang-bang-bang-bang-bang!* Bullets rained through the walls, spraying chunks of wallpaper and gypsum into the air.

The years of training took over; Striker dropped low and spun left. More gunfire thundered through the room and the front-room window cracked. One of the rounds tore through the mirror to his left, shattering it into hundreds of shiny splinters. Another bullet hit the metal frame of the door and let out a sharp *ziiiing* as it ricocheted somewhere down the hall. Others punched into the floorboards, the loud *thunk-thunk-thunk* of the breaking oak filling the air.

Striker remained low, weathered the storm.

In the living room, the woman was clambering to her feet. 'Help! Someone help me!'

'Down!' he yelled to her. 'Down! Stay *down*!'

But she wasn't listening. She climbed to her feet, turned around as if in a daze, and Striker saw the patches of red that splattered her neck and arm. She'd been hit. And by the looks of it, she was bleeding out bad. She spun around as if she didn't know where she was, ran left, bumped into the ottoman and toppled forward.

'Stay DOWN!' Striker yelled again. He kept a low stance, edged forward and peered into the room.

There was no sign of Red Mask.

The gunman had vanished.

Striker inched out further, until he could see around the bend of the wall, into the dining room. Through the back window, he caught a glimpse of the gunman. Red Mask was outside, running down the back porch steps.

Escaping again.

Striker raced across the room, up to the window, and spotted the man running between a giant pair of maple trees at the far end of the lot. He took quick aim and opened fire, shooting right through the living room window until his mag ran out of bullets.

Through the cracks of glass, Striker could see he had failed. Red Mask had already reached the lane.

Striker reloaded while running through the kitchen. The door to the backyard was open and rocking from the incoming wind. He ran up to it and scanned the narrow trail where the gunman had fled towards the lane.

It was empty.

Striker swore. The gun felt heavy in his hand, and hot. He kept it aimed ahead, his finger alongside the trigger as he made his way down the back porch steps, onto the wet grass of the lawn. He circled the garage, cutting past the small vegetable garden. By the time he reached the lane, the weak wail of far-away police sirens filled the night. Their long undulating cries were heaven to his ears.

Help was near.

Thoughts of Patricia Kwan flooded Striker's mind, the splatters of blood that painted her arms and chest and neck. Her clothes had been damn near saturated with blood. An arterial bleed, for sure, the most serious kind. He tried to push the thought from his mind and focus on the lane, on all possible escape routes Red Mask might have taken. But three steps later, the image of Patricia Kwan returned to him.

Only he could save her.

He took another hard look around the alley, saw dozens of

places the gunman could have fled, and knew he was out of options. A woman's life was at stake. He turned around and raced back inside the house. Hopefully, the coming patrol units would set up containment, get a dog track, and find Red Mask.

Before he killed again.

Fifty

By the time Courtney had gotten over the shock of what had happened and come to terms with the fact that some of her friends had been killed, her head was full of depressing thoughts and she was fighting to get herself back into that wonderful state of denial – the same one she had made use of when Mom had died. She made the decision to never think about the shootings again, if it were possible. And to divert her mind, she did what she always did.

She looked through all of Bobby Ryan's pics.

And the more she looked at pictures of him, the more she managed to drown out the depression that was creeping in. Soon it was gone altogether – or at least suppressed to the point where she could ignore it – and a low-level excitement ran all through her body as she imagined herself and Bobby together. A nervous dread filled her, too, as she flicked from photo to photo to see if he was cuddling or kissing any other girls.

When she saw that he wasn't, she felt better, but her anxiety stayed.

She right-clicked on a few of her Bobby favourites, then saved them to the folder on her desktop. When done, she opened up the one she loved most – the one with him smiling and holding a Starbucks cup – and made it her screensaver.

Finally, after what seemed like hours, she let go of him. She clicked off of the Friends tab and returned to her Home tab. She needed to add her own personal blog for the day, but all she could come up with was a big fat zero. She slumped in her chair, looked at her tagline, and felt dismayed. So far, all it read was:

The Court is . . .

She finally finished it honestly with:

Missing Mom.

But then she thought it might make her look sappy – God, what if Bobby looked at it, or even worse, that bitch from English class, Mandy? She'd laugh at her, tell all their friends. The thought was agonising, so Courtney quickly deleted the words, then changed them to:

Tired of living here with Dad.

She looked at it. Grinned. That definitely sounded better. Tougher. More angsty. A twinge of guilt fluttered in the corner of her heart, but she drowned it out, thinking that Dad wasn't even on Facebook, so what would he know? Besides, all he cared about was work and investigations and that goddam Felicia Santos.

But Felicia . . .

She would be on Facebook. No doubt about it. She was into all the cool things. Which was kind of weird, really.

Courtney typed her name in the search bar and found her in seconds.

Felicia wasn't added as a Friend yet – not that she ever would be – so all Courtney got was her main picture. But that was enough. There she was, Felicia Santos, staring back with her big pretty eyes and long beautiful brown hair brushed over her shoulders. In some ways she reminded Courtney of Raine. So confident. So alluring. And as much as Courtney hated to admit it, Felicia was pretty cool in her own right. She was hot and Spanish and had big boobs busting out everywhere and a perfect smile – all the things men liked.

Made no sense why she was into Dad. The thought made her feel miserable, and she was grateful when she saw Raine sign on with a similar message:

Raine is gonna lose her freakin' mind if Mom doesn't just BACK OFF!!!!

Courtney laughed, felt suddenly good inside. Misery loves company, right? She typed back in:

Wanna go out?

The response came back quickly:

Already am. Going to meet Que.

At Que's place?

At his friend's pad. Like he asked me to yesterday. At the restaurant. Am going for the night. Already got key. And chii-illls!

You mean ???

;0)

Courtney just stared at the screen, put a hand against her chest. Her heart was beating fast and hard. She typed back another message:

R U sure? U can stay here.

Call U 2morrow. Parade and Britney!

Call me now!

L8R.

Now.

:0)

Raine signed off.

Courtney sat there, staring at the monitor. Thoughts of Raine fell through her head. Raine out there with Que. Raine going back to his pad. Raine losing her virginity. The thought had excited her moments ago; now it made her feel completely alone. Isolated.

Trapped.

The house seemed dark and quiet and filled with so many wonderful memories that now brought her so much pain. She wished she could close her eyes, go to sleep and never wake up. And that notion made her realise one thing more than ever: she had to get away from here. Really get away. Or else she'd die. She'd really die.

Just like Mom.

Fifty-One

Over an hour later, Striker stood in the crowded admitting area of St Paul's Hospital and sipped coffee from a paper cup. The nurse had kindly brought it to him, and it was just as bad as the sludge they cooked up in Homicide.

Striker's hands shook as he held the cup. Enough to spill some of the brew over the rim and burn his skin. It was a normal reaction, he told himself. Especially after his second firefight in two days.

He only wished he could believe the inner voice.

With almost two days gone, it felt like they were losing ground. Red Mask had escaped again. And Patricia Kwan was now fighting for her life. All they'd found in the gunman's wake was a stolen Toyota Camry parked out front. Even with a priority rush, the blood results would take weeks, and he had little faith in any prints coming back.

It ate away at him.

Even worse was the woman's daughter, Riku Kwan. The girl was missing, which was only one step away from the worst possible scenario. When Felicia entered the room, Striker broke from the negativity that was sucking him down and met her in the doorway.

'Did they find her?' he asked.

'No,' Felicia said. 'Riku Kwan is nowhere to be found. We

got her flagged as a missing person on CPIC, but so far no one's got a clue.'

Striker ran through the list in his head. 'What about her father?'

'Separated from the mom, we think. Turns out he's an international lawyer. Pretty good one, too. Makes a gazillion dollars a year. He's away on business right now – somewhere in Asia. We're trying to get a hold of him, but so far no luck.'

'We got lots of luck – it's just all bad. What about the Amber Alert?'

'On all the stations.'

'TV or radio?'

'Both. They're broadcasting her name on every station.'

'And photo?'

'Not yet.'

'I want her picture up there too.'

'They're working on it, Jacob.' Felicia looked past Striker towards the Fast Track Admittance and bit her lip. 'The mother in there?'

'They took her to surgery a while ago.'

Felicia sighed. 'Let's hope she knows something when she wakes up.'

'Let's just hope she wakes up.'

The words felt heavy. And Striker couldn't help thinking things might have been different if he'd gotten there sooner. If, if, if. If Deputy Chief Laroche hadn't told Ich to shelve the feed. If they'd gotten the audio sooner. If he'd pressed just a little bit harder and stood his ground.

There were a million ifs.

Felicia touched his shoulder. 'You did good in there.'

'Not good enough.'

'Jacob—'

He pulled away. 'I had him, Felicia, I fuckin' *had* him. Damn near lined up. If I'd just been a little bit quicker, that prick would be six feet under right now.'

'And if you hadn't done what you did, Patricia Kwan would already be dead.'

'She still might be.'

'Focus on the investigation,' she said.

'Which part? We got yet another crime scene and what has it brought us? Nothing. Just a reminder that we got a bunch of dead kids already, and one more who is targeted and still out there somewhere where we can't find her.'

'We'll find her, Jacob.'

He turned his body so that he was facing Felicia. 'What we don't know is, *why*. I mean, Christ, do we have even one decent connection between these kids?'

'Three of them were members of the Debate Club.'

'What about Kwan?'

'Unfortunately, no, she's not on the list – but it's the closest thing we've got so far.'

Striker said nothing as he thought it over. Debate Club. It seemed a ridiculous notion. And Riku Kwan wasn't a member.

Just then, the door to the surgery room opened up and the doctor emerged. His name was Dr Adler – a tall, sandy-haired Australian man with an accent thicker than Vegemite. He had already taken off his surgical cap, but was still wearing the pale green gown. He looked as tired as Striker felt.

'How is she?' Striker asked.

He raised an eyebrow. 'Critical, but stable.'

'Meaning?'

'Meaning I don't know.' He scratched his nails down his face, leaving a red mark on his cheek. 'The bullet didn't have an exit wound. It fragmented, and the pieces ricocheted off the scapula, then rebounded back off her sternum – like a pinball in her thorax. It did a lot of damage to her liver and lung.'

Striker looked at Felicia. 'Sounds like a Hydra-Shok round.'

Felicia nodded, and Striker returned his attention to the doctor. 'We need to speak to her.'

Dr Adler looked at Striker like he'd lost his mind. 'Absolutely not.'

'It's not a request, Doctor.'

'It doesn't have to be. I'm sorry, Detective, but my responsibility is to the patient. Mrs Kwan is already heavily sedated, delirious, and in great pain. To try to bring her out of such a state could possibly—'

'Her daughter's life depends on it,' Felicia said.

This seemed to shut the doctor up.

Striker nodded solemnly. 'If we can't locate her daughter, the girl will be murdered. And right now the only lead we got is the woman in there.'

Dr Adler looked away, thought for a moment. The moment lasted a long time. Finally, after much obvious internal debate, he muttered something Striker could scarcely make out.

'Five minutes,' he said. 'That's it. And any signs of cardiac distress, I shut it down.'

Striker met the man's stare. 'Thanks, Doc.'

'Don't thank me,' he said quietly. 'Just find the girl.'

Fifteen minutes later, Striker stood at the third-floor entrance to the Critical Care Unit. He was dressed in a pale-green smock that barely fit around the bulge of his Sig Sauer, and a green hair-net that looked more like a woman's shower cap from the seventies than proper surgical attire. The hospital gear clung to his body like green under-armour, testifying to the thickness of his shoulders and chest.

Felicia stood beside him, dressed in the exact same fashion. She looked him over, her eyes resting on his chest.

Striker noticed. He cleared his throat, said: 'Anyone ever tell you that hair-net really brings out your eyes?'

The nurse appeared – a small chubby black woman. 'This way,' she said. She used a key card to open the door and then ushered them into the Critical Care Unit. They followed her down to room four, where Patricia Kwan was recovering.

When Striker entered the room, he was taken aback.

Everything was exactly the same as when Amanda had died two years ago. Not a damn thing was different. And for a moment, he felt sucker-punched by life. He hated this hospital. Hated everything about it.

He suppressed the feeling, got to work.

The room smelled strongly of bleach and disinfectants. Aside from the bleak light that creaked through the brown drapes, everything appeared cold and sterile. Patricia Kwan laid supine on the bed, with both bed railings locked in the up-position. Tubes and wires ran from both her arms into several machines that stood bedside, an array of red digital numbers blinking across their screens.

Her chest barely moved.

Striker moved closer, stared at Patricia. Her face looked unnatural. Swollen. The skin appeared distended and thin, like an overstuffed sausage membrane. Her dark eyes were slightly open. They were glossy, like wet candy. She moaned, a sound that was barely audible in the small room, and Striker wondered if she did this in response to their presence, her pain, or the nightmares she was suffering.

He turned to the nurse. 'She even awake?'

'Stupor,' was all the nurse offered.

Dr Adler entered the room and monitored the machines.

The expression on his weary face was one of concern, and he gave Striker and Felicia a look that suggested it was time to get things started.

Striker stepped forward. 'Ms Kwan? Ms Kwan? *Patricia*?'

The woman's eyes blinked a few times, then turned towards him.

'I'm Detective Jacob Striker from the Vancouver Police Department. I'm the cop that saved you.'

She offered no response, verbal or otherwise. She just stared at him through empty eyes.

'Patricia, I know this is hard for you right now, but these are questions I have to ask. Do you remember what happened tonight? Back at the house?'

Patricia Kwan shivered beneath the blankets. She tried to speak, only managed to croak, then began to cough. When the fit subsided, the nurse gave her water. She made another attempt to speak, and the voice which came through was low and scratchy and weak.

'The house . . . was on fire.'

'On fire?'

'*Fire*. There was fire . . . all around me . . . out of control.'

'Patricia—'

'Dragons . . . breathing fire . . .'

Felicia looked at the doctor. 'This is no good,' she said. 'The woman is delirious.'

Striker placed his hands on the bed railing, fingers gripping so tightly his knuckles blanched. As he leaned down to hear Patricia better, the smell of her body odour hit him. She smelled bad. Like she was sick. Like a dog ready to be put down. He ignored the smell, continued: 'Do you know the man who attacked you? Do you recognise him from anywhere?'

Patricia said nothing, didn't move. And for a moment Striker thought he had lost her altogether. But then her eyes grew wide and regained some clarity. She jolted in her bed.

'My daughter!'

She tried to sit up, let out an agonised wail, grabbed at her ribs and then collapsed back on the bed. The doctor and nurse immediately stepped forward to check the machines.

As they moved, Felicia's cell went off. She reached down for it, and the nurse glared at her.

'Not in here you don't.'

Striker gestured for her to take the call outside, and she did, leaving him alone with the nurse and the doctor, and he was grateful for it.

'Patricia,' he began again.

She gripped his arm. 'My daughter, please, my *daughter*.'

'Do you have any idea where she might be? We're trying to locate her.'

'Find her, *please*. You have to find her . . . find her . . .'

'Where does she go? Who does she hang out with? Is there anyone I can call?' Striker peppered her with questions. But the woman's eyes glazed, and she retreated back inside her body. Her facial muscles relaxed. She deflated against the bed like a balloon with a fast leak and sweat dappled her pallid skin.

'Dragons,' she said one last time, her voice but a whisper. 'The house was filled with dragons.'

One of the machines to Striker's left let out a series of beeps, and the doctor motioned for the nurse. She hurried over, adjusted the settings, and gave the doctor and Striker a fierce motherly look.

'That's it,' Dr Adler said to Striker. 'No more.'

Striker didn't argue the point. He retreated to the doorway, where he stopped, turned, stared. He watched the nurse and doctor fuss over their patient. Sadness swept through him, so heavy he felt the sorrow deep down in his lungs. The woman on the bed may as well have been Amanda all over again. And Striker recalled with horrifying clarity how he had felt two years ago, knowing his wife was dying and wondering how he was ever going to tell Courtney – their thirteen-year-old daughter – that her mother was never coming home again.

The memory cut into him as deeply now as it had done back then.

He stood in the doorway and stared at Patricia Kwan until the nurse ushered him into the hall. Outside, he met up with Felicia, who snapped her cell phone shut.

'That was the coroner,' she said. 'The autopsy of our remaining gunman is done.'

Striker nodded.

It was the first good thing he'd heard all day.

Fifty-Two

It was late, and the night was dark and cold. It was all Red Mask could do to keep his feet moving and his body from collapsing.

His destination – a barely noticeable hole in the wall – was an old herbal shop, on East Georgia Street. Like every other shop in Chinatown, the banner out front was red on gold: *Happy Health and Good Fortune Herbs and Pharmaceuticals.*

Sheung Fa had taken him here, many years ago, when he was young. His words had been clear: 'For you, always will these doors be open.'

And that was what Red Mask was now counting on. For in his deteriorated state, there was nowhere else to go. Certainly not home. He would never go home again. There was nothing more disgraceful a man could do than to knowingly bring evil into his father's house. And with the amount of people he had now killed, there was evil all around him. He could feel it. Like diesel fumes on his skin.

The thought landed in Red Mask's stomach like a hard stone, and his eyes welled with tears. He touched beneath his eyes. Amazement flooded him when he felt wetness. Weeping. He was actually weeping. Something that had not happened since childhood.

'What happens to me?'

The words hung there, exposed as much as the hole in his shoulder.

He killed the thought and moved on. The pain was excruciating now. If not addressed, the injury would overtake him, and he would not last long enough to find the girl.

With the stairway tilting, he descended the concrete steps and stumbled into the darkness of the alcove below. The door was locked. He knocked three times and heard shuffling feet. When the door opened, his legs finally gave way and he collapsed.

'Sheung Fa sent me,' he said.

He repeated the words over and over again as he lay on the cold wet concrete.

It was all that he could do.

Fifty-Three

Striker led Felicia out the way they'd come, cutting through the west side admittance area of St Paul's Hospital. He had just passed the waiting area, where construction was still under-way – God knows there was always a renovation underway at St Paul's – when he spotted the white unmarked police cruiser pulling into the Police Only parking out front.

The White Whale.

Deputy Chief Laroche.

'Christ, not now,' Striker muttered. And for an instant, he was tempted to turn down the nearest corridor and escape via one of the rear or side exits. There'd been enough stress over the last two days without having to deal with the white-shirted dictator again. Avoidance would have been a logical choice, for which no one would fault him, but Jacob Striker never ran from anyone.

Especially not Laroche.

'Gear up,' Striker warned.

He gave Felicia a quick look, saw the uncomfortable expres-sion masking her tired face, and barged out the exit door, into the brisk night air. The hospital door had barely shut behind him when Laroche exited the vehicle, followed by his lackey, Inspector Beasley.

'Well, he's got Curly with him now. All he needs is to find a Moe.'

'Jacob, please,' Felicia started.

He ignored her. Stopped walking. Crossed his arms. Stood rooted to the spot.

The Deputy Chief closed the car door then looked at his reflection in the side mirror. He adjusted his belt, fidgeted with his tie, then patted and combed his thick black hair back over his head while Inspector Beasley waited for him on the sidewalk. When he finally stopped fussing and stood up straight, his eyes landed on the two detectives. And his face darkened.

'Striker!'

'Laroche.'

'Jesus Christ, everywhere you go I have to set up a new crime scene.'

Striker blinked, couldn't believe his ears. Not, 'Good job at the Kwan house,' or, 'You were right, Leung *wasn't* Red Mask,' or even, 'I'm glad to see you're alive.' No, he got none of those, and there would certainly be no commendation to follow. Just more bullshit. He cleared his throat and said politely, 'Just bringing you more zebras, sir.'

Laroche said nothing. His white face turned pink. Striker expected a rebuttal of some sort, but none came. Instead the Deputy Chief swivelled his hips, found Inspector Beasley, and the two of them exchanged a nasty smirk. One that made Striker pause.

Just what the hell are they up to now?

The Deputy Chief gave Beasley a nod, and without a word Beasley returned to the White Whale, popped open the trunk, rummaged around for a second, then returned with a gun case. He handed it to the Deputy Chief, who then turned to Striker with a wide smile stretching his lips.

'The order no longer comes from me,' Deputy Chief Laroche said. 'It comes from the top, this one – right from Chief

Chambers himself. And he's made his decision clear. You have to turn in your gun. Now. It's *evidence*.'

Striker shrugged. 'I never said it wasn't.'

'You refused to relinquish it.'

'I did nothing of the sort; I promised to relinquish my gun once it was safe to do so, when the incident was over, and technically the incident was not over. Like I said before, it was a safety issue, pure and simple.'

Laroche's smile didn't falter.

'Well, there's no safety issue any more, Detective Striker. The Department will issue you a new gun, now that your old one is being seized.'

Striker dropped his hand down to the butt of his gun and ran his fingers along the grip. It was rubberised – one of the many adjustments he'd made to the Sig – and it had the flashlight attachment on the muzzle, one that needed to be made by special order.

'I've qualified on this one,' he noted.

'Chief Chambers understands your concern, so he's given you an option. If you're that concerned about being issued the new gun, then you have the right to take yourself off the road and remove yourself from the case, effective immediately, until you've requalified. So what's it going to be, Striker? Relinquishment, or Leave?'

Striker let out a heavy breath. As much as he hated to admit it, the Deputy Chief was right on this one. The exigent circumstances of the incident had long since passed, and for him to argue that the incident was ongoing because the gunman was still out there somewhere was nothing more than a technicality – especially when he was being given a new Sig as a replacement. Besides, the last thing he wanted to do was piss off the Chief. Chambers was a good man; Striker respected him.

'Well?' Laroche asked again.

Striker said nothing. He ejected the loaded magazine, withdrew his pistol, racked the slide and popped out the final round. He safed the pistol, locked the slide back, then placed it down on the hood of the Deputy Chief's car.

Laroche seized the gun.

Striker said nothing. He took the new gun case, turned, and walked away. He reached the undercover cruiser, unlocked the driver's side door and was about to climb inside when Laroche called out to him a final time.

'And Detective?'

Striker turned, waited.

'Just so we're clear, you're still in breach, as far as I'm concerned. I'll be submitting my report to Internal before the day's end.'

'Good idea, sir,' Striker said. 'Do me a favour though. On your way there, keep an eye out for a guy wearing a red hockey mask – you may not have heard this yet, but he shot up a high school yesterday morning.'

Laroche's face twisted into an angry expression, and he looked ready to say more, but Striker never gave him the chance. He hopped inside the cruiser, slammed the door, and started the engine. Once Felicia closed her own door, he tore off down Burrard Street.

The coroner was waiting.

Fifty-Four

The morgue, located at Vancouver General, is accessible only through the emergency parking on the north side. In the eight o'clock darkness, the doorway looked sinister and dangerous.

Striker parked the cruiser in Police Parking and took the cargo elevator down to the lower levels. As the booth descended, it jarred several times, causing Felicia's claustrophobia to kick in. She let out a strangled sound.

Striker gave her a smile. 'Hope it doesn't get stuck.'

'You're such a shit.'

'I got stuck in an elevator one time. Took over two hours before—'

'*Jacob.*'

He let it go. The elevator continued down, stopped hard, and the doors clanked opened. Felicia sighed with relief and bolted out like she'd been shot from a cannon. Striker followed, and they walked into the morgue antechamber.

The first thing Striker noticed was the caustic stink of body cleansers. The scent was unmistakable – almost flowery, in a sick sort of way. Then he saw the three rows of refrigerated storage chambers. Each one was devoid of nameplates – except for the final three, which read *Sherman Chan, John Doe 1* and *John Doe 2*.

John Doe 1, the headless gunman, had originally been

labelled *Que Wong*, but that name had been crossed out with thick black felt after the discovery of the real Que Wong down by the docks.

Striker had no idea who John Doe 2 was.

He stared at the chambers, losing himself, and his thoughts fell back to the past. The last time he'd been here, standing within these dreary grey walls, under the fake illumination of the humming fluorescent lights, was two years ago – just a few days after Amanda had finally succumbed to her injuries. He'd come here to identify the body – a legal necessity – and hopefully find some peace with all that had gone on.

He had found none, and to this day nothing had changed.

Felicia caught his expression, or maybe it was his posture, or maybe she just knew – she was a woman after all; they were good at that – and she gently touched his arm.

'You okay?'

'I'm okay.'

'Hasn't been that long since you've been here. And after all you went through, well . . .' Her lower lip hung open as if she'd lost the words, and she gave him a distant look before speaking again. 'You really need to tell Courtney about Amanda, Jacob.'

'Jesus Christ, you're bringing that up now? Here?'

'She needs to know.'

'Look, Felicia,' he started, but a voice interrupted him.

'Detectives?'

Striker turned and found the coroner standing in the doorway that led to the autopsy room. She was a tall woman, almost six foot, and thin – supermodel, finger-down-your-throat thin. Her long auburn hair was rolled up into a bun and tucked under a blue hairnet. The glasses she wore were large and only magnified her deep blue eyes. Morgue apparel aside, she was a Death Goddess. A knockout, but in a superficial way. Everything about her looked fake, cosmetic, manufactured. All plastic and paint.

Striker recalled her from his previous time of being here.

She walked to within a few feet of them and displayed her perfectly capped teeth. 'Kirstin Dunsmuir. Medical Examiner.'

Felicia introduced herself. When Dunsmuir looked at Striker, her eyes narrowed and she asked, 'Have we met before?'

'You worked on my wife; she died two years ago.'

'Oh.' She uttered the word without emotion, then got down to business. 'I don't have time to talk. I'm needed at Burnaby General.'

'Burnaby General?' Striker said. 'You don't got enough on your plate now?'

'It's personal.'

He gave her a hard look. 'Important enough to override school shootings? Your evidence will help me catch this prick.'

She said nothing back, and only offered him an icy stare. Striker could tell he would get nowhere with her. He wasn't into wasting his time.

'You at least get the report done?' he asked.

Dunsmuir took off her gloves, the latex snapping against her skin. 'It's not my final issue, but it's as near complete as it can get without the toxicology results.'

'I need to see it,' he said.

'It's in there,' she told him. 'Black binder on the counter, right next to Sherman Chan's body. Feel free to look through it, but leave it where you find it. Call me if there are any questions. I should be done in a couple of hours.'

As Dunsmuir turned to leave, Striker called out to her, 'You get a time of death on Raymond Leung yet?'

She never stopped walking. 'Wednesday,' she said. 'Sometime between three and eight in the morning.'

That was the morning of the shootings. The time of death was the last detail Striker had needed for him to confirm that Raymond Leung was not in fact Red Mask. He looked over at Felicia and saw that she had made the connection.

'Wrong blood type *and* outside the time of death,' Striker said, and couldn't help but feel angry that no one had initially listened to him. He stared down the hall at Kirstin Dunsmuir who was still walking away from them, her high-heeled shoes clicking oddly on the painted grey cement. It was all he could do to look at her without being irritated. Maybe it was the iciness of her emotions. Maybe it was just him, frustrated and tired. He wasn't sure. She got in the elevator, the door clanged shut, and the booth made loud grinding noises as it went up.

'Probably scheduling her boob job,' Felicia said.

Striker smiled, then turned and walked into the autopsy room.

The area where the bodies were located was labelled *Examination Room B*. Striker and Felicia stopped inside the doorway, smocked up, and put on latex gloves. Once done, they moved over to the nearest examination table. This one was labelled *John Doe 1*.

Better known as White Mask.

Striker studied him. To his frustration, when he scanned through the report binder, he found nothing new – save for one exception: the strange scars alongside the man's ribs were listed as possible shrapnel wounds. Interesting. Mode of death had been a gunshot wound. Not surprising, considering the man's head had been blown right off.

Identity remained unknown.

Striker bypassed the body and approached the second examination table. He studied the thin boy on it. There was a bullet-hole in his right cheek, the skin around the area blackened and pulled inwards. The skin of his face was looser than when Striker had last seen him, and a large Y-incision had been carved in his chest, then sewn back together.

It was Sherman Chan. Black Mask. The one Laroche had deemed 'possibly innocent'.

This was the kid Striker had killed.

He looked down at the boy. Here, dead on the table, he looked so young. Too young to be the monster he had turned out to be. He smelled bad. Of old blood and strange-scented body cleaners.

Felicia took the black binder from the counter top and flipped it open. Striker gave her time to read the report. He looked over the body and waited for her word. After a good ten minutes, she finally spoke.

'How many shots you think you fired?'

He shrugged. 'I don't know, I can't even recall changing mags.'

'Me neither, it's all a friggin' blur,' she agreed. 'Not that it matters. He took it twice. The Forensic Firearms Unit hasn't confirmed the round yet but, according to Doctor Beautiful's notes, they're going to have to test your gun first to see if the bullets match. Right now they're proceeding under the assumption that everything matches.'

'Of course.' Striker picked up a pointer from a nearby tray and placed it perpendicular to the bullet-hole in the boy's cheek. The path through was about a 120-degree angle.

'Read me the path-following entry,' he said.

She found the relevant section. 'Entered through the zygomatic arch, passed through the nasal cavity, deflected medially and inferiorly, and eventually, the remainder of the round got wedged in the rear of the skull at the posterior fissure of the parietal bone.' She looked up and smiled. 'I think that means head.'

Striker held his hand flat to the boy's chest, right at nipple level, angled approximately ninety degrees.

'And the second bullet?' he asked.

'Entrance wound was between ribs four and five, left side, right at the costo-vertebral joint – that would be the back of the rib, near the spine.'

'I know where it is.'

Felicia nodded like she didn't care, ran her finger down the page as she read: 'Says here that Black Mask must've been spinning after you got him with the first round, because the second one hit almost dead centre. It passed right through the left lung and aorta, then exited through the costal cartilage. Says here, "The resultant shock from such an injury would most likely have been fatal".'

Striker let the pointer drop to his side, then looked at the body for a long moment before finding Felicia's eyes again.

'The paragraph about the first bullet,' he said. 'It say anything about tissue damage inside the body?'

She scanned the notes. 'Yeah, she's listed a few things damaged by the bullet fragments. Occipitalis and trapezius muscles – and there's a few notes here on brain matter. Why?'

'What about the second bullet?'

She looked through the pages, shook her head. 'None yet.'

He said nothing for a long moment, then called her over. She put the black binder back on the counter and joined him beside the dead body of Sherman Chan. When she was set, Striker pointed to the bullet-wound beside the boy's sternum.

'Look at that. Not the first entry hole – I have no problem with that – but the second one.'

She did. 'Okay.'

'Now look at this.' He placed one hand under the boy's left shoulder and one under the boy's hip, rolled him onto his right side, then used a hand to stabilise him. 'Look at the exit wound of the second bullet.'

'Okay,' she said again.

'Describe the exit wound for me,' he said.

She gave him an odd look, but said, 'It's probably a half-inch in diameter, I guess, and almost perfectly circular, except for the distended skin. And it's relatively clean with distinct edges.'

'That sound like a hollow-tip round to you?'

She paused. 'Well, no, actually it doesn't – but I doubt the pathologist—'

'With all the killings over the past two days, she's had even less sleep than us. She's done her examination *assuming* the rounds were hollow-tips. But they weren't.'

Felicia looked over the wound, noting, 'That would explain why there was less internal tissue damage from the bullet fragments.'

'Because there were no fragments – it wasn't a frangible round.'

'But that doesn't make sense.'

'It makes perfect sense. Sherman Chan was shot in the back – and by a Full Metal Jacket round. They shot their own, Felicia.'

Fifty-Five

'I am glad that you know Sheung Fa,' the old man said. 'He is a good man to know. But this wound . . . the infection is very bad.' He spoke the words softly, with a sense of practicality.

Red Mask heard them like a flutter of wings as he fell in and out of consciousness. He opened his eyes and glanced around the room. He saw shelf after shelf, each one covered with different-sized jars. Hundreds of jars. Containing roots, flowers, stalks, fermented creatures and many other things he could not even describe.

'Very bad,' the old man said again. 'The arm may be lost.'

Red Mask felt removed. He looked from the flowers to the floor to the old television set, bolted high in the far corner of the room. At first glance it looked part of a video-surveillance system, all black and white and shoddy of picture, but then the BCTV News crest lit up the screen, and Red Mask realised he was simply looking at a very old television set.

The late-night news was on. *St Patrick's Peril*.

Looking in that direction hurt Red Mask's neck, and he had seen enough. He turned his eyes away from the screen.

'Bullet . . . in shoulder . . .' he murmured.

'Rest, rest,' the old man soothed.

Red Mask focused on the old man, who now stood at his

side. He was thin, with a sickly pale face. As if he had been ill for a long time. As if he, too, had come from the camps.

'The blood is dead.' The old man pointed a long brown fingernail at Red Mask's shoulder, then lightly dragged the nail around the perimeter of the wound.

Red Mask flinched at the touch, felt his entire body tremble.

'Bad blood. Dead blood. It must come off.'

Red Mask shook his head. 'It cannot.'

'It must.'

'No! I am . . . unfinished.'

The old man's eyes roamed the room, as if he was staring at things no one else could see, dissecting things in his mind. After a long hesitation, he returned to his desk, which was on the far side of the room, under another large shelf of jars. He sat and read and talked to himself in a dialect Red Mask could not understand. The words sounded lost and rhetorical and far too fast – like the clucks of chickens.

For the first few seconds, Red Mask raised his head off the table and watched the old man, but soon his shoulder throbbed and his neck shook, and he gave up the struggle. His head dropped back onto the hard wood of the table, and he moved no more. His body felt as heavy and old as the earth itself.

'I must be going,' he said.

The old man laughed. 'Are you in such a hurry to find your grave?'

Red Mask did not reply. His eyes roamed the room. On the wall hung several prayer banners. For Health. For Harmony. For Prosperity. He murmured them aloud, at the same time trying to find the source of the horrible smell that overpowered everything else in the room – even the strong stink of the ginger root. It took Red Mask several minutes before he realised that the stench came from him.

His body was turning rancid.

And all because of the *gwailo*. The White Devil.

'Ahhh!' the old man said, the word like a sigh. On wobbly legs, he stood up from his desk, then shuffled over to the sink where he gathered and mixed ingredients Red Mask could not see. When at last he turned around, he was carrying a large poultice, dripping with yellow and purple fluids, the colours of an old bruise. In the centre of the cloth, a hole had been cut. The old man draped that hole over the wound on Red Mask's shoulder.

The coolness of the compress sent tingles up and down Red Mask's neck and arm, and he shivered violently. When the old man pressed down firmly, Red Mask screamed. Thick, yellow fluid oozed out of the hole, and a deep bone pain radiated all through his body.

The old man shook his head. 'It is still in there.'

'Cut bullet out.'

'This will cause much, much pain.'

But Red Mask barely heard him. His sole focus was now on the television set, because on the screen was a picture of the cop – the White Devil who had confronted him at every turn. The News was touting this man as the one who taunted death in order to save the lives of the children. He was a legend. A hero.

The sight caused Red Mask's body to shudder, so hard it shook the table.

The old man washed his hands at the sink. When he returned to the table, a tray of crude steel tools rattled in his withered hands.

Red Mask turned his thoughts away from the pain of his shoulder, away from the tools that littered the old man's tray, and focused on Detective Jacob Striker – the cop who had almost killed him twice; the cop who had almost prevented him from finishing his mission; the cop who had killed his loved one and sent a life's worth of planning into ruin.

They would meet again. Red Mask knew this. It was unavoidable.

'Are you ready?' the old man asked.

Red Mask nodded, and moments later he began to scream.

Friday

Fifty-Six

Edward Rundell's house was worth more than most people made in their lifetime. Situated on the West Vancouver bluff, it overlooked the forked waterways and dotted isles that populated Bachelor Bay. The best view was from the master bedroom, which was set high above the water's edge, out on the precipice. The drop was straight down. Two hundred feet to jagged rock and angry frothing foam. Dangerous, and beautiful.

And the Man with the Bamboo Spine took little notice of it.

He stood in the centre of the master bedroom: a room with a vaulted ceiling, three skylights, two overhead fans, and a heated floor made from alternating stripes of white oak and black walnut wood.

The Man with the Bamboo Spine looked out the window, at the heavy darkness beyond, and he lit up a cigarette. An unfiltered Marlboro. Strong for this country, weak compared to the ones back home in Macau. The smoke tasted good on his lips, and the smell overpowered everything else. Even the stink of the blood.

'Huh . . . hu . . . hu . . . hu . . .' Edward Rundell made a series of soft sounds on the bloodstained bed, barely audible.

The Man with the Bamboo Spine ignored them as he finished

his cigarette. As always, his eyes were dark and steady. Like black marbles. Without emotion.

In his left hand was an industrial cheese-grater, almost twelve inches long. The steel was slick now, growing sticky from the brown-black blood. The holes were clogged with red chunks of meaty tissue. Most of it had come from Edward Rundell's back and the outer parts of his limbs – areas away from the major arteries. Precision was critical for this kind of work.

If Edward died too fast, his employers would not be happy. Extreme, disproportionate levels of violence was their calling card.

It fostered fear and was a tool of prevention.

The questioning had lasted for well over four hours. Edward laid prone on the bed, his thin, pale body stripped of skin and muscle, and glistening with redness. He twitched involuntarily – in the beginning this had been from the pain; now it was all shock-related – and once again let out a series of uneven, raspy breaths.

'Huh . . . hu . . . hu . . . hu . . . hu . . .'

And then the sound stopped and he became still.

The Man with the Bamboo Spine saw this, and he nodded absently. The job was complete. He finished his cigarette, dropped the stub in a plastic bag and stuffed it into his jacket pocket. Then he stepped around a pool of congealing blood on the hardwood floor and moved up to the side of the bed. He checked Edward Rundell for a pulse.

Found none.

The cheese-grater made a loud clunking sound when the Man with the Bamboo Spine dropped it. He moved into the adjoining ensuite and washed the blood off his hands – for he never wore gloves — then he walked down the hall to the front door, where he exchanged his bloodied black sneakers for a new pair of clean ones, also black. He drove away from the house in darkness, in the black Mercedes he'd been provided with, never once looking back.

Target One – the connection that linked them to the modified Honda – was down. His employers would be content.

Target Two remained unclear.

Fifty-Seven

Like the previous day, it was early when Striker awoke. The sun had not yet lightened the skies. Outside his bedroom window, the night was black and deep and cold. It was a perfect start to Halloween. Unsettling. There seemed to be something wrong with the world. Then again, maybe it was just his world.

God knows, that was how it felt at times.

He kicked the blankets off his legs. They were damp from the sweat induced by his nightmares. Too many images, all mottled together. Kids screaming, gunmen on the loose, fires and dragons and debate clubs. Amanda dying on him back at the hospital, and of course Courtney was in there somewhere.

She always was.

He got up, walked down the hall, cracked Courtney's door open and looked inside. She was sprawled out across her sheets. In her flannel PJs, she looked more doll than person.

Striker's heart pained him.

The previous five years had been hard on her, but the last two had been hell, and their constant fighting didn't help. Lately, whether she was away at school or right there in the room with him, she felt a hundred miles away. They fought, then they got over it, then they fought again. At times their relationship seemed more bipolar than Amanda had been, and he prayed it was just the teenage years shining through.

The room was cold. Striker snuck inside and pulled the blankets up to Courtney's chest. She muttered in her sleep, grabbed them and rolled over. He left the room. For a moment he considered going back to bed, but knew sleep would not come. His body might have been tired and depleted, but his mind was going a million miles an hour, and Striker couldn't help feeling he was missing something.

Something big.

He thought of all the crime scenes he and Felicia had attended – St Patrick's High, the garage where the stolen Civic had been recovered, the underground bunker where they'd found the body of Raymond Leung, the docks where they'd found Que Wong's body, the intersection of Gore and Pender where Dr Kieu and the two goons had been found dead in the white van, and lastly the shootout at the Kwan residence.

There were so many.

The Kwan residence bothered him. He'd been so busy rushing Patricia off to St Paul's Hospital in order to save her life that he had yet to spend any investigative time at the house – and he knew he had to go there or else he would never sleep again. He showered, grabbed a protein bar from the top of the fridge, and left the house.

It was barely five o'clock.

The Kwan house was under police guard.

Normally, Patrol dealt with guard duty for the first twenty-four hours, but due to the abnormal number of crime scenes, management had given the okay for the Road Sergeant to hit the Call-Out list. Striker didn't know the cop on duty – some redheaded woman with freckles. He said hello, badged her, and went inside.

The first thing he noticed was the foyer wall. Huge white

chunks of Gyprock had been torn out from the bullets, giving the entranceway a Swiss-cheese look. Air blew strong from the heating vent. Striker closed it, then walked into the living room.

He stopped in front of the TV, where Patricia Kwan had been lying when he'd first come into the house yesterday. A dark red patch stained the carpet. This section was cut off from the rest of the room by a yellow smear of police tape. To the right of the tape, the front window was cracked and full of holes, and there were jagged pieces of shiny mirror all over the sofa. Plastic numbers had been placed across the floor. Noodles or someone else from Ident had already been here.

Striker bypassed it all and circled back to the master bedroom.

The room was ordinary. Untouched. The bed was made; the dresser drawers were closed, and the closet was shut and blocked off by a hamper full of laundry. Everything smelled of lemon-scented laundry detergent. The furnace air hummed as it blew through the vents.

Striker stepped into the room and looked around. A few things caught his eye – a dresser full of knick-knacks, a pile of folded clothes on a chair and a photograph of Patricia and her daughter, Riku.

It was a grim reminder of their failure. Despite the Amber Alert and the unprecedented manpower, the girl still hadn't been found. It was distressing because everyone knew the rotten truth: the more time that passed, the less chance of survival.

Striker looked hard at the photo. Mother and daughter were at an outdoor event somewhere. Both looked hot and tired, but were smiling and drinking red punch. Striker felt uneasy while studying the photo. The people in the frame might have been

Patricia Kwan and her daughter, but it could just as easily have been him and Courtney.

He tried not to think about it, and approached the dresser.

It was made of dark maple wood. Solid. In the first three drawers he found nothing. Just socks and underwear and belts and shirts – the usual stuff. In the bottom drawer, he found something that made him pause. At first the drawer looked filled with only papers – mostly bills and lawyers' invoices – and change, but mixed in with the copper pennies and silver dimes was a glinting of dull, rounded brass.

A bullet.

Striker pulled some latex from his pocket, gloved up, then reached into the pile and plucked up the round. He held it up to the light and studied it. Forty calibre, for sure. The casing was dull and scratched, and the head was partly compressed, as if it had been loaded one too many times, which was probably why the round was sitting here in the drawer, unused. Striker looked at the top of the round, studied the inset of the head.

It was a frangible round.

Hollow-tip.

He got on his cell, called the Info channel and got them to run Kwan for an FAC – a Firearms Acquisition Certificate. Within seconds, the reply came back negative. She didn't have one now, and never did. Which begged the question: why did she have a round in her dresser drawer, and where did it come from?

The thought tugged at his mind, and he rolled the round back and forth between his thumb and forefinger. He looked at the photo again, saw the two women smiling back at him, and something grabbed his attention. The T-shirts they wore were exactly the same – dark grey with a small red and blue crest on the upper left side of the chest. Striker couldn't make out the numbers in the crest, but he was pretty certain they were 499. Which meant one thing: the Larry Young Run – an annual event funded by the Emergency Response Team. It was the same shirt Meathead had been wearing the other day.

Striker looked at the round in his hand, then back at the shirts both women were wearing. He got back on Info, ran Patricia Kwan all ways, then waited for the response. When he got it, he hung up and called Felicia. She answered on the third ring.

'Get up,' he told her.

'What? It's barely six.'

'I'm at the Kwan house.'

This seemed to wake Felicia up. 'You find the girl?'

'No.'

'Then what?'

'Patricia Kwan,' he said. 'She's a *cop*.'

Fifty-Eight

Courtney woke up and stared at the ceiling. Morning light broke through the curtains. The outside porch lamp seemed abnormally bright, and it bugged her eyes, worsened the dull thud in the back of her brain. She felt like she was hungover. Like she'd drunk a two-litre of coolers. Her mouth was dry. She needed water.

She got up, shuffled into the kitchen and poured herself a glass of water from the Brita jug. Outside, the sky was dark grey, and it matched her mood. Thoughts of Raine filled her head, as they had all night long.

Had Raine done it?

Had she had sex with Que?

The thought made Courtney frown. She wanted Raine to be happy, and she hoped her first time was perfect, but she also felt alone all of a sudden, as if Raine losing her virginity had somehow set them further apart. Raine hadn't called her since yesterday, and it felt like there was a gap developing between them already.

It worried her.

She sat down at the breakfast nook and tried to convince herself that nothing was wrong. It was just her – like it always was. She stared out the window at the Japanese Plum tree in the back yard. All the branches were bare. Everything felt so mixed up, not only in her head but in her heart. She sat there, drinking water and thinking of Raine and Que and Bobby Ryan, and then of Dad. So many strange emotions. When her thoughts turned back to Mom, she made herself get moving.

She showered and got dressed. Then ignoring a slew of missed calls from schoolfriends, she called Raine's cell.

Got nothing. She then remembered Raine was using the new iPhone Que had lent her. She called that number, too.

Got nothing but an automated message service.

Courtney cursed. She left a message, then snagged some money from the top of Dad's dresser and headed out the front door. Starbucks was only two blocks away and she wanted an Americano and something loafy. She'd barely gotten two steps down the walkway when she saw the police car out front. A hunky cop in uniform stepped out, marched towards her. He was young, about twenty-five, and *hot*. Short brown hair, dark blue eyes, and a dreamy smile.

'Back inside, Courtney,' he said.

She blinked. 'What?'

'Gunman from the shooting's still out there.'

She thought it over, nodded. 'I know – but I've got nothing to do with that.'

'Your father's orders.'

She felt her cheeks blush. 'I'm almost sixteen, I can do what I want.'

His face tightened. 'Come on, kid, you're putting me in a bad situation here.'

Kid?

She felt her warm cheeks grow hotter. Knew they were red; knew she was blushing bad. So she spun away from him, scampered back up the steps and went inside and slammed the front door behind her. For a second she just stood there in the darkness and felt the humiliation wash over her. She walked through the house to the back door, saw another marked cruiser out back, and saw the cop inside on his cell phone. The guy hung up, then looked at the house, as if he'd been warned she might come that way.

It was so totally embarrassing. She grabbed the portable phone from the kitchen, called Dad, waited. It was picked up after three rings.

'Morning, Pumpkin.'

'What the hell is going on?'

He made a surprised sound. 'What—'

'You got cops outside the house, front and back – they won't let me leave.'

'It's for your own protection.'

'I don't need any protection. I'm supposed to meet Raine and Bobby today.'

'You can see them when we find this guy.'

'Well, how long will that be?'

'A while.'

'But the Britney concert's *tonight*.'

He cleared his throat, made a sound like he was thinking. 'There's no way you're going to any concert. Not with this whack-job still out there somewhere.'

'But you didn't let me go the last time she came!'

'Oops, I did it again.'

'That's not funny.'

'It's a concert, Courtney. Nothing more.' He spoke impatiently to someone in the background. 'Look, I'm at work here and I need you safe. I need you home.'

'But the Parade of Lost Souls is also—'

'I'll make it up to you later.'

'But Dad—

'You're not going and that's final.'

'It's not FAIR!' She slammed the receiver back on the cradle and let out a scream. She picked it back up, called Raine again, and still got no answer. After the voice greeting, she left a long message about what a jerk Dad was, then hung up the phone and looked back outside. The cop was still there, focusing on the house. Really watching it. Like she was a prisoner or something. A friggin' prisoner.

She ran back to her room, looked at her Little Red Riding Hood costume, thought of the Parade of Lost Souls, and how Bobby Ryan was going to be there, and how Melissa Jones was going to be there, in her skimpy hot Catwoman costume with her big boobs hanging out everywhere – and there was no way she was going to let Bobby be alone with slutty Melissa at the Parade of Lost Souls.

No way ever.

And that meant only one thing. She was going to get out of here.

She just had to find a way.

Fifty-Nine

After leaving the Kwan residence, Striker made sure that both patrol cops – both marked units – were still outside the front and back doors of his own house on guard detail. With the discovery that Patricia Kwan was a cop, everything felt that much closer to home, and he worried about Courtney. With her safe and out of the way, he could rest easier and better focus on the investigation.

Which was now taking them to strange places.

He drove towards Felicia's, stopped for a red light at Granville. While waiting for the green, his cell went off. The screen told him it was Noodles, so he picked up.

'Friends of the Friendless,' he said.

Noodles laughed. 'You're one lucky SOB, my friend.'

'Gimme some good news.'

'How's this: got a partial print back in the van. Driver's side window.'

Striker felt a stab of excitement, leaned forward in his seat. 'Got a name?'

'Most likely, it's Anthony Gervais.'

It was a name Striker knew well. 'Most likely?'

'The print is only a partial. But I'd bet money on the ID.'

Striker nodded absently. 'I'll get right on it.' He hung up and slid the cell back into its pouch.

Anthony Gervais. Better known as Chinese Tony. To find his print in a murder vehicle was surprising.

At quarter to seven, Striker picked up Felicia. When she came out of her house – a quaint little duplex just off Commercial Drive, down near McSpadden Park – her dark brown eyes looked sharper than he'd seen them the past two days. More focused. When she hopped inside the cruiser, he handed her a Starbucks Grande Vanilla Latte and a piece of lemon loaf with strawberry icing.

She took it, didn't eat. 'Patricia Kwan's a fucking *cop*?'

He nodded, drove west on East Fifth. 'Vancouver Police Department. One of our own.'

'How? Someone would've known her. Or recognised her. Or . . . *something*.'

'She's worked the odd side for the last year, so the even guys never see her. And before that she was seconded to Surrey. One of those joint task forces – Fraud, I think. So with the exception of a few Call Outs, she's been gone for over five years.'

'She still should come up in the system.'

'She does.' Striker took a sip of his coffee, switched into the right-hand lane. 'In all the chaos no one thought to run her – we were all too preoccupied with saving her life, I guess. Not that it matters. We would've found out eventually.'

'Sooner is better.' Felicia stared out the window at the darkness of the city. 'Jesus Christ, Jacob, where the hell is this woman's kid?'

Striker wished he had an answer. After turning north on Commercial, they drove along Venables Street, over the Georgia Viaduct, into the downtown core. It wasn't until they reached Burrard that Felicia even asked where they were going.

'Comox Street.'

'Shouldn't we be getting back to Ich? The feed should be translated by now.'

'Nope. The feed isn't translated yet. I just talked to Ich before picking you up, and the translator Mosaic sent over couldn't do it. Said it was some strange dialect, and that they'd be sending someone else.'

'This is bullshit.'

'You're preaching to the choir, kid.'

Felicia looked at the tall skyscrapers that were slowly popping up, one by one, as the downtown core grew closer. 'Why Comox Street?'

Striker stopped for a bus that was swinging out into the lane. 'To see Anthony Gervais.'

'You mean Chinese Tony?'

'The one and only.'

'Why him?'

'The van we found on Gore and Pender – the one with Kieu and the two thugs inside – well, we got a partial print back on the steering column. Three guesses who it belongs to, and the first two don't count.'

Felicia frowned, said nothing, sipped her latte.

'What?' he said.

She shrugged. 'I've dealt with Chinese Tony a million times. He's a maggot, that's for sure, one of the worst property crime toads out there . . . but he isn't a killer.'

'I don't know what he is,' Striker said. 'But I do know this – he's got a condition not to be in any motor vehicle without the registered owner present, so he can have fun explaining how his prints got inside that van.'

'You said it's only a partial print – that'll never hold up in court.'

Striker gave her a quick look. 'He doesn't know that.'

'Maybe not, but he's a tough little shit. Doubt he'll talk.'

'Then we revert to plan B.'

'Plan B?'

'Yeah. I know a dark secret about Chinese Tony most others don't.' Striker flashed her a nasty grin. 'And at a time like this, I'm more than willing to use it.'

The sun was breaking through the tops of the Stanley Park trees as they drove down Comox Street and stopped in front of Hedgeford Estates. The apartment building was a twelve-storey, made of grey concrete slabs and black mirrored glass. The sunlight glinted off it.

Striker hated the place. It was a favourite abode of mid-level drug traffickers, and it pissed him off that a dial-a-doper like Chinese Tony could live here when he was collecting welfare – an amount which, on its own, couldn't pay the rent.

'His unit's right there,' Striker said, and pointed. 'The side that flanks the walkway.'

The target suite was number 112, which meant the main floor, north-east side. The ground-floor location was no fluke; it gave Chinese Tony a quick escape exit when the cops or other enemies came around.

'He'll probably run,' Felicia said.

'I'm counting on it.'

'You want the talk or the knock?'

He smiled. 'What do you think?'

'I'll flip you for it.'

'Seniority.'

'You really gonna play that card again?'

'Till the day I retire.'

Felicia frowned, then left for the building's front entrance. Striker waited just outside the patio doors to Chinese

Tony's apartment, hidden by a row of bushes. Behind him, a redbrick walkway circled the parking lot, turned north towards the tennis courts then trailed off into the lagoons of Stanley Park.

He watched the harsh fall winds blow leaves across the court. It was cold, but he left his long coat open for better manoeuvrability. He checked his watch. It was just after eight in the morning, and that was good. Chinese Tony would most likely be home. The prick did most of his crimes at night.

Striker waited for his cell to ring. It did. He picked up.

'You set?' Felicia asked.

'Do the talk.'

'Okay.' He heard, 'Police! Open up!' And seconds later, the soft grating sound of the patio doors sliding open.

Striker peered through a break in the hedge and spotted the man they were after.

Chinese Tony was a white guy – he'd gotten the nickname from being the only white kid to hang with the Gum Wah Boyz way back in the late nineties. He was a scrawny little puke – always had been, but he'd grown even thinner since Striker had last seen him.

Using his own product, Striker knew. Common mistake.

Chinese Tony's cheeks were sucked in, and his eyes were deep round hollows. New scars marked his face, the largest one trailing from his left eye and disappearing under his chin. His dark brown hair was shorter than before, cut jagged and bowl-like, real greasy. He wore the usual dirtbag attire – holey blue jeans and a black hoodie – and he came scrambling across the backyard patio like a cockroach running from the light. He crossed the yard, hopped the fence –

– and Striker nailed him in the chest with a hard elbow.

Chinese Tony went reeling backwards. He hit the gate, his

legs gave out, and he collapsed. When he looked back up again, his eyes were cloudy.

'What the *fuck*?' he started.

'Why you running from the police, Tony?'

'Who the . . . Detective Striker?'

'I'm touched you remembered.' Striker grabbed the man's arm and was surprised at the bone thinness. He flipped Tony over so that he was prone on the grass, then handcuffed him. When the cuffs were double-locked behind his back and Felicia came walking around the building into the common area, Striker hoisted him back up to his feet.

'Why were you running from the police?' he repeated.

'I got no warrants.'

'That's not what I asked.'

'I ain't breachin' nothing. Seen my PO just yesterday. So fuck you. You got nothing, man. Nothing.'

Striker grabbed him by the front of his hoodie, pulled him close, spoke quietly. 'Listen up and listen hard, you little maggot. I got three dead bodies in a vehicle down on East Pender, and witnesses are pointing you out as the driver. I'd say that's something.'

'I was home.'

'Did I even say when this happened?'

Chinese Tony licked his lips, said nothing.

'Also, we got a couple prints off the steering wheel,' Felicia added. 'Good ones, too. Or else we wouldn't be here wasting our time.'

'I was sleeping, see? Ali K was here, too. He'll tell you that.'

Striker looked at Felicia, and she smiled. The only person who could possibly be Chinese Tony's alibi would also be the same person who had been the passenger in the stolen van.

Striker grinned. 'Ali's prints are in the vehicle, too, Einstein. Got any other stories you want to throw out there?'

Chinese Tony's mouth dropped open, but no words came out.

Striker made a point of laughing. 'Your story's got more holes than a box of Cheerios.' He tightened his grip on Tony's hoodie, pulled him even closer. Whispered, 'I don't give two shits about the motor vehicle breach, got it? What I care about are the dead bodies.'

'I already told you, I wasn't even in no van.'

'Did I ever say it was a van?'

The words caught Chinese Tony off guard, and he stuttered, 'I w-want my l-lawyer.'

Striker nodded, never letting his eyes deviate.

'Those bodies might be linked to a lot of dead kids,' he said. 'Now I don't know how you got involved in this, but I do know one thing – you were in that goddam van. So you can 'fess up now and tell me what your part is, or we can do it the hard way.'

'I want my fuckin' lawyer.'

Striker turned to Felicia and smiled. 'Awesome. Plan B it is.'

Sixty

The table was wet when Red Mask awoke, and his body was slicked with sweat. The room was cold. So terribly cold. And there was that smell again.

He heard the sound of running water and saw the old man standing by the sink, his arthritic spine all twisted from the rear view. He was washing off steel tools.

The old man must have sensed something, for he turned around. Found Red Mask with his eyes. 'You fell into unconsciousness.'

Red Mask tried to think back. There was no memory. 'Is bullet removed?'

The old man shuffled over to the table and dropped the lump of mashed lead into Red Mask's palm. 'The bringer of so much sorrow. It is yours. Well earned.'

Red Mask looked at the source of his pain; it was so small.

'I must go,' he said.

The old man grimaced. 'You can go nowhere. Your body is weak. Very weak.'

'My spirit is strong.'

'The spirit is housed by the body.'

Red Mask sat forward, and let out a cry. The pain was just as intense as before, but different. Less sharp, more diffuse.

He swung his legs off the table and carefully stood. His legs trembled but did not give out.

'I owe you much.'

The old man put a vial of pills into his hand. 'You must take these. Every hour. To fight off the infection.'

Red Mask stuffed the vial into his pants pocket. Then the old man touched him.

'Your body needs rest.'

'I will rest when dead.'

'That will not be long if you persist.'

Red Mask walked to the exit. Before leaving, he did something he hadn't done in as long as he could remember – he cupped his hands together and bowed low to show his respect and gratitude to the man who had saved his life.

Or at the very least delayed his death.

Outside, the steep incline of concrete stairs took every bit of energy he had left to climb. Once at the top, he stepped out from under the awning and the rain hit him. Just a soft spatter of rain, but that was all it took. And within seconds, he was back there.

Back then . . .

Red Mask was small again. Weak. And alone.

A child.

Child 157, to be exact. It was his label now. He stood on his toes, terrified, but daring to peek through the iron bars of his window, into the pits of D Block below.

That was where the old man had been taken. It would be his final resting-place.

'Who is your employer?' the inquisitor with the blue sash demanded.

The old man before him trembled. He was seated on his

knees, his chest and torso exposed, his rice-thin pants torn. Sweat and blood dripped down his sunburned brow and along the sides of his leathery wrinkled face. His long, uneven beard was patched with grey.

'No one, there is no one,' the old man said, and the desperation in his words was painful.

'What is your former occupation?' the blue-sashed man demanded.

The old man raised his branch-thin arms in the air, as if pleading for mercy. 'I have told you many times—'

'Put him in the tank!' the inquisitor snapped.

The old man screamed and waved his arms, but when the guards came – and they *always* came, wearing that horrible, drab grey clothing – they took him easily, for he was too thin and too weak and too old to fight them off. They tied his arms behind his back, then dragged him across the room to the iron tub. It was filled with water, and the stink of it reached Child 157's nose. It was the same water a hundred others had died in – including the old man's wife just before midday.

'I have done nothing!' the old man cried out. 'Nothing! I am inno—'

The guards forced his head beneath the water, cutting off his cries. Loud splashes filled the room. Frantic sounds, like a fish fighting for life. The old man's legs kicked and his body bucked, and the water thrashed and spilled.

Child 157 watched from his window. He could not look away.

The room was hot and sweltering in the summer heat, but he felt cold now. Cold with fear. He watched for a long time as the guards continued the pattern – yanking the old man's head from the tub, demanding answers from him, then slamming his face back into the water when they did not get the words they wanted. Every time they did it, more water splashed across the floor and wall, the odd splatters hitting Child 157 and wetting his skin.

The violence went on for a long, long time.

But eventually the old man's body gave out. Or perhaps they held him under the water a second too long. The reason did not matter. When they pulled him from the tub, his neck fell forward limply and his face slammed hard on the lip of iron.

It was over.

Uncle was dead.

The inquisitor wrote something down in his book, then turned his eyes towards the iron-barred window of the cells. He found Child 157 and fixed him with a cold stare.

'Bring in the next,' he said.

Red Mask startled as he awoke from the memory. Cold water splashed his face, and it took him several seconds to realise it was not water from the drowning tub, but rain from above. Simple rain.

'Uncle,' he murmured.

It was a word he had not said in decades.

Confused by the recall, he turned and headed south. For Kingsway and Rupert. To meet the man who controlled his life every bit as much as the spirits controlled his destiny. His childhood mentor. His only grace. His last chance in this unforgiving world.

Sheung Fa.

Sixty-One

The Vancouver Jail was slower than usual. No arrestees were in the holding cell, and none were in the search bay. When Striker learned that Jail Sergeant Connors was away on sick leave, it was a stroke of good luck. Connors was newly made, and anal about the booking rules and procedures. For what Striker had planned, the procedures would be thrown out the window.

It was better for everyone not to have Connors around.

Striker told the wagon driver to leave Chinese Tony inside the back of the wagon, in the dark with the heat cranked up to full. He locked his Sig in the jail's gun-locker, then stood outside the pre-hold and waited for the guards to buzz him in. They did, and he walked right through to the front desk. The jail guard was one he'd never seen before, a young black guy with huge glasses and a weary expression on his face.

'Got a prisoner in the wagon,' Striker told him. 'Keep him in there.'

'Sure thing, Detective.'

Striker went alone. Felicia had gone over to Headquarters at 312 Main to do some more searching on the Debate Club lead, and Striker was thankful for it. They needed more information, and he needed some space. Especially here and now.

Some tactics worked better old school.

He walked through the jail. In the thirty years it had been

open, not much had changed. There were new policies and procedures, new forms and safety checks, but the essence of the jail remained untouched. It was a bad place. An unforgiving place. The walls were dark and dreary, the lighting was poor, and the place stank of piss and puke and shit and bleach.

Cologne of the Skids.

Striker went over his plan. He picked Cell Block 2 because there was a psychological advantage to having an inmate walk down the stairs, deeper and deeper into the bowels of the jail. And he chose Cell 9 because it had been recently revamped into a temporary holding cell for high traffic times. Being revamped meant it had once been a search room for recently booked prisoners, and being a search room meant it was one of the few places in the jail that had no cameras.

The cell door was open. Striker stepped inside. The small ten-by-ten room contained two bunk beds and two fluorescent bulbs. It was too bright for his liking, so Striker climbed up on the top bunk and removed one of the bulbs, making the cell even darker.

'You owe us big for this,' a voice behind him said.

Striker turned and spotted Constable Chris Pemberton and Detective Pinkerton Morningstar – two of the biggest men on the force. Each man was at least six foot six and over three hundred pounds. Dressed in white, paper-like prisoner gear, Pemberton looked like a square-faced enforcer from the Aryan Nation, and Morningstar looked like the meanest blackest motherfucker ever to grace these prison walls.

They were perfect for the part.

Striker looked at Morningstar. 'I pissed in the cell so it feels real for you.'

Pemberton chuckled, Morningstar did not. 'Let's just get this over with,' he said.

Striker couldn't have agreed more. Time was everything.

Pemberton and Morningstar stepped inside the cell, Striker shut the door on them, and then he went back upstairs and got to work. Within ten minutes, he had Chinese Tony run through the search bay and dressed in his prisoner digs. The man talked big and strutted around, giving everyone the gangster show Striker had seen a thousand times over. Striker walked Chinese Tony down the north stairway, gave him a smile, and said, 'Dead Man Walking.'

Chinese Tony didn't react.

When they reached Cell Block 2, Tony beelined for Cell 6. Before he got there, Striker grabbed his arm.

'Slight change of plans.'

'What the—'

Striker shoved him along the narrow grey corridor until they reached Cell 9, where Pemberton and Morningstar were waiting inside. A steel hatch covered a small pane of rectangular viewing glass, inset in the green steel door. With a quick flick of his finger, Striker opened it to reveal the two thugs inside.

'How's it going, ladies?' he said. 'Can I interrupt this Mary Kay meeting?'

Morningstar kicked the door. 'Fuck you!'

Pemberton just stood there and looked menacing.

Striker grinned. 'You getting all acquainted with one another in there?' He looked at Pemberton and laughed mockingly. 'Is it true what they say – once you have black . . .'

'Go fuck your mother,' Pemberton said. 'You lying prick, Striker! You said you owed us one. Said you'd look out for us. You're a lying fuck!' He stepped forward and kicked the door so hard it shook and the viewing hatch closed.

Chinese Tony reared back nervously.

Striker held him steady. He flipped the hatch back open and

made eye-contact with the two men inside. 'Don't get your panties in a knot, ladies, I brought you some fresh meat here. Now you can have a ménage-à-trois – Hotel Skid-style.'

A nervous whimper escaped Tony's lips and his entire body tightened. 'No fuckin' way I'm going in there.'

Striker just smiled at him. 'Hope you smuggled in some lube.'

'I'm gonna tell my lawyer!'

'Go ahead and tell him whatever you want. But he won't get down here for at least three hours after the call is made. Plenty of time for some good old-fashioned lovin'.'

Chinese Tony's face hardened. 'Stop fuckin' round, Striker.'

'You should really consider your words better when you're about to go in the can, Tony. You see the big black dude in there,' he pointed through the glass window at Morningstar, 'there's a reason I picked him to be in your cell. And the white wacko, too. See, they were both victims as kids. Sexual molestation cases. Anal rape – real bad stuff. They've suppressed most of it, but I bet they'll remember it all when I tell them your dirty little secret.'

Tony's face paled. 'I ain't got no secrets.'

'You're a skinner, Tony.'

'Fuck you, I am.'

'Like the little boys.'

'This is bullshit.'

'Every cop knows it – and they're just waiting for the information to nail your tight little ass to the wall.' Striker pointed into the cell. 'And soon they will, too. Unless we talk. Up to you really. You wanna talk to me – or you wanna take your chances in there with Ebony and Ivory?'

Tony's chest was heaving and sweat dappled his skin, as if the Cell Block 2 was suddenly too hot.

'Go fuck your mother.'

Striker didn't hesitate. He opened the door, shoved Tony inside, and Tony let out a terrified croak.

'Striker!'

'I told you, Tony, I got dead kids on my hands and a crazed gunman out there. I'm willing to break all the rules on this one. And a piece of shit like you means nothing to me.' Striker grabbed the edge of the door, looked at Morningstar and Pemberton, and smiled. 'I told you guys I'd look out for you, and that I'd owe you one. Well, here it is. The name of your new cellmate here is Chinese Tony. He's a *skinner*. Have fun with him.'

Striker slammed the door shut and the harsh metallic sound echoed throughout the halls. Not a second later, Chinese Tony let out a horrible cry and started pounding frantically on the door.

'I'll talk, I'll talk, I'LL FUCKING TALK!'

Striker opened up the door, saw Chinese Tony on his stomach, trembling, crying, his prisoner clothing already half-ripped from the lower part of his thin white body. His ass was hanging out. In behind him, Pemberton and Morningstar stood with strips of Tony's prison clothes in their hands. Striker turned his eyes down to Tony.

'You'll tell me everything?' he said.

'Everything, Striker, *everything*. I swear!'

'Good. Because you shut me out again and you'll be right back here – and next time, this door won't open back up.'

Sixty-Two

Ten minutes later, Striker sat across from Chinese Tony in one of the interview rooms located behind the main booking area. The air was cooler and much more comfortable here, and the lighting was brighter. The room was secure.

'Have some water,' Striker said, and slid bottled water across the table.

Chinese Tony accepted it with trembling hands. He tried to uncap it, couldn't, and Striker did it for him. He passed the water back and tried not to notice the bad smell in the room.

Chinese Tony had pissed himself.

Striker put down his water, fixed Tony with a hard look. 'The van,' he said. 'Start talking.'

For a moment, Tony's deep-set eyes took on a distant look, and he drank more and more water as if trying to delay the inevitable. After a few seconds, water spilled from the corner of his mouth onto the desk.

'We just stole it, is all.'

'Stole it?'

'*Stole* it. We was out lookin' for something – Ali K and me – and then we headed up through the back lane of Pender there.'

'The south lane.'

He shrugged like it didn't matter. 'Yeah, I guess. We cut into one of them underground parkades, and then we heard this motor running. So we turned the corner and looked up, and there it was – this white van someone left running. One of the back doors was open. Like they was loading it or something.'

'And then?'

'Well, we just ran up to it and saw no one was there, so we slammed the back door and hopped in each side and drove it out of the underground.' He stopped speaking, took in a long breath. 'Underground was dark. Wasn't till we got out on Georgia we realised there was those bodies in the back. And then – just like that – there was these cops behind us, and we just kinda panicked. We dumped the van and ran outta there, ran straight through the projects.'

Striker said nothing as he thought it over. The story made sense – Chinese Tony was a prominent car thief, and vans were his MO – but the odds of finding that van were bullshit. Striker fixed him with his best cold look.

'One more lie and you go right back to the tank.'

'I told you—'

'You didn't just happen across that van and steal it, Tony, someone hired you to do it. Who?'

'I told you—'

Striker stood up. 'Let's go. Back to Cell 9.'

'They'll kill me if I tell!'

Striker said nothing. He stood by the door and studied Chinese Tony. The man looked frail, terrified. He was shaking so hard, the chair rattled against the floor. Striker leaned forward, down to Chinese Tony's eye-level. 'No one will ever know but you and me.'

Tony looked down, his lips trembled.

'I promise you that,' Striker added.

Chinese Tony wiped his eyes with the sleeve of his prison gear, then let out something between a laugh and a cry.

'Kim Pham,' he finally got out.

The name was familiar to Striker, and then he recalled – Kim Pham, the manager of the restaurant that owned the van.

Striker watched Tony's face for any change in expression as he asked, 'Who the hell is Kim Pham?'

'He's their leader.'

'Whose leader? Leader of what?'

'The Shadow Dragons.'

Striker stopped. All at once, Patricia Kwan's nonsensical words came back to him: '. . . the house was filled with dragons . . .' He let it hang in the back of his mind.

'This Kim Pham,' he said. 'Did he contact you directly?'

Tony shrugged. 'Well, no, not directly. He usually does. But not this time.'

'Then how? Who?'

'Some woman. Never heard her voice before. Left a message on my cell that they needed me again. Said it was urgent. But I never saw her, never got no name or nothing. Just did what I was told. Like I always do.'

'Why did she hire you?'

Tony shrugged again. 'To get rid of the van, to dump it in the river.'

'Did you know why?'

'I never knew there was gonna be any bodies inside, that's for sure. I thought it was for insurance stuff.'

Striker thought about it, went over the timing and connections. If Chinese Tony had done his job right, the bodies would have ended up in the bottom of the Fraser River. Same place as where they'd fished out Que Wong.

'What else can you tell me?' he said.

'That's all I know.'

'Should we revisit Cell 9?'

'That's all I know, man! Honest. There's nothing else, they don't tell me nothing. All I ever get is cash up front from one of their drop-off guys and then I never hear from them till they need me again.'

Striker studied the man, saw his fear, believed him.

He escorted Chinese Tony to an empty cell in Cell Block 2, then went outside and retrieved his gun from the locker.

It was time to pay a visit to the Fortune Happy restaurant.

Sixty-Three

The Golden Dragon Lounge was packed with the noon rush, so Red Mask circled around the large tinted-glass windows to the back lane, where the busboys were throwing out the trash. One of them, a young boy named Gock, recognised him.

Red Mask stopped him with a soft word. 'Boy. You know my face?'

'Yes, sir, I do.'

'This is good. I must speak with Sheung Fa. Ask him to hold tea with me.'

The boy nodded and ran inside. Five minutes later, he returned and motioned for Red Mask to follow. He led him through the kitchen area, down a long hallway, then up another series of stairs until they reached a large wooden door.

'He waits for you inside.'

When the boy turned to leave, he fled more than walked. Red Mask watched him go until he had descended the stairs and was no longer in view. Then he turned and entered Sheung Fa's office.

Inside, the air was overly warm. Sheung Fa sat behind a desk made from a whitish wood Red Mask had not seen in twenty years. Out of respect, he bowed – as low as his body would allow in his injured state – and he held it until Sheung Fa told him otherwise in his gentle but commanding tone.

'Stand freely.'

Sheung Fa's face had changed since he had last seen him. The differences were almost imperceptible, but there was enough to show that no man escaped time. Not even Sheung Fa. His dark eyes stuck out against the silver of his recently-cut hair, and his goatee and moustache were freshly trimmed to match. Everything about Sheung Fa's appearance was proper, professional, and exemplified great care.

'Come forward,' he said.

Sheung Fa spoke in English, for their dialects were too far apart. He gestured for Red Mask to sit in the chair opposite him, and Red Mask did as ordered. Sheung Fa then picked up the teapot and poured black tea. He did so slowly, as if the pouring of the tea was more a ceremony than a simple task.

Red Mask watched the steam rise from white china mugs. He waited for Sheung Fa to pick up his own cup, then followed suit. The tea was hot and tasted wonderful, if a little bitter. It was the first thing to pass his lips in twenty-four hours.

'Thank you, *Dai Lo*. For tea and time.'

Sheung Fa put down his cup. 'You are man of middle age now, so far from the youth I remember of years gone by. How is your father?'

Red Mask looked down. 'Father is good. But time thins him.'

'Time, or the past?'

'I think both.' He looked up again. 'You and I not speak for years, *Dai Lo*, but never do I forget all you do for me in past.'

Sheung Fa smiled, but there was sadness in his eyes. 'You were but a boy then, a child. You would not have made it.' For a moment, Sheung Fa turned his head and looked at the triangular pennant hanging in the corner of the room, the bright fiery red standing out against the black wood walls. When he spoke again, his voice was reserved, but strong. 'I do not think of the past much these days. There has been enough pain. It is not good to allow it back.'

Then Sheung Fa's pale face darkened. 'I know of what transpires, and I am sorry for your loss. But your actions have caused great concern.'

'I act only necessary.'

'Do you? Was killing Pham a necessity? This has caused us much trouble and much work. We have taken action and disposed of the body. But the other three you left behind have been found, and they will surely be a problem.'

Red Mask met Sheung Fa's stare. Explained. 'Pham tried to end my life. To put fault at my feet. The plan, *Dai Lo*, was not mine, but Pham's.'

'And the responsibility?'

Red Mask looked down. 'This is mine alone.'

Sheung Fa finished his tea, breathed out slowly. 'Your honesty is refreshing.'

'When Pham and the doctor attack, I react.'

Sheung Fa leaned forward and steepled his fingers. He thought in silence for a long moment before speaking. 'The concern comes not from this office. It comes from higher up. Overseas.'

Red Mask felt his mouth go dry. '*Shan Chu?*'

Sheung Fa nodded. 'I will speak with him on your behalf. I will try to steer him towards right thoughts. But this is all I can promise.'

'Thank you, *Dai Lo*.'

Sheung Fa stood. He was taller than Red Mask remembered, nearly six feet, and slender. He rounded the table. When Red Mask started to bow, Sheung Fa stopped him with a soft hand. He pulled Red Mask close and gave him a long hug. 'It is good

to see you again, little one. Now tell me: how many can identify you?'

Red Mask pulled away from the contact. 'There are two.'

'And that is all?'

'Yes, *Dai Lo*.'

'And one is left from your mission?'

'Yes.'

Sheung Fa nodded. 'It is as we thought. These three will be
Shan Chu's greatest concern.' He handed Red Mask a thin
manila envelope.

Red Mask opened it and pulled out five pages. Four were
written information on Homicide Detective Jacob Striker; the
last was a photocopied picture of the man.

'Is this correct?' Sheung Fa asked.

'It is him.'

'The better you know your enemy, the greater your chance of
success.'

'Success?'

'It is a pivotal time, little one. Follow the path and there yet
may be a meeting for you with Shan Chu.'

Red Mask smiled, for the message was clear.

There was still hope. A new life for him, in Macau.

All it would take to get there was three more kills.

Sixty-Four

The Man with the Bamboo Spine remained standing behind the closed door until Sheung Fa told him to enter the office. He opened the door and stepped inside. The air was warm and smelled of black tea. Behind the large teak desk, Sheung Fa sat with his hands folded on the blotter.

The Man with the Bamboo Spine approached the desk, stood there silently, waited. He felt the draught of the air conditioner on his back, heard the ruckus of the patrons in the lounge, and smelled the tea and the sage scent of burned incense.

And still, he waited.

It wasn't until almost five minutes had passed – a total of ten since Red Mask had departed – that Sheung Fa finally spoke in his native tongue of Cantonese, a language the Man with the Bamboo Spine fully understood.

'Be his shadow,' Sheung Fa said.

'Yes.'

'Assist him.'

'Assist?'

'*Assist*. But be discreet.'

'Until?'

'Until instructed otherwise.'

The Man with the Bamboo Spine nodded, signalling his

understanding of the instructions, as confusing and unexpected as they were. He left Sheung Fa's office, closed the door behind him and lumbered through the smoky darkness of Golden Dragon Lounge into the grey light of the outside world.

Assist. It was exactly what he would do.

Until instructed otherwise.

Sixty-Five

Striker and Felicia reconnected back at 312 Headquarters, got into their cruiser, then drove down Gore Street in one car. They parked a block away from the Fortune Happy Restaurant, at the corner of Gore and Pender – the crime scene of the van and three bodies.

Ident had already been on scene and left. The yellow tape had been taken down. The van had been towed to the police garage with the bodies still inside. Soon they would be transported to the morgue for autopsy.

Now it was just an empty intersection.

Felicia ran the name Kim Pham in the computer. To Striker's surprise, the guy was a no-hit, meaning he had no history, criminal or otherwise.

'Play with the dates of birth,' he told Felicia, and she did.

When something came back, she said, sounding displeased, 'Just a driver's licence. Maybe the name is an alias.'

Striker doubted that. Kim Pham owned a BC Drivers Licence, his name was listed as the primary operator on the insurance papers, and Chinese Tony had been terrified of the man because he was leader of the Shadow Dragons – a gang Striker had never heard of. He turned in his seat to look at Felicia.

'You ever hear of the Shadow Dragons?'

'They a Chinese version of the Jonas Brothers?'

Striker smiled. 'Not quite.' He filled her in on his dealings with Chinese Tony and told her what he'd learned about the existence of a Shadow Dragons gang as they headed for the Fortune Happy restaurant.

Once on scene, it didn't take long for them to get the run-around. A Chinese lady in a black silky dress with red Chinese characters sewn into it, who looked part dragon herself, used her small, lithe body to block Striker's way. The boldness of her stance gave him little doubt she held power of some kind among her peers.

Striker flashed the badge. 'Where is Kim Pham?'

'Kim Pham out. He away. Long time.'

'Where?'

'He go to Hong Kong. Father very sick. Very ill. Might die.'

'When will he be back?'

'Not know. He not work for very long time. On holiday. Holiday very much.'

Striker was getting tired of the run-around. 'Then who are you? What do you do here exactly?'

'I hostess. I restaurant hostess.'

'But *who* are you?'

'I hostess. I fill in.'

Striker had had enough of the charade. 'I want ID,' he told her.

She gave him a stubborn look, then returned to the hostess podium and came back with her wallet. She handed him several documents, including her immigration papers.

Striker sorted through it all. 'Annie Ting,' he said.

'I return to work,' she said.

'No, you stay with us. We'll be needing you for a while. But you can put your wallet back.'

She appeared less than happy, but did as told.

While she was gone, Striker turned to Felicia and smiled. 'I bet if you ask for the special menu you can order Annie-Ting.'

She grinned, and the hostess soon returned. Striker told her to take them around the restaurant. She did so, making no attempt to hide her reluctance.

The tour was brief. Three large dining areas all coloured in gold and red, with white-clothed round tables and black high-backed chairs. A fourth dining area was closed off for private parties, though it looked very much the same as the previous three.

Annie Ting led them on. 'The kitchen,' she said, and gave a half-hearted swing of her hand to show them.

She moved on, Striker did not. He stood at the entranceway to the kitchen, which was covered by nothing but a red hanging sash, and breathed in the smell of lemon and chicken and garlic and green onions. It smelled good. Made his stomach rumble. He realised how long it had been since they'd eaten.

'Over here is office,' Annie Ting said. 'This way, this way here.'

But Striker still did not move. He was looking at an unmarked door that sat just between the kitchen and pantry. It was painted black and had scuff marks in the bottom.

'What's in there?'

'Pantry. Office this way, this way here.'

'I thought that was the pantry,' Striker said, and pointed to the other side of the kitchen.

'Have two. Need much. Very busy restaurant. Office this way.'

Striker paid her no heed. He glanced at Felicia, and when she gave him a nod, he stepped up to the door and turned the knob. It was locked, didn't budge. He listened, and could hear clatter on the other side. He turned back to Annie Ting, saw the hardness of her stare, and knew they had found something.

'Always lock the pantry?'

'Door is broken, we never use.'

'Well, you can either fix the broken door and let us in there, or we can use other methods.'

'Door broken,' she said again.

Striker stepped forward and landed one hard kick alongside the door knob. The door burst inwards, taking a chunk of frame with it and filling the kitchen with the sound of snapping wood. On the other side of the door was a short hallway, leading back to another series of rooms.

'Stop, stop!' the hostess said.

'Big pantry.'

'You need warrant!'

Striker heard Felicia tell the woman to shut up as they walked down the hall. They'd barely gotten ten feet when the air thickened with smoke, and the smell of whisky and other liquor filled the air. At the end of the hallway was another sash. When Striker neared it, he could hear chatter and a clattering noise, like pebbles being dropped on hardwood. He knew what it was immediately.

Pai Gow tiles.

They'd walked into a backdoor gambling ring. Nothing out of the ordinary for Chinatown.

He pushed through the red sash and stepped into a large room with many tables full of gamblers. Some were older, most were middle-aged, but all were Asian. Looked fresh off the boat. Cantonese filled the air, loud and excited tones. Serving boys scurried from table to table, and a few older gentlemen in tuxedos served whiskys and cognacs. At the far end, two large men in golden suits eyed him warily but did not approach.

Striker turned to Felicia. 'Those suits look familiar?' he asked.

'Same as the men in the back of the van.'

He nodded. 'Keep an eye on them and the dragon lady while I look around.'

The hostess, Annie Ting, narrowed her eyes at the comment. 'You need warrant!' she said again.

Striker ignored her. He walked in between the tables, and some of the guests stopped gambling and looked at him suspiciously, as if they had just realised that a white guy had invaded their Chinese gambling den. Others gave him indifferent glances and made more bets.

At the right end of the room, a narrow stairway descended. Striker approached it, stared down. At the bottom was a closed door. He motioned to Felicia that he was going to check it out.

The stairs were wood and they creaked under the weight of his boots. When he reached the alcove, it was dark, the only light bulb in the hall being burned out. The sign on the door was readable and in English.

KEEP OUT.

Simple, but effective – for those who weren't police.

Striker opened the door, stepped inside the room, and was bathed by fluorescent light. The room was long and rectangular. It might have once been an office, or a meeting room. It was difficult to tell because it had been completely gutted, and recently. The carpet was torn up, and the walls were painted, though not with paint but grey primer. Striker rubbed his hand across the wall and felt a few rough areas where the filler had not been properly sanded.

A rush remodelling job. There had to be a reason.

He walked through the room, studying the floors and walls, and finding nothing of interest. When he turned back to the doorway and was about to exit, something caught his eye.

He looked up at the hard-foam ceiling tiles. Each square was a perfect twelve-by-twelve inches and mottled with black specks. The nearest tile had a small hole in it, at the far edge, near the doorframe. At first glance it looked to be part of the design, but this hole was larger than the others, and it went in at an angle.

Striker pulled over a pair of paint cans, stood on them, took a better look, and knew what he had found. It was a bullet-hole. And given the connection of the dead men in the van and the information he'd gotten from Chinese Tony, there was little doubt what this place had been.

A murder room.

Sixty-Six

Over an hour later, at just past one o'clock, Striker and Felicia dropped by Forensic Audio, obtained a hard-disc copy of the audio feed from Ich, and headed for Worldwide Translation Services. Translating the feed was their next best bet because things at the Fortune Happy Restaurant weren't going so well.

Annie Ting wasn't saying anything, and neither were any of the people who worked there. Striker had expected as much. He lodged everyone in jail while Ident processed the scene.

It was the best strategy possible. Sometimes a few hours in jail made people talk. And when it didn't, some hard forensic evidence often did the trick. Regardless, they were stuck in another waiting game, and that was a game Striker didn't want to play.

They reached the corner of Grant and Commercial, where Worldwide Translation Services was located. It was a place Striker was familiar with, having been here a dozen or so times over the years, when the clumsy and inadequate translation people of the police departments failed them – which was too damn often.

Striker sat in the waiting room, the latest disturbing events circulating in his head. He turned to Felicia. 'You call the hospital again?'

She nodded. 'Yeah, no change with Patricia Kwan. Dr

Aussie's gonna call us back when he has any information.' She pulled a Caramilk bar from her jacket pocket.

Striker stared at the chocolate bar. 'Jesus, do you eat anything else?'

'Yeah, Snickers.' She broke off a piece and dropped it in his hand. 'Have some. If things keep going the way they are now, it might be the only nourishment you're going to get today. Besides,' she smiled wryly. 'I've kept it close to my heart for you.'

Striker smiled back at the comment, and popped a Caramilk square into his mouth. He wasn't the chocolate fiend Felicia was, but it was the only thing he'd eaten today since whatever it was he'd had for breakfast. He let the chocolate melt in his mouth and scratched at his face. He hadn't shaved for two days now and the growth was bugging him. He let out a frustrated sound and muttered, 'Any news on the Amber Alert?'

'No, the Kwan girl is still missing. But we've called every relative she's got, and have every jurisdiction looking for her.'

'We find a cell number for her?'

Felicia made a face. 'She's on a prepaid and it's run out. Found the phone in her bedroom.'

Striker said nothing, just groaned.

'Relax, Jacob. This is what kills you – stressing about what you can't control. We're here to translate the disc. Focus on that until we can do better.' She offered him another piece of chocolate. When he declined, she grinned. 'It's a substitute for sex, you know.'

'If I used it for that, I'd be three hundred pounds.'

Magui Yagata opened the office door and entered the waiting room. Striker looked her over: she was in her late fifties, and the lines around her eyes and lips showed it. She was a hard-looking woman, and her mannerisms were no different.

Before Striker could even say hi, she reached out and grabbed the disc from his hands.

'Blu-ray, huh?' She snorted. 'You're a lucky man, we just got a new reader for this type of media; some asshole broke the last one.'

'Nice to see you too, Magui. How's life treating you?'

'Like a used condom. Follow me, both of you.'

Magui turned and left the room, expecting them to follow. Felicia gave Striker a look as if to say, *What's up her ass?* and he just shrugged.

That was Magui for you.

They followed her into the adjoining room. It was another featureless office – tables, chairs, a video unit. Striker and Felicia took a seat at the table and waited as Magui looked at her watch and frowned, as if she had other pressing matters to attend to, matters much more important than this one. She turned on the television, loaded the disc, hit play.

And all at once, Striker was watching the shooting again.

What struck him as odd this time was his own reaction – it was no different from any of the other times he'd seen the footage. By now, after seeing it so many times, he'd expected its impact to have lessened, at least a little.

But no, it was just as devastating.

When the video was finally over, he unclenched his fingers and looked at Magui. The scorn on her face had been wiped away, but it was not replaced by shock or pity or even terror. A look of dark intrigue covered her face, ugly as a birthmark. Without saying a word, she got up and fiddled with the Blu-ray player.

Felicia leaned into him and whispered, 'This bitch gives me the creeps.'

Striker nodded. 'Maybe so, but we need her – she speaks

eleven languages, for Christ's sake.' He looked back at Magui, and got down to business.

'Can you tell me what they're saying, or not?' he asked.

'Don't be absurd. Of course I can.' Magui reset the disc and replayed the feed. When they reached the point where the gunmen came face to face, just prior to dragging out and killing the boy dressed as the Joker, they began to talk. Magui translated.

'Target One and Target Two eliminated. Target Four not located.'

Striker listened to the words. '*Target?*'

'This is the most correct translation.'

Striker retreated into himself, let the words sink in. Target. The word disturbed him, not because of the meaning, but because of the context; it had been used with purpose, instead of 'she' or 'he' or any real names. There was only one reason to do this, and that was to dehumanize the victims and desensitise the gunmen. Even worse, it wasn't the language of some sociopathic students or crazed murderers. It was the language of mercenaries. Soldiers of Fortune. Pros.

It was goddam *military* speak.

Striker looked at Felicia, who had stopped eating her Caramilk bar. She caught his stare, bit her lip.

'This is not good,' she said.

'Couldn't be much worse.'

Magui spoke loudly, cutting them both off. 'The greater concern,' she said, 'is not what they are saying, but how they are saying it.' When Striker didn't respond and just waited for more information, she continued: 'They're speaking *Khmer*.'

Felicia shrugged. 'Which is?'

'Well, essentially, it's Cambodian. But the words are more clipped and more formal than that of the modern-day society.

Which would suggest that these two men grew up in the seventies – a very bad time for that country. Mass murder. A full-out genocide.' She sat down in one of the office chairs, swivelled to face them. 'You ever hear of the Killing Fields?'

Striker nodded. 'You're talking about Pol Pot's regime.'

'That is exactly what I mean.' She gestured towards the two masked gunmen on the feed. 'You may well have uncovered someone who was a part of that regime – or even worse, a survivor of it.'

Felicia, who had remained patiently holding her tongue, finally leaned closer to Striker and spoke up. 'Okay, forgive my ignorance here and fill me in – who the hell is Pol Pot?'

Striker looked at her like she was crazy. 'He was a dictator, Felicia. One of the worst the world has ever seen. Killed three million people.' Striker gave a deep sigh then continued, 'Pol Pot turned children into soldiers. Made them kill their parents. Ordinary women and children were starved and raped and tortured into giving false confessions. Almost a quarter of Cambodia's entire population died because of his regime.'

Striker looked back at the image of Red Mask displayed on the monitor and recalled the eyes of the gunman. So dark. So cold. So *dead*. When he saw the morbid curiosity in Felicia's eyes, he didn't want to say the words, as if speaking them might make it true.

But she had to know it.

'We're talking about the *Khmer Rouge*.'

Sixty-Seven

The midday sun ruled the sky, one giant ball of white flame. It gleamed off the steel gates of St Paul's Hospital and glinted off the damp red brick of the building.

Red Mask saw this spectacle, and all at once, he reared at the memories the image brought back. Reared so hard, he almost dropped the jar he was holding, and that most certainly would have been a great – perhaps deadly – mistake.

His body trembled. He wavered on the hospital steps, recollecting the images of Section 21. They were horrific. And he could not understand why they preoccupied his mind. He had not thought of that dark place in years. In most ways, the two buildings were entirely different. Style, size, even colour.

But something took him back to the time when he was eight years old. The worst time of his life. And then, without searching, he found the answer. It was the sun, beating down upon him with the same blinding white intensity it had every single day of the Angkors' occupation of Cambodia.

Beating down upon his father as he toiled in the Killing Fields fourteen hours a day, his frail accountant's hands cracked and bleeding, under the watchful eye of machine-gun guards.

Beating down upon his mother as she was hog-tied and raped for eleven days before the guards got bored and slit her throat.

Beating down on him and the other children as they were thrown together into that dusty pit where there was no food or water or safety from the guards.

Beating down upon them all with as much mercy as the Angkor offered.

Which was none.

Red Mask felt his body wilting from the cruelty of his thoughts. Where were these memories coming from? He was a man now, not some eight-year-old child – not Child 157. That boy had died long ago.

'The spirits,' he found himself saying. For there could be no other reason.

He closed his mind and willed his feet to move. And though his body listened, his mind was not as obedient. With every step, the memories of that time became clearer. The images more vivid.

Until he relived the nightmare all over again.

And Mother was screaming.

Screaming.

Screaming . . .

Her ungodly cries filled the camp all night. Like the other nights, there was much laughter from the guards – cruel reptilian sounds – as Mother cried out for her ancestors to save her, or at the very least deliver her quickly into death. But the hours passed and her cries went unanswered.

Child 157 balled up in his cell, in uneven rows with the other children. Some of them writhed in hunger, some in pain. Others had not moved for a very long time. He barely noticed them; Mother was all that mattered. Her voice was everything. He tried to drown out her cries, to pretend he had no knowledge of what was happening to her. But he knew. He always knew.

At day's end, when the guard entered to pour broth, Child 157 was quick to steal the key from the ring the man so lazily left hanging on the wall. The moment the guard finished his duties, Child 157 began prying the thin flesh of his ankle out of the shackle that bound him to the floor.

It was a slow and agonising task.

By the time he freed his leg, it was deep into the night, and even later before the pain subsided enough that he could walk on it. His bloodied foot was now a lump of ragged flesh, yet he limped to the door, unlocked it, and slipped outside.

He had no plan. No training. Not even any knowledge of the camp layout.

But he also had no choice.

Father was gone, for many days now. Too many to count. Taken to the Killing Fields, from which no one returned. Sisters Du and Hoc were dead, their necks broken with steel bars so the guards could save bullets. The only ones left were himself and Tran – Child 158 – and somewhere in the east building with the other infants was baby Loc.

Child 157 knew the truth. He was the eldest. Only he could save Mother.

The night was hot and black. Child 157 limped across the camp, with only the moon as a guide. He was only eight years old, and small for a boy. 'A field mouse', as Father often called him. The runt of the litter. He had barely gotten halfway across the camp when One-tooth caught him cutting in between the sacks of rice.

'Rule-breaker, rule-breaker,' the guard sang, his voice thick with cruelty. He pounced on Child 157 and dragged him out by his hair. He pulled him close, smiled. 'You want to see much, then I will show you much, rule-breaker. Show you much, yes.'

Child 157 tried to break free of his grip, but that only

angered One-tooth, who rose up and screamed in his face. Beat him down into the dirt. Beat him until he tasted his own blood and could not move. Beat him until One-tooth's fists grew tired.

One-tooth then called the other guards, and together, they dragged him to the hollowed grounds east of the main building. Where the grass was always red and the earth was soft and mushy.

In the centre of the hollow stood the Nail Tree – a thick-trunked, knobby tree that was almost dead. Its branches had been sawn off and large nails driven into the bark. At the base of the tree were many bones.

The remains of the little ones.

'We have a show for you,' One-tooth told him.

And before Child 157 understood the meaning of One-tooth's words, two of the other guards came out of the nearest building. They carried with them a small sack. At first he thought it rice, or grain – maybe they were going to eat in front of him and laugh at his starvation. But then a tiny arm dangled out, and he realised with horror:

'Baby Loc!'

Child 157 rose up. He struggled to free himself, desperately, with all the strength he owned, but One-tooth held him in place with little effort.

'Release me, RELEASE ME!' He bent his head down and bit One-tooth on the hand as hard as he could, his teeth tearing into the flesh and drawing blood; when the guard screamed and let go of him, he raced for Baby Loc.

But he did not get far.

One of the other guards knocked him down, and before he could stand back up, One-tooth was on him, pinning him down in the grass, holding him firmly – the weight of a grown man's body on that of an eight-year-old child's.

He was helpless.

One-tooth yanked his head back, forcing him to look at the Nail Tree.

'Bye, bye,' One-tooth sang. 'Bye bye, Baby Loc.'

He nodded to the two guards. One of them undraped the sack, then grabbed hold of the infant by both his legs. Child 157 screamed and struggled to get up, but One-tooth held him down firmly, laughing at his weakness.

Baby Loc was crying now, reaching out for Mother, but finding nothing. The guard holding Baby Loc's ankles swung him around like a piece of wood, his head flying towards the Nail Tree. And there was a terrible crunch.

Child 157 screamed for Baby Loc. It did nothing.

The guard holding baby Loc swung him again. And again. And again. *Crunch, crunch, CRUNCH.*

The sound of Baby Loc hitting the Nail Tree stayed in Child 157's head like a bad ghost. It would never leave him. When at last One-tooth climbed off of him, something snapped inside Child 157's mind. Like a twig that could never be whole again. The pain was gone, the fear was gone. Everything was gone – replaced by a complete and total numbness.

It was all he knew.

Sixty-Eight

Striker and Felicia left Worldwide Translation Services and climbed into the cruiser. Striker sat behind the wheel, his mind working in overdrive, searching for a connection between a group of suburban kids from a sleepy Dunbar school, the Shadow Dragon gangsters, and the Khmer Rouge war which was thirty years over and two thousand miles away.

He found none. Their best lead now was Patricia Kwan – who lay unconscious in the hospital. Doctor or no doctor, weak or strong, it did not matter. Patricia Kwan was the only chance they had of finding her missing daughter.

She would have to be woken up again.

'Saint Paul's,' Striker said. 'You drive.'

They switched places, and Felicia drove west on First Avenue. As they went, Striker logged onto the laptop, then initiated PRIME, the report programme all the municipal forces had adopted ten years earlier. Every Patrol call written was in this database, and it was one more check box on his list.

Felicia switched to the fast lane, looked over at him. 'Any theories?'

Striker pulled out his notebook and set it down on his lap. 'I'm running every damn name we got through the patrol database. See if we can get even a weak connection. Right now I'd be happy with anything.'

Striker got to work. He typed in the names of all four kids involved – the ones that were known targets: Conrad MacMillan, Chantelle O'Riley, Tina Chow, and the still-missing Riku Kwan. A few minutes later, he deflated.

'Nothing,' he said quietly. 'Jesus Christ, not a one.'

Felicia looked over. 'What do you mean, not one?'

'I mean they're not even in the system as entities. Goddam zilch.'

It was frustrating. Not one of the kids had a youth record, or any criminal history in any of the information systems. Not one was even listed as a Witness or a Property Rep, or even a Person of Interest, much less a Suspect Chargeable. The closest matches Striker could find were Patricia Kwan and Archibald MacMillan – the parents of Riku and Conrad. Kwan, as they now knew, was a Vancouver cop. Her entity was automatically entered into the system upon hire date. And Archibald MacMillan was a fireman, so he was listed the same way.

Striker told this to Felicia.

'What hall is Archie at?' she asked.

Striker scoured through the report. 'Hall Eleven. Got a notation here in the remarks field – says he's specialised. HAZMAT.' Striker looked over at Felicia. 'They deal with chemical spills, explosive substances, meth labs, unknown terrorist devices – all that shit.'

Felicia turned south on Main. 'I know what HAZMAT is, Striker. Christ Almighty, how junior do you think I am?'

'Stands for Hazardous Materials.'

She peered at him out of the corner of her eye. 'You're such a shit. Any of the other parents come up?'

He focused back on the computer screen, scanned through the electronic pages. 'No, not that I can see. The only Chows listed are all low scores, and there isn't even an O'Riley on file.' He used the touch-pad to close the extra windows, bringing him back to his original request of Archibald MacMillan. 'Interesting though. Hall Eleven is at Victoria and Second – that's District Two.'

'What's interesting about that?'

'Both Archibald MacMillan and Patricia Kwan work in District Two, yet they live in Dunbar. And both their kids go to the same school.'

Felicia shrugged as if to say, *So?* 'A lot of cops and firemen live in Dunbar,' she said. 'It's a good family place. Try to cross reference them.'

Striker read through their histories. There was a lot.

Patricia Kwan had written over two hundred calls the past year. Pretty standard for a patrol cop. Everything from Break & Enters to Homicides. Archibald MacMillan had been to sixty-three calls, most of which were gas leaks and car accidents.

Striker cross-referenced their names. 'Interesting . . .' he said.

'What you got?' Felicia asked.

'Nothing astounding, but they've only been to one call together. Just a few months back, in fact. A house on Pandora Street, Seventeen Hundred block.'

'That's the industrial area,' Felicia noted. 'What kind of file is it?'

He clicked on the link and waited until the incident number popped up.

'Okay, there's actually two calls here,' he said, 'and they're linked. First one came in as a Suspicious Circumstance, then later the same night, it was linked to an Arson call at the same address.' He queried the number and got back a generic CAD call with only the address and time listed. There was nothing in the remarks field. Not even a name. Frustrated, he ran the incident number for a report and got back a three-word message.

'Event Not Found,' he said. Meaning it was either non-existent or locked for security reasons.

'Any badge number associated?' Felicia asked.

'Nothing.'

Striker called Info, asked if they could bring up the report. But the same message came back to them as well. Irritated, he closed the CAD call.

'I want to see that house on Pandora,' he said.

'It'll have to wait,' Felicia told him. 'We're here.'

Striker looked up from the laptop screen and saw the tall steel gates and old red brick of the hospital before him.

They had reached St Paul's.

Sixty-Nine

Red Mask stood in the east wing of St Paul's Hospital and looked through the windowed door that led into the Critical Care Unit. In there was Patricia Kwan.

His next target.

He was dressed in janitor's clothes, which he'd taken off the old man he'd killed in the next wing. He also wore latex gloves – so he would leave no prints – and a gown overtop his clothing. With only one good arm, the baggy gown hampered him in reaching his pistol, but the uniform was necessary to enter the CCU. So he left the back straps loose.

It was the best he could do.

On the other side of the doorway, Patricia Kwan's room was under guard. Red Mask had expected no different. A young cop, about twenty-five years old, leaned on the doorframe. He looked bored. With the exception of the nurses and orderlies who roamed the walkways, no one else was around.

And this was to Red Mask's benefit.

He carried the jar and duct tape in his left hand. The weight of his tools was not much, minimal really, but the stress it put on his shoulder was alarming. He closed his mind to the pain and focused on the task at hand.

In his right hand, he carried a small oxygen tank, one he'd stolen from the cancer ward. He had taken two of them, and purposely left one by the CCU entrance doors. The tanks were pressurised and heavy, about thirty pounds.

It would be more than enough.

He waited patiently for the nurse to leave, then swiped the keypad with the janitor's access card and entered the Critical Care Unit. He looked at nothing as he made his way down the corridor, just kept his eyes straight ahead, as if he were a tired man finishing his shift. When he neared the cop, he glanced left. Saw that the man wasn't paying attention.

It was the only opening he needed.

Mustering as much strength as his shoulder would allow, he swung the oxygen canister; the cop spotted the movement and raised his arms – but the reaction came far too late. The oxygen tank impacted with his face, smashing his head into the door and breaking his nose. He dropped to the floor, as limp as rice noodles.

Red Mask took no chances. He drove the tank into the cop's face one more time, then opened up Patricia Kwan's door and scanned the room. When he saw no one but the woman on the bed inside the room, confidence filled him. He placed the jar and tape down on the nearest counter, then set the oxygen tank down on the floor, just inside the doorway.

He dragged the cop inside and removed the man's pistol. He released the mag, racked the slide, and expelled the chambered bullet. Then he threw the Sig Sauer in the garbage can and dragged the cop into the washroom. When the door closed, he and Patricia Kwan were alone again.

It was time to get to work.

He grabbed the duct tape and jar and walked up to the bed. Patricia Kwan lay still under the blankets, locked between the raised chrome bed railings. It seemed so long ago that he had last seen her. How odd it felt.

And how wonderful.

Patricia's face was whiter than before. The skin now sagged around her cheeks. Her chest rose and fell in slow intervals. Tubes ran from her wrists and forearms to three different machines. One of them reminded Red Mask of the electric current machines the guards had used to obtain confessions in Section 21. The thought manifested dark emotions, and he killed them immediately.

Emotion was weakness.

The bed was too high. Red Mask lowered it with the electronic control, then leaned over Patricia Kwan. She sensed the movement, and her face tightened. Red Mask smiled.

He could bring her back to consciousness.

First he put on two pairs of latex gloves, then tore off a strip of duct tape. He placed it across her mouth, then grabbed her wounded shoulder and gave it a vigorous squeeze.

Patricia jolted like she'd been electrocuted. Her eyes opened. They scanned the room, stopped on him, and widened. She jerked under the sheets, and one of the machines made a high-pitched, beeping sound.

'Be still,' Red Mask ordered. He pointed to the tape covering her lips. 'I am removing tape. Understand –' he held up the jar of clear fluid '– this is *nitric acid*. Nothing more painful in world. You scream, I make you swallow.'

Patricia Kwan's eyes filled with terror. Tears spilled down her cheeks.

'Understand?'

She nodded slowly, and Red Mask peeled back the tape.

'Please,' her voice was weak, scratchy, 'I'll do anything. Anything you want. *Don't kill me.*'

Red Mask placed the jar on the bedside table, directly within Patricia's line of sight. 'I not lie to you, Patricia Kwan.

You will die. But you can go in pain or no pain – the choice is for you.'

Her response was a whisper: 'Please – God – why? Why are you doing this?'

Red Mask just looked at her and tried to analyse the twinge of emotion he was experiencing. Something was stirring inside of him, somewhere deep, a tickling sensation. Like a name he could not recall.

'You show great disrespect. That will not – *cannot* – be tolerated.' He gave her an odd look. 'Do you think no one would discover?'

Patricia Kwan's eyes took on a distant look. 'But I don't know what you're talking about. I'm innocent!'

'No one is innocent.'

Red Mask looked over at the clock. Already several minutes had passed. Soon the nurse would return. Seconds were valuable. He leaned forward, so that he was looking right down at her, and he suppressed the pain he felt, for there was no time for pain.

'I ask you one more time, Patricia Kwan.'

'Please, I—'

'Where is daughter? Where is Riku Kwan?'

Seventy

When the phone rang, Courtney was in the shower. She heard the rings, almost didn't bother with it, but then thought of Raine and wondered if she'd gone all the way with Que. With mango-scented soap dripping into her eyes, she slid the shower door to the side, hopped out, snagged a towel from the rack and scurried half-naked down the hall.

She snatched the phone up on the fifth ring – one before the machine picked up – and looked at the caller ID.

Quenton Wong.

She knew it was Raine and said, 'Jesus, I've been calling and calling you, like, forever. Why don't you pick up?'

'Sorry, Court. My cell crapped out.'

'I've been calling Que's, too.'

'Thing's a piece of junk. He dropped it in the tub once and it's constantly on the fritz. Sometimes it works, sometimes not.'

Raine stopped talking, and there was a moment of silence on the line. Finally, Courtney asked, 'Well? Did you do it?'

'He's . . . he's not here,' Raine said.

'Not there? Where are you?'

'At Que's friend's pad. You remember, that one we met when we saw Avatar? The one with the bad skin?'

'Oh yeah, Mr Creepy.'

Raine laughed at the name. 'Yeah, well, Mr Creepy has his own place. Up here on Adanac.'

'Is Que there?'

Raine made a sound somewhere between embarrassment and frustration. 'No one is. And Que hasn't come back all night. I dunno. Maybe he wasn't really that . . . into it.'

Courtney felt the water trailing down her legs and feet, forming a small pool on the hardwood floor of the den. She didn't care. 'God, are you kidding me? He was, like, so all over you at the restaurant. Something must have happened.'

'Like what?' Raine asked.

It was something Courtney hadn't really considered, and the thought bothered her because Que was either out with some other girl or he'd gotten into some kind of trouble and was probably in jail or something.

'Maybe he got drunk again and was sent to the drunk tank.'

Raine's tone turned defensive. 'He only did that once.'

'I'm just saying—'

'I know, I know. Look, Court, what you doing? Wanna come down and see me? I could use the company. All I been doing is powering through *Twilight*. It's good, but if I read any more, my eyes are gonna fall out. And besides, I sure as hell can't go home right now.'

'Why not?'

'You kidding? After staying out all night at Que's, I'm as good as grounded for the rest of the year. I got my Britney ticket, I got my dress. I ain't going home again till after the Parade of Lost Souls and the concert.' She paused, cleared her throat. 'Hey, it's almost two o'clock now. Parade starts in three hours – why don't you head down now and we'll start partying.'

Courtney thought of the two cops guarding her home. 'About that . . .' she began.

'I talked to Mandy and she said Bobby was asking about you.'

'Really?'

'Said he was gonna be in the park before the show started, just having a few drinks and stuff, wanted us to come down.'

Courtney closed her eyes, cursed Dad. It was so unfair. *He* was so unfair. Mom would never have held her back like this. She thought about the two cops positioned out front and back of the house and wondered if there was some way she could give them the slip. Maybe out the side window, over the fence through the neighbour's yard. Or even the other way through the park. There had to be a way.

'You coming?' Raine asked again

Courtney took down the address. 'Be there in an hour.' She said goodbye, hung up the phone, and stood with only the damp towel to protect her from the cold draughts of the house. Already, her body was chilled. She started back for the shower, stopped, covered herself up as best she could, and looked outside the front-room window.

No cop car was out there.

She turned around, stepped into the kitchen and stared into the back lane.

No cop car was there any more either.

'Strange,' she said, but counted her blessings. She hurried back for the shower and finished washing her hair. She had to get ready. There was a lot to do before the party started. A whole lot.

Raine was waiting for her

And so was Bobby Ryan.

Seventy-One

Striker and Felicia took the east wing elevator to the third floor of St Paul's Hospital. When they reached the locked entrance to the Critical Care Unit, Striker grabbed a gown from the bin and put it on. He tied the ends behind his back and looked around for a nurse. Moments later, the same nurse he'd dealt with last time came out of the staff lounge. He called her over and requested the doctor.

She furrowed her brow. 'He's on break.'

'This is a police matter.'

'It's the first break he's had in nine hours.'

'And we haven't had one in twelve. Get him. I wouldn't be asking if it wasn't crucial.'

'I guess I could try paging him.' She spoke the words with obvious reluctance, then walked down the hall without so much as another word.

Striker watched her go, then looked at Felicia. 'Is she getting him, or not?'

Felicia threw up her hands. 'This is bullshit. Wait here, I'll find one myself.' She marched down the south branch of the hallway, turned the corner, and disappeared from Striker's view.

With the nurse and Felicia gone, the interconnecting area of the hall was empty, and Striker was alone. He thought of

Courtney, as he'd been doing all day, and of the fight they'd had two nights ago.

The guilt, it was always the one thing he could count on.

He pulled out his BlackBerry, called home, got nothing. He tried calling her cell phone and got the machine. She was screening the calls, he knew. Avoiding him. Like she always did when she got pissed. He waited for the beep, and was about to leave a message when he peered through the windowed door into the Critical Care Unit and noticed something that bothered him.

The cop guarding Kwan's room was gone.

Striker snapped his cell closed. He took a quick look around for a nurse, doctor, janitor – anyone with a pass card to get him through the door – but found no one. The place was as devoid of life as a mausoleum. He got on his cell, called Dispatch and asked them to radio the cop who was guarding Kwan's room. He was put on hold for nearly two minutes, and when the dispatcher came back on the line, her voice sounded concerned.

'He's not responding.'

'Get units here now. Code Three.' Striker pocketed the phone and kicked open the door. The swipe receptacle snapped off the frame and a loud, high-pitched alarm filled the halls. Striker ignored it. He drew his Sig, ran thirty feet down the hall to Kwan's room, and threw open the door.

In the far corner of the room, Patricia Kwan lay on the bed. Standing to her left, his back to Striker, was one of the hospital janitors. The man was cleaning the array of hospital equipment that flanked Kwan's bed. Besides the missing cop who was supposed to be guarding the room, nothing seemed amiss.

Striker relaxed a little, let his gun fall to his side. 'Hey, man, have you seen the doctor?'

'On break. Come back ten minutes.' As the janitor spoke the

words, he glanced back over his shoulder, and Striker saw his eyes – those cold, dead eyes.

Red Mask.

'Don't fuckin' move!' he yelled, and raised his gun.

But Red Mask had already reacted. The gunman spun around, crouched, and took cover behind Patricia Kwan. He raised his gun over her bed and began shooting.

Bullets slammed into the wall behind Striker. He dropped low, took aim – and couldn't get a shot off, not without hitting Patricia Kwan, who still lay helpless in the hospital bed. Without cover, he was screwed. He scampered leftward across the room.

Red Mask remained hidden behind Kwan's bed. He pulled the trigger fast, in rapid fire – four shots, five, six, seven – and all of them punched into the wall to the far right of Striker.

Three feet from their intended target.

At first, when the bullets missed him by several feet, Striker counted his lucky stars. But then a cold feeling ran through him. He'd battled Red Mask twice now, and the gunman was no novice. He had displayed *exceptional* gun-fighting skills back at the high school and at the Kwan residence, where he had kept Striker pinned down in the foyer with suppressing fire.

There was no way his shots would be that far off their target.

Unless Striker was not his intended target.

Striker kept low and looked in that direction. What he spotted made his heart race – someone had left an oxygen tank directly beside the door, and the bullets were landing all around it.

If the tank got hit, it would damn near obliterate him.

Striker lunged to the washroom door, reefed it open, and spotted the dead cop inside. The sight of the body slowed him for a split second, and in that moment, one of Red Mask's bullets finally struck the oxygen tank.

The entire room shook with the boom.

One moment Striker was scrambling into the washroom; the next, a thunderous explosion filled his ears and he was sent flying forwards, arms wind-milling and body twisting, until he slammed hard into the toilet and wall. He dropped to the ground, landing half on top of the dead cop, half on the hard white floor tiles. A high-pitched ringing filled his ears, and yet everything was quiet, muffled.

The gun –

Where the fuck was his gun?

He spotted the Sig behind the toilet base. Snatched it up. Gun in hand, he climbed back to his feet, stepped out of the washroom, and fell sideways onto the ground.

The room was spinning. His equilibrium was all but gone.

He raised the gun and scanned the room, but saw no sign of Red Mask. Where the oxygen tank had been sitting a giant hole had been blasted into the wall, and the entire doorframe had been blown out in the process. The door lay flat in the middle of the hall.

But where was Red Mask?

Striker struggled to get to his feet. As he did so, his head pounded and his stomach tightened. He fought off the urge to puke, stumbled to what was left of the doorway, and glanced down one end of the hall.

Halfway down, he spotted Red Mask. The gunman was running, his pale green gown flapping behind him. When he reached the end, where Striker had kicked open the CCU doors, he stopped, spun about and opened fire.

Again, his bullets were way off the mark, and when Striker looked ten feet down the hall, he saw another oxygen tank. He ducked back into the recovery room, preparing himself for another explosion, but none came.

When the sound of the bullets ceased, Striker peered back into the hall. The oxygen tank was still there, but there was no sign of Red Mask.

Striker raised his pistol and entered the hall. He moved east down the corridor, keeping close to the wall, out of the centre line of fire. When he reached the doorway and entered the cross-section of diverging halls, he ran right into Felicia. She had her gun out. At the sight of him, a look of horror covered her face.

'Jacob, you're bleeding!'

He reached up with his free hand, touched his brow and felt the warm stickiness of fresh blood. He pulled his hand away, saw red.

'He's here. In a hospital gown. Red Mask.' Striker looked around. Felicia had come from the south, and he had followed from the west, so there were only two ways the gunman could have fled. He ordered Felicia to take the north while he searched east.

At the end of the hall, the door to the outside fire escape was ajar. Striker kicked it open and stepped outside. He looked down and found a discarded pale green gown and janitor clothing. But the rest of the staircase was empty. As was the alley below.

Red Mask was gone.

Striker reached for his cell phone to call for units to Burrard Street, then realised he'd lost it somewhere in the mayhem. No radio either. And with the time already passed and Red Mask nowhere in sight, Striker knew they had lost him.

Again.

He scanned the streets below and the buildings all around

him. Across the way, on the rooftop of the next building, a tall Asian man stood looking at him. He was thin, with overly long legs and arms, and his face looked tight and angled wrong, as if his skull was too big for his skin. He stared back at Striker, offering nothing. Not a wave, not a smile, not anything.

Striker called out to him. 'You see a guy run down these stairs?'

The man looked back, said nothing.

'You see him?' Striker asked again.

'No.'

Striker stepped back inside and slammed the fire-escape door closed. Dizziness overtook him. He leaned against the wall, felt a moment away from collapsing. He fought through the weakness, returned to the hallway and spotted Felicia. She gave him the thumbs-down gesture.

'No luck.'

'He went that way,' Striker said, and passed her by. She asked him something he couldn't make out, but he ignored her and hurried back down the hallway to Patricia Kwan's room. As he marched through the blown-apart doorway, he heard agonised sounds coming from the bed.

What he saw took his breath away.

Felicia entered the room just behind him. She saw Patricia Kwan, stopped hard and put a hand over her mouth. 'Oh dear *Christ.*'

'Just get a fucking doctor.'

Striker ran to Patricia Kwan and reefed her out of the bed, so hard he tore the IVs from her arms. He dragged her limp body into the washroom, turned on the water and began flushing her face.

He prayed to God he wasn't too late.

Seventy-Two

Half an hour later, Striker sat on the examination table with his shirt off and an Intern assessing his head wound. His head was ringing and all sounds were dull, but what bothered him most was how weak he felt. Despite the lean muscle that covered his body, he felt thin, exposed. Had he not already been in such good shape, he would have broken down by now.

He wanted sleep.

The Intern was a young blonde girl. Striker allowed her to do her thing, all the while letting his own mind wander to the Critical Care Room, where Patricia Kwan was being treated. The thought of her made his head hurt – almost as much as his hands. He turned them over, studied his palms, and assessed the redness. When he made a fist, the skin felt swollen, like it might tear if he tightened his fingers too much.

The Intern took notice. 'Doctor Hart is the Specialist. He'll look at that. Should be here any minute.'

A knock came on the door, and Felicia entered the room. 'Hey.'

Striker looked at her, not wanting to know but having to ask. 'She okay?'

'Patricia?' Felicia shrugged. 'Gonna take some time to know.'

'What about her daughter?'

'No news on Riku Kwan either.' Felicia moved around the

Intern, sat down on the only chair the room offered, and pulled a Cadbury chocolate bar from her coat pocket. She caught Striker's stare and held it up for him to see. 'Hazelnut. Got it from the vending machine in the staff lounge.' She broke off a piece, leaned forward and stuffed it in his mouth. 'For the pain.'

Striker chewed. The chocolate tasted wonderful, and he realised how hungry he was.

The Intern tutted as she assessed the gash that ran horizontally across Striker's upper left brow. She wiped away some blood and said, 'This is going to require stitches. But first we'll have to get you in for some scans.'

Striker looked at her. 'Scans? What kinda scans?'

'CT. X-ray for sure.'

'How long will that take?'

'A few hours.'

'Absolutely not. Just stitch me up.'

'You hit your head pretty hard, Detective Striker,' the young woman began. 'I would really recommend—'

'Just stitch the goddam thing.'

The Intern frowned. 'Very well. Hold this against the wound.' She then turned and headed out of the room, presumably to get supplies.

As she left, the Specialist walked in. Dr Hart was a tall man, terribly thin, with a face so long and gaunt it made Ich look tanned and square-jawed. He offered only the briefest introduction to Striker and did not so much as look at Felicia. He turned Striker's hands over, asked him to make a fist, then nodded sagely.

'Minor burns,' he finally said. 'Chemical. Not quite second degree. You're lucky.'

'Don't feel so lucky,' Striker told him.

'Have you seen Ms Kwan?' The doctor spoke the words without emotion. 'Trust me, you're lucky.' He pulled out his prescription pad, scribbled on it. 'Get this cream, apply it several times a day for two weeks. It will help with the skin elasticity. The scarring will fade over months.'

Striker nodded. 'What the hell was it – battery acid?'

'No, much worse. It was nitric acid, and in a highly concentrated form. Corrosive on human flesh and extremely disfiguring.'

Felicia interrupted. 'Nitric acid? I've never heard of it.'

The doctor cast her a sideways glance, as if her comment was an annoyance. He finished working on Striker, then turned around and without another word, headed for the exit. When he reached the doorway, Striker called out to him.

'Hey, Doc, tell me . . . Patricia Kwan – is she going to make it?'

Dr Hart stopped in the doorway. He gave Striker a long, hard look and raised his hands in a *who-knows* gesture.

'Keep the stitches clean,' he said, and left the room.

After the Intern stitched the gash on Striker's brow, Striker and Felicia left the treatment room. Felicia walked slowly, and Striker loved her for it. Every muscle in his back felt bruised, deep down into his bones.

'How's your head?' she asked.

'Attached.'

'The doctor said you have a concussion.' She held up three fingers. 'How many fingers am I holding up?'

'Tuesday,' he said, and smiled.

'You're such a shit.'

They continued on. Striker steered Felicia away from the east hallway, where Patricia Kwan's room was located, and where there were now an entire slew of cops guarding and taping off the scene. No doubt Noodles would be there, or at least on his way. And Deputy Chief Laroche, too.

Striker was in no mood to talk to him.

They took the east elevator down to the first floor, then went outside through the north side exit. The sun was out, fighting through the cloud. The moment the hospital door closed behind them, Striker spotted the very people he was trying to avoid – Inspector Beasley and his diminutive leader, Deputy Chief Laroche.

They were parked out front.

Striker studied him through the windshield. The Deputy Chief's face looked tired, like he hadn't gotten his full ten hours' sleep last night, and there was plenty of agitation in his tight facial muscles. The sight should have made Striker smile, but he didn't. Oddly, he felt for the man.

Much as Striker hated to admit it, Laroche had his own stresses, too.

Laroche exited the White Whale, which was parked at the kerb. As he slammed the passenger door, he spotted Striker. Instantly, his dark eyes narrowed and his white face turned red.

'What the hell have you done now, Striker?' he asked.

Striker stopped walking. 'What have *I* done?'

'You're damn right, *you*. Everywhere you go I have to follow with more men and more crime scenes. We got six of them now, and that's just the primaries, set up from here to Dunbar. Department's running out of goddam crime-scene tape, and I'm out of men. You've effectively killed our budget for the entire year.'

Striker looked back, deadpan. 'Yes, I know you're very concerned about your budget, sir. And I'm sure Constable Kwan will be too – *if* she survives her injuries.'

Laroche's eyes narrowed. 'I'm not the one who put her in that position.'

'Of course not, because you don't do anything. Only thing you do well is your hair. You got one out of place, by the way.'

'Striker—'

'You know, Kwan might care about your budget, too. *If* she survives her injuries. And *if* we can find her daughter.'

'Don't be so—'

'Riku Kwan is still missing, by the way, in case you weren't aware of that. I know she's just a young girl and her safety doesn't rank up there with your fiscal matters, but I thought you should know.'

Laroche pointed a finger. 'I'm writing you up, Striker. And I'll be forwarding this to Internal. Today.'

The Deputy Chief turned away from Striker, towards Inspector Beasley, and began giving the man shit about something. Striker ignored them both. There were more important things to focus on right now. In order to learn Red Mask's identity, they were going to have to learn more about the Shadow Dragons.

And that meant using every resource Striker had.

He got on his cell and called up Meathead, the man who had the most connections to experts on Asian gangs. Meathead answered on the second ring, and Striker filled him in on what kind of expert they needed.

'So?' Striker asked. 'You know of any?'

Meathead's reply was quick and definitive. 'Yeah, just one. *The Lamb.*'

Seventy-Three

Red Mask cut down the south lane of East Hastings Street. Pain and confusion ruled his mind. He had no idea why he was taking this route, only that it was away from St Paul's Hospital, where he had completed the first step of his mission. Patricia Kwan had been fortunate to survive the first attack in her home; she would not survive this second one at the hospital.

The thought brought him no happiness. No contentment either. Just one step closer to mission completion.

To the Perfect Harmony.

Huddled in an alcove at the left side of the alley were three women. Crack whores. One of them – a blonde with pock-marked skin – gave him a wary look. He ignored her, and at the next alcove took shelter from the afternoon winds. They blustered through him with enough force to hamper his speed.

The smell of piss and shit hit him. The Downtown East Side. This festering place. The sickness of the city was bested only by the sickness of his body. With every step, the weight of his shoulder bones tore open his wound a little further.

Not that it mattered.

He reached inside his pocket and took out the vial of pills. White and yellow ones. He couldn't remember what the old herbalist had said, how many to take, so he dumped a few of each in his mouth and chewed them into paste. He had just finished swallowing when he spotted the man. Around fifty, and six feet tall – large for an Asian – he wore a baggy coat that offered perfect cover for weapons holstered beneath. The man entered the lane, casually looked in Red Mask's direction, then disappeared between the apartment complexes on the south side.

Red Mask felt his jaw clench. This was not the first time he had seen him. The man stuck out. His walk was distinctive, as if he had something wrong with his back. As if his spine was made not from bone and ligament, but wooden rods. When he walked, he took long stork-like strides.

Red Mask recognised this walk. He'd seen it back home in Cambodia. This was the result of disease. Some villagers called it 'Tree Spine' or 'the sickness from the North', but Red Mask knew the real reason for it. It was punishment.

Bad karma.

The first time he had seen this man was just after leaving Sheung Fa's office. And that thought weighed heavy in his chest because it meant only one thing.

This man was an assassin.

Red Mask returned to the main drag of East Hastings. At the corner, he entered the Jin Ho Café. The waitress hurried over and offered him a seat, but he ignored her, going immediately to the narrow hallway that led down to the washrooms, and turning to spy out of the glass front window.

Within a minute, the strange man reappeared on the sidewalk out front, his stiff legs plodding him along with surprising speed and grace.

One look from this closer distance and Red Mask felt a coldness sweep through his belly. The man's face was angular, like those from the north, with high, thick cheekbones and narrow hard eyes. Red Mask recognised him. It was the Man with the Bamboo Spine. A man he hadn't seen in over twenty years.

He was here to kill him.

Seventy-Four

It was almost three in the afternoon by the time Striker and Felicia made it to Simon Fraser University. The campus was located high atop Burnaby Mountain, a good half-hour drive from the downtown core. Rush hour had been bad.

After they parked in the top lot, Striker walked with Felicia by his side through the outdoor breezeway of the convocation mall that was flanked by cafeterias, coffee shops and bookstores. It was cold and windy out. Even the rays of sun, breaking through the red and yellow foliage of the trees, seemed cold.

Winter was slowly edging out the fall.

As they passed a small sitting area where the crowd thickened, Striker studied the students around him. He was struck by how much older they seemed than the high-school kids. The majority were in their late teens and early twenties. Adults. Most noticeably, a lot of them were dressed in costumes. Today was Halloween after all, Friday, and the crowd was littered with everything from nurses to ninjas. The masquerade gave the campus a dark but exciting aura, and it made Striker feel like he was back at St Patrick's High School.

The thought turned his palms sweaty.

He tried to lighten the mood, divert his worries. He looked

at a young blonde woman, her big breasts barely contained by her sexy nurse costume, and he smiled at Felicia.

'Don't you have one of those outfits?'

'Yeah, but it's more the Kathy Bates type.'

'You gonna hobble me?'

'Believe me, some days I'd like to.'

He laughed, and the release felt good.

They walked to the end of the breezeway, where the mustering crowds thinned, and Striker was thankful for it. They paused at another square, and Striker milled about while Felicia searched for a directory. They needed to find the auditorium. That was where Grace Lam was speaking at the International Gang Conference.

Striker looked forward to seeing her. She was supposed to be a guru in the world of gang intelligence. From what Striker had learned from Meathead, Grace Lam had started her career in Los Angeles, studying the Grape Street Watts gang, then gotten herself an interview with the infamous Monster Cody Scott when no one else could. After that, she'd been mentored by some of the finest gangologists Los Angeles and New York had to offer. When she'd earned the distinction of being a certified gangologist, she'd started her own thesis, focusing on South Asian gangs. That work had landed her in Vancouver.

It was a telling statement of the underground activity that existed in Canada.

With this thought in mind, Striker approached a water fountain that sat nestled in between a concrete bench and a Japanese plum tree. Being the end of fall, the leaves were still red, but slowly turning purple and yellow and brown.

The area had a certain serenity. Striker wished he could enjoy it. He looked across the square. On the other side of the concrete expanse was a row of terminals at a coffee shop. Internet access. Thoughts of the nitric acid attack on Patricia Kwan returned. He crossed the breezeway and entered the shop. He sat down at one of the computers, then started up Google. He was into his sixth link, reading through the long article, when Felicia found him.

'I located the auditorium,' she said, then leaned down and stared at the screen. 'Nitric acid – what did you find?'

He sat back in the chair, an uncomfortable plastic thing that groaned and stretched beneath his weight, and pointed at the photo of a disfigured woman on the screen. 'This acid is the stuff of nightmares,' he said. 'It's deadly. Turns flesh to jelly, mutates the hell out of it. If not treated immediately, the effect is permanent.'

'Then you were lucky.'

He focused on a few jpegs on the screen – horrible images of mutilation – and continued explaining what he'd read: 'Here in Canada, nitric acid is mainly used for industrial reasons – processing and manufacturing, stuff like that. But overseas, this shit has become the weapon of choice in some countries – for the humiliation that the disfigurement causes as well as the pain. And to inspire fear. It's used quite commonly as a repayment for adultery . . . the list of victims just goes on and on and on.'

'What countries?'

'Hmmm. Mostly the Asian ones. Hong Kong. The Philippines. But the Middle East, too.'

'Cambodia?'

Striker shrugged as if to say, who knows. 'Did you find Grace Lam?'

'One better,' she said. 'I spoke to her.'

'And?'

'She'll be meeting us in twenty minutes. At Legal Grounds.'

*

Legal Grounds was a small but chic coffee shop away from the clatter of the university crowds, near the bottom of the Burnaby Mountain. The place had been built without a dime spared. The walls were oak, the floors were birch, and throughout the room were loveseats and high-backed armchairs – all of them supple burgundy leather.

Behind the counter was a young brunette, about twenty, dressed in an outfit that resembled a tuxedo. On the wall behind her was a large golden image of the Scales of Justice. Striker stared at it as he bought Felicia one of her fancy lattes – the Charter, as they called it. It was nothing more than an expensive vanilla latte with chocolate sprinkles. Striker bought himself an Americano, black. Then they took their drinks to a small secluded nook in the back.

'Thanks for the latte,' Felicia said.

'Yeah, sorry it took so long, I had to sign a loan to get it.'

She smiled and sipped her drink, and Striker joined her after taking off his long coat and draping it over the back of the chair. They sat there, waiting and going over the case. To Striker, the moment felt surprisingly wonderful. It was the first respite they had had, even if it was forced.

Twenty minutes later, Grace Lam appeared. She walked into the lounge, and Felicia stood up and waved her over.

Striker had expected someone elegant and mature, someone professor-like. But Grace Lam was none of that. She was young, maybe thirty years of age, not an inch over five foot and easily two hundred pounds. Her body and face were equally round, like two perfect circles. In contrast, she had small, hard eyes and lips so thin she looked perpetually angry. Sweat trickled down the sides of her cheeks as she hurried in.

Striker looked from Felicia to Grace, then back again. 'You could be sisters,' he said.

Felicia gave him an unimpressed look. 'You're a bastard.'

Striker just smiled and sipped his Americano.

After Grace had bought a coffee – something sweet like Felicia's; Striker could smell it – she sat down in a chair facing both Striker and Felicia. In her hands was a silver-and-black ToughBook laptop, which she placed across her knees, and a thick brown briefcase, which she set down beside the table.

'So how did you come to find me?' she asked. 'I'm actually on leave.'

'First off, thanks for seeing us,' Striker said. 'Especially on your leave.' When Grace said it was no problem, he continued. 'We found you through Meathead – I mean Hans Jager; he's a part of the International Gang Task Force. He said you were the one to talk to.'

Grace got a strange look on her face, and Striker wondered how Meathead had managed to offend her, too.

'And this is about?' she asked.

'The massacre at Saint Patrick's High.'

The mention of the shooting made Grace's expression tense up a little. It was a small change, barely noticeable, but all the easiness left her face.

'Gangs?' she asked.

'Shadow Dragons,' Felicia said.

From his coat, Striker produced some of the Ident photographs of White Mask's body and showed them to Grace. 'Here is a partial tattoo on the base of the neck, there,' he said. 'He also has a number 13. Crudely done though. A home job.'

Grace looked at the images for only a few seconds, before saying, 'The partial tattoo is the tail end of a dragon.'

'Dragon?' Striker asked.

Felicia leaned forward. 'How can you be so sure?'

Grace pointed to the photo. 'By the colour and location. Red and gold are the colours of prosperity and good fortune; the left side is the sinister way, and the dragon looks backwards across the shoulder – a spiritual protector from one's enemies.'

'Sounds like superstition to me,' Striker said.

'It is,' Grace replied. 'In fact, I'm surprised that you found one at all – it's a rather old tradition. New members never do it. In fact, they're no longer getting tattoos at all nowadays – makes them too easy to identify that way.'

Felicia cut in: 'I've never heard of this gang before today, not even once.'

'That's because the information is misleading.' Grace opened her briefcase and sorted through a pile of manila folders. After some searching, she found the correct one, flipped it open and set it down on the table.

The first thing Striker saw was a huge number four, followed by the image of a red triangular flag.

Grace noted his stare, and explained: 'The pennant is triangular, representing the three basic forces of the universe – Heaven, Earth and Man.'

'I've seen that pennant before,' Striker said, 'but I didn't know it represented the Shadow Dragons.'

'It doesn't.'

Striker gave Felicia a glance, saw the confusion masking her face, and he felt it, too.

Grace continued: 'The Shadow Dragons are nothing in the big scheme of things; what they are is the tail of the beast. If you want to define them – categorise them in some way – they're a feeder gang, just puppets, doing the nasty work for their superiors back East and hoping to one day become an accepted part of the real gang.'

'And what real gang are we talking about here?' Felicia asked. 'The Angels?'

Grace shook her head, suppressed a laugh. 'Sorry. Everyone says that. No, it goes further back than that, I'm afraid. And worlds away. What you're dealing with here is the Fourteen K.'

Striker stiffened. 'Fourteen K? Aren't they a division of the Triads?'

Grace nodded slowly. 'That's exactly what I mean.'

'The Triad Syndicate.' The words felt strange on Striker's tongue. 'I thought they were dismantled. Folklore.'

Grace raised an eyebrow. 'They would like you to think so. Though the folklore stuff isn't too far off when you consider the Triad ways. And their history.' She turned to Felicia. 'The Triads were born out of secrecy, you know, by refugee monks.'

'Monks?'

'Well, they were essentially rebels back then – revolutionaries determined to overthrow the Qing or Manchu Dynasty. We're talking way back here.'

'When exactly?' Striker asked.

'The seventeen hundreds.'

Felicia made a sound. 'Christ, that's ancient.'

'Maybe so, but even today, the history lingers. To be accepted into the gang is a complicated process involving swearing thirty-six oaths before the altar, and with many convoluted rituals and sacred phrases. *Sham Tai Wang Fung* is one of them.'

'*Sham Tai* – what?'

'*Sham Tai Wang Fung* – Extensive Transformation and Uniting Heaven.' Grace took a sip of her coffee. 'The penalty for betrayal is death by "a myriad of swords and thunderbolts". Or at least, that is the oath. As you can tell, this stuff is extremely outdated, but the ceremonies remain, especially in the Far East where they are very superstitious.'

'The Far East as in Toronto?' Striker asked.

'As in Hong Kong. Their headquarters.'

Felicia put down her latte, wiped her mouth. 'Not to be rude, but it sounds ridiculous.'

Grace nodded. 'To the Western world, yes. Every belief the Triads hold is logic mixed with superstition. Strategic yet tempered by mysticism, planned thoroughly yet done so with numerology.'

'Numerology?' Striker asked.

Grace nodded. 'Oh yes, numerology is *huge* in the Triad Syndicate.' She turned the folder pages until she found a listing. 'Here, look at this. The list ascends in order of status.' She turned it so that Striker could see.

Numerology of Triad Hierarchy

426 – Red Pole. Brigade Enforcer.
415 – Pak Tsz Sin. White Paper Fan. Senior advisor.
      Knowledge of Triad history.
438 – Sheung Fa. Canada Liaison Officer.
483 – Fu Chan Shu. Deputy Leader.
489 – Shan Chu. King Daddy. Dragon Head.

As Striker read the list and made notes in his notebook, Grace spoke. 'You say this guy had a number 13 tattooed on his body. Where was it?'

'Chest. Left side.'

Grace nodded. 'The number 13 covers the heart because it's out of respect for the thirteen monks.'

Now Striker felt completely lost. 'What monks?'

'The Shao Lin monks, in the Fujian Province. We're talking four hundred years ago, but it does show you who – and what – you're dealing with here. The Triads have alliances all across the seas: in the Philippines, Hong Kong, Macau, Cambodia, Viet Nam – the list is as long as there are places. And they will never go away.'

Striker thought this over for a moment. Then: 'What I still don't get is how a group of teenage kids from Saint Patrick's High School got tangled up with a global gang.'

Grace agreed. 'I really see no connection, Detective. The Triads are a very secretive group. They would never be involved in something like this.'

'That's the problem,' Striker said. 'They are.'

Seventy-Five

Que Wong's friend, better known as Mr Creepy to Courtney and Raine, had his own pad in the 1800 block of East Georgia Street – a bad part of town but perfect for the girls as it was only four blocks away from Commercial Drive and Venables Street, the starting point for the Parade of Lost Souls party.

The building was old, even for Commercial Drive, made up of cracked grey concrete and filthy windows. Out front, a small grassy area was blocked off by a rusted iron fence. Inside it was a teeter-totter with a swing set, neither of which looked used.

Courtney reached the front entrance. Dressed in nothing but her Little Red Riding Hood costume, she felt exposed, a step away from being naked, and she suddenly realised how much of her ass the costume revealed. It was too much. Hadn't seemed like this in the change room. And she was cold, wished she'd brought a jacket or something.

From somewhere above, maybe on the third floor, she could hear a baby crying and a couple arguing. The man's voice was slurred and distorted. Trying to ignore the clatter, she pressed the building buzzer and found it broken. She pushed on the front door and it opened anyway.

Once inside, a musty smell hit her; it seemed to come from the worn-out brown carpets. The building interior was cold and dark. Mr Creepy's apartment was on the sixth floor. One look at the small rickety booth of an elevator convinced Courtney to take the stairs, which were equally narrow and confining. When she reached the sixth floor, she stepped into the hallway and heard the loud ruckus of a party going on. As she walked down the hall and around the corner, she realised it was coming from Mr Creepy's place.

The front door was wide open, and people were spilling out into the halls. The air was heavy with cigarette and pot smoke. It made Courtney hesitate, unsure.

But then Raine poked her head out, spotted Courtney and let out a squeal. 'Oh my GOD – you look so *hot* in that costume.'

Courtney looked down at herself, felt suddenly self-conscious. Her cheeks blushed and her throat went dry. She looked back up at Raine, saw her huge boobs busting out of her nurse's costume, and knew she could never compete with that.

'You look great, too,' she said. 'Every guy at the party's gonna wanna be with you.'

Raine laughed, pulled her inside where the music was louder. Something heavy, pounding. Bad-ass Rap. 'I'll get you a cooler – strawberry or peach?'

'Peach,' Courtney said, and looked around.

The crowd was a blend of weirdos and strangers. Out on the sundeck was a handful of Asian guys, all with tinted blond hair and leather and red gangster hoodies. They were smoking up some pot. In the kitchen was another group of guys and girls, mixed races, most of them looking older than her and Raine. A *lot* older. Some of them wore torn-up jeans and black jackets and had a biker look to them. They were drinking hard stuff. Jack Daniel's. Rum. Vodka. In the far corner, a group of Asian girls were hanging out in a closed-off circle, a few of them constantly looking over their shoulders at her and Raine.

They looked mean and tough. It gave Courtney an awkward feeling, and she covered herself up by folding her arms across her chest, then moved in behind the bend of the hall to get out of their line of sight.

'We're the only ones wearing costumes,' she suddenly noticed.

Raine shrugged. 'So? We're hot.'

'Who are all these people?'

Raine opened the fridge door, looked around. 'I dunno, they just showed up.'

'Showed up?'

Raine handed her a peach cooler. 'Yeah. They're friends of Mr Creepy. Said the party was planned for weeks. Said that everyone knew. They just walked right in like they owned the place. What was I gonna do, not let them in? I just got the ice outta his fridge and loaded up the sink. Next thing I know it was filled with booze. Everyone's bringing something, and I've just been helping myself.'

Courtney didn't drink her cooler right away. 'Maybe you shouldn't have let them in.'

Raine gave her an impatient look. 'You're not gonna go all nerdy on me again, are you?'

'No. Of course not.'

'Good. 'Cause I just got off the phone with Bobby Ryan and he's already on his way over.'

Courtney felt her insides explode with butterflies. 'Now? He's coming *now*?'

'Actually, that was over a half hour ago. He should be here any minute.'

'Oh GOD.' Courtney's fingers suddenly felt clumsy on the bottle. She leaned against the wall, looked down at herself and started fussing with her costume.

Raine grabbed her hand, stopped her from playing with the dress. 'You look hot, Court. *Super*hot. So chill.'

'You think?'

'They do,' she said with a laugh, and pointed at a group of guys hanging out in the den where the Vancouver Canucks were battling the Washington Capitals on the big screen. That Russian superstar guy was centrescreen.

Courtney let her eyes fall from the game to the group of guys.

A few of them – all way too old, like, ten years too old for her – had turned around from the game and were staring at her and Raine. The nearest one, a long-haired white guy with a few days' growth on his face, had on a black sleeveless T-shirt that showed off his heavily muscled arms, both of which were covered with tattoos. She met his stare, hoping he would look away. When he didn't – and offered her a dirty grin – she pretended not to see and looked down from him.

'They're gross.'

Raine laughed. 'You just need to chill, Court.' She grabbed the bottle of peach cooler in Courtney's hand and lifted it to her friend's mouth.

Courtney took a long gulp, hiccuped, and laughed.

'Better?' Raine asked.

'I dunno. Maybe. A little.'

'Good,' she said. 'Because Bobby just walked through the door.'

Courtney didn't reply. She froze to the spot, couldn't move. A part of her wanted to turn around and face Bobby boldly, but she couldn't. Another part of her wanted to avoid him and run away from the party, but she couldn't do that either. So instead she just stood there like a statue and drank down her entire cooler. When it was done Raine handed her another one, and she drank that, too.

It was too much, she knew. Too much for a girl who never drank.

But she couldn't help herself. She finished it and started her third. The music blasted all around her and people started making out in the corners. She spotted Bobby across the room, saw him looking back at her. He began to cross the room, and a small smile spread over Courtney's lips.

Maybe Raine was right, after all.

It *was* gonna be one helluva night.

Seventy-Six

Striker and Felicia met Delbert Ibarra at Strike Force HQ. Ibarra, Vancouver's only Mexican cop, was the Inspector in charge of Strike Force, the city's best covert surveillance unit. For five years now, Strike Force had been massing up piles of information through Project Pacific – a joint task force initiated to identify the numerous unknown entities of the ongoing Asian gang warfare.

The information Striker and Felicia now had was straightforward. The gunmen were somehow linked to the Shadow Dragons, which was something of a feeder gang for the Triads. And the most likely division of the Triads they were dealing with here just so happened to be the most powerful faction – the 14K. So the goal here was simple: find some pictures of these guys. ID them. Then find the link to the school.

The photographs of Project Pacific were their best bet.

'Haven't looked at these for months,' Delbert Ibarra said as he removed a thick folder of photographs from the cabinet.

Striker nodded. 'Let's just hope they got something we can use.'

He waited impatiently in the corner of the Strike Force projector room while Ibarra – Taco Del, to all those who knew him – went through the surveillance folder for Project Pacific. Felicia, the more reserved of the two, sat tilted back in one of the office chairs.

'How long was Project Pacific?' Striker asked.

Ibarra unconsciously patted down the sides of his handlebar moustache, grown for the undercover operation he was halfway through. He flipped through the folder, looking at the dates. 'Sixteen months. Sixteen long friggin' months.'

'What exactly was this project?' Felicia asked.

Ibarra continued picking at the handlebars of his moustache. 'Multi-jurisdictional surveillance project, set up by a coalition of deputy chiefs. Goal was to gain information on the growing diversity of Asian youth gangs. We had the Strike Force working in two teams, twelve-hour shifts, seven days a week for almost a year and a half. Burned everyone out. Caused a lot of transfers when the gig was up.'

'Fed money?' Striker asked.

'What else? God knows, *we* couldn't afford that. Most of the information we got never went to charges. But it's been a valuable resource for the IHIT and the IGTF.'

Striker nodded. The Integrated Homicide Investigation Team and the Integrated Gang Task Force were in the public eye a lot nowadays. He looked at the file, saw how thin it was. 'That's all you got?'

Ibarra laughed, his entire face lighting up. 'These are just the reference numbers – the entire file is on the database.'

'We'll want to see that then.'

Ibarra started the nearest computer and initiated the log-in sequence. As he did so, Striker studied the man. At five foot ten and one hundred eighty pounds, Ibarra was of average height, average weight. He had brown eyes, shaggy brown hair, a bushy brown moustache, and a face people would forget after ten minutes – which was exactly why he had been known as the Surveillance God for the past ten years.

The computer booted up, and Felicia joined Striker and Ibarra at the row of terminals. 'We need pictures,' she said.

Striker clarified: 'Of suspects only. No vehicles or institutions.'

Ibarra used the mouse to navigate through the subsystem. When he found the folder he was looking for – *Project Pacific* – he craned his neck and gave them both a quick look. 'This is related to the Active Shooter at Saint Patrick's?'

Felicia nodded. 'We think so.'

'How?'

'It's convoluted,' Striker said, and left it at that.

Ibarra let his stare hang on Striker for a few more seconds, then turned back to the computer. 'I've given you the okay to see this stuff, but you still got to be logged in the book. Procedure.'

Striker nodded like he didn't much care, and Ibarra opened the search menu bar. 'Can I narrow this down for you?'

'Shadow Dragons and Triads and anything connected,' Striker said.

Ibarra did a double-take, as if he didn't believe they could be involved, then just shrugged and ran through the subdirectory. When he found the folder labelled *Triad Syndicate*, he opened it up. There were three more folders inside: *Triad Divisions. Triad Associates. Triad Feeder Gangs.* He got up from the computer and offered Striker the chair.

'These are all photos,' he said. 'Most of the jpegs are named. The ones with generic numbers are listed in the file folder. You'll have to cross-reference them to see if their details match. I'll be in the other room, just grab me if you need something.'

He left the room.

Striker sat down in the chair Ibarra had deserted; Felicia pulled over another one and joined him.

The computer screen was tinted with soft blue and white, and showed the three folders Ibarra had navigated. Striker opened the folder labelled *Triad Divisions*. Within it was a long list of subfolders, all countries – Canada, the US, China, Hong Kong, Australia and more. When Striker searched through them he found even more subfolders and directories, breaking down into states and provinces, then cities.

None had what he was looking for.

He cycled back to the original page and opened the folder labelled *Feeder Gangs*. Like the other folder, this one broke down into countries and then cities. Striker clicked through the subsystems until he found a folder named *Vancouver and the Surrounding Lower Mainland*. He opened it up, hoping to see a listing for the Shadow Dragons, but was not so lucky. Inside the folder, in page-long lists, were a series of jpeg images. He scrolled through them with the mouse.

'Jesus, there must be thousands,' Felicia said.

Striker nodded. 'All the more reason to get started.'

He switched the view settings from List to Thumbnails, and the computer started making loud grinding noises as the hard drive loaded the images. One by one, they popped onto the screen. Slowly, methodically, he and Felicia went through every one of them, maximising and ruling them out. The process was slow, arduous, and after forty long minutes, Striker's eyes were irritated. It was another twenty minutes before he found anything valuable. He clicked from one photo to the next, then made a soft sound that got Felicia's attention.

'What?' she asked.

'Weird scars on this guy's torso. Left side.' Striker thought of the Medical Examiner's findings of their headless shooter, White Mask.

'Shrapnel wounds?' she asked.

'Might be. And there's some kind of tattoo on the neck. Left side.' Striker sat forward in the chair and narrowed his eyes. 'A dragon maybe.'

Felicia rolled her chair nearer to his as Striker maximised the photo.

On the screen was the colour image of an Asian male, mid-to-late thirties, with a long angular face. His height was difficult to guess, but his build was average, lean. He wore white shorts, a pair of black-and-gold wraparound sunglasses, and looked like he was walking along a beach somewhere. There was water in the background.

Striker looked at the scars all along the man's side. They were thick and long and uneven, and looked as if they'd been splattered there. Like specks of white spackle. Striker felt a surge of adrenalin. He looked at the tattoo on the neck. It was left side, and it was long and somewhat cylindrical. But the detail was poor, difficult to see.

He magnified the image over the tattoo.

Two times, four times, six times, then eight . . . and Striker felt the breath escape his lips as the image became larger and more distinct. The tattoo looked like a seahorse on the man's neck, but Striker knew it was really a dragon. Red and gold. The tail trailed down the left side of the neck, the head looked back across the shoulder.

Striker panned in on the chest, left side. There was a number 13.

An overwhelming sense of excitement flooded him. The caption under the jpeg read: *Tran Sang Soone*, and Striker read the name several times, as if disbelieving the words.

Tran Sang Soone.

He had found White Mask.

Seventy-Seven

Striker wanted all the information the Inspector had on Tran Sang Soone. According to the chart, there was a separate folder on the man, but it was not filed in its proper place. Ibarra left the room to check the backup files, and Striker and Felicia continued scanning through the pictures for the one man they wanted most.

Red Mask.

Striker had seen his face in two of their three gun battles, and it was a face he would never forget. Like Tran Sang Soone, Red Mask was thin and wiry in build, and of average height. But it was the eyes that gave him away – sitting deep behind heavily boned cheeks, their stare deep and hollow and empty. In his sixteen years of policing Striker had never met a stare like that, and the thought reminded him of Magui Yagata's words back at Worldwide Translation Services, when she spoke of the Khmer Rouge.

'A *survivor*.'

The more Striker thought about it, the more he believed her words. He let the thought take him away for a bit, then snapped back to the task at hand when Felicia looked up from the folder she was perusing and said, 'Found some info on Tran Sang Soone. Date of birth: January 15, 1964.'

Striker moved closer. 'Sixty-four? Are you sure?'

'That's what the file says. Info comes from Immigration. Says here the place of birth is Phnom Phen, Cambodia.'

'Then who knows what his real age is. Cambodia doesn't exactly keep good records.' The thought of Cambodia was disturbing to Striker. 'That date and location correspond perfectly with Pol Pot and the Khmer Rouge. What else is in there?'

She read on. 'He's got an extensive criminal history. Christ, there's everything in here! Charges for Assault, Trafficking, Running a Common Bawdy House, Running a Gambling Den, Uttering Threats – the list just goes on and on.'

'Any of the charges go through?'

'Nope. All stayed, every single one of them. Must have one helluva lawyer. He's listed as a Person of Interest in a dozen murders from Vancouver to Toronto. Even one back in Hong Kong. But he's never done time for any of them. Never done time for *anything*.'

'He's doing time now,' Striker said. 'And hopefully the furnace is cranked. He got a list of associates in there?'

She shook her head. 'Not in this folder. But there are lists of other Shadow Dragons.'

Striker logged onto CABS – the Criminal Automated Booking System – and brought up the query box.

'Let's go through them,' he said. 'One by one.'

Felicia read the first name out, Striker typed it in the box and hit send. Seconds later, the photo popped up. It wasn't Red Mask, and Striker deleted it. Then they started all over again.

Twenty minutes and twenty-nine associates later, Striker brought up the last image, found it didn't match, and cleared the search bar.

'Next one,' he said.

'That's it, we're done.'

'Done?' Striker made a frustrated sound, then thought things over. 'Okay, what other gangs was White Mask – Tran Sang Soone – connected to? We'll start with the most likely, then fan out from there.'

'The Golden Lotus,' Ibarra said, stepping back into the room.

Striker wrote the name down in his notebook. 'I've heard of the Lotus before, but never the Golden Lotus.'

'That's because they're from Toronto.'

'Toronto?'

'Yeah, I got bad news for you,' Ibarra said. 'My team followed these guys around for the better part of a year – the gang brings in a lot of off-shore help. China. Singapore. Macau. There were so many faces we could hardly keep up, even with twenty-four-hour surveillance on them. Much as I hate to burst your bubble, this guy might be from overseas – a FOB-K.'

Felicia looked at Striker, then at Ibarra. 'FOB-K?'

'Fresh off the boat killer.'

Striker said nothing. It was a thought he didn't want to entertain. Having an overseas gunman would mean more time, more agencies – Interpol, FBI, the Feds – and the list went on. In the end, an overseas gunman would mean less chance of identification, and it would keep them stuck in this constant cat and mouse chase, where the only way to catch Red Mask was to wait for his next attack.

And who knew how many more deaths that would mean.

Ibarra held up a thin folder. It was beige and dusty, and the corners were turned over from being compressed. 'This is all I got on Tran Sang Soone.'

Felicia took the folder from Ibarra and opened it on the desk. As she went through it, Striker continued scanning through the surveillance photos of 14K Triad members and suspected associates. He reached the end and was about to put them away when something made him pause. In one of the surveillance photos, Tran Sang Soone was seated at a banquet table. He was laughing heartily while talking to another gang member. Behind him, the waitress was bringing more platters out from the kitchen.

'Where was this taken?'

Ibarra leaned forward. 'That photo was taken over a year ago, at the Chongmin Banquet Hall. Used to be a big splashy place. Closed down now though. Got caught running a gambling den and a common bawdy house out of the back.'

Striker looked at the photo, stared at it for a long time, and spotted a tall man in a white apron in the doorway. He pulled the photo closer. The background was grainy, hard to make out, but something clicked in Striker's mind.

'Who is this guy?' he asked, and pointed to the man in the apron.

Ibarra looked over his shoulder. 'The cook.'

'You run him?'

Ibarra nodded. 'We ran everyone who so much as farted in their direction. Believe me, anyone who's got any known criminal involvement is listed under the associates.'

'So who is he?' Striker pressed.

Ibarra took another look at the photo. 'Don't know the name. I remember him though. Real oddball. Just stood there staring off into space half the time. Most the guys thought he was on the nod, or something. We checked him out though, and he was completely negative. Nothing criminal in his past, nothing even remotely suspect. Shit, I don't think he even had a speeding ticket.'

'That means nothing,' Striker commented. 'Seung-Hui Choi had no criminal history either, but that didn't stop him from killing thirty-two people at Virginia Tech. What's the cook's name?'

Ibarra couldn't remember, so he took the image number from Striker and started flipping through the pages of the *Project Pacific* folder.

While waiting, Striker searched through the rest of the restaurant photos, scanning each one with deliberation. It was on the eleventh photograph that he found the cook again, in a strange pose. He was out in a laneway with his shirt removed. His body was tattoo-free with beige skin; his build was lean and wiry. Striker studied the man's physique, then his face. And then he knew.

It was the eyes. That cold, vacuous stare.

Felicia, reading over the *Tran Sang Soone* folder, made an excited sound and looked up. 'Jesus Christ, he's got a brother!'

And before Striker could react to this, Ibarra found the name connected to the image of the cook. Striker snatched the paper from his hands and read it over. He turned to face Felicia.

'Call Dispatch,' he ordered. 'Call the papers. Call every TV station you know.'

Felicia stood up from her chair. 'Red Mask?' she asked.

Striker nodded. 'His name is Shen Sun Soone.'

Seventy-Eight

Shen Sun Soone stood rooted to the spot. The sweet aroma of Chinese pork buns filled the air around him, but it did not stir his hunger. All he thought of was the Man with the Bamboo Spine.

The 14K assassin.

The Man with the Bamboo Spine was Dai Huen Jai, a former Big Circle Boy – one of the Vietnamese National Liberation Army soldiers turned mercenary. These men had a willingness to resort to unnecessary torture. And they did so in horrifically creative ways. Death by slow boiling; death by skinning; death by disembowelment – all procedures conjured up to inspire fear in their enemies.

And it worked with great success.

'Take seat,' the waitress said to Shen Sun. 'You take seat. You order food. Eat much.'

Shen Sun left the restaurant, feeling divided. A part of him longed for Macau, where Shan Chu was located. If only he could go there and hold tea with Shan Chu, then there might be hope. But that was impossible. Shan Chu was Dragon Head, above even Sheung Fa. He did what was necessary to protect the syndicate. And because of that, the order for Shen Sun's death was understandable. The Triad need for secrecy superseded everything else. So when Shen Sun's photo started popping up on every TV screen around the city, his fate was sealed.

The news media had ordered his death, every bit as much as Shan Chu.

The door to the Jin Ho Café slammed shut from the wind, the glass rattling. It tore him from his stupor. Woke him to the harsh truth. There was no future – not for him. Perhaps there never had been. Perhaps he had died that day in the camps, and now he was nothing more than a shadow wandering this earth.

He stood on the corner of East Hastings and Hawks and stared at the cold expanse of sky. Moments ago it had seemed sunny. Now it was grey.

He reached under his shirt, pulled the Glock from his waistband and placed the barrel flush against his temple. His finger rested heavy on the trigger. The steel was cold. But there was an easiness now. Peace. He gently squeezed the trigger.

And stopped.

Something had caught his eye. Something across the road. It was subtle at first, like the softest change of wind. But it was there. It was undeniably there.

And it was *magnificent*.

Across the road, on the north side of Hastings, was the Sunshine Market. The store awning was old and yellow with a dozen golden pennants hanging down. Each one boasted a symbol – Peace, Strength, Prosperity, Wisdom. The wind tilted them all towards the west.

All except one.

In the centre hung a single red pennant. Triangular. And on its face was the character for Perseverance. Unlike all the other ones, this pennant tilted towards the *east*. Against the wind. And Shen Sun could not believe his eyes.

It was a sign, he knew. A glorious rescue. He stared at that red triangular pennant tilting towards the east, and felt his eyes turn wet. Soon tears ran down his cheeks, tasting salty on his lips.

'Tran?' he asked.

The wind died and all the pennants stopped flapping.

Shen Sun let the gun fall to his side. Smiled. He would finish the mission. And he would survive. Like he always had, no matter what came up against him, be it the Khmer Rouge, the Shadow Dragons, a Big Circle Boy. Or some gwailo cop chasing him down at every turn.

Nothing could stop him.

He looked east, in the last direction he had seen the Man with the Bamboo Spine marching. Only a few blocks away was Raymur Street. And that told Shen Sun the true destination of his newfound enemy. The Strathcona Projects.

The Man with the Bamboo Spine was going after Father.

Seventy-Nine

When the Man with the Bamboo Spine got the call, he was already walking under the Hastings Street overpass. The cross-road below the pass was Raymur Street, and it was home to most of the cross-dressers and transsexuals Vancouver had to offer.

The overpass was in shadow, not only from the overhang of the road above, but from the cloudless sky. A grey darkness had slowly crept into the city, smothering it like a giant slate cover.

The Man with the Bamboo Spine did not notice the sky. He marched along Raymur Street, staying close to the railroad tracks that ran on the east side of the road. The tracks were set slightly off the main path, on depressed land – decent cover if shooting started. And it probably would. For though he had not seen Shen Sun Soone in over two decades, he knew the kind of man he was. A survivor.

Much like himself.

The phone call he was waiting for finally came. It was inevitable, and had been ever since Shen Sun Soone's face had been plastered on every TV set in every window. The Man with the Bamboo Spine picked up.

'Yes,' he said.

The voice on the phone was Sheung Fa, and his tone was unusually low, distant. There was regret in his words, and grief, so much it was palpable. 'The situation has changed for the worse.'

'Yes.'

'There is no longer an alternative.'

'No.'

'Do what must be done.'

'Yes.

The Man with the Bamboo Spine snapped the cell phone shut and put it away. He looked across the road into the Raymur projects and saw the townhouse address of 533. The man who lived here was Lien Vok Soone – the father of Tran Sang Soone and Shen Sun Soone. Judging by the photographs, he was an old man, short, thin and frail, and from the history in the package, he was the owner of a small convenience store. A simple but honourable man. Another survivor.

It changed nothing.

The Man with the Bamboo Spine was going to kill him first.

And then he would find Shen Sun.

Eighty

Once Striker had identified Red Mask as Shen Sun Soone, the information was sent to every district in every department. His name was flagged on CPIC, meaning the information would be shared not only in Canada, but the rest of the world. Everyone from border patrol to the coast guard was notified, and no less than fifty units were searching possible hideout locations. But so far the search had come up negative.

It made Striker take a different path.

It was five-thirty p.m. with no end in sight when he got on his cell and called up an old acquaintance – the Hall Eleven Fire Chief, Brady Marshall. Years ago, Brady had started his career as a cop before switching to Fire three years in. The hours were better, he had said, and the pay and benefits similar enough. Striker got along well with the man.

Brady answered on the third ring and Striker gave him a quick rundown on the situation, emphasising the Suspicious Circumstance call that had been linked to an Arson call on Pandora Street.

'You gonna be there a while?' Striker asked.

'For this, of course.'

'Be there in fifteen.'

Striker hung up, and Felicia looked over at him and raised an eyebrow. He offered her nothing and kept thinking over the events that had transpired. Moments later, he pulled out his cell and dialled Courtney's number.

It went straight to voicemail.

'She screens her calls one more goddam time, I'm gonna take away her cell.'

Felicia said nothing. It was for the best.

They sped down Hastings Street into the 1700 Block where a McDonald's was located on the north side. Striker's stomach growled at the sight, and he detoured. He cut through the Drive-Thru, ordered them a couple of Big Macs, fries and coffees. Five minutes later, they were back on the road, heading for the Fire Department.

Felicia sorted through the bag of fast food, handed Striker a burger. 'Why Hall Eleven?'

He accepted it, tore off the wrapper. 'I know the Chief there. Brady Marshall. He's a good man, and he owes me one.'

Felicia removed her own burger from the bag. 'How can he help us?'

'He can give us paper on the Pandora call – the house fire. God knows, we can't find any reports at the Vancouver Police Department, so we'll get them from him.'

'They'll be different. Less detail. You know how Fire writes things up.'

'If they have anything, I'll be happy. They're all we got.'

Striker ate while driving, careful not to spill anything on his suit. They turned left on Victoria Drive and drove south.

Felicia swallowed a mouthful of burger, grumbling, 'We should be out there looking for Shen Sun, not visiting Fire Halls.'

Striker put his coffee into the cup-holder. 'Fifty units are already doing that. What we need now is a good, solid motive. If we can find that, then we'll be one step closer to solving this thing. All we've got right now is a mishmash of theories, none of which come together very well.' He gave her a questioning look. 'Unless you can connect it all.'

Felicia shook her head and pulled out her cell phone. She ate her burger and went through her emails; Striker was grateful for the silence. He used the time to down his own food and go over all they had done, making sure they had all their bases covered.

He thought they had. He'd been precise.

Damn near everyone in Operations had been called out. Mandatorily. Both Strike Force Teams were set up on the fly – Team One on a possible location for the Shadow Dragons' Headquarters, way down in the 4800 block of East Pender; Team Two on the suspected 14K Triad Headquarters up on Kingsway and Kerr. All four Emergency Response Teams were on scene as well: Team Blue on Shen Sun's apartment on Hastings, Team Green at St Patrick's High School, Team Grey at the Kwan residence, and Team Red at the only other known associated address.

Shen Sun's father's place on Raymur Street in the Strathcona Projects.

And that was to say nothing of the Investigative Units. Detectives had been pilfered from every section – Robbery, Assault, even DVACH, the Domestic Violence and Criminal Harassment section. They were sent to assist the gang squads with anything required, no matter how important or trivial the task.

The entire Department was on high alert, as were all the surrounding areas – New Westminster, West Van, Port Moody, Abbotsford and the RCMP. All were geared towards the same goal: finding Shen Sun Soone. He was arrestable for murder on multiple counts, and considered the highest level of threat.

Flagged as a possible suicide-by-cop, because there was little doubt he intended to have police kill him in a gunfight.

Like leaves caught in a whirlpool, the thoughts circulated in Striker's head. He drove past First Avenue and the Fire Hall came into view.

Fire Hall Eleven was located on Victoria Drive, just east of Commercial. Situated north of McSpadden Park, it was shrouded by the darkness of the forest overhang. When Striker pulled into the driveway, at just before six o'clock, the only light chasing away the charcoal greyness was that of the car's headlights and the hall itself.

Striker parked in front of Bay Three and walked inside.

Fire Chief Brady Marshall was dressed in a creased white shirt. He looked like an average guy, five foot ten and maybe two hundred pounds. A bit of a belly. Harsh blue eyes that were partly hidden behind bushy grey eyebrows. He sat behind a large desk that was so clean it looked polished with wax. A half-empty bottle of apricot brandy sat on the desk in front of him.

Striker pointed at it. 'I thought rum was your drink of choice.'

Brady smiled behind his walrus moustache. 'It is, and it's gone.'

'We'd get fired for that,' Felicia said.

'So would we – if anyone knew.'

Brady let out a boisterous laugh and waved Striker and Felicia closer. His cheeks were ruddy, as if he'd been out shovelling snow all day.

'I got the folder you wanted,' he said. 'Though I'll tell you, it was a bit of work. Thing got filed in the wrong place.' Brady reached into the drawer, pulled out a thick green file. He met Striker's eyes, looked truly concerned. 'Any luck out there?'

'Yeah, all bad,' Striker said tiredly. 'We know the gunman's identity, but we can't locate him.' He stopped talking for a second and looked at Felicia. She was standing there, playing with her phone. She flipped it closed, looked up.

'This is my partner,' Striker said. 'Detective Santos.'

'My pleasure,' Brady said. He didn't stand, but he did reach out and shake her hand.

'Likewise,' was all Felicia said.

Then Striker got down to business. 'So what can you tell me about this Pandora Street fire?' he asked.

Brady shrugged. 'Kind of what you'd expect. Typical Suspicious Circumstance call that turned into an Arson. I've given the report a quick read. It's not overly detailed, but it's not lacking either.' He flipped through the pages. 'Why you so interested in this anyway?'

'I think it's somehow related.' Striker circled the desk, looked over Brady's rounded shoulders. 'What are the specifics?'

Brady ran his finger down the page. 'Accelerants were used, which is typical. White gas, most likely.'

Striker thought it over. 'How long it take for your units to respond?'

'We were on scene in less than ten minutes from the time the call was made.'

'That about right?'

'Depends on the night, but yeah.' Brady picked up his coffee cup, snagged the bottle of brandy, and poured some into it. Striker could smell the booze. When Brady looked back up at Felicia, he smiled.

'On my time now,' he said in his defence. He offered them some, and they both declined.

Striker took the report from Brady's hands and flipped through it until he reached a page with a header that read:

Pertinent Structure Details. Reading through it, he found some interesting details.

'Says here something about stasis-foam being used . . .'

Brady finished sipping his apricot brandy and made a smacking sound with his lips. He wiped his hand under his overgrown moustache and nodded. 'Yeah, we lucked out on that one. The fire was going good when we got there – a real beast – but, thankfully, the house was filled with that stuff.'

'Stuff?' Felicia interrupted. 'What exactly is stasis-foam?'

Brady looked up at her. 'Well, essentially, it's just insulation. But it's a high-end quality product – kind of like a flexible, mouldable foam. We don't see a lot of it, since it's cost-prohibitive. Used mainly in high-friction areas where heat might be a factor.'

Striker noted this. 'Such as?'

'Well, hot machinery, for one. Super computers, too, because it's also a fire-retardant.'

Striker flipped through the rest of the pages, then closed the folder and sat down on the desk. The entire structure squeaked and moved beneath his weight. He looked at Brady for a long moment, then asked, 'You seen any other houses with this stuff?'

'Not many. Like I said, it's expensive. 'Bout ten times the cost of regular insulation. And not all that easy to get here in Canada. You got to order it in from the States, so you get stuck with the extra shipping costs as well.'

'That's what I thought.' Striker held up the report. 'Can I keep this?'

'Sure.' Brady raised his cup. 'It's a copy. But make sure you destroy it when you're done.'

'Thanks, Brady. It helps.'

'Just find this fuck.'

Striker nodded. He and Felicia left the fire hall the way they'd come and hopped back in their cruiser. When Striker started the engine and drove onto Victoria Drive, he headed north this time, and Felicia gave him a questioning glance.

'Where we going?' she asked.

'To where this entire nightmare started.'

She furrowed her brow. 'But Saint Patrick's High is *west* of here.'

'We're not going to the school,' Striker said. 'We're going to that house on Pandora Street. All the answers are there.'

Eighty-One

Shen Sun hung up the pay phone. This was the third time he had called Father, but he was not home. Which meant he was at either the Chinese Society Social Club on Pender or playing Mah-jong somewhere in Strathcona.

His absence put Shen Sun at a disadvantage.

He slammed down the receiver and turned away just in time to see a patrol car drive by. Inside the cruiser were two young cops – a man and a woman. The woman cop gave him a long, hard look, said something to her partner, and the car immediately turned at the corner.

Circling the block.

Shen Sun cut into the north lane. His head felt swollen from fever and his legs moved like a pair of rubbery stilts. He passed through the industrial section to Raymur Street, below the overpass, where the she-males and transsexuals plied their trade. This was the so-called bad area, a place of drugs and sex and violence. Yet it was also a good place. A lot of honest hard-working people lived here. Poor people.

Like Father.

Shen Sun crossed the road and hurried across the train tracks, under the cover of shadow. On the other side of the gravel path, the ground swept upwards. It was steep, but Shen Sun climbed it. At the top, he followed the bush line a few hundred metres south to a small hollow. He crept inside. From this vantage point, he could see the valley below – the train tracks, Raymur Street and, most importantly, Father's small town home.

Everything appeared calm.

Father's unit faced onto Raymur Street. The front door was closed, the drapes were open. However, the living-room light was on, which was disturbing, because Father had grown up poor. Lost electricity was lost money. Leaving a light on was something he never did.

Shen Sun watched and waited. Inside the unit, there was only stillness. No one appeared to be home. And no one was on the streets either.

That bothered Shen Sun even more than the light being left on.

He had spent ten years living here. Never was Raymur Street so quiet. Since setting up in his vantage point, he had not seen one police car drive by. And that was highly unusual. It told him one important thing: undercover cops were around.

Minutes ticked by slowly. The stillness made him edgy, made him want to return home. But if Father had taught him anything in this life, it was the importance of patience.

And so Shen Sun waited.

Just as he had waited so many years ago, in the forest brush that flanked the east end of Section 21. The memory was hot, blending in with his fever, and before Shen Sun knew it, he felt as small as a child again.

As small as Child 157.

Eighty-Two

As Striker and Felicia drove towards the 1700 block of Pandora Street, angry stormclouds floated in from the north, threatening rain and turning the grey twilight a purplish black.

It was fitting for the area. Everywhere Striker looked there was nothing but square concrete building after square concrete building. Some were brown, some were grey, some were a dirty, time-stained beige. But all were the same ugly industrial design.

It was half past six, and there was little sign of life on the street. Just the odd hooker working her corner, and the binners and homeless camped out between the lots, scavenging what they could from the trash cans. Striker watched one girl take note of the undercover cruiser and drop back into the shadows.

When they reached the 1800 block of Pandora Street, the darkness deepened. There were only two sources of light: the streetlamp at the end of the road and the yellow neon glow from Tony's Autobody Shop, on the south side. The shop was closed for the night.

Halfway down the road, Striker spotted the building he was looking for. It was the lone house – or what was left of it – sitting on the north side of the road. Nestled between a condemned warehouse and an empty lot.

As they drove nearer, the extent of the damage to the house became clearer. Half the exterior was damn near demolished.

The other half, barely standing, was nothing but a burned-out shell.

Striker glanced at Felicia. 'Looks like the last time you tried to cook.'

She smiled. 'This coming from the man whose daughter makes his every meal.'

'Point taken.' Striker frowned. The mere mention of Courtney gave him pause. He tried her again, at home and on her cell.

Nothing.

'Give it up,' Felicia said, sensing his thoughts. 'She's a woman, she'll talk to you when she's ready.'

'Which means never.' He opened the car door, got out. The overpowering stench of chicken guts hit him immediately. The smell filtered down from the slaughterhouse which sat a half block to the east, and it permeated everything.

Felicia brought a hand to her nose and winced.

Striker moved on.

A narrow cement path led from the sidewalk to the remains of the house. By the time they'd reached the front porch area, the chicken smell had been overtaken by the reek of burned wood and insulation. Impressive, considering the fire had been out for weeks. The front door and frame were completely gone. On the floor, just inside the foyer, a leftover string of yellow police tape stretched horizontally from beam to beam. Hanging from the tape was a sign: *Condemned by the City of Vancouver*.

Striker ran his finger along the yellow tape, feeling smoothness and grit. He stepped into the hallway, the burned hardwood clunking and creaking beneath his boots. All around him, blackened pillars rose up like gnarled fingers. Some of the beams continued up past the first floor; others were burned so badly they'd broken and toppled over. Striker crossed into the room and found the one area that was least affected by the fire.

He stopped, studied the wall. Said: 'Come here. Look at this.'

When Felicia joined him, he pointed to a series of hollows in the leftover, grey-foam latticework. He gloved up, reached out and took hold of the remaining shelf of foam. Despite the intense heat of the fire, the material had remained supple. It bent as Striker yanked on it, but remained firm.

'This is it,' he said.

'It?'

'The key to all this.'

'*This*?' Felicia looked at the burned-away insulation. 'What is it?'

'It's the stasis-foam. What Brady was talking about.'

'I don't get it.'

He smiled. 'You will.'

Felicia made a face, and Striker gestured for her to follow. He led her from one room to another, through the empty pockets of blackened framework. This second room looked no different than the first, except in the far corner. A warped metal box lay on the ground with piles of what looked like melted wire surrounding it. Striker picked the box up, forced it open and studied the inside. Most of the inner panel was a clean grey colour, except the bottom half, which was blackened.

'Fuse box. Source of the fire.'

Felicia furrowed her brow. 'Brady said they used white gas.'

'They did – for the second fire.'

'*Second* fire?' Felicia looked at Striker, then at the destruction all around her. 'You think there were two fires?'

'I'm betting on it.' He walked to the window, where no glass remained, and stared outside, down into the north lane of

Pandora. Outside, a series of industrial garbage cans lined the lane.

'Follow me,' he said.

They tried to go out of the kitchen door down into the back-yard, but the stairs were all but burned away, so they cut back through the house, went out through the front door and took the sidewalk around the house. Once in the rear lane, Striker flipped open the first of five huge garbage containers. He looked inside, but could see little in the darkness.

'Lot of garbage cans for one place,' Felicia noted.

'Exactly.'

Striker continued flipping open the rest of the lids. When done, he took out his Maglite and shone it inside the garbage cans, one at a time. The first two were empty. At garbage can number three, he stopped, reached inside and pulled out three empty plastic cups and the remnants of two very large fans. The fan blades were covered in soil. He held one of them up and muttered, 'Jesus Christ, could it be that simple?'

Felicia frowned. 'I'd say no, since I have no idea what the hell you're talking about.'

He threw the box back into the garbage can and met her stare. 'It was a grow-op, Feleesh.'

'A pot palace?' She looked doubtful. 'There's no record of a grow-op ever being here.'

'Exactly. So why not? That's the million-dollar question, ain't it?' He looked at the array of plastic cloning cups in the next garbage can and shook his head. 'There has to be documentation somewhere.'

Felicia got out her cell. She called Info and requested an Incident History Location on the address. After a couple of minutes, the operator got back to her, and she hung up the phone.

'Nothing new,' she said. 'All that's listed here is the first Suspicious Circumstance call, and then, a few hours later, the Arson.'

Striker walked around the far side of the house, searching through the burned refuse. When he found nothing of value, he hiked back to the front. Analysed the devastation the fire had caused. Saw the *Condemned by City* sign.

'With a fire of this magnitude, they'd have to shut off the power first,' he said. 'Get an engineer to attend. Electrical and Structural. I know some people at the City – you got any contacts with the electric company?'

'Yeah, I got one at BC Hydro. Just up the road from here.' She looked at her watch. 'But it's getting late though. She might not even be there.' She flipped open her cell again. 'Hold on, I'll see what I can get.'

As Felicia made the call, Striker walked back to the roadside. Once there, he scanned the street for any video cameras, found none, then spotted the only other house that still survived on this block.

Sitting under the lone working streetlamp was a rickety old two-storey, covered in blue-painted stucco. A rusted iron fence ran around the yard, which was covered mostly by crabgrass and other weeds. Out front of the yard was a collection of old metal garbage cans, most of which had no lids and were dented.

Striker detected movement in the upper window of the house. Peering out from between the curtains was a thin, old woman. The moment Striker met her eyes, the curtains swished shut, and she was gone.

Felicia came up the walkway. 'Okay,' she said. 'I've got someone at Hydro who'll help us, but we've got to go now.'

Striker kept his eyes on the house across the street. He

hesitated. Something about the old woman struck him as odd – no doubt, she was one of the many fruitloops in this area; everyone down here was wing-nut crazy – but the way she had ducked out of view told him something was up. He turned to Felicia and threw her the keys.

'Meet me back here when you're done.'

'You're not coming?'

'No,' he said, and flashed her a grin. 'I think I just found us a witness.'

Eighty-Three

The memories of being Child 157 settled in Shen Sun's brain like cold fall mists in the Danum Valley. They left him fragmented and drained. As they always did. Amidst the fading recollections, a light clicked on and stole him from the stupor. He focused left. There, in the first ground-window of a nearby house, an old white woman was having tea.

For a moment, Shen Sun almost ignored her. He was tired and felt weak – as thin as rice paper. But something in her living room caught his eye. The television screen. The news was on, with a blonde woman reviewing the high-school massacre. Behind her pale face flashed the image of the gwailo.

Detective Jacob Striker, the headline read. *Hero cop.*

The image twisted Shen Sun's guts. He turned his whole body away, and the bundle of papers Sheung Fa had given him fell from his pocket.

Information on Detective Jacob Striker.

Shen Sun picked the paperwork up, stared at it with bad thoughts. As he flipped through the pages, the last one – the photocopy of Jacob Striker's picture – unexpectedly broke into two, and Shen Sun realised there were actually two pictures stuck together. He separated them and studied the photograph he had not seen.

The image was that of a young girl. About sixteen, with

long, curly, reddish-brown hair, milky skin and light freckles. Her eyes were a soft, sad blue.

The image filled him with excitement and renewed vigour. And he laughed out loud, silently praising Sheung Fa for protecting him still. It all made sense to him now. He had found The Way.

He would kill the Man with the Bamboo Spine, saving Father. And then he would repay Detective Striker for all that the man had stolen from him – Sheung Fa, Tran, his future with the Triads, his entire *life*. Shen Sun stared at the picture of the young girl and felt everything fall into place.

A daughter for a brother. It was more than fitting.

It was karma.

Eighty-Four

Striker watched Felicia drive away, south towards Hastings Street. When the roar of the Crown Vic faded, the sound of the wind became more prominent, howling between the burned framing of the house.

Striker spotted the old woman peering out between the drapes again. She pretended not to see him, then slowly backed away from the window. This time, Striker knew he had something. He used his cell to call Info, queried the address, and discovered there were numerous calls to her residence – all of them labelled as EDP.

An Emotionally Disturbed Person.

Commonplace for this area.

He headed up the block. By the time he had crossed the street and made it to her lot, the curtains were pulled shut and the interior and exterior lights were turned off. From here, the house looked empty, abandoned. And it gave him the creeps.

He took the stairs two at a time until he came flush with an old screen door. It let loose a creaky protest as he swung it open and knocked three times. He'd barely finished the knock when the door opened and a tiny old woman stood in the doorway.

She was an even five foot and about one hundred pounds.

Her rail-thin body had a look that suggested she was either on the way out of this world, or suffering from crack addiction, and her face was deeply lined with wrinkles. The three coats of make-up that plastered her skin were thick and oily.

'Hello,' Striker said.

'Hello, Officer,' she replied, her voice smoker-rough. 'I'm Phyllis. I've been expecting you.'

Five minutes later, Striker stood inside a crowded living room that stank of decade-old cigarette smoke and mustiness. The walls were now smoker's-teeth yellow, and everywhere he looked, ashtrays full of cigarette butts covered the tables.

He tried to ignore them and looked around the room. Old newspapers were piled up high in every corner, as were mountains of rocks and artistic stacks of Diet Pepsi cans. The sofas were brown, sat in an L-formation, and were covered in a clear plastic so old it was cracked and discoloured. When Phyllis offered him a seat, Striker politely declined and remained standing. He moved left, nearer the window, and knocked over another stack of Diet Pepsi cans.

He looked up at Phyllis, forced an embarrassed smile. 'I'm sorry.'

Phyllis picked up the cans, restacked them. 'Diet Pepsi, kid. Nectar of the fucking gods.'

'Not a Coke fan?'

She humphed. 'Coke? That stuff is shit. Know why? It's not the original – all they did was steal the Diet Pepsi formula, 'cause they knew it was better than the poison they were selling. They stole it and they renamed it Coke Zero. Read that in one of those supermarket papers.'

Striker nodded. 'There sure is a lot of information out there nowadays, isn't there?'

Phyllis lit up a smoke, inhaled deeply. 'Coke fuckin' Zero. Pfft! Know why they call it Coke Zero? 'Cause only a zero would drink it!'

'Hey, I hate the shit.'

Phyllis gave him a queer look, as if trying to either believe or disbelieve his words. Finally, she shrugged like she didn't care one way or the other and brushed her skin-and-bones fingers through her long, yellow-grey hair.

'So I know why you're here, Sugar. Came 'bout that fire, I betcha.'

Striker's interest piqued. 'Bang on, Phyllis. You see it?'

'Damn right I saw it. Big production. All them firemen runnin' round with their big hoses and their big red machine. Smoke was so bad it turned the entire neighbourhood into a black cloud. Stunk up the place worse than the chicken choppers down the street. Then the cops came and they tried to make me leave, but I wouldn't go. Said I was the last house on this block, I did, and I'd be keeping it that way till the day I die.'

'Well, hopefully that won't be any time soon.'

She took a long drag on her cigarette. 'Soon enough, Chuckles. Know how old I am? Ninety-two. Ninety-two goddam years old, and I been smoking Camels for seventy years and using aspartame for forty. Been drinking Diet Pepsi! Tell that to those organic-loving granolas!'

'Drinking Diet Pepsi, not that Coke Zero shit.'

She nodded. 'Fuckin' Coke Zero. Always trying to make it look like their recipe is such a big secret when all it is is fuckin' caramel and water! Everyone knows that. Except in the old days when they tried to hook everyone with the cocaine they put in it.' She snorted once, dropped her half-smoked cigarette into the ashtray, then took out a bright pink plastic tube.

'Damn cigarettes always wipe off my lipstick.' She put on another smear, lit up another cigarette, then took a long drag.

Striker looked at the ashtray full of pink goo and cigarette butts, and shuddered. 'So about the fire . . . can you tell me if there was anything unusual about it?'

'Everything down here's unusual. Makes the unusual look usual, know what I mean?'

'Sadly, yes I do. Did you know your neighbours before the fire?'

'Neighbours? Ha! If you can call them that. Never saw them, not once. They always came in the back lane. I heard them though. Always coming in with those big delivery trucks. Sometimes twice a day.'

'Twice a day?' Striker tried to sound casual. 'You ever see what they dropped off?'

'Who knows? Shoulda been fire extinguishers. Ha!'

Striker grinned. 'For sure. Not that it would've done a whole lot of good. That was a pretty bad fire.'

'The second one was.'

Striker gave her a hard look. 'Second one?'

'Yeah. The second fire. There were two, you know. First one happened earlier in the night – five, maybe six hours earlier – just a little bit of smoke coming out the window, the front one there. But they got it under control. Police came anyway, and the next thing you know, people are being taken out and the entire place is roped off.'

'Roped off?'

'Yeah, yellow tape everywhere.'

'Crime scene.'

'Sure, whatever. The whole place shuts down, and you think the show is over. But naaaw-aaahh. Suddenly, the cops're back, hauling shit outta there. Then there's another fire – the real one

this time – and the whole place goes up. Fuckin' *whoooosh*!'
Phyllis let out a loud phlegmy cough, took another drag on her
smoke, then reached for more lipstick. After smearing it on, she
continued, 'All I know is, someone musta fucked something up
real bad, because soon after that, we got the City out here and
the entire place is condemned.'

Striker let her finish talking, and he was glad when she
reached for another cigarette. The momentary silence gave him
a chance to think things over. So he had been right. There had
been two fires, hence the two calls. But the two calls had been
written up under one file number, then linked. Interesting, but
just that. It still left too many unanswered questions. He looked
out the window at the blackened shell just down the road.

'You ever wonder what they were bringing out of there,
Phyllis?'

'You mean, the people that used to live there before the fire?
Or the cops after the fire?'

Striker frowned. 'Both.'

'No, and I don't rightfully care.' She downed her Diet Pepsi,
pulled another one from the mini-fridge beside her chair, then
cracked open the tab. 'But one guy did.'

Striker blinked. 'One guy?'

'Yeah. The one guy who kept coming round here. Chinaman.
Hard face. Real thin.'

'When did he first come around?'

'Oh . . . right after the first fire. And he waited for a long
time, just over there.' She pointed her knobby finger out the
window, to a small patch of bushes that ran between two autobody shops. 'Stood there in the shadows for *hours*, just
watching everything.'

Striker thought this over. 'So to clarify, he got there after the
first fire had started, and watched it burn?'

'Yes. Well, it was already going when I saw him.'

Striker nodded. 'And he stayed long afterwards, till after the second fire?'

'Yeah. In fact, he stayed there till after the place had burned down. Just watching. Always watching.'

Striker absently rubbed the skin of his left hand, where the acid had splashed him. The skin around his fingers was raw, swollen. 'You ever tell the cops about this guy?'

'Nope.'

'Why not?'

'No one asked.'

Striker let this go without comment. 'And then what? He just leave?'

'Yup.'

'You ever see him again?'

'Sure. He come right back the next day. Musta spent, oh, two, three hours in the house there, just lookin' at things.'

'Things?'

'Yeah, you know, in the house. Lookin' at the walls, the floor, the ceiling. Seemed like he was lookin' for something real specific, trying to figure things out. Like a Chinese fuckin' Matlock.' She sipped her Diet Pepsi and shook her head. 'I dunno, I'm just an old woman, what do I know?'

Striker felt a twitter in his chest. Nervousness. Excitement. Hard to define. He took out his BlackBerry and brought up the images of Tran Sang Soone and Shen Sun Soone he'd downloaded from Ibarra back at the Strike Force HQ. When the images were completed, he held the phone up for Phyllis to see the screen.

'Look familiar?'

She put on her glasses, pointed at the second image – the one of Shen Sun Soone. 'Yep, that's him.'

Striker put the BlackBerry away. 'Thanks, Phyllis, really, you've been a great help.' He headed for the door, stopped, handed her a business card. 'You mind if I come back if I have any more questions?'

'Come anytime, darlin'.'

Striker gave her the thumbs-up. 'Fuck Coke,' he said.

'Amen to that, Chuckles.'

He left Phyllis alone in the room with her pink lipstick and Diet Pepsi, and closed the door behind him.

Eighty-Five

The muscles of Shen Sun's legs were cramping when he spotted the first sign of movement. It was subtle, almost indiscernible.

But he did see it.

A man, clad in black clothing, combat vest and long gun, changed his position from the parking lot near the boarded-up warehouse to the bushes down by the train tracks. The darkness was heavier now, and Shen Sun wondered if the man thought he was concealed.

Shen Sun watched him hightail it across the road, with surprising stealth for someone so large. Soon, a second man followed, much smaller. The two paired off on either side of the bushes.

Police, he knew. Emergency Response Team. Which meant there were at least eight more here somewhere in the darkness.

Shen Sun felt nothing at the sighting. No fear, no anger. It was expected. Just one more of the reasons why he could not go home.

Inside Father's apartment, nothing had changed. The interior remained quiet and still and shrouded by dimness. Only one lamp was on. In the living room.

Everything appeared ordinary.

And then there was movement inside. It was fast – just a blur in front of the lamp – and then gone.

Shen Sun twitched. He leaned forward, extending beyond

the bushes. The only door to Father's town home was at the front on Raymur Street. If someone was inside, they had been in there for forty minutes.

The thought was unnerving. Shen Sun watched the window, waiting for another sighting. When the image came, he flinched. A man lumbered across the room, his walk rigid and uneven, as if all the joints of his long legs were fused.

The Man with the Bamboo Spine had beaten him here.

The assassin walked into the living room. Stopped at the kitchen sink. Turned on the water. Washed his arms and face.

Shen Sun felt the last traces of his world slip away. He could not see it – he did not have to see it – but he knew what the Man with the Bamboo Spine was doing. He was washing away the blood.

Father was dead.

Shen Sun closed off any emotions he might have felt, and watched the town home – not as a son, but as a soldier, for it was all he could do now.

The Man with the Bamboo Spine finished wiping himself off on Father's quilt, then threw it in the corner. He walked to the front door, opened it, and stepped outside.

Shen Sun gripped the Glock with care. This was a hundred meter shot. Extremely difficult with a pistol. Even more so with only one good hand. He brought up his left hand and tried a two-handed grip on the Glock, but the pain of his shoulder was too much to bear. His left arm fell away.

'POLICE! Don't move!' someone cried out.

Shen Sun looked down below and spotted the two Emergency Response Team members leaving concealment. Both had machine guns out – MP5s, by the look of it – and were fast crossing the train tracks.

The Man with the Bamboo Spine was quick, so quick he

astonished Shen Sun. In one fluid motion, he turned away from the police as if he had not heard them, and drew his pistol. He left it hanging by his side, partly hidden by the long tails of his trench coat.

One of the cops gave the order: 'Put your hands in the air where I can see them!'

The Man with the Bamboo Spine did nothing at first; he only stood still and assessed the two men who had him lined up in their sights. The calm he displayed was amazing. And Shen Sun realised the assassin was lulling the cops in.

Preparing to shoot it out.

But then more cops appeared; they exploded from the shadows, every bit as deftly as the spirits that plagued Shen Sun's life. They came in pairs, long guns out, a semi-circle of warriors. And in the blink of an eye there were twelve.

Big Circle Boy or not, the Man with the Bamboo Spine was hopelessly outgunned.

Shen Sun saw the expression on the assassin's face turn from hard preparation to logical surrender. He was going to give up. Turn himself in.

And Shen Sun would not allow it.

He raised his Glock. Lined up the assassin. Opened fire.

The silencer was long burned out, but still managed to stifle the first two shots, allowing only a soft thunder to emit from the barrel. But the third and fourth shots were full bore. They sounded every bit their 40 calibre, and the entire valley below the overpass resonated with gunfire.

'Gun! Gun! GUN!' one of the cops screamed.

Shen Sun fired again. That first shot went high and wide, the second and third ones went too low, slamming into the earth at the assassin's feet. The Man with the Bamboo Spine reacted the only way he could. He raised his own gun.

And an eruption of gunfire filled the night.

It was over in seconds. The police carbines and MP5s shredded the Man with the Bamboo Spine, waking the neighbourhood and filling the night with brilliant flashes. The assassin jerked, spun left, and fell backward.

Shen Sun could not tell where the assassin had been hit, or how many times, but he was dead. Over ten cops had been shooting, and with high-powered assault rifles. No one could survive that.

Not even the Man with the Bamboo Spine.

Eighty-Six

Striker was standing in the centre of the burned-out framework of the house when Felicia finally returned. He checked his watch. It was seven now, and it felt even later. The sun was lost to them, and the coal-coloured clouds, which blocked the incoming stars and moon, killed any natural light that was left.

The wheels of the cruiser crunched loudly as they slid on the gravelly road and came to a stop. Felicia climbed out, leaving the engine running and the headlights on. In the aura of the beams, her face looked like a compilation of satisfaction and exhaustion. The shirt she wore was looser now, partly untucked on the left side of her hip, giving her an almost slutty look. It stirred something in Striker he hadn't had the time or energy to feel in days, and despite the weariness he suffered from and the shit they were dealing with, he couldn't help but notice – she looked sexy.

'You get the report?' he asked.

She held up the electric company's folder, a dark manila one with *BC Hydro* written across the top. 'Take a gander.'

Striker took it from her and glanced at the tab, where only the date was written and a BC Hydro case number. 'Have you read it yet?'

'I've perused it.'

'And?'

'Well, you were right about this place being a grow-op. In this report there's a list of all the supplies found: soil and seeds, lamps and fans, ozonators and filters – you name it.'

The confirmation gave Striker more confidence. He opened the folder, but it was too dark outside to read. He pulled out his flashlight, turned it on, and scanned the light across the pages.

The report was detailed, listing where the power had been bypassed and where the fire was believed to have started. The source was exactly as Striker had suspected – some kind of electrical problem in the fuse box, most likely caused by the increased power consumption of the lamps.

'There's our file number for the Arson,' he said to Felicia, pointing to the top of the page, 'and here's one that isn't linked in our system. Run this incident number, and I bet you find the grow-op report.'

Felicia returned to the car, then came back with the laptop and they went inside the burned-out house. Striker took the laptop from her and set it down on a small portion of kitchen counter that had not been completely burned away. On the counter, next to the laptop, he opened up the Fire Department's folder, and next to that, the BC Hydro file.

He pointed to the CAD call on the computer screen. 'So this is the first call Dispatch gets of someone yelling and smoke coming out the window. It comes in anonymous as a Suspicious Circumstance and turns out to be a fire from a grow-op.' Striker ran his finger down the page. 'Police attend and call in Grow-busters.'

'And then they call for the City and the electric company.'

'Right. But only after the fire is dealt with.'

Felicia nodded. 'And then six hours later, we have the big fire – the arson. A coincidence?'

He gave her a sideways look. 'There are no coincidences. And here's the real connection – look at the name of the engineer who attended for the electric company.' He turned the page and pointed to the author's name. 'Stanley Chow.'

'Tina's father?' Felicia asked.

'None other.' Striker picked up the Fire Department's report, then jabbed at the author's name. 'And look who wrote *this* one.'

Felicia read the last line. 'Archibald MacMillan – Conrad's father.'

'And who was here for *our* file number?'

'Patricia Kwan,' Felicia said. She scanned through the Fire Department's report, frowned. 'That still leaves one name missing – O'Riley. I've run Chantelle through the system ten times. No one in her family shows up for anything.'

Striker smiled. 'Look at the Fire Department's report. See the structural engineer who attended for the City.'

Felicia skimmed down the page, found the name. 'Pevorski. Polish person.'

'Stefana Pevorski,' Striker said. 'Now run her in PRIME.'

Felicia did. When the name returned, she made a surprised sound. 'It's a perfect hit,' she said, meaning all the details matched.

'That's because Pevorski is Stefana's *maiden* name. She's been married twice and she's never corrected it on the work system. Her current married name is O'Riley.'

Felicia looked up from the report, an excited look covering her face. 'They're all there then. We got Kwan—'

'Vancouver Police.'

'And Chow—'

'Structural Engineer for the City.'

'And O'Riley—'

'Electrical Engineer for Hydro.'

'And MacMillan.'

Striker tapped on the Fire Department's folder. 'Our HAZMAT guy for grow-ops.'

Felicia looked up from the file folders and smiled. 'That's a parent for every kid targeted. All four names. Connected.'

'Plus it explains why Doris Chow and Margaret MacMillan would never have made the link – they probably never even knew.' Striker bit his lip. 'We've been looking at this the wrong way ever since this nightmare began. The kids aren't the problem here, Feleesh, they never were. They're simply pawns in it all.'

Felicia shook her head absently. 'But why? For a friggin' grow-op? That doesn't make sense. We close down pot palaces all the time, so what was different here? What could these people have done that would warrant such a horrific response from any gang?'

Striker led her into the other room, where a large part of the wall was still intact. He pointed at the grey insulation lining all the walls.

'This is it here, the key to all this.'

'The stasis-foam?'

'You bet. The report says it's more than just a fire-retardant, it's impossible to X-ray through. And drug dogs can't detect smells through it. These pockets in the insulation aren't areas that the fire burned away – look at the ridges, they're completely uniform.'

'Then what are they?'

'They're prebuilt vaults. For *cash*. We're standing in the middle of a huge underworld bank, Feleesh. Even this one room alone could hold millions – and we have no idea how many other vaults were burned away in the other rooms. For all we know, the whole house could've been built this way. The money stolen could be in the *tens* of millions.'

'But why would a gang use a grow-op for a bank when there's such a high risk of fire?'

'That's the key – there's not. The stasis foam should have prevented that, but this place wasn't designed for being doused with white gas.'

Felicia ran her finger down the supple edges of the stasis-foam. 'So you're saying that Kwan and Chow and MacMillan and O'Riley are . . .'

'Thieves. Nothing more.'

Felicia thought it through silently, while Striker went on: 'They found the grow-op, did their due diligence, and later, after the drug teams left and everything was evacuated, they somehow discovered *this*.' He pointed to the series of vaults in the walls. 'A payday beyond what any of them could fathom. More money than they could ever have dreamed about, even collectively. So they took it – maybe as much as thirty million dollars – and then used accelerants to set the house on fire. They thought the place would burn to the ground and cover up their trail. Then they'd lay low for a few years before taking off somewhere else. They thought the gang and the police would never know better.'

'But they hadn't counted on the stasis-foam,' Felicia said. 'It slowed down the fire and gave the next Fire crew enough time to put out the blaze.'

'Exactly. And they hadn't counted on Shen Sun watching from the shadows. My witness, Phyllis, saw him there. Monitoring what they were doing. He knew something was up. Later, he did a thorough investigation of the house, figured out their plan and reported it to his bosses.'

'The Shadow Dragons?'

Striker shook his head. 'First off, don't confuse the gangs. The Shadow Dragons are nothing but a feeder gang for the real baddies – the Triads. More specifically, the 14K Triads – the strongest faction of the worldwide gang. They're the one every East Asian criminal wants to be a part of. They have all the power, all the history, all the *respect*. In Canada, their main liaison officer is Sheung Fa, who acts as kind of a bridge between the Shadow Dragons of Vancouver and his boss in Macau – the guy everyone calls Shan Chu. The Dragon Head.'

Felicia made a lost sound. 'My head is spinning. When did you work all this out?'

'When I finished talking to Phyllis and was waiting for you. It came together slowly, when I realised what the stasis-foam was being used for – and when Phyllis told me about the Asian guy watching the police from the bushes. That was Shen Sun Soone. So when Pevorski's married name came up as O'Riley, all the connections were there. Kwan, Chow, MacMillan and O'Riley were stealing from the Triads, and Shen Sun Soon and his Shadow Dragons were sent to deal with it.'

'So this was all just one big payback? Nothing more?'

'Oh, it was payback,' Striker said grimly, 'but that and a whole lot more. This is the Triads we're talking about. The 14K. Follow them back throughout their history and they have one main rule: disrespect the gang in any way and you will lose what is most precious to you.'

'Your children?'

'Your firstborn,' Striker said. 'It was a message being sent – to those who were guilty, and to the rest of the criminal underworld: steal from us – *disrespect* us – and this is what it will cost you.' He let out a sour laugh. 'Jesus, we thought Kwan was delirious back at the hospital, yammering on and on about the house being on fire, and dragons rising up all around her.'

'She was telling us exactly what we needed to know.'

'It also makes sense why some of the parents weren't too willing to meet us. They were afraid. Of us and the gangs. Some of them still have other children to lose.'

Felicia looked ready to say more, but Striker's cell went off. He snatched it from his belt and stuck it to his ear. 'Detective Striker, Homicide.'

'Shipwreck, it's me.'

'Meathead?'

'Yeah. We're at Shen Sun's father's place, down here on Raymur.'

'And?'

'It's all over,' he said. 'We got the fucker. He's *dead*.'

Eighty-Seven

Once on scene at Raymur, Striker made his way towards the group of ERT cops standing around the fallen gunman on the front lawn. He was almost there when his cell phone rang. He hoped it was Courtney, calling to see if he was all right, calling to say hi, or even argue – he just wanted to hear her voice again.

'Detective Striker,' he said.

The voice that responded was high-pitched and nervous, jittery. 'Detective Striker, it's me. It's Joyce.'

It took Striker a second to place the name and voice. Joyce Belle was the mother of Naomi, one of the girls on Courtney's last softball team. He hadn't spoken to the woman in over six months. Not since Courtney and Naomi had stopped being friends over liking the same boy. It alarmed Striker that she was calling. His first thought was of Naomi – was she one of the fallen? His mind frantically raced back through the names of the dead, but he couldn't recall if Naomi had been one of them.

'Joyce,' he acknowledged. 'Did Naomi . . . make it home okay?'

'Oh, she's fine, she's fine, thank Christ she's fine – thanks to you.'

Striker let out a sigh of relief. Stopped walking. His head was pounding. 'Look, Joyce, not to be rude, but I'm at a crime scene right now—'

'Oh, no problem, no problem at all,' she said. 'I wouldn't normally even call you, especially when you're at work, but Naomi just got home, and well, I thought I should tell you. Do you know where your daughter is?'

Striker thought of the two cops guarding his house. 'She's at home. Why?'

Joyce cleared her throat. 'Well, Naomi just got home from the mall. She says that not a half hour ago, she saw Courtney down there at the Skytrain exchange. Says she was all dressed up as Little Red Riding Hood and heading down to Commercial Drive for the Parade of Lost Souls. Said she was pretty drunk.'

Strike paused. 'I thought they cancelled that thing because of the shootings?'

'They did,' she explained. 'But then they put it back on in memory of those who were killed – kind of like a mass teenage catharsis for the kids.'

Striker cursed under his breath, wondered what the hell had gone wrong. 'Joyce, hold on for one second, will you?'

He cut across the road to the Emergency Response Team and borrowed the radio from Jake Holmgren, Team Leader. He got on the radio, then asked Dispatch to raise the units outside his house. Within thirty seconds, her response came back:

'I have no one on that detail.'

Striker felt his mouth go dry. 'There should be two cars on my place – one out front, one out back. We stationed them there this morning.'

'Let me check the local log,' she said. The sounds of typing filled the air and then the dispatcher came back on. 'Here we are. They were released from the detail at fourteen hundred hours.'

Striker's fingers tightened hard on the phone. 'By whose order?'

'The Deputy Chief,' she said. 'Laroche. I think it was a man-power issue.'

Striker swore and threw the portable back to Holmgren. He turned away from the group and got back on his cell. 'Joyce, you still there?'

'Yes, I'm here.'

'You're right, it's her.' Striker pinched the bridge of his nose as he spoke, felt the headache coming on like gangbusters. The Parade of Lost Souls. Christ, it was anarchy down there. And if Courtney was drunk, he'd kill her. He didn't need this. Not now. He checked his watch, saw that it was fast approaching eight o'clock, and realised that the huge Halloween bash would already be well underway.

'I have to go, Joyce,' he said, 'but thanks for calling. I'll head right up there and see if I can find her.'

'Don't hang up!'

The shrillness of her voice startled him, and Striker held the phone away from his ear for a second. When he brought it back, he said slowly, 'Joyce, is something wrong?'

'She wasn't alone,' the woman said breathlessly. 'She was with that friend of hers – Raine.'

'So?'

'You're looking for her, aren't you?'

'No, not that I'm aware of.'

Joyce paused, then said: 'You know who Raine is, right?'

'Well, I've never actually met her.'

'Raine is her nickname. Her real name is Riku. Riku Kwan.'

Striker felt a stab of cold in his chest. '*What?* How the—'

'Patricia wanted Raine to keep some of her heritage,' Joyce explained, 'so she legally named her Riku. But everywhere else, she was listed as Raine, because Patricia wanted her to fit in as well. I thought . . . I thought you knew this. I thought *everyone* knew this.'

Striker made a frustrated sound. Nothing in the case had been easy from minute one.

Felicia, watching him from the debriefing, caught his expression and gave him a *What's up?* look. He ignored it, told Joyce to let him speak with Naomi, and got all the details. When he finally hung up, Felicia had left the ERT pack, moved closer, and was still watching him.

'What was that about?'

Striker gave her a weary look. 'That was the mother of one of Courtney's friends. Apparently, Courtney's been out drinking all afternoon and she's buggered off to the Parade of Lost Souls.'

Felicia shrugged, grinned. 'She's fifteen, what else is new?'

'She was with Riku Kwan.'

The grin fell from Felicia's face. 'Riku? But how . . . why would . . .'

'Courtney's friend Raine *is* Riku. Raine's her goddam nickname. She's been within reach all along.'

'Holy shit. Give me the details, I'll call it in.'

Striker handed Felicia his notebook. While she got on her cell and called Dispatch to have this latest information broadcast, Striker tried to clear his mind. He marched up the hill towards the group of ERT guys and spotted Meathead, his six-foot-four frame towering above the rest of the men. Meathead spotted him, too, and stepped away from the group.

'You can buy me a bottle later,' Meathead said to Striker. 'Jack Daniel's. Legendary Blend.'

Striker looked past where the group was standing and stared at the mangled mess of flesh lying on the grass. The entire body was riddled with bullets – stomach, chest, and face completely blasted away. Striker winced. 'You turned him into Swiss-cheese, man.'

'I hate cheddar.' Meathead laughed at his joke.

'We wanted him alive.'

'No choice. Fucker drew on us.'

'He drew on you? Twelve guys?'

Meathead pointed towards the apartment. 'It's a murder-suicide, Shipwreck.'

'And his family?'

'Let's just say there won't be any more Father's Day cards sent here.'

Striker looked at the door for a long moment, couldn't help but feel something was wrong. He marched towards it.

Meathead stepped after him. 'Hey, Shipwreck, you sure you wanna go in there?'

'No.' He opened the door and stepped inside.

The front room was hot, as if someone had turned the heat on full blast. It was the first thing Striker noticed, then the smell hit him. Meathead joined him in the foyer, and the two of them made their way to the bedroom.

Striker stopped just inside the doorway. It was like nothing he had ever seen before. Lying sprawled out on the bed were the grisly remains of Lien Vok Soone – father of Tran Sang Soone and Shen Sun Soone. He was in the supine position, eyes open, arms out to the side, palms facing up towards the ceiling, as if he'd been crucified on an invisible cross. His mouth was wide open. It looked like he was screaming. Even now, in death.

'Jesus Christ.' Striker brought the sleeve of his suit up under his nose. 'What the fuck did he do to him?'

'Skinned him alive,' Meathead said, and for once there was no humour in his voice.

Striker moved towards the body.

'Don't touch nothing,' Meathead warned. 'Noodles ain't been here yet.'

'Fuck Noodles.'

'The Deputy Chief is on the way—'

'Fuck Noodles, fuck Laroche, fuck them all, Meathead – I don't care any more.'

Only one light was turned on – an ordinary lamp on the nightstand – leaving the room illuminated, but still relatively dim. Striker took out his flashlight, shone it down on the bed for a better visual. What he saw almost brought up his burger. The sheets were splattered with red gooey clots and covered in thick, uneven shavings of human skin.

'Look at the blood,' Striker noted. 'It's dark, almost brown.'

'So.'

Striker gave him a hard look. 'It's venous blood, not arterial. Means he lived longer through the process.'

Meathead said nothing, and Striker continued to study the body. When he shone the flashlight on the crotch and saw the peeled-away flesh and dismemberment, he closed his eyes, looked away, and turned off the flashlight. He let out a heavy breath.

'Seen enough?' Meathead asked.

'Too damn much.'

Striker exited the town home, stopped just outside the front doorway, and took in a deep breath of the clean, cold air. It felt wonderful in his lungs. Like it was cleaning his insides of the terrible odours he'd breathed in.

Felicia neared, asked him what had gone on in there, but he couldn't answer her. Flashes of the brutality bombarded him, and the scene still felt wrong.

'Something here doesn't make sense,' he said roughly to Meathead.

'What doesn't make sense?'

'The murder-suicide.'

'It makes perfect sense,' Felicia interjected. 'Shen Sun couldn't face his father. Couldn't tell him that Tran was dead. Couldn't tell him about the horrible things they'd done. So he murdered him and then killed himself. Who knows why? Some twisted form of family honour. Shame. Embarrassment.'

Meathead agreed. 'Yeah, shit, who ever really knows why?'

Striker ignored Meathead, looked back at Felicia. 'You wouldn't say that if you had been in there. That man is completely stripped of his flesh. Skinned alive. It's one thing for Shen Sun to murder his father and then commit suicide, but why the torture? That makes no sense at all. It's something he would never do.'

Never do.

The words hung there, and they made Striker reflect on the whole situation. A thought occurred to him, a nasty one, and he turned to face Meathead.

'Who identified the gunman?'

Meathead said nothing at first, he just scratched his head and looked at the group of ERT guys behind him.

A sinking feeling invaded Striker's guts. '*Who* identified him?'

Meathead flustered. 'It's him, Shipwreck. He drew down on us.'

'Jesus fuckin' Christ – no one's done it, have they?'

'I think Holmgren might—'

Striker pushed past Meathead, shoved through the cluster of ERT members, and knelt down in front of the body. The face was obliterated, and it reminded him of Tran Sang Soone – White Mask – back at the high school. There wasn't much to go on. At approximately five foot eight and one hundred thirty pounds, the physical frame of the corpse somewhat matched that of Shen Sun Soone. Lean, wiry, and that of a middle-aged man.

Striker turned back to Meathead. 'Gimme your knife.'

'Noodles hasn't even—'

'I don't give a fuck about Ident, just give me your goddam blade!'

Meathead removed the knife from his belt and handed it to Striker, who flicked it open, slid the blade under the dead man's shirt, and cut away the fabric. The first thing he saw was the tattoo on the man's right shoulder – a circle, drawn crudely, with a Chinese character he didn't recognise in the centre.

Striker stood up with a jolt.

'You stupid sons-of-bitches,' he said. 'It's not him.'

Eighty-Eight

Shen Sun crept out of the bushes and turned away from the police. He moved steadily into the adjoining cul-de-sac and began trying the door handles of the parked cars. He tried four of them before finding one that was unlocked – a grey, older model Honda Civic.

His favourite type.

He jumped inside, searched for a hidden key, found none. Taking his gun, he unloaded the clip and chamber, then used the butt end to break the ignition. Once the console was split open, he hotwired the car. Seconds later, he reloaded his pistol with the few bullets he had left, then drove south down Glen Street until he found a clearing.

He turned off the headlights, left the car running. From this vantage point he could see the group of cops on Raymur Street below. They were still standing out front of Father's apartment. Before, they had been calm – now they were arguing. And in the centre of them all was the Homicide Detective. Jacob Striker.

Something bad was happening. Shen Sun could see it in the cop's face.

He waited with great patience until the gwailo signalled for the woman cop to join him and they both jumped into the car. They did a quick U-turn, tires skidding on the road, then accelerated north on Raymur before turning east.

The lane was one that Shen Sun knew. It rounded back onto East Hastings Street. Sure enough, thirty seconds later, the cruiser breached the roadside, turned east, and sped down Hastings at a high rate of speed.

Shen Sun put the Civic in drive and followed them, flooring it to catch up. The road was busy with Friday-night traffic, made worse by the Halloween crowds. Shen Sun used this to his advantage. He followed the undercover police cruiser east. When the tail-lights lit up and the car came to an abrupt stop on the corner of Venables and Commercial, Shen Sun knew exactly where they were going.

The Parade of Lost Souls.

He pulled over not a half block away, and watched the two cops get out. He smiled when they both pointed at the crowd of costume-faced partygoers and hurried up the Drive. There was urgency on the gwailo's face. More than Shen Sun had seen before.

The sight intrigued him. Jacob Striker had been the calmest adversary he had ever faced – back at the school, at the Kwan residence, at the hospital. He had been a man of ice.

So why this sudden urgency?

The answer came to him like flowers blossoming in his heart. Only two things would cause this emotional reaction from the hero cop: either he was going after Riku Kwan, or he was going after his daughter Courtney.

Shen Sun leaped from the Civic, stuffing his pistol down the back of his pants. A momentary euphoria flooded him as he hurried towards Commercial Drive. He was nearing the end of his journey; he could feel it. And it now seemed so long ago that Kim Pham had come to him with the promise of a place in Macau, sent down from Shan Chu himself. The question of why the Triads had chosen him for the St Patrick's High mission never crossed Shen Sun's mind. Not once. He *knew* why. It was because he was logical. He was ruthless. He was without emotion.

But more than all that, he was a *survivor*.

The Angkor had proven that.

The St Patrick's High mission had been simple and straight-forward: kill the firstborn of every individual who had disrespected the gang and dared to steal from the underground bank on Pandora Street. Almost thirty-eight million dollars had been lost. And all of it 14K property.

It was sacred.

The most frustrating part was that the plan had been perfect. The firstborns would have been killed, the parents made aware of the cost of their larceny, and then the issue of interest-owed repayments would have been addressed.

Unless they wanted to lose their other children, too.

Fall guys had all been put in place. Sherman Chan, Que Wong and Raymond Leung would have been labelled as teenage spree killers, thereby keeping the police and public anger contained. And when the police eventually did discover that there were other possible suspects – through times of death and blood testing – Shen Sun and Tran would be long gone.

Far, far away in Macau.

In the criminal realm, every gangster would have known the real reason for the killings – because no grapevine was stronger than that of the underworld. And word of mouth aside, every-one in that world already knew the rules of the business. This was the ultimate cost of Triad betrayal.

Your firstborn.

As it always had been, throughout the centuries.

Shen Sun had needed no motivation for the job. Not when the reward for such a mission was to be the White Paper Fan at Shan Chu's side in the glorious city of Macau.

That was the Perfect Harmony.

That was *power*.

Shen Sun stepped onto the Drive and gaped at the frenzy before him. The Parade of Lost Souls was an outdoor costume ball with more than ten thousand people in attendance. His employers had provided him with photographs of Riku Kwan and Courtney.

One of these girls was here in the crowd.

Shen Sun knew this undoubtedly. And this time, the night would be his. For Tran was with him, somewhere in the night, his spirit floating in the October winds. It gave Shen Sun the edge he needed. The confidence. This time he would be unstoppable. The gwailo would fall. And Shen Sun would take his rightful place in Macau. It was a goal he had been working towards for twenty long years. A goal that had cost him Father and Tran. A goal that would come to fruition.

All it would take was two more deaths.

Finale

Eighty-Nine

Grandview Park was packed by the time Courtney and Raine got there. They'd left the party at Que's pad in full swing, and headed for the Parade of Lost Souls on Commercial Drive. Much to Courtney's delight, Bobby came with them, and he brought a new friend of his, Tom or Shaun or John or whatever his name was. She couldn't really remember – she'd had three coolers and two Cokes with cherry brandy – but he was tall and good-looking.

And good for Raine. Que had screwed her over again – but that was good anyway, because she seemed to like Bobby's friend. The two were walking side by side and talking, Raine dressed in her naughty nurse uniform and him dressed up like that bad guy from that superhero movie.

Bobby looked at Courtney, grinned. 'You look great, Court.'

It was the first thing he'd said for the last two blocks, and it made her more nervous than the uncomfortable silence.

'Raine picked it for me.' She gave him a quick glance, making eye-contact for a second then looking away. It was enough to send her heart into twitters. He was dressed all corny, in a Star Trek uniform. A yellow one, like he was Captain Kirk, or something.

'Well, she did a good job,' he replied. 'You look amazing.'

She looked back at him again and smiled. When his eyes

stayed on hers, intense and heavy, she felt her cheeks grow hot. She looked away from him, studied the crowd.

On the east end of Grandview Park, the band was setting up the stage. It was monstrous. There were a ton of lights, all red and white and blue and green, and some of them were already flashing. Loud explosions of firecrackers filled the air, sharp like gunfire, and a smoky haze floated through the crowd – firework and pot smoke, for the most part.

This was Commercial Drive, after all.

They all stopped a few feet from the stage and Bobby put down the backpack he was lugging around. It was a small dark blue thing, and it looked heavy the way he hoisted it. From it he took a two-litre bottle of Coke, a bottle of Jack Daniel's, one of cherry brandy and some plastic cups.

Courtney looked at the booze, shook her head. 'I'm done, my head's swimming.'

He acted like he didn't hear her, filled the cup with Coke, then added a heavy dose of cherry brandy. He handed it to her.

'Really, I've had—'

'Come on, Court, enjoy yourself. The Parade only comes once a year.'

She looked back at him, at the cup in his hand, and was about to say no again when she caught Raine's stare. She was giving her one of those *Don't-be-nerdy* looks, and so was Bobby's friend.

So she forced a smile, took the cup, and brought it to her lips. The cherry brandy smelled stronger than it had before, still good but really sweet, and her stomach quivered. She brought it to her lips, however, took a small sip. As she did so, Bobby reached out and lifted the bottom of the cup, forcing her to down more than she'd wanted. She almost choked, pulled the cup away from her lips, and stammered, 'B-Bobby!'

He just laughed, and stared at her with those suck-me-in eyes of his. 'You're beautiful, Court,' he said.

He grabbed her chin, tilted her head back and kissed her. His lips were soft and warm, and tasted of Jack Daniel's and Coke. They felt oh-so good. Her entire body tingled and she didn't want to stop. Even with Raine and Bobby's friend right there watching them, she didn't want to stop. She wanted him to keep kissing her forever.

Touching her. Feeling her.

He finally pulled away, and she felt a dizziness spill over her, fought to keep her balance.

'I want to kiss you again later,' he whispered. 'When we're alone.'

'Okay,' was all she got out. And before she knew it, he had refilled her cup with Coke and cherry brandy. 'It's enough,' she said.

But he just smiled and kept pouring.

Ninety

Striker waded into the sea of masks. They were all around him. Ninjas covered with head-to-toe blackness. Clowns with sad and angry faces. Superheroes complete with capes and masks. Everywhere he looked it was nothing but hidden face after hidden face. And he knew that Shen Sun could be one of them.

Hiding somewhere amongst the crowd.

The situation couldn't have been worse. Shen Sun had seen his face twice now, at the Kwan residence and at St Paul's Hospital. If that wasn't enough to etch it into the gunman's memory, Striker's face had been plastered on every TV screen around the city, twenty-four hours a day, for two straight days. In the end it meant one thing:

If Shen Sun was here in costume, he had the advantage.

'Just keep moving,' Felicia said, her voice sounding far away in the din of the crowd, even though she was just a few steps behind.

He nodded and pushed the bad thoughts from his mind. He marched slowly but determinedly through the crowd, focused on the immediacy of their situation.

The air stank – of pot, beer and body odour. Firework smoke saturated everything. And despite the October chill, it was hot and stuffy. Too many bodies were around him, tripping over and banging into each other. The crowds were like little whirlpools, turning this way and that.

'Courtney!' he called out. 'Raine!' But his voice was barely audible above the constant roar of the crowd. People were yelling and laughing, some dancing in the streets. A half block down, someone set off a series of firecrackers, and the explosions had Striker reaching for his pistol before he realised what they were.

'Easy, Big Guy,' Felicia said, and she put her hand against his back to let him know she was there.

When he made it to Grandview Park, he was blocked by an enormous stage, and had to circle round the band as they set up their gear. He grabbed the bass guitarist, a guy dressed up like a modern-day vampire, and asked him if the microphone was working yet.

It wasn't.

Striker cursed. He left the vampire guitarist and pushed on through the thickening crowd. When he reached the end of the park, he stopped on the corner of Charles Street and turned to wait for Felicia. Her face was tinted by the blue glare of neon stage lighting and her skin was damp with perspiration.

'This is no good,' he told her. 'We got to split up.'

She agreed. 'They're probably together.'

'If you find them, just get them out of here,' Striker stressed. 'Away from the crowd. Immediately. Get them down to the station.'

Felicia nodded. 'Put your cell to vibrate – you'll never hear it in this crowd.'

Striker did so, then pointed back at Grandview Park. 'You take north of the stage, all the way down to Venables; I'll take south and go to First. And if you see them . . .'

'Just get them out of here.'

'Right.' Striker touched Felicia's arm, pulled her close so she could hear better. 'And remember, Raine probably doesn't know about her mother yet, otherwise she would've gone home.'

A sad look crossed Felicia's face. She loosened her dress jacket so she could access her firearm more quickly. When she looked back up at Striker, there was concern in her eyes. And she gave a quick look at the crowd around them before speaking.

'Be careful,' she said. 'If this prick wants to attack us, there's no better place.'

Striker forced a grin. 'He's already struck out three times.'

Felicia moved forward. She wrapped her arms around the back of his neck, pulled him close, and gave him a long, hard kiss.

'What are you—'

'Just be careful out here. We have unfinished business, you and I.' She winked, turned around and set off through the crowd once more.

Three steps later she was swallowed by the masses, and Striker was alone again. He didn't delay. He spun around and pressed southward along the Drive. Into the endless flow of roaming smoke and angry masks and undulating bodies.

Into chaos.

Ninety-One

Shen Sun had lost sight of the Detectives, and that frustrated him. He speared through the crowd, shoving a pair of drunken clowns out of his way. The crowd was packed worse than cows at an auction, and the air smelled as bad. Most of the people were taller than him, but young. Drunk, high, out of control. To his right, at the beginning of Grandview Park, he saw a girl dressed as a French maid. She sat half-propped up against a tall oak tree, her left breast hanging out for all to see. He watched her sitting there, dazed, off-balance, bringing the cider bottle to her lips. A few seconds later, someone tried to help her up. He was tall, skinny, dressed in a black outfit with a white hockey mask.

It was perfect.

Shen Sun watched the boy take off the hockey mask and place it on the ground beside them. When the girl started vomiting, and the boy held her hair back from her face, Shen Sun took advantage. He snatched up the mask, then moved on through the crowd. As he went, he pulled it over his head, feeling the cold plastic stick to the flesh of his face. His body became flushed with adrenalin. It was as if he was back at the school again. Back at St Patrick's High.

At the beginning of the mission, and not at the end.

On the far side of the park, away from the hustle and bustle of the Halloween bash, a white catering van was parked alongside the kerb. *Hobbes Meats*. Sitting in the passenger seat was a fat white man. A *jin mao ho*. Shen Sun seized the moment. He quickly crossed the park.

When he came up beside the driver's window, he looked around and, seeing no sign of the cops, he rapped on the glass and got the man's attention. 'Why are you not in celebration?' he asked.

The man rolled down his window. As he turned his head to speak, he coughed violently and his many ripples of neck fat quivered. He snorted and spat out the window.

'Hockey mask. Nice costume, kid – you spend all night dreamin' up that one?'

'Why you wait?'

The man nodded at the roadblock on Charles Street, where bundles of partygoers were waiting for the band to start playing. 'Who are you, the parking police? It's my last load of the day, and I got here late. Can't make my drop till they lift the roadblock.' He sighed tiredly. 'What do you care anyway?'

'Drive down alley,' Shen Sun replied. He pointed back across the road. When the man turned his head to look, Shen Sun brought up his gun and smashed the butt end down over the back of the man's head. The driver let out a soft moan, his body went limp and he slumped down between the seats.

Shen Sun opened the door, pushed him right off the seat, and climbed in behind the wheel.

'Head . . .' the driver muttered. 'What hap . . . what . . . what . . .'

'Remain silent.'

'You . . . you can't—'

'I can.' Shen Sun brought the Glock down as hard as he could on the back of the man's skull, several times. He did this until the grip of the gun was wet and the man made no more sounds, but just lay there like one of the sacks of meat he was delivering.

Strapped to the man's belt was a set of keys. Shen Sun removed them. He climbed out of the vehicle, opened the back doors to be sure the keys worked, then locked them, feeling pleased.

Everything was set.

Hockey mask on, Shen Sun walked back across the park to the Drive.

Up ahead, a man dressed as a red devil set fire to a pair of metal balls on chains, then started swinging them in large figure eights. The crowd made a long *ooooh* sound as the fiery balls rolled through the air in wide uneven circles.

Shen Sun took the opportunity to study the faces. So many wore masks, and that was frustrating, but he believed that neither of the girls would do this. Why hide themselves? They were beautiful young girls. Ready to mate. No doubt they would dress in something to attract the opposite sex.

He was counting on it.

Sixty seconds later, the fire-show continued and Shen Sun finished surveying the crowd. Neither girl was in the immediate vicinity, so he moved on. He passed the bus stop, where a clown and a fairy were making out, and was about to continue when he came to an abrupt stop.

The woman cop was there. On the sidewalk. Her face was grim, but there was something else in her expression, too. Nervousness? Anxiety? No, that was incorrect.

Relief.

She had found something.

He watched her intently as she hurried south along the Drive, then crossed the street to the east. He followed, keeping close, and heard her call out: 'Courtney! Courtney!'

Shen Sun's heart constricted in his chest like a knot of rope. He followed the woman cop with his eyes, making certain he did not lose her. Moments later, when she pushed past a group of boys dressed as pirates, Shen Sun caught his first glimpse of Riku – the girl who would make his mission complete. And of Courtney – the girl who would serve as a cruel reminder for the rest of Detective Striker's life.

The girls were together.

Together.

Shen Sun smiled at his good fortune.

Ninety-Two

Striker reached First Avenue, where one of the Special Constables had set up a roadblock, preventing the traffic from turning north on Commercial. The Constable was a young kid, about nineteen, with a hooked nose.

'Hey, kid,' Striker said. He held up his badge to get the boy's attention. 'You see either of these two girls?' He showed him his BlackBerry and paged between the photographs.

The kid scratched his chin. 'There's been a lot of girls.'

Striker's BlackBerry buzzed. He turned away from the boy, looked at the screen, and read the incoming text: *Got them B4 U. Turks Coffee Shop.*

Striker replied immediately: *Only 5 blocks. Meet U there.*

He looked down the Drive. Turk's Coffee Shop was not far under normal circumstances, but in this crowd it seemed like miles. Everywhere he looked, something blocked him – a guy on stilts, roaming the street; a tall makeshift billboard, selling next year's Parade; and the outcrop of the stage, which cut Commercial Drive in half. Compounding all this was the firework and firecracker smoke – it floated through the air, ghostlike, greying everything in its path.

Striker frowned. Something didn't feel right. His instincts were screaming. And before he knew it, he was fighting his way through the crowd, shoving people out of his way.

'Asshole!'

'Jerk!'

'. . . the hell he think he is . . .'

The comments were endless, and he didn't care. He pushed on with even greater force, until he made it to within a block of the coffee shop. At first, he saw nothing, and he hoped they had already left for the police cruiser, but then he spotted Felicia and the girls a half block down.

A cop, a nurse, and Little Red Riding Hood.

Striker crossed Charles Street, spotted the man in the hockey mask, and his entire body tensed. Flashbacks of the school shootings bombarded him, and at first, he thought he was reliving memories of the past.

But something about the man gave Striker the creeps. He was facing Felicia and the girls, just standing there, watching them. They were his entire focus. They were everything.

Striker ran towards them.

As he did so, the bass guitarist from the band jumped up on one of the stage speakers and began his intro. 'You monsters having a good time?' he yelled, and the crowd began to cheer.

Stage fireworks exploded, sending waves of green and red and orange flame into the air, and were followed by more trails of thick grey smoke. Someone set off a series of firecrackers. *Bang-bang-bang-bang-BANG!*

Striker sprinted down the sidewalk, slicing the crowd in two, knocking people over and sending them onto their asses. When the crowd thinned for a patch, Striker scanned the area, but could no longer see Felicia or the girls. An icy coldness pierced his heart, and he knew instinctively:

Shen Sun was here.

Ninety-Three

Shen Sun saw the two girls – one dressed in red and black, the other dressed as a nurse. The woman cop was beside them. They were so close. A gift from the spirits.

A gift from Tran.

He adjusted the mask, reached behind his back and felt the gun. The magazine had five rounds left, which was not a lot. He didn't want to use one single bullet.

Not yet.

With this in mind, Shen Sun cut across the road, snaking in between the partygoers. They danced and stumbled and paraded all around him, each trying to close in on the stage as the band geared up and blasted their music into the night. The burned-gunpowder scent filled Shen Sun's head as he closed in on his targets.

The woman cop was looking the other way.

In one quick motion, Shen Sun pulled out his Glock. He held it by the barrel, raised it high, then slammed the steel butt down towards the back of her head. She sensed the blow coming, and at the last second turned, but it was too late. The gun smashed into her face with as much force as he could deliver.

Her head snapped hard and she dropped. Both the girls screamed, and suddenly one of the teenage boys dressed in a yellow uniform reached out for Shen Sun. Shen Sun easily pistol-whipped him to the ground. Another boy standing nearby took off through the crowd.

'Get away from us!' Courtney screamed. The girls turned and confronted him.

He pointed his pistol at them. 'Escape is forbidden. If one runs, both die.'

Courtney's mouth opened and she nodded slowly, as if understanding the command, or at the very least understanding the direness of the situation. Riku Kwan just stood there, her hand over her mouth. Her drunken face was a smear of disbelief.

'Felicia!' a voice called. 'FELICIA!'

Shen Sun turned. He looked south and spotted the gwailo. The cop was rampaging through the crowd. People were flying in his wake. The rage and fear and determination on his face were palpable. Simple escape was no longer an option. He needed something to slow the cop down. A diversion. Chaos. Pandemonium. Like . . .

A frantic mob.

Shen Sun aimed his pistol. He fired twice, once to the east, where the crowd was massing in front of the stage, and once to the south, where the gwailo was coming from.

The blasts were loud, deafening, unlike any of the firecrackers; and for the first time, people stopped partying. They turned around and looked at him. Really looked at him. At his stance. At his mask. At the gun in his hand.

A scream filled the air: 'She's been shot – someone shot her. She's been SHOT!'

And more followed:

'Gun gun gun – he's got a GUN!'

'Fuckin' nutcase! *Run!*'

The crowd exploded. Turned mob. Survival instincts took over. The partygoers scrambled in all directions. Dropping their drinks. Fighting for escape. Crushing the others before them.

When Shen Sun turned back to face the girls, they stood frozen. He reached out and grabbed hold of Courtney, pointed his pistol at Riku Kwan.

'Move away from crowd.' He flicked his pistol to show the way.

When Riku hesitated, he struck her across the face, splitting her lips.

She let out a wail. 'Please, we don't even know—'

'Move, or be killed!'

He wasn't sure if she heard him or not, but the pain woke her. She did as instructed. When the crowd thinned, Shen Sun turned the girls through the rolling masses into Grandview Park. Towards the van he had commandeered.

Escape was just a grass field away.

Ninety-Four

Striker saw Shen Sun cut north through the crowd with both Courtney and Raine as his hostages. One moment they were there, the next they were gone, swallowed up by the mob.

'COURTNEY!' he screamed.

He plunged forward, fought to race after them, but was knocked back by wave after wave of terrified, drunk party-goers. People screamed, cried out, grabbed on to him and begged him for help. He shoved past them all. Courtney was out there somewhere. He had to get to her.

She was everything.

He worked his way north, paralleling the coffee shops and convenience stores of the Drive. When he reached Turk's Coffee Shop, he found Felicia squatting on her knees against the patio railing. Trying to get up.

She'd be trampled if she stayed there.

In one quick motion, he reached down, snagged her wrist and hauled her to her feet, out of the path of the frenzied mob. She teetered momentarily, but managed to stand.

'You okay?' he asked her.

She looked back vacantly, blood running down the left side of her chin. Then mumbled, 'Go after him.'

Striker held her up on her feet, moved her to the safety of the coffee-shop entrance and got her to lean on the wall. With her safely out of the way, he then grabbed on to the drainpipe and climbed on top of the steel gate that separated the coffee-shop patio from the sidewalk. He scanned the mob.

It took ten seconds to find them.

Shen Sun was forcing the girls across the field, deeper into Grandview Park.

Striker jumped down. He told Felicia to stay put, then dove through the crowd. When he reached the other side of the Drive, he hopped onto the stage and raced across it. He leaped off the other side, entered the park, and spotted Shen Sun slamming shut the rear door of a white commercial van.

'SHEN SUN SOONE!' he bellowed.

He raised his pistol, took quick aim, and lost the gunman when a swarm of teenagers fled in front of him. Gun in hand, he raced through the park. He was barely halfway across when the van's tail-lights flashed red. Threequarters across when the van pulled out of the parking spot and sped north on Cotton Drive.

'Stop!' he screamed. 'STOP!'

Cotton Drive was a dead-end road. It connected with William Street and turned west, away from Britannia High School. Away from the Drive.

Striker angled his run across the park towards the school. He reached the common area just in time to see the white van speed west on William Street, turn north at the next block, and like a drowning person, slip just out of view.

Striker snagged his BlackBerry from its pouch and dialled 911 while running. When the operator answered, he blurted out his badge and rank and told them his daughter had just been kidnapped by Shen Sun Soone. He gave the location, a description of the van, and the last known direction of travel. With his lungs burning, he reached Odlum Street.

The van was nowhere to be seen.

He sprinted down to Napier.

Nothing.

Down to Parker.

Nothing.

Then all the way down to Venables Street, running till his legs ached and he felt he would collapse.

And still nothing.

Finally, he stopped. Let his hands fall to his sides. The only thing he felt was the heavy pulse of blood thudding through his temples. Gone. Courtney was gone. Taken by the madman just as God had taken Amanda.

He had failed her.

Ninety-Five

Courtney felt the van tilt as it turned hard somewhere on the road. The unexpected motion made her stumble and almost fall onto her side. Instead she hung on desperately to the inside edge of the rear door of the van, and tried to clear her head of her drunkenness and terror.

The movement made her head spin, and she vomited in the darkness. But that was okay. She felt better from it.

And maybe it would help her sober up a little.

There was no light in the back of the van, and only the whimpering sounds of Raine, who was somewhere deeper towards the back of the compartment. She felt around the walls and ceiling for a switch, found one, flicked it, and a small light came on.

The first thing Courtney saw was Raine. The girl was sprawled out on the cold floor of the van, on her stomach, head tilted to the side, in between the boxes of meat. Her lips were split, and blood trailed down her chin, onto the white surface of the van floor.

'You okay?' Courtney asked.

Nothing.

'Raine, you okay?'

The girl just laid there, a look of shock on her face.

'He has a gun,' she finally said.

Courtney remembered it well. She'd seen the gunman slam it into Felicia's head before turning it on them. It was a pistol; she knew that much. But what type or calibre, she had no idea. It was a big gun, and he would kill them with it.

The gunman had taken her cell, so she looked to Raine. 'You got your phone?'

'I dropped it . . . in the crowd somewhere.' Raine started to cry.

Courtney made her way over to the girl. All around them were boxes. Courtney opened the nearest one. It was full of steaks: thick, frozen slabs of meat. She grabbed the frozen slabs and started tucking them into Raine's costume.

Raine gasped with shock as Courtney shoved package after package down her top, sliding them down to her stomach and lower back area, then adding more. Courtney had no idea if the frozen meat was strong enough to stop a bullet, but it couldn't hurt. When she had Raine completely layered with frozen meat beneath her costume, she looked down at herself.

Grabbing a few packages of frozen steak, she shoved them down the front and back of her costume, padding the waist as best she could. It was so cold, it froze her skin, and she felt nauseous from the booze and fear.

The van tilted hard again, to the left, and she tumbled into Raine. The girl let out a sharp cry, as if the contact had finally woken her. She looked up at Courtney.

'It's the same guy from the school,' she said.

'I know.'

'The one who killed all the others.'

'I know.'

'He's going to kill us, too.'

Courtney saw the fear and desperation on Raine's face,

which mirrored her own emotions. And she said nothing, because there were no words of comfort. She simply put her arm around Raine and felt the van turn and tilt at every corner, as they were driven further and further away to an unknown location.

Ninety-Six

Striker had no idea how many minutes had passed by the time he'd made it back to Commercial Drive. His head felt clouded; his senses distorted. Already there were police cars everywhere. One cop guarded the dead van driver who had been dumped on the west side of Grandview Park. Another cop took custody of a deceased girl Shen Sun had shot near the front of the stage. And one was parked in front of Turk's Coffee Shop, where a paramedic was patching up Felicia.

Striker hurried up the Drive, red and blue flashes of police lights reflecting off the lingering smoke. The strip was now deserted. As he neared Felicia's side, she pushed past the paramedic and stumbled up to him. She stopped at an arm's length, a question in her eyes.

'He got away,' Striker said. 'With the girls.'

'Did you see what he was—'

'A white *Hobbes Meats* truck. Already broadcast it.' The words fell oddly from his lips, sounding hollow, forced. He felt like a dam full of holes, ready to crumble at any second. When he spoke again, he fought to maintain control of his emotions. 'They could be anywhere.'

'Let's go back to the car – we'll find them.'

Striker looked at her face, saw the dried blood on her chin and neck, the swollenness of her jaw. He nodded, and they turned north on Commercial. They'd barely gone ten steps when his BlackBerry vibrated against his hip. He lifted it so he could read the call display, and felt a stab of electric fear and hope in his heart when he read the name: Courtney.

He picked up fast. 'Hello?'

The voice that replied was masculine, clipped, and brief: 'Ironworkers Bridge. Halfway.'

'Shen Sun?'

'Block traffic at both ends of bridge. And come alone, *Gwailo*. Otherwise, both die.' The line went dead.

Striker stood there, dumbfounded for a moment, then turned to look at Felicia, who had heard every word.

'He wants you alone on the bridge? What, does he think you're out of your mind?'

'I'm going.'

'Jacob, you can't—'

'I have to, Felicia. Why do you think he called? He could have escaped by now, but he didn't. It's no longer about the theft or the murders or the position he was promised – it's about him and me now. *I'm* what he wants.'

'Just stop for a second. Slow down. Think about this. It's what *he* wants, Jacob. Jesus, at least wait for a sharpshooter.'

'There's no time.'

She grabbed his arm, got in his face. 'Jacob, it's *suicide*.'

Striker pulled away. 'He's got Courtney, Felicia. He's got my little girl.'

Before she could respond, he marched back to the police car, thinking over the words Shen Sun had spoken. The orders were clear. Meet halfway across the bridge. Shut down the bridge at both ends. Those two sentences alone told Striker everything he needed to know about the situation. A negotiator would be of no use.

Nothing would be.

Shen Sun wasn't planning on surviving the night.

Ninety-Seven

The Ironworkers' Memorial Bridge was a 1200-metre, six-lane steel monstrosity that spanned the Burrard Inlet, connecting the city of Vancouver to the Northern Shore. It was built up high, on concrete pillars that rose from the foaming, turbulent waters below like a series of grey gnarled fingers. A perpetual fog brooded around the structure, one so thick it made the paved lanes seem more like a witch's cauldron than a roadway. The bridge had been built in 1957, and in the process of construction had cost 136 workers their lives.

Striker prayed it would take no more tonight.

It took him and Felicia less than four minutes to reach the south on-ramp. Already, a marked patrol car had blocked off the entrance, its red and blue emergency lights reflecting off the heavy fog that roamed the pavement like a crawling beast. Next to the police cruiser, a patrol cop dressed in orange and yellow reflective gear waved him over and said, 'Park it there, Striker.'

He did.

When he climbed out, he recognised the man. It was Chris Mathews, from the Two-Eight squad. Striker walked towards him, his head feeling as fogged as the roadway. He'd barely gotten ten steps when a white unmarked cruiser came speeding up the on-ramp behind them. Its lights were flashing, the siren turned off. The cruiser slid across the wet asphalt, coming to a slow stop not five feet away. The driver's door opened and a man in a white shirt hopped out.

One look at him and Striker stopped cold.

Laroche.

The Deputy Chief came stomping around the cruiser, his face pale and twisted in the harsh glare of the headlights. He was followed by Inspector Beasley.

'Striker!' he called, his voice cracking in the cold. 'Where the hell do you think you're going? I've already got ERT and a negotiator on route.'

Striker turned to face the man. 'Did you pull the units from my house?'

'That doesn't concern you.'

Striker took a step closer, his hands balling into fists. 'I asked you a question, Laroche. Did you or did you not have patrol guard removed from my house?'

Laroche raised a finger and pointed it in Striker's face. 'You're damn right I did! My men aren't your personal—'

Striker punched the man square in the face, sent him sprawling backwards. The Deputy Chief hit the pavement, landing hard on his ass. Stunned, he sat up, touched his lip, then looked at the blood on his fingers. Disbelief coloured his face, quickly replaced by anger.

'How *dare* you strike a commanding officer! I'll have your badge for this—'

Striker stepped forward, grabbed the Deputy Chief by the scruff of his shirt.

'Let go of me!' Laroche screamed.

Striker ignored the order; he dragged the man back to the police cruiser, opened the rear door, and threw him inside. When he slammed the door closed, the Deputy Chief let out a frustrated howl and grabbed the door handle. He tried to open the door, reefed on it hard, but the safety lock engaged. He pounded his fist on the glass.

'Striker! Striker! Open this door immediately! It's an ORDER!'

As Inspector Beasley started for the car, Striker stepped in his way, fixed him with an icy stare.

'My kid's up there. *I'm* going up. No negotiator. No ERT. No Air One. No goddamn nothing.' He stabbed a finger towards the Deputy Chief. 'That little prick gets out and in any way endangers my daughter's life, and I'll shoot the fucker. I mean it, I'll goddam shoot him and you can arrest me for it later.'

Inspector Beasley's mouth dropped open.

Striker continued, 'And if Laroche comes up there and any bad shit happens, I will hold you personally responsible, Beasley. Got it?' Without waiting for a response, Striker turned away from the man and found Felicia. He came up in front of her, spoke softly. 'Don't let *anyone* up this road.' He then took her pistol as a spare and tucked it in the back of his belt.

'Be careful,' she urged.

There was nothing to say, so he just nodded, then turned away.

It was time to face Shen Sun Soone.

Ninety-Eight

Striker marched quickly up the bridge deck. The asphalt was damp, and covered with metal and plastic fragments from an earlier accident. His boots slipped as he hurried on. With every step he took, the bridge inclined, becoming steeper and steeper, and he rose higher and higher into the fog. Until it felt like he was walking into the cloudbanks.

Up ahead, the headlights of the *Hobbes Meats* van came into view. The sight hit Striker like a physical force and he stopped. He looked back the way he'd come and saw the flashing red and blue gleam of the police lights. From this distance, saturated by the heavy blanket of fog, they looked small and faint, like tiny bulbs on a Christmas tree.

He was alone on this one.

And the girls' lives depended on him.

The Sig Sauer sat snugly in its holster – and he dropped his hand down to the butt of his gun for comfort as he marched on. The rubber grip was cold, harder than usual in this freezing weather, almost slippery from the icy moisture. Striker wrapped his fingers around the grip, squeezed tight, moulding it to the flesh of his palm.

The wind kicked up, strong and fierce, blowing his hair in all directions and sending the flaps of his suit jacket whipping to the sides, exposing his gun. And though he knew undoubtedly that Shen Sun would expect him to be armed, there was no point showboating it. He pinned the jacket down with his elbow, kept his fingers loose and ready.

The bridge lamps, weak against the heavy fog, shed a minimal light. Striker could barely make out the vague shape of the van as he closed in, just the halogens. He strained his eyes for any sign of Shen Sun or the girls – for any sign of movement at all – but saw none.

From far below, he heard the rushing sound of water as the Fraser River slammed into the bridge foundation. Striker was well over the waterway now, had been for the last fifty metres.

He marched on. After another twenty feet, the van lights mutated from a single globular glow into two clearly distinct headlights. And soon Striker could hear the heavy rumble of the engine, and smell the dirty diesel in the air. Ten steps later, the outline of the vehicle became sharper. Ten more steps, and he could make out the blurry lettering on its side.

'You stop now.' The voice was quick, hard, angry.

Striker did as instructed. He looked ahead, tried to figure out where the voice had come from. But all he could see was the bright piercing glow of halogen headlights. And he realised that the van had been parked this way to blind him.

He stared into the piercing light, raised a hand to ward off the glare.

'I'm here, Shen Sun. You got what you wanted. Now let the girls go.'

'What I want?' The voice was mechanical, numb, spoken more like a statement than a question. 'Never do I have what I want.'

'Where are the girls?'

'Your daughter? She is here. I give proof.' There was a brief pause, and suddenly a scream filled the air.

'You twisted little fuck.' Striker started forward.

'Come, and they die.'

He stopped cold. Said nothing. Just waited. Listened. Tried to focus and calm the panic. *Think.* Judging by the direction of Shen Sun's voice, Striker figured he was near the tail end of the van. Left side. A tactically sound position.

One Striker would have chosen himself.

Striker took a small step to the left, inching his way out of the worst of the glare. And for the first time, he spotted a vague outline behind the lights. A wide blur – three bodies, crammed together – between the rear of the van and the bridge railing.

Two were standing. One was seated.

'What do you want, Shen Sun?' Striker asked. He took another small step out of the glare.

'What do I want?' His voice was hollow, eerie. 'I want my brothers back. My sisters. Father. Mother. This is what I want.'

Striker listened carefully to the words. The man was making no sense. Striker inched over a little more, tried to give his eyes time to adapt.

'What do you want *from me?*'

'I tell you what I want from you, *Gwailo.* I want you to feel the pain I felt, when you ended my mission, when you killed Tran. And Father.'

'I never killed your—'

'Yes, you did!' Shen Sun snapped. 'The man was here because of you – *only* because of you. You destroyed my future. My life. Everything! And now you have same pain I have – and you must choose.'

Striker raised his hands in the air, purposely to distract the gunman, and inched his way a little more to the left. 'You're talking in riddles.'

'Then I speak simple. I have gun against daughter's spine.'

Striker moved a little more left.

'And here is Kwan child,' Shen Sun continued. 'The one we both search for.'

A little more left . . .

'I give you choice, *Gwailo*. Simple. Choose Kwan child and she live. But I shoot daughter in spine, and you watch for rest of life knowing your fault.'

'Shen Sun—'

'Or choose your daughter – but Kwan child dies.'

'That's no option at all.'

'It's all you have.'

'It's nothing.'

Shen Sun cocked his head, spoke softly. 'Family, or honour?'

'I can't—'

'*Family – or honour!*'

Ninety-Nine

Shen Sun watched the gwailo's hopeless expression with a sense of euphoria. He was exhausted; his shoulder seared with pain. And there was no chance of him escaping this situation alive.

None of that mattered.

All that existed in the moment was the terror of the girls before him, and the heavenly desperation of the cop ahead. And he laughed out loud, for he could not help himself. All his life he had strived to be 14K – to be with Shan Chu, the King Daddy himself, the Dragon Head – and before the mission had started, he had been promised a swift trip back to Macau if things at St Patrick's High had gone well.

But things had not gone well. The whole mission had been disastrous. All because of Detective Jacob Striker. Shen Sun had been forced to improvise. To alter the plan. It had been the only way to keep his dream alive. The only way to reach the place he called home.

And to find the Perfect Harmony.

How odd it was. Here at the end of his life – for that was surely what this was – he had found it. And unexpectedly so. Not in a place, or an object, or even through some achievement. No, he had found it through a state of mind. And that was what it was, wasn't it? The Perfect Harmony. Finding whatever it was that you were missing inside, that one lost piece that would make a man truly whole. Well, he had found it. At long last, he had found it.

And it was *power*.

'This isn't necessary,' the cop said.

'Make choice, *Gwailo*.'

'We can find another way.'

'*Make choice, I say.*'

To Shen Sun's lower left, Riku Kwan let out a sob. He pressed his foot down harder on her ankle, making certain she remained seated. Not that she would attempt escape. He had made it quite clear: any attempt to escape would result in a quick death for both of the girls.

'Shen Sun,' Striker said. 'I'll do anything—'

'Choose!'

To Shen Sun's right, Courtney squirmed. He clutched the hood of her Little Red Riding Hood costume, twisting his fingers deep into the material. She let out a cry as his fingernails dug into her back, but he held her tight.

'I won't make that choice,' the cop finally said.

The words hit Shen Sun like the end of a whip. And for the first time since the gwailo had set foot into the headlights, he felt his euphoria seeping away. The pain in his shoulder became sharper, the throbbing of his head more violent. His body was sweating and shivering, and the weakness of his legs had returned, keeping him off-balance.

'You will not . . .' he began. Then Shen Sun Soone felt the world fading on him. He looked up at the cop, standing in the circular glare of the fog-veiled headlights, and suddenly he could see him for what he was – for what he had always known Jacob Striker to be – ever since their first encounter back at the school.

An evil spirit in human form. An earthbound demon.

It made no difference.

'Make choice!' he demanded for the last time.

And the cop did.

He reached down, drew his pistol, and ran forward. And just like the evil spirit he was, he fell out of the light into the darkness, and vanished from sight.

One Hundred

The seconds felt like hours.

Striker burst forward, cleared the glare of the headlights and took quick aim the moment the two girls and the gunman came into view. Raine was grounded, on her knees, sobbing but out of the line of fire.

Courtney was not.

She was held tight by the madman, pulled close, a human shield. There was little room – definitely not enough room for a shot. And yet Striker knew he had no choice. If he didn't act now, Shen Sun would kill her. He squeezed the trigger, heard the blast shake the entire area around them . . .

And then heard Courtney's agonised scream.

She collapsed onto the wet concrete of the sidewalk, then rolled off the kerb into the lane. Even in the poor light, the dark, glistening splatter that covered her belly was obvious. And Striker realised it hadn't been him who had fired the shot.

Shen Sun stepped forward. Into the light. Raised his pistol.

Striker saw the motion out of the corner of his eye. He darted left, took aim again, and heard three shots blast off. He felt bone-breaking pain as his chest and ribs cracked from the impacts. The force sent him reeling. He landed hard on his back, in the middle of the road, fighting to breathe, but still managing to pull the trigger in rapid fire.

Bang-bang-bang-BANG! The shots rang out, too many to count.

And then there was more screaming. The girls were screaming.

Striker rolled left, propped himself up on one arm, and scanned the sidewalk. He spotted Shen Sun, hobbling like an old, crippled man across the sidewalk. Towards Raine. His left arm hung limply and his right leg didn't work right.

Striker raised his gun and drew down on the man. But he couldn't get the shot off – not without hitting Raine. The girl screamed out in terror as Shen Sun grabbed her from behind, hoisted her to her feet, and pulled her into him.

'Please!' she screamed. 'PLEASE!'

Shen Sun ignored her. He reared up to the bridge railing, wrapped his arms around her, and then found Striker with his eyes.

'History is circle, *Gwailo*. Past is also future.'

There was no time left. Striker kept his aim tight, the sights lined up on the centre of Shen Sun's face, and he pulled the trigger. All he heard was the god awful *click-click-click* of an empty chamber.

Shen Sun smiled. Smiled as if all the pain and rage and fear had left him and he had found peace. For a moment, he looked calm, serene . . . harmonious. Then he threw his body backwards.

In one quick, horrible moment, Shen Sun and Raine slipped over the railing and were swallowed up by the greyness beyond. Nothing was left behind in their wake, except a young girl's cry that would forever be embedded in Jacob Striker's mind.

Epilogue

One Hundred and One

Three weeks later, early in the morning, Striker pulled into the visitors' parking lot of the G.F. Strong Rehab Centre and felt his BlackBerry vibrate on the side of his belt. The caller was Sergeant Ronald Stone from Internal. He didn't answer, but punched the ignore button instead. There was enough on his plate today without having to deal with Professional Standards.

He locked the car and headed for the main building. The sun was out and the sky was blue, but the air was crisp and cold. Snow had fallen the previous morning, testament to the fact that winter had definitely arrived. The cedar bushes that flanked the walkway were clean and white, and decorated in Christmas lights.

Red and blue.

The snow from Striker's boots turned the hard tiles of the hospital floor slippery, and he walked carefully as he made his way from the admitting area down to Rehab. Once in the wing, he stopped by the Christmas tree planted beside the nursing station and smelled the strong scent of pine in the air. He scanned the area and spotted the Occupational Therapist, a middle-aged East Indian lady. She was only five feet tall but built like an aircraft carrier.

'Mr Striker,' she said at the sight of him, and offered a wide smile.

'Janeeta,' he said. He took a long hard look down the hallway, in the direction of Courtney's room. His nerves felt on fire. 'How's she coming?'

'She's coming well, Mr Striker.'

'But will she walk normal again?'

Janeeta looked at the chart she was holding, flipped through the pages, then looked back at Striker and gave his arm a soft rub. 'Why don't you go talk to your daughter, Mr Striker?'

He nodded, then walked down the hall to Room 14.

'Hey, Pumpkin,' he said as he stepped through the door.

Courtney was seated on the bed, looking out the window. She wore a burgundy pair of track pants from *Roots*, complete with a matching sweat top. At the sound of his voice, she looked over her shoulder at him. Her expression was unreadable.

'Snow,' was all she said.

'Yeah, first time in two years. Christmas is coming.' He pointed to her tracksuit. 'Got your colours ready, I see. Very festive.'

Courtney didn't smile. 'It hasn't snowed like this since Mom died.'

The words punched through Striker, took his breath away. Mainly because she was right. The last time it had snowed was the night Amanda had taken off, when she'd driven for her friend's house on the North Shore and never made it back. The memory seemed like yesterday. And Striker wished he could forget it all.

He approached the bed, crested it, and rubbed his hand over the top of Courtney's upper back – away from her healing scar – in his best attempt to show support. He stared outside at the snowy roadway, thought about what his daughter didn't yet know, then sat down in the bedside chair and faced Courtney.

'You know, we've never really talked about that night,' he said softly.

'You've never wanted to.'

He nodded. 'There are reasons, Pumpkin. Ones not too nice.'

He spoke the words reluctantly. When he looked up and saw the seriousness of her stare, he considered letting the subject go, once again burying it with the rest of the past. But this time, he could not. Everything was different now. It was time for a clean start. Time for honesty.

He closed his eyes, trying to think how best to word it. 'Things between your mom and I weren't as good as you remember them, Courtney. Our marriage wasn't perfect. To be honest, it wasn't working all that well.'

'I know, Dad.'

He blinked. 'You do?'

'Yes. I know about the affair.'

He twitched in his seat. 'Affair? What affair?'

'With you and Felicia.'

Striker let out an exasperated sound. 'You think *that*?'

'Well, what am I supposed to think?'

'Jesus Christ,' he said. 'No wonder you've been acting the way you have.' He rubbed his hands over his face and sighed deeply. 'It's my fault. All my fault for not telling you.' He leaned closer, took her hand and said, 'Courtney, I never cheated on your mother. Me and Felicia never so much as dated until seven or eight months ago.'

Her face took on a confused look. 'Then what—'

'Your mother wasn't well, Courtney. In fact she was quite sick. Clinically depressed. She wouldn't even leave the house half the time. It was an issue – her bipolar diagnosis – and we always tried to hide that from you, but I guess . . . I guess it was wrong of us.'

'Bipolar?'

'She was on medication and seeing a specialist in Kerrisdale.' He took in a deep breath, studied the shock on her face, then told her the worst of the truth. 'The night she left home, I didn't let her drink and drive, Courtney. In fact, she hadn't drunk a drop.'

'But then how . . .'

Striker said gently, 'The Dinsmore Bridge . . . it's straight and flat. And there was no traffic that night. When your mother drove off the bridge, Courtney, it wasn't an accident. It was her own doing.'

The words made Courtney flinch, and she almost pulled her hand free from Striker's grip. He watched her intently, expecting her to cry and crumble, or at least get angry and lash out. But she did neither. She just stared out the window, at the snowy hills outside, and her face took on a sad look.

'You okay, Pumpkin?'

'I think I always knew,' she said in a low voice. 'I just didn't want to believe it.'

'I'm sorry about your mother, Pumpkin. And about Raine.'

Courtney looked up at him and her expression was wretched. 'It's so strange. When Raine and I were in the back of that van, I thought we were going to die, I really did. And Raine was just out of it. Like in shock or something. So I stuck a bunch of frozen steaks down the front and back of her shirt. I thought that it would protect her if he started shooting, but now . . . now I wonder if that was what weighed her down. Maybe that's why she couldn't swim to shore. I killed her.'

Striker looked into her eyes. 'The fall killed her. And the currents are strong. She never would've been able to swim out.'

'I just feel—'

'You did all you could. And thank God for those frozen

steaks. They may have deflected the bullet a bit. The doctor says you'll walk again.'

'But how well?'

Striker held her hand. 'I don't know.'

Courtney didn't reply. Moments later, a few tears slid down her cheeks.

Striker stood up and wrapped his arm around her, gave her a long hug, felt her warm breath under his chin, smelled the lemony scent of the laundry detergent on her clothes. She held him, too, and just as tight. When her arm finally relaxed a little, Striker pulled back and looked at her face.

'What do you want for Christmas?'

'Getting this bullet out of my spine would be a nice start.'

He laughed, genuinely and hard, and touched her face. 'I love you, Pumpkin.'

'I love you, too, Dad.'

He fetched her suitcase from under the bed, made sure it was locked and secure, then helped ease her off the bed into the wheelchair.

'Come on,' he said softly. 'Let's get the hell out of here. We're going home.'

One Hundred and Two

Striker had just finished getting Courtney seated and buckled into his Honda CR-V when the sound of squealing tires filled the underground. He turned and spotted a small car speeding around the bend in the dark parkade. Instinctively, he swept his hand under his jacket flap and touched the butt of his pistol. As the car drove closer, Striker saw that it was a silver Volvo, a car he recognised well.

Laroche.

Striker let his fingers slide off the butt of his gun as the Volvo came to a stop ten feet away. Even in the darkness, Striker could see the angry expression on Laroche's face. The Deputy Chief climbed out, slammed the car door.

'Striker!' he roared.

'This is a hospital, sir – the mental institution is down the road.'

Dressed in civilian attire, Laroche looked even smaller than he did in his dress pants and officer's shirt. Beads of sweat rolled down his face, making his white skin appear even more sickly. He stormed up to Striker, his hands balled into fists.

'It was you, wasn't it?' he demanded.

'Me, sir?'

'I know it was you, Striker!'

'I have no idea what you're talking about.'

'The complaint to Internal. The subsequent review over my handling of the Active Shooter file.' When Striker said nothing, Laroche continued, 'I'm getting demoted, Striker. *Demoted!* You've ruined my bid for Chief. Ruined it. My entire career!'

'That's very unfortunate, sir.'

Laroche's eyes darkened and his face reddened till all the white had left his cheeks. 'You think I don't know you did this, Striker? You think I'm some kind of fool?'

'Think, sir?'

Laroche swore out loud, raised a finger. 'I don't care if it takes the rest of my goddam career, I'll make you pay for what you've done.'

Striker waited for Laroche to finish his rant, then stepped calmly forward and said quietly, 'Let me give you a little bit of advice, *Superintendent*. When you're in a field full of horses, don't go looking for zebras. All you'll find is more horses.'

Then Striker turned around, walked away from Laroche and climbed into the CR-V. Moments later, he and Courtney drove out of the underground parkade into the cold brightness of the blue-skied winter day. Courtney was returning home. Felicia was coming over for dinner. And Laroche was screwed. Striker let out a satisfied breath.

What more could a man ask for?

One Hundred and Three

Three hours later, Striker sat in the passenger seat of the under-cover police cruiser. Felicia was driving. The sun was still out and the sky was an icy, cloudless blue – perfect for such a cold wintry day. Courtney was at home, being tended to by the out-reach occupational therapist, so it gave them some time.

They were headed for the Ironworkers' Bridge.

They took First Avenue out east, all the way to the Trans Canada Highway. As she drove, Felicia rambled on, mostly about the upcoming changes in Homicide, and also relaying the latest gossip of who was screwing around with whom – a topic that never got old at the Department.

Striker barely heard any of it. He was deep in thought, and way tired. There had been little sleep for him since the shootout on the bridge. Too many ideas and notions lingered in his head. Some things were entirely clear; others were not.

There was no doubt that Tran and Shen Sun Soone had been two of the three gunmen during the St Patrick's High School massacre, and that they had recruited outcast Sherman Chan into becoming the third. From what Striker could piece together, Tran had been one of the planners of the attack; he was never intended to be one of the gunmen.

But when Que Wong failed to show, everything changed.

The order to kill the kids had come through Kim Pham – the

manager of the Fortune Happy restaurant and *de facto* leader of the Shadow Dragons. His body had been found a week ago, in a stolen Toyota Camry that was dumped in the Fraser River – not overly far from the docks where Que Wong's body had been located.

Kim Pham had been shot twice in the chest, once in the head. And Striker liked that discovery.

It had a little bit of irony to it.

The real mastermind behind it all had been Sheung Fa, who had carefully *suggested* the idea to his Shadow Dragon underlings. Sheung Fa was the known liaison officer – the White Paper Fan – of the 14K Triads in Vancouver, despite the fact that he passed himself off as a simple Chinese merchant. Striker had attempted to interview him numerous times, but Sheung Fa knew his charter rights better than anyone. He'd lawyered up, wasn't talking, and Striker knew he never would.

The whole thing angered Striker so much he couldn't sleep.

Sherman Chan, Que Wong and Raymond Leung – who was now known to be Que Wong's distant cousin in from Hong Kong – had all been pre-planned fall guys from the very start. All three were bad people. Murderers without a conscience.

Striker had no pity for them.

But he would have loved to offer them deals on their testimony. Unfortunately, dead men don't talk. Everywhere Striker looked, there were connections and coincidences and implications that singled out Sheung Fa.

But none of the hard evidence needed for court.

The more Striker went over it, the more it all made sense to him, in a twisted crazy way, and he let out a long, slow breath. He was tired. So goddam tired. And Felicia was still going on and on about work issues.

'. . . and then Meathead suddenly tells everyone that Jay Hall is dating Ashley Grey – you know, that new girl that transferred over from Port Moody? The superhot one that looks just like Megan Fox?' Felicia stopped talking and gave him a rap on the arm. 'Hey, you even listening to me?'

Striker offered her a weak grin. 'Yeah, Jay Hall is dating Megan Fox.'

This seemed to satisfy Felicia. They turned north on the Trans Canada, heading towards the North Shore, and Felicia continued chatting on until the Ironworkers' Bridge came into view. At the sight of it, she stuttered, and Striker realised that all her small talk had been nothing more than a diversion from dealing with the situation at hand.

She dropped her eyes, got quiet for a moment. 'What do you think's gonna happen to the parents?'

Striker shot her a look. 'Nothing worse than has already happened. Patricia's still in critical, so who knows with her. But the rest have all hired Robicheaux, and from what I hear, he's a pretty damn good lawyer.'

'You think they'll get good jail time.'

'They'll have to. Twenty-two kids died because of their actions.'

'But they obviously didn't expect—'

'You don't steal millions of dollars and not think some kind of violence is coming your way.'

'I agree with that, but—'

'Twenty-two kids, Felicia.' Striker left it at that.

When they circled the bridge towards the south side, Felicia fixed him with a nervous look and said, 'I don't know why you do this to yourself.'

'A young girl died because of me.'

'She didn't die because of you, Jacob, she had a chance to live because of you.'

'And I failed her.'

'It was an unwinnable situation. Jesus, it's a miracle both girls aren't dead.'

Striker pointed to the halfway point of the bridge. 'Just stop there.'

Felicia pulled the car over, then put on the emergency lights so no other vehicles would smash into them from behind. The flowers Striker had brought – an arrangement of white roses – lay flat on the back seat.

Striker picked them up and left the car.

Then he did what he had done a dozen times since that horrible Halloween night – he stood out on the bridge deck and relived all that had happened. Every goddam second of it. He looked at where the van had been parked, where Shen Sun and the girls had been positioned, and he recalled the pitch fog of the night, illuminated by nothing but the van's glaring headlights.

Now, it all felt like a movie in his head, one which would never end. The scenes were with him throughout the day, and at night they haunted his dreams, leaving him exhausted come the morning sun.

'Jacob.'

He blinked, turned and looked at Felicia, who still sat in the police cruiser, parked in the slow lane. 'What?'

'You were just standing there, in a daze.'

'I was . . . thinking.' He moved down the bridge, then turned about and retraced his steps, going over the soundness of his tactics – how he'd approached the van, his stance towards the gunman, the way he'd improvised when Courtney fell forward and Shen Sun ran for Raine. He went over it again and again and again until his head hurt and he could feel the blood hammering behind his temples.

Drained, he approached the railing where Shen Sun had pulled Raine to her death. On all the other days he'd come here, he'd bent down and propped her flowers against the steel railing. Today he walked right up to the railing, looked down and stared at the turbulent green waters below. The flowers slipped from his fingers, and Striker watched them fall, counting the horrible seconds it took for them to hit the water.

Four and a half.

Striker frowned. The terror Raine must have felt before slamming into the cold, hard waters and being sucked down by the unforgiving currents. He counted the seconds in his head, over and over again. And another dreaded duty was yet to come. Patricia Kwan had been stabilised, and Dr Adler said he would be taking her from her induced coma soon.

Then Striker would have to inform her of Raine's death. He could get someone from Patrol to do it, but knew he wouldn't. Raine's death had occurred because of his failure.

He would tell Patricia so.

Felicia came up to his side, and rubbed her hand on his back. Striker shook it off, not because he resented her touch, but because his ribs were still sore – broken from the bullets that had tagged him on the bulletproof vest that night.

'It's over,' Felicia said. 'And neither Raine nor Shen Sun Soone are coming back. You have to accept that, Jacob.'

Striker said nothing. He simply looked across the water to a small sandy inlet, just south-east of the native reserve. That was where the frogmen had finally found Raine's body some six hours after her fall.

Shen Sun's body had never been found.

Striker doubted if it ever would. The gunman had manifested into Striker's life like a ghost from another realm, and he had gone out in much the same manner – there one moment, gone the next. Vanished soundlessly, like a fading phantom.

The thought made Striker shiver, and he recalled the gunman's last words:

'History is circle. Past is also future.'

Striker understood the hidden message in those words: that their paths would cross again one day, in this life or the next. The saying was old. A Chinese superstition. And Striker hoped it wasn't true. God knows, he'd already suffered enough pain for this life and the next.

But if it did happen, he would be ready.

Felicia gave him a nudge. 'You okay?'

He nodded. 'I'm more than okay, I'm alive.' He pulled her close and gave her a long, passionate kiss. When he pulled away, her cheeks were rosy and her lips stretched into a smirk.

'Does this mean we're on again?' she asked.

Striker raised an eyebrow and smiled at her. 'Let's just say, you won't be needing chocolate again for a long, long time.'